The Power of Water

Book One of The Doom of the Gods

James Grimm

YUMEBOOK

Cover design by Miblart https://miblart.com/

Visit the author's website at http://www.author-jgrimm.com

Sign up for the author's newsletter: https://www.author-jgrimm.com/landing-page

Use the contact form on the author's website for permissions requests: https://www.author-jgrimm.com/contact

First Edition 2024

ISBN: 978-1-963553-00-0 (ebook)

ISBN: 978-1-963553-01-7 (paperback)

ISBN: 978-1-963553-02-4 (hardback)

Contents

Maps Before the Wall of Destruction

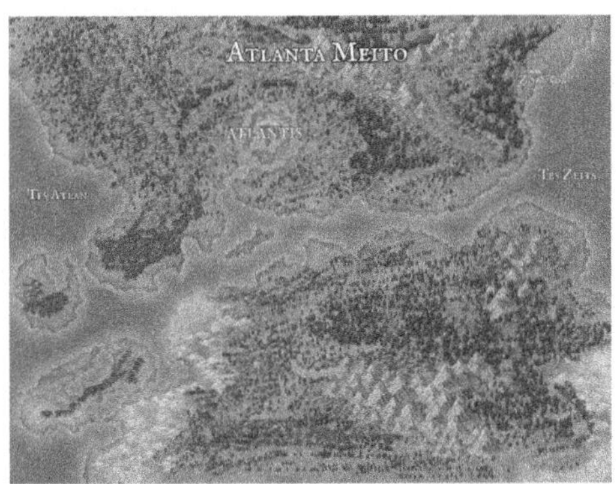

Atlantis before the Wall

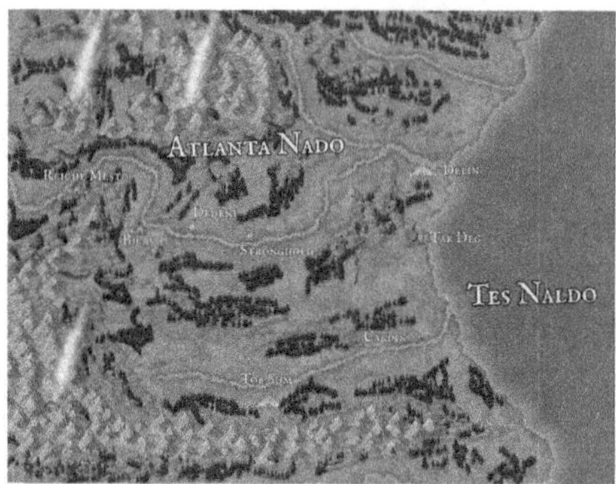

Atlanta Nado before the Wall

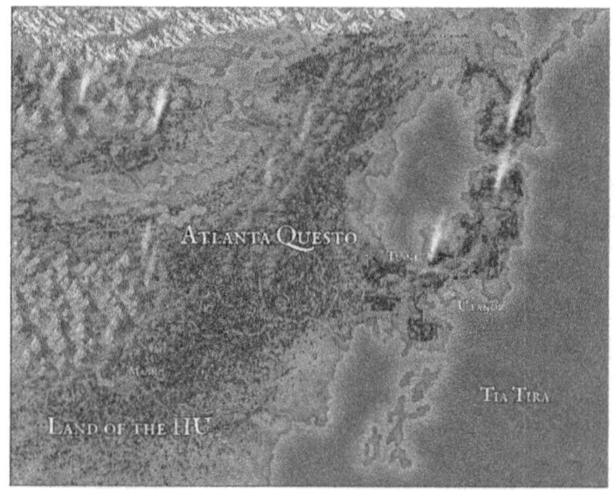

Atlanta Questo before the Wall

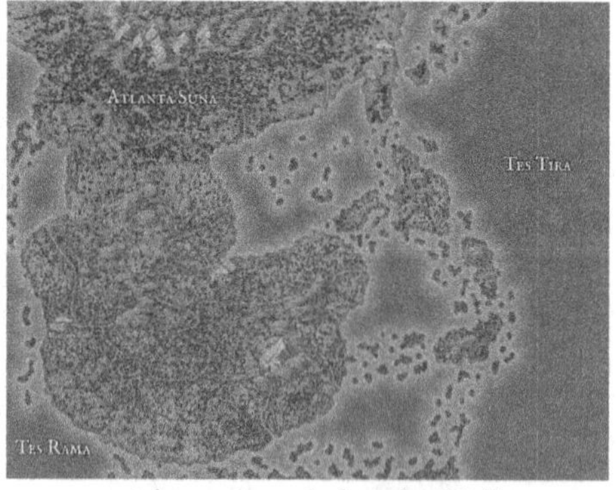

Atlanta Suna before the Wall

Altai before the Wall

PROLOGUE

Around 22,000 BC Atlantis

S ilenus, the teacher to the Gods, loves to drink with humans and be entertained by them. On one particular visit to King Ceros' court, a few survivors
of an attacked caravan are present. They told the tale of how a pack of Harpies
ruthlessly destroyed a merchant train from a nearby land. These survivors are
from a company of Atlantean soldiers that encountered the Harpies devouring
the caravan members' remains.

The survivors stood in front of a hushed crowd, their expressions heavy
with grief and exhaustion. They explained how the Harpies' thick, scaly armor
effortlessly deflected arrows and how close combat was a death sentence against
their razor-sharp claws and teeth. Out of eighty soldiers, only seven made it
out alive, and even then, most were severely injured. The senior survivor's voice
trembled as he declared, "We are no match for these creatures; the gods have
bestowed them with near impenetrable protection."

Silenus stands up slightly drunkenly. "Ney, brave warrior, the gods created
these creatures but do not protect them. They are sport for the hunts."

"Sport or not, they are too much for us, and Poseidon does not heed our pleas
for assistance," Ceros snarls, flinging his chalice to the tiled floor in disgust. The
silence is palpable as everyone holds their breath. All eyes are on Ceros, and no
one dares move or make a sound except for the crackling of the fire in the large
hearth and the torches burning in their sconces.

Silenus throws his head back in loud laughter, pounding the table with mirth.
Most of those gathered here think he has gone crazy or is drunk - as is his wont.

Ceros, drained of mirth with such evil tidings, warns, "Silenus, you show disrespect to my men. I think it best you retire for the night."

A tense silence permeates the air, every soul present frozen in fear. Not a single person dares to utter a word lest they invite the wrath of this divine being. For all, imagine that asking such a god to leave could be suicidal. Silenus gradually settles down. "My King, I meant no disrespect. I was just thinking about something which I find humorous." His chuckles resume, and he reaches for his drink, ignoring the anger on the King's face.

Fingers drumming dangerously on the throne's arm, Ceros inquires, through a clenched jaw, "What do you plan to do, Silenus?"

"I'll give you the knowledge to create weapons powered by Aether. This way, we can even the odds against these creatures and chase them out of your lands." Silenus snickers, taking a sip from his cup, nearly spilling it all over himself.

The gravity of what he said hits everyone like a thunderbolt; Atlanteans know of Aether weaponry wielded by gods and heroes but lack the knowledge of how to manipulate the source. Here is an intoxicated demigod offering to teach them this secret.

Ceros starts to laugh as well. "Well, Silenus, that is great news indeed and the sign of a dear friend. Come tell us what we need to do to use this source."

Silenus says, "Fetch your priests since prayer is required. Have your son pick a group of men and maidens to participate."

"Why, my Lord?" asks Prince Tolenar, standing beside his father.

"Because, my dear boy," then shifting his look to the King, "Power corrupts, and this is the power of the Gods." Turning back to the crowd, "Good mortals you may be, above those poor fools that know nothing of wine, but you are not strong enough to resist the power of Aether." He finishes his cup, taking the pitcher from a nearby servant.

Ceros looks at Silenus, trying to decipher the secret of the warning he just gave. "Dear Silenus, what do you intend with my son?" A group of priests enters the hall.

Silenus stands and stretches. "I do this to help you and save you. For once I give you the secrets of Aether, the gods will be angered. The idea of power-hungry mortals with the power of the Gods does not sit well with them. What they will do, I am not sure. I might be consigning you and yours to death."

Prince Tolenar, standing near the dais, asks, "Then why give us something that might have us punished with death?"

With a huge grin, Silenus looks at the Prince. "Didn't I tell you? I will not give you the secret. You must ask for it. Now you know the possible cost. You know your risk with full knowledge that this could kill you." Looking back at the King, "My King, shall I continue?"

Ceros surveys the crowd, taking in the familiar faces of family and friends. He knows the Gods have many weapons and tools powered by Aether. Could his people also build such things with the knowledge that Silenus is offering? Should his people become Gods?

King Ceros looks at his son, who reluctantly nods, "Silenus, please share the secret with us."

The demigod's jubilant expression fades to solemnity. "King Ceros of Atlantis and the Seven Isles, you are asking to unlock the Well of Knowledge, even though it could bring great ruin to your people. Is this correct?"

Ceros eyes Silenus warily, doubt assailing him. Looking over his nobles, he sees many eagerly awaiting him to proceed. Licking his lips, "Yes, we seek the knowledge of Aether."

Silenus' mirthful aspect returns. "Wonderful! And so it shall be. You know, I am intrigued by what will happen." He plucks a flute from his robe and plays a short tune, then beckons: "Pandora, be a dear and present us with the Well of Knowledge."

Everyone looks around for this Pandora. Silenus continues to stare out the window, a smile on his face and arms out wide, but nothing happens. People start to talk, with snippets of "it's a joke" rising above the rumble of dozens of side conversations. Then, the hall fills with a fragrant smell of fresh flowers, and a ray of moonlight slices through one of the windows. The crowd grows silent when down that moonbeam comes the most lovely young maiden any of them have ever seen.

She carries a small onyx box and walks to Silenus. He gives a fatherly smile and says, "There you are. Good."

He turns to the priests and the Prince with his selected men and women, "Form a circle of priests and one for the prince's followers." They look to the King for guidance.

Silenus bellows, "Hurry now, the moonbeam will soon go, and so must Pandora." Pandora smiles a sad smile.

Both groups swiftly form circles as the rest of the crowd shuffles closer. The King remains on his throne, wholly captivated by the unfolding events.

Silenus calls to the Prince. "My Prince, come here. To you shall be the honor or curse of opening the Well of Knowledge." The Prince makes his way toward Silenus and Pandora.

Looking between them, the Prince tentatively touches the box. He locks eyes with Pandora and inquires, "Is this your box, Pandora?"

Before she can answer, Silenus impatiently motions for the Prince to continue. Looking annoyed at Silenus' interruption, the Prince fiddles with the latch and is rewarded with a spring-loaded needle pricking his finger. He jumps back, holding his finger. Glaring accusingly at Silenus, "You didn't say it was armed."

Sheepishly, Silenus glances at the Prince, then the King, "You didn't ask if it was armed, now did you?" With his previous mirth returned, he opens the box.

Silenus intones, "To protect from any mortal gaining too much knowledge and power of Aether, Pandora's box holds two smaller boxes. One for each group. The knowledge of Aether shall forever remain separate and flow down through time as thus."

Lifting one of the small boxes, he walks to the circle of priests and enters the ring. "To the priests is given the knowledge of channeling Aether into Mother Stones. Yours will be the creation of the lines of power." He opens the box, and a strong wind comes forth and swirls around the priests. "This understanding must be taught to other priests who are worthy." All the priests swoon in the winds and fall asleep. "Disturb them not. They will awaken in due course."

Silenus returns to Pandora, taking out the second small box. "This is the secret to manipulating the power. While the priests can charge devices, they can not wield Aether." He walks to the Prince's group.

Looking at the group, he continues, "To you is the gift of power. Some of you will create tools powered by Aether that all can use. Once the Aether store has been exhausted, the priests must recharge it. Others will learn the secret to drawing from the lines into tools only Aether users can manipulate. Your bloodlines will be sensitive to this gift."

And with that, he opens the box, and a cloud envelops them. Cries of shock and bodies collapsing to the ground echo through the thick air. "Do not come any closer. This is for them alone. The cloud is poison for all others."

The crowd recoils in fear of touching the cloud. When the cloud dissipates, Silenus stands amongst the fallen people. He returns to Pandora and returns the second box to Pandora's box.

"You may go, child." He says to Pandora, who curtsies and steps onto a moonbeam before dematerializing as the moonbeam wanes.

A thunderclap proceeds massive lightning a few seconds later. "Ah, Zeus is aware," Silenus marvels.

Ceros joins Silenus. "Dear Silenus, what does Zeus say?"

Closing his eyes, Silenus cocks his head toward the windows. "He is furious, but Poseidon intervenes on your behalf and speaks of our agreement."

The fallen start to stir, most with wonder in their eyes. Some try to stand but cannot without assistance.

Thunder and lightning intensify until they shake the Great Hall of the Sea King. People cry out in alarm but can barely be heard due to the constant rumble getting louder and louder. Many fall to their knees and pray for forgiveness or protection, depending on the God or Goddess they revere. Prince Tolenar staggers to his father and Silenus.

Ceros falls to his knees and begs Poseidon to save them. In mere moments, only Silenus and Prince Tolenar remain standing. The Prince is dazed, swaying slightly to an unheard beat. Tumultuous rumbles shake the hall to the core, like massive waves crashing against a rocky ocean-side cliff in a storm.

Mere moments later, the clamor fades away like a singer's parting note. Then, shattering the eerie silence, Silenus's voice booms forth, "Now comes the final Doom of the evening." he declares, his words carrying a weighty gravitas that seems to fill the entire hall. "Teach those who hold the power of the Gods to wield it with humility. There will come a time when they believe themselves equal to deities and act accordingly. The Gods will test the faithfulness of Atlantis, seeking to remind them of this sacred pact we make today. And if they dare defy these warnings, they will feel the full force of divine wrath – for the Gods are fiercely possessive of their power, and mortals cannot withstand their fury."

FOUR MONTHS BEFORE

Around 11,000 BC ATLANTA SUNA

Whistling while walking back onto the base, Risor thinks, *"Comfy assignment, beautiful beaches, great food, occasional combat but not too intense, yup, I have it good. Well, as long as this war doesn't screw it up."* He heads to the base's Mission Command building for a brief on their upcoming mission. His squadron, the Falcon Claw, and two others will soon go on a mission to strike a grave blow to the Rama Empire and her allies in this decade-long war.

Entering the general's office, Risor greets General Varno, the base commander, sitting at his desk with others already seated. Nodding toward the open seat, Varno turns his attention back to the screen on the opposite wall displaying a map of a base.

The intelligence officer waits for Risor to sit before starting his brief. The Aether-powered map projector displays a map of the Rama military base in Taxila.

The officer starts, "My Lady and Lords, our target for this mission. Intelligence states that they are building some type of powerful new weapon there. Your mission will be to capture or destroy this weapon and all its data if you cannot bring it back."

Risor asks, "Lieutenant, what type of weapon is it?"

"We are not really sure. The evidence provided by the Shigar is pretty scant..."

Lady Jana Kalin, the commander of the Wave Rider squadron, a Shigar party member and commander of the mission, interrupts. "Does it really matter? Just do what you are told."

Before Risor can respond, she turns to Varno. "General, I request that the Falcon Claw squadron perform the feint mission."

Turning back to Risor. "No offense, Commander Tarnor, but I want someone who follows orders and doesn't endanger the mission with frivolous questions watching my back."

Risor shoots back, his anger getting the best of him. "You mean you want Shigar to get all the glory?"

General Varno interrupts, "Okay, people, we are on the same side." Taking a deep breath before continuing, "Let's keep politics out of it, okay? I agree with your request, Commander Kalin."

Jana and the other squadron commander, Lord Jamal Fera, leader of the Sun Darters, look disdainfully at Risor.

Fingernails digging into palms and jaw clenching, Risor stares daggers back at Jamal when he receives a stern look from Varno. Risor relaxes slightly. He nods, and Varno signals the intelligence officer to continue.

Once the intelligence officer completes his brief, Varno states, "If no further questions, you are dismissed to your squadron briefings. Risor, a word."

All of the officers stand at attention and salute. Lady Kalin, Lord Fera, and the intelligence officer leave the office. Risor keeps standing at attention, afraid his anger will betray him.

Once the door is closed, Risor spits out. "Sir, I could have supported her just fine."

"Yes, Commander."

Risor pauses at the general's lack of response. Varno continues, "But if things go wrong, she will blame you and Nalos. There are tensions enough between the two parties."

Not quite ready to give in, Risor responds. "Sir, I would not let our political issues get in the way of my duties."

Sighing, Varno gets up and walks towards the door. Risor is still standing at attention. "Yes, Commander Tarnor, I believe you, but I have heard of Lady Kalin, and we both know about Jamal. Trust me on this. Dismissed."

Not entirely satisfied with the general's answer, but knowing he can't keep arguing, he performs a parade-ground salute and exits. General Varno does not understand; he is not a Nalos member like Risor.

Walking out of the command center, he feels cheated. Annoyed by the events in the office, he thinks, *"This day started so good."* But by the time he gets to his barracks, he wonders if that is not bad.

On the base's flight line, many Vailixi, silvery, box-shaped craft powered by Aether, are parked and loading troops. A few Vailixi fly high overhead, providing a defensive patrol for all the craft on the ground. The air over the base shimmers slightly, signifying that the base's shields are active.

Troopers in Aether combat armor stand in line, boarding the Vailixi. The bulky armor covers their entire body with red Skor metal plating. Skor, a gift from Poseidon long ago, is created by armorers and priests, and when infused with Aether, it is difficult to pierce and takes the shape of the body armor. But without Aether, it collapses into a pool of a rubber-like substance that is easy to transport and store. It also provides enhanced visuals and can communicate with other armored teams, Vailixi, or, if in range, bases.

Risor's second in command, Tilor Togolan, a noble from one of the smaller colonies near Risor's home of Altai, stands with him near the rear of their craft with the troopers for their Vailixi already boarded. They stand watching Lady Kalin and Lord Fera talk a few Vailixi over.

"Happy lot they are. We are better off doing the feint, sir. No backstabbing." Tilor states, then spits on the ground.

Smiling, Risor responds, "Backstabbing? I doubt they would go that far. She writes her ticket in the Shigar if this is successful. She won't screw with her chances."

Shaking his head, Tilor gives Risor a severe look, "Yes, sir, but General Varno is right. If it fails and we are central to it, she would blame you and Nalos for causing the failure. It's better this way."

Nodding in agreement, Risor turns to them again and sighs, "Party politics is such bullshit." Turning back toward the open bay of the craft. "Shall we go?"

Tilor gives one more look toward the other commanders. Grins and states, "Besides, Jamal and his Darters are fuck ups waiting to happen. They would probably screw up the feint and need our assistance to save their asses."

With the rear ramp door closing, he adds, "Definitely better this way."

Overlooking the beachside military base stands a small hut at the edge of a hillside orchard. Four people around a fire watch the Vailixi take off and head toward the northwest. As the last craft recedes into the distance, one of the four turns and enters the dwelling.

One man of the three remaining people stands, shading his eyes, and asks, "How many did you get?"

The sole woman answers, "I counted forty-five. About three squadrons."

The last man, still squatting near the fire, nods his head at the woman's pronouncement. The standing man nods and goes into the hut. In a dark corner of the hut sits the man who entered earlier, talking into a mirror-like device glowing with the power of Aether. He turns at the intrusion.

The man entering the hut walks to the other man and says, "Tell them we see three squadrons heading in a northwest direction."

The woman from outside comes in and asks, "Shall we tell them the rumors we heard from the other villagers?"

Nodding, the standing man states, "Yes, tell them we believe that the target is Taxila."

ATLANTA RAMA

A dogfight occurs over the targeted military base near Taxila between Vailixi and Vimana. Vailixi are small and fast. Vimana, the flying craft of the Rama Empire, looks like small step pyramids, correspondingly slow but heavily armed.

The Vimana are outnumbered and losing. Their saving grace is the ground-to-air fire support they are getting from the base's defenses. The base defenses consist of large cannons that throw up clouds of Aether streams to deny an area to the Atlanteans. Below the dogfight, some of the base's buildings are on fire or smoking from strikes by the Atlanteans.

Vailixi swarm around the base like wasps around a hive. Defending Vimana circle above the base, relying on its defenses to ward off the Vailixi ships coming from various angles. The Vailixi group into three or four craft, concentrating on one Vimana at a time. They try to breach the target's shields before nearby Vimana can swat them away with overwhelming firepower.

The command bridge of Risor's Vailixi has four consoles in the forward section: weapons, two probers that feel and see what is around the vessel, and shields. Behind this console row are three more positions. First is the navigator position, Tilor's seat, followed by Risor's spot as the craft commander. The communications position is to the right of the commander's seat, and on the left is a passageway leading to the lower passenger deck below.

Each console glows a soft blue with Aetheric energy. Aether flows through the conduits connecting to the console dishes, causing them to glow. The navigation console emits a fast pulsing rhythm. The other consoles pulsate, too, but slower.

The communications officer, Dimera, turns to Risor. "Sir, Lady Kalin wishes to speak to you."

Risor swings a smaller dish, connected to his station's chair, into position in front of him. "Pass to my console."

Jana's face appears on the screen, "Commander, break off to commence your mission."

"Yes, my Lady." Risor swings the dish back to the side.

"Tilor, the queen has spoken. Time to head towards Taxila." Tilor grins and turns back to prepare the orders.

Jana's Vailixi lands among others in a clearing. The rear ramp opens, and power-armored troopers armed with an Aether spear disembark and start heading into the woods. Each Vailixi unloads ten troopers, then takes off and is replaced by another.

Jana walks down the ramp with powered armor on and her helmet off, talking to her second, Nailos Dentam. He is in a standard flight suit and remains on the ramp.

"Keep half the squadron here and send the others to assist Jamal."

He nods and looks like he wants to say something. She motions for him to talk. "Yes, my Lady. Could I not go with you? I would feel better," he pleads.

Jana grips his shoulder with her armored hand and tightens her grip until Nailos winces in pain. With a cold voice, she says, "As I said before, I don't need your protection, Nailos. I could cut you down in seconds."

Lines crease his forehead, and his lips pull back into a grimace of pain. He hurriedly responds, "Forgive me, my Lady. I do not mean offense. I just... well... us..."

Releasing his shoulder, she takes a deep breath, "I know what you meant, but just do what I say."

Putting on her helm, she turns and, with her escorts, bounds off into the forest after the other troopers. He watches until she disappears in the woods. Massaging his shoulder, he retreats up the ramp as it closes. The craft lifts and speeds away.

Hours before, the meadow was tranquil, and a dirt road traversed through the woodlands to the base's gate. Now, troopers in power armor have taken up positions within the trees, exchanging fire with Rama soldiers who have barricaded themselves among the base's buildings.

The meadow separates the forest from a wooden and stone fence, scattered with now burning watch towers. The Rama troops are equipped with leather breastplates, helmets, and greaves; they cling tightly to their Aether bows. Made from metal and armed with a glowing string, these weapons can shoot out a bolt of Aether when pulled back and released. It is similar to the Aether spear wielded by Atlanteans, which emits a discharge of Aether when its trigger is pressed.

Jana reaches the tree line and assesses the situation. The enemy seems to be heavily outnumbered. Without hesitation, she issues the order to advance. The troopers emerge from the trees in a skirmish line. Jana remains behind them, orchestrating their movements.

At her command, a handful of troopers dart forward using their power armor's enhanced speed. Shrugging off enemy fire, they perform a power-assisted leap over the wall and ditch to the other side. With weapons blazing, they charge toward the closest buildings to create a bridgehead along the base's perimeter. Enemy fire concentrates on the advanced team, desperately trying to collapse the position before reinforcements arrive from the forest line. The enemy's efforts to dislodge the bridgehead play into Jana's plans. Their concentration allows the rest of the troopers a chance to move forward under weak fire.

Jana, in mid-jump, targets a group of defenders behind a nearby barricade. She hits two of them with successive shots. Discipline fails, and they scatter, abandoning the barricade to her forces. Landing gracefully, Jana takes in the chaos around her - seeing a nearby trooper hit by multiple blasts. His body flung back into the ditch. Others are hit while landing and another falls, but most charge forward successfully. The battle rages on intensely, each trooper fighting for survival and victory against a determined enemy selling each building dearly.

Jamal and his Sun Darters try suppressing the ground fire while battling the remaining Vimana over the base. Three of his squadron complete a dive into the base to strafe some buildings where a large concentration of defenders are massing. They start walking their fire down a row of buildings, successfully breaking up the enemy formations.

The three Vailixi start pulling up and away when a few buildings fall apart to reveal Aether cannons. Two of the three Vailixi are right in the path of the cannons and disintegrate under fire. The last one is able to pull up and away but is leaving a trail of smoke. It will survive to fight another day but is already returning to base at a much-reduced speed.

Jamal's communication officer breaks his concentration, viewing the demise of his squadron members. "Commander, scouts are reporting a large number of Vimana inbound from the south."

He swings his Aether dish into position and sees the reported inbound targets.

"Get me, Lady Kalin. Order the squadron to break off. We will strike these new Vimana. Tell the Wave Riders to continue to support the ground forces." His staff gets to work on passing his messages.

The front viewer shows the open sky as the craft ascends to combat altitude. Other Vailixi form up on his craft.

"Commander, Lady Kalin."

Sitting up straight, Jamal lowers the privacy shield over his seat. This will keep their conversation private while allowing him to see the rest of the command deck.

"My Lady, a large Vimana force is coming from the south. We will engage and leave your Vailixi to support you."

He sees Jana think that over. "Fair enough. We are starting to breach the perimeter. Any word on what the Falcon Claw is encountering?"

"No word yet, my Lady. I will check."

An earth-shattering explosion fills the air, and Jana tightens her grip on her weapon. Buildings around them have been razed to their foundations. Dead defenders, with the occasional Atlantean power suit, litter the streets while many of the buildings burn.

The defenders are making the Atlanteans fight for each building by firing from windows, roofs, or the sides of buildings. The fires burn out of control - fueled by the highly charged Aether energy released by both sides.

Jana is under no illusion that they can hold this ground. She has a short window to get to the research buildings and take this discovery or at least destroy it. They are only a block or two away from the target buildings.

The air is thick with the smells of smoke, blood, ash, and the metallic tang of Aetheric energy released in the raging battle. Indrajit, a tall, powerfully built young man, stands near the corner of a building a few blocks from Jana's location. He has an Aether bow strapped to his back and a large blade in his hand. There are another thirty Rama soldiers around him.

Peering around the corner with a small mirror, Indrajit sees a few Rama soldiers down the road falling back ahead of the enemy's power-armored troopers. Aether streams whiz back and forth between the two forces. Most of those defenders will probably not return to the protection of the building where Indrajit waits.

He turns to his friend, Zhenjin. "Zhen, when they get closer, I will charge out. Signal the strike at the same time."

With a worried look, "Are you sure about this, my Lord? You are quick, but I think Aether is faster."

Indrajit gives Zhen a quick grin and a pat on the shoulder, "Aether, maybe, but not those troopers."

He peers around the corner and notices that most retreating soldiers are past him or down. The enemy is almost even with the corner, maybe three meters away, and paying attention to the last of the defenders trying to get around the corner of the building on the opposite side of the street.

Zhen shakes his head and puts his horn to his mouth, watching his lord and friend. Indrajit cocks his head to listen for the coming footsteps, then takes a deep breath.

Jumping out from behind the corner of the building, Indrajit lands with his blade, igniting into Aether flames. He swings at the first Atlantean trooper's head. The God-crafted blade easily slices through the enemy's armor, and the helmeted head smacks the wall a meter away.

Before the body hits the ground, Indrajit is driving his sword into the chest of the next trooper. Grabbing the dying soldier's Aether spear and aiming it back toward the oncoming troopers, he shoots the next trooper.

Zhen blows the horn and, with the rest of his men, starts to run around the corner to fight the oncoming Atlanteans. Being a God-blessed hero with superhuman speed, Indrajit is already attacking the next trooper about two meters from the corner. Before the Atlanteans could concentrate their fire on Indrajit, Zhen and the other Rama soldiers filed into the street, firing.

Jana and her team quickly move through the cluttered office, rifling through drawers and flipping through stacks of paper scrolls. The two large desks dominate the room, each covered in piles of papers and writing implements. Along two walls stood floor-to-ceiling shelves overflowing with more scrolls and parchment. Unlike the more advanced Atlantean society, the Rama empire relies heavily on written records. Scrolls of aged paper are treasured here, symbolizing tradition and history. Though the Atlanteans had long ago abandoned paper in favor of Aether-powered tablets, the Ramans clung to tradition. However, they also adapted to technological advancements. Like their Atlantean counterparts, they utilize Aether tablets for more complex matters. This decision reduces the workload for their priests and requires less Aether power to maintain compared to the extravagant systems of Atlantis.

A trooper shoves a stack of captured tablets into a bag. At the same time, Jana and the others concentrate on reading scrolls to reduce the load they must take.

Explosions continue to shake dust from the rafters over those rummaging in the office. Occasionally, Jana blows dust from the screen of her Aether tablet, which she holds over a scroll she is translating. Unlike those around her, she uses the tablet's translation capabilities because she cannot read Rama's script.

She clenches her fists and tosses the scroll with a loud thud. Looking up, she sees a chaotic scene of discarded scrolls strewn around the room. Piles upon piles of delicate parchment lay scattered on the floor, while a towering mountain of unexamined texts is precariously balanced on the tables. Grinding her teeth, she breathes loudly through her nose and dives back into the task.

"My Lady, Lord Dentam advises that Lord Fera is on the line."

She pulls back from the table, raises her arm, and then taps a device on her wrist. A 3D image of Jamal appears. "What is your status, Jamal?"

The floating head responds, "My Lady, we are getting beaten back. There are too many. We can hold them here, but not much longer."

"Did you hear from Commander Tarnor?"

He nods, "Yes, he is encountering stiffening resistance. More Vimana are joining the battle all the time."

Frowning, "Losses?"

"He reports near full strength. I am down to almost half."

"I have lost a few here. I will send you some."

A new trooper rushes into the office. Everyone looks at the intruder. "My Lady, they have a hero and are counter-attacking with a massive force."

Jana stares at the new trooper briefly, then sees her communicator flashing. She touches another button on her armor. Another 3D image of Dentam appears.

He bows, "My Lady, we have a large force of Vimana coming from the north. I need your support craft to join me."

Turning slightly red and visibly trying to keep control, she turns to one of her team still reviewing scrolls. "Tell me you have found something of value?"

The man looks a little frightened. "I'm sorry, my Lady. It's mostly inventory reports, and they're not even interesting."

Fighting the anger, she growls, "You said this was the base research administrative office."

Swallowing, "That is what Intel said. And the sign near the door says it, too." Others in the room nod their heads in agreement.

She is ready to send some fighters to Dentam when another trooper enters the room. This one has a deep gash in his arm. Blood dripped onto the floor. The trooper quickly exclaims, "My Lady, they are getting closer. We can not stop this cursed hero."

Everyone is watching and awaiting her orders. She turns back to the images. "Dentam, patch me through to Commander Tarnor."

She looks at Jamal, "Commander, fall back to our position as fast as you can."

He nods and then blinks out. In seconds, Risor replaces Dentam as well.

"Commander, fall back to our position. I fear we have sprung a trap, and I will make them pay."

Looking a little surprised, he said, "Yes, my Lady." He looked away from her for a second, "If it's a trap, should we not retreat? There seems to be much more than we can handle coming into range."

"Do as I say."

He nods and disappears. Her anger flares since he broke the connection with a senior. Dentam's image returns, looking worried.

"He broke the connection, my Lady."

"I know what he did." She snaps and turns to the people in the office. "Prepare to fall back to the perimeter."

Everyone starts moving. The image of Dentam disappears.

The Atlanteans have been pushed out of the base. A firing line is forming at the forest's edge, with most troopers already in the forest.

The Rama defenders take up positions within the buildings near the perimeter fence. Shots are traded between the two groups as an overhead dogfight heats up. More Vailixi arrive to overwhelm the few Vimana that remain.

Jana sighs in disgust. She is back to where she was just a few hours before. Through her suit, she calls a floating image of Jamal.

"Commander, how are we doing?"

"My Lady, we are beating them back. But we don't have much strength left."

Jana calls up another image of Risor. He acknowledges her. "Commander, where are you now?"

"We are about five minutes out. The enemy is about six minutes behind us."

Jamal asks, "Risor, how strong of a force do you have?"

He looks away momentarily, "We have ten effective craft, and about twenty enemies are chasing us."

Jamal is about to say something but looks away. When he looks back, he looks worried. "My Lady, the enemy has another force coming from the south. About 20, from what we see. Plus those here and those following Risor, about four to one."

Jana quips, "We are better." Looking at Risor, "Commander, when you get here, land your craft and have each ship deploy three crew to assist in the ground assault. I want to make them pay."

Risor looks at her for a few seconds without acknowledging the order. Then he slowly starts, "My Lady, I .. will .. not. We are outnumbered in the air, and it seems the enemy kicked you out of the base. You will have us destroyed."

Jamal shouts, "Commander, remember your place. Lady Kalin leads this mission."

With resolve stiffening, he said, "I believe Lady Kalin does not see the full picture and is in error. As the commander with the largest remaining force, I am taking command and ordering a retreat."

Slightly shocked at his statement, but before she can respond, Jana sees a person carrying a fiery sword speed into the woods further down the line.

To Risor, "I am in charge here."

She is again interrupted when a ground officer breaks into her communications on the emergency channel.

"My Lady, I apologize for interrupting, but the enemy is advancing into the woods. Their hero is already amongst us, and we can not hold much longer."

She looks down the line at the enemy in the meadow before the forest. Her troopers are vastly outnumbered.

"Order the retreat back to the landing zone. Commander Fera, pick up my force. Commander Tarnor, provide air cover."

Both subordinate commanders nod and disappear. She and the remaining troopers start to disengage in an orderly manner. She knows that today is not only a military loss but also a political one.

ATLANTA SUNA

Back at their base, General Varno listens to Jana, Jamal, and Risor discuss their understanding of the events that unfolded at Taxila. Dentam, Tilor, and Jamal's second-in-command sit in the row behind their commanders.

Jana states, "Commander Tarnor knowingly disobeyed my orders to land and assist in the ground assault. He is a coward and should be brought up on charges."

Jamal, his lieutenant, and Dentam nod. Risor prepares to respond when Varno answers first." Thank you, Commander, but I remind you that I decide who is brought up on charges and don't need your opinion. Is that understood?"

Jana blanches, "Yes, sir."

Varno sighs. Continuing in a neutral tone, "I understand he did disagree with your orders, and it was borderline mutiny. But he also points out that you were on the ground and did not have a view of the entire battle space. Commander Fera, would you agree?"

Jana gives Jamal a hard stare. Jamal looks down and then back up at the general without looking at Jana. He responds, "Yes, General. She was on the ground and did not have access to all the information."

Dentam interrupts, "My Lord, we passed her all pertinent information. She..."

Varno slams his hand on the table, giving Dentam a stern look. "Sub-Commander, if I want your opinion, I will ask for it. You will shut your mouth unless asked. Do I make myself clear?"

Sitting up board-straight, Dentam quickly states, "Yes, my Lord. I apologize for my outburst."

Jana gives him a warning look when he opens his mouth to continue. Sighing, he closes his mouth and looks down, clenching his teeth.

She sighs, then turns back to the general, "My General, I understand your position and accept it. I do believe Commander Tarnor was insubordinate and should be punished. Someone from a great house of Atlantis has a responsibility to uphold the order of our society, and refusing orders is anti-Atlantean. It shames his family in front of his people, his peers, the Emperor, and the Gods."

She turns to Risor with a slight smirk only meant for him. Continuing, "As a noble of Atlantis, I demand punishment for this behavior, so it is not rewarded or encouraged among the commoners."

Vigorously nodding, Jamal states, "I must also agree with this, my general."

Risor's face turns red, eyes straight ahead, and neck muscles straining; he remains silent.

Varno takes a few seconds. "Your point is noted, Lady Kalin. While I might not be your social equal and understand the shame you speak of, I am the ranking officer in this region. I believe his following your orders afterward proved he was not mutinous and was acting in the best interest of our people."

Jamal tries to interject, "My General..."

General Varno points a finger at Jamal, shutting him up. "This is my decision, and it is final. I am ordering the Wave Riders and Sun Darters back to Atlantis for overhaul."

Jana nods her head while Jamal slumps a little. She quickly glances at Risor. He smiles at her, intensifying the fire in her eyes.

Varno continues, "Risor since your squadron is the most complete, your squadron will remain until I can get a replacement to cover. Jamal, your people can take leave until the Shilots have fixed your craft. Risor, your people will get to take leave when they return to Atlantis later. Questions?"

Jana shakes her head in the negative. Jamal is still looking down, and Risor seems relieved.

"Dismissed."

All the officers start filing out. Jana moves quickly to leave and talks to no one. Dentam and Jamal follow after her.

Risor and Tilor walk out with a spring in their step. Tilor turns to Risor and says, "A double vacation? No, Jamal and his cronies, and then back to Atlantis."

Chuckling, Risor responds, "That does have a nice ring to it. And you can see Lena."

ATLANTA RAMA

Taxila is a major center of commerce along the Sarasvati River. Like most Raman Empire cities, it is either along the coast or navigable river. And like most Rama cities, it is primarily two-story buildings.

The city's layout is built on a grid system with block buildings surrounding a central courtyard with a fountain shared by all in that block. While there are highly adorned temples to the Gods, most of the city's external appearance is relatively mute. That is not the case with most of the interiors, though.

The city council chamber is near the public market. It is not a very large building, but it is used mainly for council meetings during public sessions. The rest of the city's administration resides in other buildings scattered around the city.

While not a public session on this day, they meet in this council chamber because it is larger and allows room for several spectators. Eight elders are seated at a semi-circle table facing Indrajit, who stands in the middle of a mosaic circle. To the side and behind the circle are spectator bleacher-style benches facing the council table.

Zhenjin stands a little behind Indrajit with a big grin on his face. A group of twelve other officers stand behind Zhen, representing the different forces that partook in the battle at the base. Most of them are also smiling. It was a great victory.

Kiran, an older man who sits at the head of the table and is the council's leader, talks to Venkat, Indrajit's father and a council member. Of the other council members, only Kali smiles back at Indrajit. She is a priestess or mantrik, as they are known in Rama—a wise yet frail woman and mentor of Indrajit.

Indrajit summarizes the victory over the Atlanteans at the base. "So the surprise was total. We destroyed over 20 Vailixi, killed 53 armored troopers, and captured 27."

Kiran supplies, "Yes, our spies report that quite a few of the Vailixi that returned were heavily damaged."

Displaying his frustration for all to see, Indrajit states, "If it was only so successful every time, we need to hit them back. If you could just ask the Emperor, I can lead a force to attack Atlanta Sunda while they are weak. I know I can hurt them badly."

Kali raises her hand to gain the attention of her pupil, "We know you could, my hero, but we have another task to ask of you."

She nods to Kalpana, her young assistant. Kalpana walks up to the council table near Kali, bows to the council, and then faces Indrajit.

She states, "My Lord, there is Atlantean activity in the northern ice pack, and we want to know what they are doing. We think they are Shilots studying the ice. We want to know why."

Zhen, never known for keeping his council to himself, speaks up, addressing Kali. "Master, why would they or us be interested in the ice? It's always been there."

Kali smiles, "That is the question, warrior Zhenjin. We need to know what the Atlanteans study. If it is a new weapon they seek, then we must get it first."

Indrajit, as a God-anointed hero of his people, knows his duty. "Then we will go."

Indrajit looks to Zhen, who nods in agreement.

Venkat asks, "Mantrik Kali, when will he need to go?"

"It is reported that they are preparing to send a party to the area north of Tes Naldo. We do not know how long they will stay."

Venkat nods his thanks.

Kiran states, "There is another task we would ask of you. Our allies, the Tugar, need Aether weapons. They have lost much in the new Atlantean offensive in their territory. The Greeks normally supply them but are also being pressed hard. Could you deliver a load of weapons to them first before going to the ice pack?"

"Of course. I will gather a team and leave when the weapons are ready."

Kalpana continues, "My Lord Indrajit. Please remember we need the Shilots alive and brought back here."

He nods, "We will not fail you."

Kiran stands, "May the Gods protect you on your journey."

The meeting is over, and all of the council stands up. Venkat signals Indrajit to wait. He walks up to Indrajit, with Zhen standing a respectful distance behind him. Kali is also walking slowly up to him.

Venkat talks to his son, "Come home for dinner tonight. Zhenjin, you are also welcome."

Zhen bows to Venkat and smiles at the thought of a good meal.

Indrajit frowns, "I will try, Father, but I need to get our people selected and ready."

Zhen frowns. Kalpana is leading Kali closer to them.

Venkat sighs, "Son, your mother will never forgive you or me if you do not stop by. We do not know how long you will be. You know how she is."

Kali nears them and says, "Go to dinner, my hero. I will not deny beautiful Sita her son's presence or suffer a mother's wrath."

They all laugh. Kali nods to Venkat and takes Indrajit's arm as they exit the chamber. Venkat, Kalpana and Zhen follow behind. Zhen is smiling.

Curiosity sparkles in Kalpana's eyes as she asks, "Why do you smile, warrior Zhenjin?"

Zhen's grin widens, "His mother's cooking is legendary. I will die happy afterward."

Venkat chuckles, "Protect my son, and you will have his mother's gratitude and a special meal."

Zhen's smile widens even more, and Kalpana can't help but laugh with them.

Up ahead of them, Kali tells Indrajit, "My hero, be careful on the ice. There are many hidden dangers: thin ice covering deep crevices and deadly predators."

Smiling and patting her arm, "We will, my teacher. I have survived much worse."

Stopping and facing him, "Do not trust God's blessings that much. They have blessed you with strength and power, but that does not mean you are invincible."

Indrajit looks more thoughtful. "I understand my teacher. I must admit, the death of Satyaki was a blow to my confidence."

They turn to start walking again, and she states, "As it should be, my hero. Heroes are not immortal. The Gods select their champions in times of need, but the other Gods work to kill them."

They are near the door to the council chamber. She continues, this time patting his arm. "Anyway, go enjoy your mother. Tomorrow, you can prepare."

Perched on the outskirts of Taxila, nestled among rolling hills that overlook the bustling town, lies Indrajit's spacious abode. While most of the city's buildings are unremarkable, those with power and wealth tend to have grander residences outside its borders. And Indrajit's family home is no exception -

a stately two-floor structure flanked by smaller buildings on either side. Its intricate design and sprawling grounds suggest a life of luxury and privilege within its walls.

His family and Zhen sit at the dinner table while servants clear the dishes. They watch the news on their Aether viewer, a sizeable mirror-like device displaying news of a battle near the Atlantean city of Moia, far to the east and north of Atlanta Sunda.

The announcer pulls up a detailed map of the region around Moia and then cuts to scenes of Hu warriors mounted on sturdy horses galloping past the viewpoint. The sunlight glints off their long spears and elaborate armor as they thunder down the valley.

"The Hu smashed the Atlantean forces and their allies with heavy losses before retreating back to the plains of their homeland. In other news..."

Indrajit raises his glass in a toast, "To the Hu, fierce and honorable warriors."

They all toast. Sita, Indrajit's mother, turns to Zhen. "Zhen, were your brothers there?"

"I believe so, Mother Sita. I have not heard from them in a while. They are strong and will do their duty."

Venkat nods, "Yes, but it would be better if we no longer fight."

Indrajit signals for a servant to bring more wine. "Yes, Father, but Atlantis will not give us peace, right? How are the negotiations?"

Shaking his head, Venkat responds, "Difficult. Their Shigar party wants to destroy us. Regrettably, the Nalos party is not stronger in their government. We would have a chance for peace, then."

Zhen shrugs, "Nalos, Shigar, they are all the same. Atlanteans that want to control the world. Curse their Gods forever giving them Aether."

Venkat sighs, "Zhenjin, there are good Atlanteans, as there are bad people in every society. We just need the right partners for peace. Their emperor seems to be a good person. Just surrounded by those that are drunk with power."

Indrajit finishes sipping his refilled wine glass and then thoughtfully asks, "Can we win, Father?"

Venkat looks back at the screen and then at his wife. "Can we beat them? No, I do not believe so." His wife looks worried. He smiles and continues, "But maybe we can fight them long enough for the people to become war-weary and give Nalos a chance to gain control of their government."

His comments did not reduce Sita's worry. She asks, "Is that likely?"

Patting her hand, he responds, "I do not know. Our spies say that the people are still not hurting from the war."

Indrajit softly whistles, "Even after ten years?"

Venkat chuckles, "Yes, we have the power to protect our cities and keep our people safe but do not have the power to take the fight to them. They have the power but do not have good leadership. They fight too arrogantly and usually suffer for it."

Looking determined, Zhen declares, "Then we must keep hurting them." Indrajit shares that determined look.

Sita sighs, "That is enough talk of war. You both leave tomorrow for unknown dangers. That is enough worry for me." She turns to the viewer, "Music."

The monitor changes from news to a singing and dancing group. Indrajit gets up and goes to his mother. He hugs her, "Yes, mother. And we will return safely before you know it."

ATLANTA NADO

The dying Sun touches the peaks on the horizon, creating a fiery crown. Shadows start to creep up the massive walls of the stronghold. It was not a structured castle from one of the more technologically advanced combatants of the war. This is a stronghold of the Tugar, a junior ally of the Rama, the enemy of Atlantis.

A junior partner to the Rama in feats of Aether, but not in spirit. They have been fighting the Atlanteans for most of the ten years of the war with little assistance from Rama. Their land is a chain of river valleys surrounded by mountains and a minor front in the global war. This fact probably has much to do with them not being overwhelmed yet.

Perched atop a towering cliff, the stronghold commands a view of the river stretching below. The stronghold is an imposing sight, with the rugged cliffs providing natural protection on over half of its exterior. The massive structure is built from monolithic stones, carefully stacked and arranged to create a labyrinth of tunnels and platforms that resemble a great hill in the fading light. But it's not just the impressive design that makes this fortress formidable - defensive weapons such as catapults and Aether cannons have been strategically placed throughout the stronghold. In this age of Aether, defensive structures must withstand heavy assaults.

An open field surrounds the outer portions of the stronghold. In the forest beyond, facing the stronghold, the Atlantean infantry awaits. Those closest to the forest edge stay undercover, still within range of the defender's arrows and

Aether blasts. Luckily for the attackers, the defenders have very few Aether weapons.

In the woods, near the cliff's edge, stands Rogat, the leader of a 22-person section. He is distracted from his work by a herd of woolly mammoths across the river, drinking at the river's edge. Their braying provides constant background noise to an otherwise quiet sunset. Most of his section rests amongst the trees around him. Three lookouts are closer to the stronghold, watching the enemy.

The Atlanteans are armed with a short sword, buckler, and Aether spear. They are further equipped with a leather breastplate, greaves, and helm. This is standard Atlantean infantry equipment.

Rogat sighs, then returns to his Aether-powered viewing tablet. Currently, it displays the stronghold and surrounding force dispositions. Near him, his friends and senior troopers of the section, Noko, Teado, and Migu, wait.

Walking up to Rogat and his team, 1st section, 3rd Piilo or company, comes the captain of the 3rd Alta Faltan infantry battalion, Captain Skerios. He is a serious-looking man of noble birth and a good leader who cares for his people.

Rogat comes to attention, placing his right hand over his heart with a slight bow. "Sir, the first section is ready for action."

Those near him also rise and stand at attention.

Captain Skerios stops in front of Rogat, quickly putting his hand over his heart in acknowledgment. Captain Skerios is not one for ceremonies in the field or behind closed doors.

"Good, we will move soon," Skerios said, motioning for everyone to return to their business. "Just waiting for the Vailixi to strike first."

Noko speaks up respectfully, "Sir, they know where the enemy is, right?"

Heads nod, and a few grumblings of agreement arise from those in hearing distance. It is known that sometimes a Vailixi pilot might start shooting before they line up the target, leading to friendly fire hitting Atlantean infantry positions. Rogat turns and gives all a "shut up" look that quickly silences the sentiment.

Skerios smiles at Noko. "Yes, trooper, I believe they do. To be safe, do not get excited and run too far ahead of the line."

Many chuckle at the idea. Migu, another of Rogat's friends, snorts, "No worries with this one, sir." Hiking a thumb towards Noko. "He only moves quickly for food and wine."

There is more laughter from the section, all know Migu is the biggest smart-ass of the section. He is also one of the laziest, spending more effort trying to get out of work than he would be doing it. Usually to the amusement of those around him. Teado, the last of Rogat's constant companions, punches Migu in the arm and says, "Look who's talking, slacker."

Even the captain laughs. Everyone loves to see Migu lowered a notch or two since he spares no one his barb-filled humor.

The captain quickly regains his serious composure and motions for Rogat to follow him. "Rogat, a word."

They walk back about ten meters from the rest of the section. "Yes, sir?"

"This is probably gonna be a bloody affair. You being a new section leader, I need you to ensure your troopers do not cut and run."

Rogat sighs, "I wish you had not given me this role. I am not sure I am ready, but I will make sure we do our part."

Skerios claps him on the shoulder. "That's the spirit. Remember, you lead the section now—not just you and those misfit friends of yours. You lead all of your people. So make sure as many of them come back as possible."

"Yes, sir." He responds, looking back at the section. Skerios nods and moves off toward the next section.

In the distance, a group of Vailixi soars just above the river, trying to stay low and quiet to avoid detection by the defenders. The Aether engines on these flying machines produce a distinct whirring sound as they move through the air.

While flying so low along the river hides their approach to the defenders, it does not go unnoticed. The mammoths on the opposite side of the river trumpet their displeasure with the craft's whirling noise as they pass by.

Close to the target, the flight commander sees the topmost portion of the stronghold, still shining in the last rays of the Sun.

The craft gun their engines as they start to increase altitude. The commander worries the defenders will hear the whirl of the Vailixi the closer they get. She is hopeful that they will not know the direction of the source before it is too late to bring their guns to bear.

Before they reach the lip of the cliff, the flight screams overhead as they go full throttle. The forest and open area before the stronghold swiftly pass by, with the target looming large in front of them. Just as they pass the ground troop positions, the stronghold opens up with its anti-air weapons.

The craft take hits, but mostly, their shields hold as they drop Aether bombs on the stronghold. Massive explosions rip the darkness as the bombs explode within the stronghold. With a lucky drop near an entrance, the Aether plasma flows inside the tunnels and over the catapult emplacements. The rest crashes harmlessly over the large stone blocks.

One of the craft has its shields flare brightly before quickly disappearing to be replaced by smoke billowing from the rear of the craft. The stricken craft makes it over the next hill and drops out of sight as the surviving squadron craft rise and veer over the distant mountains. An explosion outlines the next hill in a brief blue glow before a fiery pillar rises high, most likely signaling the death of the craft and crew.

Rogat's troopers are ready to go. They hear the distinctive whirling sound of Vailixi engines, but the surrounding forest blocks their view. The whirling sound gets louder as they return for another run, and then explosions in the stronghold follow.

"Okay, people, keep low and stay together. Forward!" The unit starts moving forward through the trees. Near the forest's edge, an arrow hits one of the most forward troopers. He is hit in the arm, losing his balance and falling back. Another section member grabs him and returns him to the Somena, or healers.

"Take cover." The unit goes to the ground before an object falls near the edge of the treeline and explodes with Aether power.

"Great, they have Aether artillery." Migu bemoans.

Teado looks at him, "Didn't the strike against the Vailixi clue you in? At least they don't seem to have powered throwers. Those must be mechanical."

Another bomb hits near the location of the first one and explodes.

"I think they do not have many since that hit near the other." Rogat declares as he crawls behind the log that his friends are behind.

Another explosion kicks dirt up and sprays them. Flinching, Migu quips, "Always the optimist, eh Rogat?"

Noko slaps Migu on his helm. "Shut up, fool. Don't let the Gods hear you and curse us."

There is another explosion further down the line out of Rogat's area, and then more. Eventually, an air strike occurs with no return fire from the stronghold.

Rogat looks over his people. All crouch behind logs or trees about ten yards from the tree line. "Everyone forward to the tree line."

The section quickly moves forward to take cover near the tree line. Another Aether bomb lands in the area between his group and the next.

Rogat taps Teado on the shoulder, "Teado, how far to the walls?" Teado rises above the log, squints, and gets a good look at the wall. An arrow whizzes by his head.

Noko barks while pulling Teado down, "Look quicker."

"Yes, be careful cuz I am next if you die." Migu grins.

Rogat clamps his big hand down on Migu's shoulder as Migu winces. Rogat grins and declares, "No, Noko will be, but we will throw you out there to draw their fire."

All who are within hearing distance laugh.

Teado, ever the serious one, looks at Migu, "If you are done being a smart ass." Looking at Rogat, "I estimate 100 meters."

Cocking his head to the side, Rogat hears the whirl of the Vailixi getting louder. He decides, "Okay, next strike, we run for the wall. I believe the Vailixi will keep their heads down."

Grunts of agreement and people start tensing for the next strike, which is coming soon as the whirl gets louder.

"When?" Noko asks. The whirl gets louder still, and then the sound of the Vailixi firing.

"Now!" The whole section starts moving into the clearing between the forest edge and the wall. Twenty individuals run out to the wall as explosions in the stronghold ring out. A few arrows come down. Rogat glances down the tree line and sees other units start to charge the stronghold but are well behind his unit.

As they run, the Vailixi flies past, and shouts of alarm come from the stronghold. Rogat and the team are about twenty meters from the wall when more arrows start coming down. His team and the other units are firing back but with no accuracy. The others running for the wall get heavily peppered by the defenders, including Aether bombs.

One of Rogat's team members goes down, and another stops to pick the person up. The person is pin-cushioned with arrows.

"Hurry, leave the wounded." Rogat barks as he pours it on with everything he has to get to the base of the wall.

Fourteen get to the four-meter-high wall. Breathing heavily, they wearily look up and fire on defenders that stick their heads out to try to shoot down at Rogat's team.

Other units of the first wave are still at a distance from the wall and are getting torn up. The second wave is at the tree line and trying to fire at the defenders, but the distance is too great for accurate fire. The defenders respond with Aether bombs and some arrow fire.

Teado, standing next to Rogat and watching the wall above him, states, "Rogat, we can't stay here long, or they will tear us apart."

Noko chimes in, "We can climb up or go to the entrance further along the wall."

Rogat, using his Aether spear, shoots at a head that appears above, getting a scream of pain for his efforts. "I don't like either."

Migu shoots at another person as an arrow sprouts from the ground less than a meter from his foot. He looks at the arrow and then at Rogat. "Yes, I am kinda addicted to living. And being in one piece."

Rolling his eyes, Teado quips, "Migu, I can't phantom why the Gods allow you to live."

Noko, staring above them, says, "We are cursed, and he is our punishment."

Looking back toward the forest, Rogat waves his Aether spear to get the attention of the second wave. He points up to the defenders atop the wall. Pulling off his climbing rope and twirling it, he stops and looks to the tree line. One of the soldiers at the tree line raises his spear in an up/down affirmative motion.

"Guess the decision is made," Teado states while grabbing his climbing rope.

Rogat readies his throw. Looking at the rest of the team, he states, "Yup. Alright, people, climbing ropes for A squad and B covers."

Team members nod, with some people grabbing ropes while others move further out to get into a better firing position. Those in the tree line start firing and moving forward. The other units of the first wave make the wall.

Rogat twirls his hook. Migu is behind him, looking up to fire at anyone who peeks out.

Rogat's gaze fixes on Migu. "Make sure you shoot straight."

Migu's fingers flex around the firing lever, his brown eyes flickering with mischief. "Of course," he quips back. "I promise not to shoot you in the ass."

Shaking his head in mock exasperation, Rogat mutters, "One of these days, Migu."

Rogat and A squad throw their hooks over the wall—most catch. Further back, 2nd section is a good distance into the open fields firing at the walls above. From the tree line, another wave, the 3rd section, moves to the edge of the tree line to get into a supporting position. Squad B moves further away from the wall to get better shooting angles.

Another Vailixi strafing run comes in, hitting near the section's position. Rogat and his team scamper up the ropes. Shots from 2nd section hit the top of the wall, and Aether shots from below fly near Risor. With the Aether spear strapped to his back, he nears the top of the wall. Getting a good grip on the rope with one hand, he pulls out his short sword.

An enemy archer rushes Rogat, trying to stab him as he tries to lift himself over the top of the wall. Fending off the attack with a well-timed parry, he gains the upper hand and plunges his short sword into his opponent's armpit.

Gaining the battlement, he clears an area to allow his people to join him.

Behind the wall, a small plaza of massive non-uniform stones placed perfectly together has some apparent Aether fire damage from the Vailixi. Two tunnels appear opposite the battlement. One tunnel leads up to the next higher level, and another leads down and further into the stronghold.

Teado climbs over the wall and gets back to back with Rogat. There are four of his section over the wall, while the enemy has ten archers. The archers are armed with daggers, and the Atlanteans have short swords. More enemy archers and swordsmen run out of the tunnels. Some archers try to fire arrows at Rogat and his people, while others rush forward with daggers or swords.

More of Rogat's unit comes over the wall. Eventually, twelve of his people are on the plaza.

Teado quickly jabs Rogat to get his attention, "Second section is coming up the wall now."

Nodding, Rogat roars, "Squad B, use Aether spears."

Rogat and Squad A continue to use swords while those that just came up to the battlements unshoulder their weapons and fire at the enemy.

The Atlanteans are in a semi-circle around a few climbing ropes while the Second section starts to gain the battlement. B squad shoots between those with swords while the next unit's troopers reinforce them with Aether spears blazing.

Another Vailixi strike hits the far wall and kills several enemies. The remaining enemy flees back to the tunnels.

Seeing the enemy losing their nerve, Rogat calls out, "Atlanteans, after them." He and the rest of his people follow the enemy to one tunnel. A group of the enemy is cut off from the tunnels and cut down with no mercy. More troopers come over the wall.

Rogat nears the tunnel entrance when an arrow hits him in the arm. His friends pull him away from the entrance. Migu and Noko hold him against the wall while Teado breaks the exposed length of the arrow. Roaring in pain as the arrow is broken and pulled out, he steadies himself.

Most of his team are near the mouth of the tunnel, firing down the tunnel with their Aether spears. Once the wound is bound, Rogat hefts his short sword and then nods to his friends to release him.

"Don't let them regroup." He orders.

He and his fellow troopers continue to push the enemy back up the tunnel. Aether fire sizzles past his head to the enemy up ahead. The tunnel continues to slope up, and light is in the distance.

Noko comes up to Rogat, who is holding his arm, "Rogat, you should fall back and let us take this."

Through the pain, "No, we can not slow down, or they will prepare their defenses. Keep moving forward."

Dead or dying Tugar and Atlanteans litter the tunnel. They are near the exit of the tunnel, and resistance is weaker. A few soldiers from the second section pass Rogat and his tired force and burst free of the exit. Rogat is near the exit and sees those soldiers die in a crossfire.

He calls for a halt to the advance. The exit is clear of live enemies, and the viewable plaza from the exit has a few bodies besides the fallen troopers.

"What do you think, Rogat?" Teado asks. Those nearby gather around them. Rogat is nursing his arm.

"I think they have some positions to the sides that we have to exit to see. Puts us in a kill zone."

Migu looks at the exit and casually asks, "Whose gonna check to see if you are right."

"Thanks for volunteering." Rogat smiles. A few soldiers from Rogat's and the other unit clap Migu on the shoulder and not-so-gently push him forward. The soldiers are about three meters back in the tunnel. Migu gives Rogat a sour look.

"Remind me to keep my mouth shut next time."

"Don't worry, Migu. The Gods are still not done cursing us. They will keep you alive," Noko says with a semi-serious look. Others grin and smile. He continues, "But just in case, be careful."

Moving forward, Migu creeps up one side and looks out. Further fighting, Aether blasts and explosions ring in the distance — Migu strains to see past the exit. An arrow ricochets off the wall next to him, cutting his cheek.

An Aether bomb flies through the air and lands before the exit. Migu scrambles back two steps and then dives back down the tunnel. The others also dive for cover. The explosion rings through the tunnel.

The Atlanteans reposition a few meters further down the tunnel. Migu gets up and shakes himself off. He returns down the tunnel toward his friends, opening his jaw and shaking his head.

"I believe you know what they have now," Migu yells in a smart-ass manner, rejoining Rogat and crew. Everyone motions for him to lower his voice. He continues to shake his head.

Rogat tries to peer through the smoke at the mouth of the tunnel. Failing to discern anything, he looks over at Migu.

"Could you see anything?"

Migu takes a drink from an offered water skin. Starting loud but self-correcting and getting back to a reasonably normal volume. "Not much, but there are a lot of them out there."

Rogat looks at another soldier. "Report back that we have taken the first battlement, but the tunnel leads to another plaza further up, and we can not proceed further." The trooper leaves.

Teado asks, "What do you want us to do? Also, you need to go back and get fixed up."

Migu chimes in, "Me too, that arrow cut me good."

Noko grabs Migu's face and looks at it, then pushes his face away in mock disgust, "Migu, that is barely a cut." Others laugh and push Migu around.

Rogat looks back at the mouth of the tunnel, then at the bodies around them. "Stack the enemy bodies into a barrier. Get our dead back down the tunnel. Wounded go, too." He goes up to one of the dead enemies and cuts a swath of uniform to rebandage his blood-soaked arm.

Teado touches Rogat's shoulder, "Rogat, go get that healed. I imagine we have a priest on the battlement by now."

Noko agrees, "Ya, we can watch the tunnel."

A senior trooper from the 2nd Piilo approaches the barrier made of enemy dead. "Who's in charge?"

The plaza smells of the stench of death. The bodies have been removed, but the pooled blood remains. Rogat's team is relaxing around the battlements, and their energy is spent from hours of fighting. A huddled group of Tugar prisoners are escorted from one tunnel to another. Heads hung low and spiritless.

The conquered looked defeated as they resigned themselves to their fate at the hands of their conquerors. They would likely face internment, interrogation, and forced labor until their nation was defeated. Then, they might be allowed to return home or live as slaves if they had angered the Empire. Slavery was uncommon in Atlantis, but it was used for captured warriors or those who rebelled against the Empire. After a few years, they would be tied to the land in a settler program. There, those who didn't cause problems were granted their freedom, land, and, in time, citizenship if they paid their dues and proved their loyalty. Through hard work and determination, this process helped rebuild former enemies into patriotic citizens.

Rogat contemplated the stars above. This plaza faced the river; in the distance, he could hear the large herd animals trumpeting challenges at night. Looking over the parapet and through the moonlight, he could see some massive mammoths. They grouped to protect the young or old from predators, like the saber-tooth cats or packs of grey wolves.

Migu brings him back to the plaza. "Think we will go back to Delin?"

Noko responds, "I think they will have us push on to the next stronghold."

There were a few groans from all those around Noko. They have been out for two months, taking strongholds along the river. There are many more to go, but the unit is worn out. Rogat watches a withering of the team's spirit. The last stronghold they had lost their previous Sergeant. He is happy they did not have that problem after taking this stronghold.

There is silence, broken by an explosive sigh and quip from Migu. "Must you always be so pessimistic? The Gods are probably bored with all your doomsaying."

Teado shakes his head, "Migu, be careful..."

Migu interrupts Teado, "Yes, Yes, I know. The Gods will curse me if I am not careful."

Rogat warns, "Migu."

Migu turns to Rogat and gives him a conspiratorial smile. "Ah, the voice of reason. Come Rogat, tell them they are too serious."

"Let it be Migu." Sighing, Rogat continues, "Yes, our Gods have not blessed us with heroes in the last few thousand years. But it is said they still guide us."

Noko jumps in, "The Gods are real. Many cultures still have God's blessed heroes. And our Gods have given us Aether and our strength. They watch us still."

Teado voices his opinion around a mouth full of rations, "It doesn't matter, just don't tempt the Gods as long as you are near us." Many around them agree.

Rolling his eyes and raising his hands, Migu responds, "So much for an entertaining and stimulating conversation."

He gave Migu that warning look a million times: "Shut up, Migu. You talk too much."

Many laugh at that, and even Migu can not contain a grin. Captain Skerios walks up out of the upward-bound tunnel. Everyone slowly starts to rise to attention.

"Good work today. Bloody business, but the stronghold is ours."

Migu speaks up first, "Sir, will we be able to rest?"

"Yes, you will trooper. We will send you back to Delin. We suffered a lot of casualties, so we will rebuild."

Everyone perks up at that. Before they could all cheer, Rogat asks, "Sir, who will man this stronghold?"

"Some of our allies will arrive in the morning. Not sure who yet. The good news is that your whole unit can rest. The 5th Piilo will be responsible for security tonight since they were the reserves and saw little action."

No longer able to contain themselves, the troopers cheer. The prisoners shoot fearful looks their way. Momentary fear of not knowing why the enemy is cheering is replaced by weary dejection when they realize that the enemy will not harm them.

Teado, holding a tin of field rations up, "Sir, will we have decent rations tonight?"

All cheering stops as they wait to hear what the captain says. He holds his answer for what seems like an eternity before breaking up in laughter: "Yes, trooper, the cooks should be making the rounds and will get here soon, I imagine."

Further cheers, the team becoming very animated. Rogat moves closer to the captain. "Sir, will we have a chance to go home?"

Skerios thought momentarily, "Yes, I believe you will get at least a month or two with that wound. Back to Altai, eh?"

"Yes sir, I received word my friends are also heading back."

"The Vailixi commander, right? One of the lords of Altai?"

"Yes, sir, Lord Tarnor. He commands the Falcon Claw squadron. We have been friends since we were kids."

The captain grips Rogat's good shoulder. "I see. Well, yes, I believe you deserve it. You have permission to leave as soon as we return—after you report to the Somena, that is."

THREE MONTHS BEFORE

ATLANTIS

S tretching, Tolen glances out the window of the passenger version of a Vailixi to see nothing but clouds with a fiery hue from the setting sun. They had been in flight for the last six hours and would land in an hour. It would be near sunset when he arrives in Atlantis.

Turning to his seat's console, he activates the flight tracker. The craft is slowing down and nearing Atlanta's continental shelf. It will not be long.

At the southern tip of the peninsula of Atlanta Meito is the Belt of Hercules, a strait over 100 kilometers long and three wide at its narrowest point. Toward the western end, on the northern shore, lay Atlantis, the Eternal, the city of Poseidon.

Tolen stares at the console. He thinks of the 30,000 years of history that have made up Atlantis. Smiling, he considers what the early Kings of Atlantis would think of the Empire and what it has become—from a people that sought to befriend others and bring them the gift of civilization to now, a people that wishes to rule the world.

"I am sure Hercules would have a thing or two to say to the emperor." Turning off the console.

"I'm sorry, sir. Did you need something?" the stewardess asks, walking up the aisle behind him.

Fumbling with his papers, "Oh, sorry, could I please get a quat."

She smiles and moves off to fulfill his request. Shaking his head, he chuckles.

She returns with his quat. The aroma of the drink is truly an addiction for most Atlanteans. He heard a rumor that even those of Rama are addicted to it. Different variations are coming from the remote reaches of Alta Cieto and Atlanta Suna. He even heard that some enterprising merchants were trying to grow it beyond the imperial borders in Atlanta Luxa.

He wonders if those who love quat in the Rama Empire grow their own beans or if the rumors are true that some merchants have set up creative distribution channels to get quat to Rama. What would he do if he could not get any?

He sips the drink and sighs. Nectar of the gods, he thought. Not the cut stuff that some of the more unsavory merchants try to ply, using burnt husks and some roots as an additive to a few quat beans. Holding the cup with two hands and staring out the window, he fantasizes about picking his beans and making the best cup of quat possible. Musing, maybe he should try to grow his own.

Dropping below the clouds, the Sun sets on the horizon. According to the priests, God Helios's Sun chariot is driven along the path of the sky. Being a scientist, Tolen knows that the Earth follows a path around the Sun. That means his home across the ocean, far off Altai, is enjoying a mid-morning sun.

Smiling, he watches the Sun sink further down behind the horizon. Continuing his thoughts, some of Atlantis' more primitive neighbors think the Sun goes in a hole in the ground and follows a tunnel to the west through the lands of Hades. There, it exits to go back into the sky. No matter how many times his people tell them differently.

"Some people always believe they know better," he said aloud.

He adjusts the seat's console viewer to bring the inspiring sight of Atlantis growing larger before the craft. The Sun sets the highest buildings ablaze with vibrant hues, casting a breathtaking glow over the city. The undersides of clouds are painted with fiery oranges and reds, illuminated by the fading rays of sunlight. Amidst the billowing clouds, glimpses of stars twinkled against the darkening sky. It is a surreal and awe-inspiring scene, like a painting come to life.

Below, the pyramids, with their glowing capstones, stood majestically over the rest of a darkened Atlantis, the fading Sun surrendering the building tops to the embrace of darkness. Only the tip of the pyramids is ablaze in golden light. Tolen considers himself lucky. The fabled Blessing of Poseidon is about to occur.

The craft turns north, blocking Tolen's view of the rest of the city. Heading north, it banks steeply to give all passengers a view of the spectacle about to happen. As the light last touches the capstone, it flashes brilliantly in all directions, becoming a dazzling spectacle. In the viewer's mind, the image of the God Poseidon smiling directly at the viewer occurs to all that look up at that moment. It is said that even foreigners experience this blessing.

Tolen knows it is a trick of optics but is still unsure how it occurs. It even happens to those viewing the image via Aether viewers. So alluring is the image that there is a law on days when the spectacle will occur; all Aether from the pyramids is stopped in the city, shutting down all operations to ensure no one gets hurt while mesmerized by the image of Poseidon. Of the pilots of Vailixi, the large view screens are not allowed to be on.

Moments later, the image recedes from Tolen's vision. A warm feeling of love and safety enwraps him and his fellow passengers as the Vailixi descends to Atlantis' aeroport.

The Imperial Academy of Science loomed over the surrounding neighborhoods of Atlantis, a towering behemoth of marble and stone that stretched six stories high, one of the tallest buildings in the city beside the power pyramids. It resides on the third ring of the city, a sign of the Academy's independence from the undue influence of the other functions of the Empire, which reside in the inner rings of the city. Intricate carvings depicting the history of science and discovery adorn its entrance. This magnificent structure, built thousands of years ago, is a beacon of knowledge and innovation in the city and the Empire.

The Academy is a gathering place for esteemed members to share groundbreaking research and ideas. Today, military members and government ministers are also in attendance, a testament to the importance of this event.

Standing confidently at the podium before his peers, Tolen takes in the grandeur of the auditorium. The stage stretches out in front of him while the most senior members of the Academy sit on his left. This is a momentous occasion on which he will have the opportunity to showcase his discoveries to those who hold power and influence in society.

Behind him, a large Aether screen displays the northern ice sheet covering most of the planet's northern climes.

Tolen judges the audience has had time to grasp the vastness of the ice sheet. He continues, "Altai had recently dispatched an expedition in their area. The ice lakes there were averaging 500 meters deep." The map shifts down to the ice sheet above the continent of Alta.

"The last expedition north of Atlantis, three years ago, discovered the ice lakes in that region were, on average, 700 meters deep."

The image shifted to the north of Atlanta Meito. Large blue areas materialized on the map, showing the discovered ice lakes.

He continued, "The estimated amount of water in this region would raise the sea levels nearly three meters worldwide."

There are murmurs in the crowd. The sergeant at arms pounds his ceremonial staff on the ground and yells for silence. Once the crowd quiets, Lord Tolloc, the Prime Minister, asks, "That is all fine, Shilot Dekarn, but what does that mean to the average citizen? Is Atlantis in trouble?"

Tolen looks over the crowd. "Three meters would not be a major problem to Atlantis, Prime Minister. It would cause the sea to encroach on some of our colonies and swamp some low-lying farmlands."

Next to the Prime Minister is Lady Tomar, a leading member of the Shigar party and the military's General Staff. She puts her hand on the Prime minister's arm and asks, "So it will not cause any problems." Huffing loudly, she asks, "Why are we here?"

One of the peers on stage stood up. Shilot Dentian is very old and a very respected member of the Academy. Tolen defers to her.

"As you probably know, these are not the only ice lakes, general."

A warning flashes in Lady Tomar's eyes—a warning that Dentian ignores by smiling at the general. Fighting to maintain composure, Lady Tomar responds, "No, but the chances of all breaking are limited, correct? So, there is no concern right now. Right?"

Shilot Dentian nods to Tolen to continue.

"No, Lady Tomar, that is not exactly true. If the ice walls continue to melt, we can not determine when each will fail and if the ice lakes behind them will drain."

"So we are guessing, is it?" Asks the Prime Minister.

"That is why we must further research and measure, Prime Minister. The release of one of the ice lakes could cause a shift that would cause other ice walls to break."

"Again, you are guessing, right?" quips Lady Tomar.

Frustration rising, Tolen responds, "That is why we need to continue researching. We have not encountered such an issue in the thousands of years of our Empire. From what we have measured, there is enough water to raise the sea levels much higher."

Lord Tofiz, sitting next to Lady Tomar and the commander of the armies of Atlanta Luxa, joins the discussion. "How much Shilot Dekarn?"

"We are not sure yet. We need..."

Lady Tomar interrupts, "Sounds like you do not know a lot of things."

The crowd is getting agitated. Many Shigar and Nalos supporters are starting to throw accusations and counter-accusations. Lord Rosan Tranor, Risor's father, sits ten people down from the Prime Minister. He stands up and faces Lady Tomar.

In a loud voice to quiet the crowd, he said, "Lady Tomar, the pursuit of knowledge is not gained in guessing but in pursuing facts. That is what the Academy is doing."

Lord Tofiz stands up and faces Rosan, "We have spent enough money for this lack of knowledge, and we have a war to prosecute."

The crowd noise increases. Lord Tofiz, Lady Tomar, and even the Prime Minister are all Shigar members, while Lord Tranor is a leading Nalos member. Others throughout the crowd stand up and argue with opposing groups around them. The Academy's sergeant of arms fails to quiet the crowd with his natural voice or the pounding of his staff.

The sergeant of arms activates his staff, which starts to glow. The glow increases to a blinding and piercing brilliance. His voice is amplified around the hall. "Silence! This is a house of learning, not a pub to brawl in."

The crowd, adequately chastened, quiets.

Rosan bows to the Prime Minister and then the academy members on stage, "Forgive the outburst and my interruption, Prime Minister and members of the academy."

Lord Tolloc stands up, looks around, and nods to Rosan, who returns to his seat. Lord Tolloc looks the crowd over with a look of disdain.

"An unsightly scene by all. The question remains. Do we not know what and when?" He finishes by turning to Tolen.

"No, Prime Minister. That is why we must continue sending expeditions to the ice packs to measure the ice melt rate and the size of the ice lakes."

Lady Tomar stands up. "It sounds like these dangers that Shilot Dekarn mentions might come to pass, but I have been told, on good authority, that it is still a long way off. We are at war and should spend what we can to defeat this enemy threatening our way of life."

Someone in the crowd yells, "It is us that threatens Rama's way of life."

The crowd goes wild again. Most members are standing and arguing again, with some pushing and shoving.

Tolen stares at Lady Tomar with a barely contained, fed-up look. Lady Tomar, for her part, looks back at him with disdain.

Lord Tranor's mansion in Atlantis is a mini-palace. The Tranors are an old family that has been a power broker in Atlantis from its founding. Rosan, the current patriarch of the family, has kept the palatial residence even though the family mostly lives in Altai now. Altai is across the ocean and one of the oldest colonies in Alta.

The senior council member of Altai sat at the head of the table. His wife, Miana, and son, Risor, who is on leave awaiting his squadron's repairs, are on his right. Tolen, a childhood friend of Risor, sat on his left. Risor's younger sister is next to him.

Everyone laughs but Tolen and Rina. "Risor, stop it. Tolen does not think it is funny."

With a raised eyebrow, Rosan gives Risor a warning look. Realizing he is outnumbered, Risor grins, "Oh, okay. Tolen, forgive me, my friend. But it is what the Shigar do. Is it not?"

"Yes, that is the case. They ignore what they do not wish to understand."

Risor takes a drink and holds the cup up for a servant to refill, "Yes, which is everything."

Tolen stares at his cup, "Yes, but even the Prime Minister is acting this way."

Risor shrugs, "He is Shigar, after all."

Rina looked from father to brother. "He is supposed to be for everyone, right, Father?"

With a sad smile, Rosan responds, "Yes, he is."

Everyone seems to catch Rosan's melancholy attitude. Silence as everyone considers what he means.

Tolen breaks the silence, "Risor, you said you crossed Lady Jana too?"

Risor smiles, "Yes, she wanted me charged with mutiny."

His mother touches his shoulder, "Come home with us. We leave at the end of the week. Get away from here."

Rosan pats Miana's hand and smiles, then looks at Risor, "It would seem that you put our family on the target list for the Shigar. Son, be careful."

Chuckling, "I seem to recall you helped get us on that list, too, Father." When no one sees his humor, he grins. "They are not a concern. I worry more about some poor Raman soldier getting a lucky shot at my Vailixi than them."

Tolen, taking on a serious tone, "My friend, the lucky shot by our enemies is one concern, but the well-placed blade or word to a Shigar fanatic is doubly dangerous. Especially since they will not stop with you."

Miana rubs Risor's shoulder with a concerned look, "Please think of the family, Risor."

Rosan toys with his cup, "It would probably be best to return to Altai as soon as possible. Maybe reschedule for tomorrow. To let things blow over."

Risor drains his cup, waving off the server. "Well, I have a few weeks of leave. It will take that long for these learned ones to refit my squadron." He winks at

Tolen, although Tolen is not one of the Shilots that can manipulate Aether to make the devices Atlantis uses.

Giving Risor a hard look, Rina says, "It's the Gods that grant us these powers."

Acting surprised, Risor responds, "Truly, Rina? If they could only take care of the Shigar too."

Miana hisses, "Risor, do not blame the Gods."

A scandalized Rosan adds, "Do not worry, my love. Our SON was not being disrespectful. Right, Risor?"

Realizing his humor is unappreciated, he says, "No, Father. Mother, I meant no disrespect. And now I am off to meet my people." Standing, he turns to Tolen, "Tolen, care to join?"

Tolen stands with him. He looks at Rina and smiles. "No, I have had enough excitement today and am happy to finish with this wonderful meal. A word with you, Risor?"

They walk out of the room together. Rosan calls after them. "Risor, remember, keep the peace."

They are near the front door, and a servant opens the door.

Tolen stops and turns to Risor, "Risor, be careful, my friend. I think things are coming to a head with the Shigar. I fear we are looking at something outside of the normal animosity."

Clapping a hand on Tolen's shoulder, "You worry too much, my friend. Think more of my sister. She couldn't take her eyes off of you."

Coughing and turning red, "Well, yes, I think highly of her."

Hugging his friend, "You two were made for each other."

Later that night, Risor sits in the squadron's home bar with members of his squadron. They have just arrived in Atlantis the day before. Their squadron's Vailixi getting their chance at overhaul after the battle at Taxila.

The Sun Darters and Wave Rider squadrons have almost completed their repairs. Upon completion, the Sun Darters will return to Atlanta Suna. Risor didn't know where the Wave Riders would go, but they would probably stay in Atlantis.

The bar is softly lit, with numerous tables empty. The night is still young. An Aether display sits in the corner, turned to a news channel that discusses the Empire's news.

Those with Risor are mostly from his own Vailixi. Most squadron members have already departed for their home regions to visit their families.

Unlike infantry units, mainly formed from a single town or region, Vailixi squadrons require people who can manipulate Aether. This brings people from all over the Empire together. Those operating shields, weapons, communications, and engineering can use Aether. The commanders do not require this talent. They are primarily nobles.

Risor sits with Tilor, a noble like him. Dimera, Imshina, and Milo are with them. The non-team member is Geiro, the commander of the squadron's number three Vailixi and one of its newest members.

Risor raises his glass, "To the empire." The others repeat the toast, and all drink deeply.

"Sir, are you going to go back to Altai?" Tilor asks.

Risor nods, "Yes, with all the passions in Atlantis, it's best to leave for a while. You are staying for a while?"

All at the table smile. Tilor grins, his eyes follow one of the waitresses at another table.

Geiro volunteers, "I will visit family south in Atlanta Luxa."

"Me too." Chimes in Imshina. She is also from Atlanta Luxa.

Dimera said, "I will return to Altai, as well."

"Oh, then join my family on our return. I think we leave the day after tomorrow." Risor said while getting the attention of the bar owner.

"Sir, I can not afford those flights. I will catch the next boat to Neptius, then see if I can catch a hop to Altai."

Risor smiles. "Nonsense. You will be my guest. Milo, what about you? Are you heading home?"

Finishing his beer and wiping his mouth on his sleeve, "Nah, I think I will stay here and enjoy some of the local entertainment. Besides, Tilor can not stare at Lena every day, so I will keep him company."

They all laugh as Tilor's stern look returns with a barely passable, innocent look from Milo. The door opens, and another group of flyers comes in. The mood turns somber as the other group is recognized.

Milo sighs, "Well, there goes the neighborhood."

In a near whisper, Dimera says, "Sir, they are Wave Riders."

Tilor looks at them disdainfully, "At least Jana is not with them. But that fool Dentam is."

With a worried look, Imshina adds, "Not too loud, Tilor."

Tilor is about to say something when Lena, the barmaid and girlfriend Tilor, comes up. He smiles at her, but she gives him a worried look.

"Tilor, please be careful." She says as she picks up the empties and wipes the table.

He pats her hand, "Don't worry, baby, we will not start anything."

Risor stands up, "I think I need to make more room. Another round, Lena dear."

Risor enters the bathroom when Dentam from the Wave Rider table calls out. "What do we have to do to get service here?"

Lena looks at Tilor and then goes to the other table. Tilor is watching her, and Dentam sees that. He gives her a lewd look and puts his hand on Lena's butt. She slaps it away. Angered and shocked, Dentam stands up and looks like he is about to hit her. She flinches. Tilor's table stands up. Then, the Wave Riders do the same.

Tilor belts out in a commanding voice, dripping with disdain, "Touch her, my Lord, and I will cut that hand off."

"What, this whore? She assaulted me and will pay for it."

"You grabbed me," Lena states as she tries to escape, but another of the Wave Riders grabs her arm.

"Silence bitch. You do not address your betters that way." The man who held her said.

Tilor moves towards Dentam with Milo behind him. The others stay near the table.

Tilor stops before them, looking between Dentam and the man with Lena's arm. "Same thing to your dog if he doesn't shut his mouth and let her go. Lena, come here." He holds out his hands.

Lena pulls free from the man and moves towards him when Dentam grabs her arm again and pulls her to him. The crowd goes silent while both parties move closer.

Risor comes out of the bathroom and stops, seeing the commotion. He looks at the owner, who looks fearful. The Wave Riders, all Shigar, are known for their anger.

Lena whimpers, the crowd is silent, and Tilor bursts with anger. Risor slowly moves behind the Wave Rider table, whose occupants are all turned towards Tilor and the group.

One of the Wave Riders moves toward Tilor. With a haughty look at Tilor, he turns slightly to speak to his group. "My Lord Dentam, maybe we should show his lordship here what she really wants. Barkeep, how much to take her for the night?"

Dimera's shoulders slump, "Oh shit."

Tilor roars and punches the guy in the face. Both groups start toward each other. Dentam pulls back with Lena, who is whimpering, letting his people move forward to Tilor.

Fists are flying, and Dentam, still holding Lena's arm, feels something and turns. Risor grabs a handful of his hair and yanks back hard. At the same time, he gives him a kidney punch. Dentam expels and lets go of Lena.

She runs away while the two groups thoroughly go at it, and the rest of the crowd pulls back from their tables. Risor, still holding Dentam by the hair, slams his head into the table a few times.

The bar is a disaster zone, with overturned tables and chairs strewn about. Broken glass litters the floor from one of the windows, having been shattered by someone being thrown through it. The garrison troopers escort the members of the Wave Riders back to base.

Risor emerges from a conversation with the duty officer of the garrison, his charm having convinced them that his team was innocent in the brawl. Approaching his team with a cocky grin fades, seeing their injuries. Lena tends to Tilor's cut lip, while others sported bruises and black eyes. Dimera held an ice pack to her swollen eye. Clearly, their victory did not come without consequences.

"Okay," he asks Dimera, pulling her hand and towel away to see the shiner starting to discolor.

She gives him a painful look, "I will live. Are you okay?"

He touches his nose and wipes under it with a finger, noticing no blood. He smiles, "Nothing a little special attention wouldn't cure."

Looking at the others, he settles on Geiro. "Geiro, you okay? You look terrible."

Geiro winces, turning his whole body to face Risor. "Thank you, my lord. I think I will be happy to take a few weeks off."

Imshina looks like she barely broke a sweat. "I will make sure he gets home okay."

Risor nods and stands up. He helps Dimera get up as the others start standing as well.

"Okay, I think it's definitely time for all of us to leave Atlantis for a while. Lena, I think you should go too."

Tilor nods, "Don't worry, I will take her on vacation. If you are okay with that, Lando?"

They all look at the bar owner. Lando looks up from cleaning up some of the mess behind the bar. He gives a non-committal shrug and wave of dismissal in their direction.

Risor looks at all of them, "It's okay. He is a little sore from the place being busted up."

"Gee, imagine that," Milo said.

Looking slightly worried, Lena said, "I should stay and help."

Risor shakes his head and smiles, "Nonsense. He will be paid well for today. I will give the bill to the Wave Riders."

They all look a little shocked. Tilor, becoming serious, says, "Sir, that will not endear you to them."

Risor nods, "Probably so, but they started the mess and deserve it."

With a worried look, Dimera asks, "Didn't you say your father wanted you to be low-key this evening?"

Grinning, "Fear not, my lady, this is a little friendly one-upmanship between squadrons." Seeing some of them do not understand, Risor sighs and continues, "See, no one wants this reported. Dentam agreed to pay the damages and bills for everything. The duty officer accepted that and escorted them back to base to ensure their night was over. Dentam will pay the bill in the morning, and only our two squadrons will remember this."

Geiro chimes in, "Sir, they are Shigar, and most of us are Nalos. Maybe it won't be forgotten so easily?"

Tilor agrees, "I think Geiro is correct, sir. They will be gunning for us, especially you."

Risor smiles innocently and shrugs, "We shall see. Come, let us let Master Lando close his bar."

They gather their stuff, and Risor returns to the bar. Lando and his other staff are cleaning up the mess.

Starting somewhat contritely, "Master Lando, again, I am sorry for what happened here tonight and for taking Lena." He fishes a large golden imperial out of his pocket. "For your troubles." Then pulls out another two smaller silver coins. "And for your people." The amount he gives would take them all a good part of a year to make. He smiles, having an idea. "I think I will send the bill to the Shigar party."

Lando looks up, worried, "My Lord, I do not want trouble with the Shigar nor for you."

"More trouble?" Tilor asks, coming up to them.

"I will send the bill to the Shigar party with a little note for Dentam." Risor raises his eyebrows repeatedly at his cleverness.

Tilor shakes his head. "You are looking for them to shoot you down in mid-air, aren't ya? The bad thing is that we are gonna go down with you."

"Do not worry, my friend. They will pay and not do more. It's an honor thing." He gives Lando a wink.

Atlantis is a large city with nearly 100,000 inhabitants. With the concentric island rings surrounding the central Imperial sector, it is even larger in area than some would think. The waterways between the island rings constantly flow with traffic. Wind-powered or Aether-powered merchant and passenger ships come from all over the globe.

For most people, ships are the means of traveling between regions. The rich take passenger Vailixi, and the rest take ships. If lucky and willing to pay enough, they take Aether-ships, which move quickly and do not depend on the vagaries of the wind.

Many of those ships would pass the military headquarters complex on the second ring, which is significant in area but only three stories high. Lady Tomar, Commander of the First Front and a faction leader of the Shigar party, stands on her office's balcony, watching the ships sail by towards the open sea.

Her aide interrupts her musings to announce that Lady Kalin has arrived. She nods and watches the Sun lowering to the horizon for the coming sunset and the Blessing of Poseidon.

Jana stands at attention in front of her desk. Lady Tomar walks to her side of the desk and picks up a viewer tablet.

"What is with you and Commander Tranor?"

Anger flashed through Jana's eyes, "I should have demanded his trial."

Lady Tomar points the viewer at her, "You let him get to you."

Ready with a sharp response, Jana checks herself and then, taking a barely noticed breath, forces out, "That man vexes me. One day, I will find a way to repay him."

"First, taking command of the assault, making you look weak and uninformed. Then he adds insult to injury with this bill."

Lady Tomar tosses the viewer to Jana, who starts reading it.

She continues, "Do you know what this is about? Your man started this?"

Coloring slightly, Jana nods, "Yes, I did not know the damage was so great."

With disdain, "So you have again been shown up by Lord Tranor. Frankly, Lady Kalin, I wonder if I made a mistake supporting you."

Returning to attention, "No, my Lady. I am yours and will make up for this."

"Really? Can I trust you?"

"With my life, I am yours to command."

Lady Tomar stares at Jana for a while, enjoying her unease. Then she starts walking towards the balcony again, beckoning Jana to follow. She is satisfied to see a humbled Jana walk up next to her at the balcony rail.

Looking toward the west and the sunset, Lady Tomar remarks, "Another chance you will have, but my patience is wearing thin with these failures."

"It will not happen again."

Giving Jana a look, "See that it doesn't. But he is no longer an issue. Have you heard of the Hand of Aries?"

"Rumors, my Lady, but nothing more."

"Go get the viewing tablet."

Jana brings the viewer, offering it to Lady Tomar. Lady Tomar puts her hand on the tablet, "Open Hand of Aries project."

The viewing tablet screen changes, and an aerodynamic missile with writing on the side comes into view. Lady Tomar gives the viewer to Jana. The more Jana reads, the more incredulous her face becomes.

She gasps, "The gods, what have we wrought?"

Lady Tomar turns back to the sunset. "The ultimate weapon, and you will use it against Rama. Then we will take care of our internal problems."

ATLANTA QUESTO

Tolen Dekarn stares out the window. Long white robes marking the wearer as a Shilot, or scientist, clothe him. Most of those sharing the ride with him wore expensive tunics or dresses that marked them of the nobility or wealthy merchants.

The craft crosses the shoreline and is now over Atlanta Questo. It is early morning, and the Vailixi swings onto a southerly course along the coast. The Sun's blazing glory spears through each window on the left side of the cabin.

Tolen squints and tilts his head away from the Sun's rays. He watches Tu-ne grow in size as they decrease the distance. Tu-ne is a large active volcano with a constant plume of smoke exiting its crater.

The Atlantean city of Utanor is on the coast near the volcano. He wonders why the original colonists built their colony so close to an active volcano. When they have a moment, he resolves to ask Choka, the head Shilot of Utanor.

The city of Utanor rests at the mouth of a wide and flat river valley. To the east is the ocean, Tes Tira, and to the west, Tu-ne, standing alone above the low mountain range surrounding it.

Like Tu-ne, the governor's palace stands majestically above the rest of the city on a massive, rocky outcrop. Most of the city is two or three-story buildings below the outcrop.

When the Vailixi lands at the airport, it is mid-morning. The aeroport is on the rise a kilometer or so outside of Utanor. When Tolen exits the Vailixi, he can see the Tes Tira behind the city. It is a beautiful sunny day.

While most passengers exit the Vailixi and board an Aether wagon, Tolen walks toward three officials similarly attired as him. Choka, the head Shilot in Utanor, stands smiling with two assistants behind her. She is young for her position, which reflects her brilliance in metallurgy.

"Welcome to Utanor Shilot Dekarn. I trust your flight was comfortable?" She said with a warm smile. They have been working together, but remotely, on the problem of the ice packs for two years.

Shaking her hand, "Finally, a chance to meet Choka. And please, call me Tolen." She is not of the nobility and thus only uses a first name. "Yes, it was mostly a good flight. Passed through a storm over the ocean, but the pilot was skilled in skirting the worst."

"I have not had a chance to fly over the great oceans, but I have heard it can be rough." She signals her assistants to take his bag and shows him to their Aether wagon. Smaller than the airport's wagon, this one is owned by the science academy.

Driving through Utanor on the way to the palace, Tolen watches life go on as it would in his home of Altai. Large open streets with small crowds of people walk along the sidewalks. Shops open to the street, followed by gated homes or apartments for the common folk.

Choka interrupts his reflections. "We will meet Yanis and the rest of the Academy after lunch. It should give you some time to relax."

"Thank you, Choka. I would be happy to meet Shilot Yanis beforehand. I would like to go over the route one more time."

She chuckles. "Even in a new place, all business. Oh, and later this afternoon, we will meet the Utanor council. They would like to hear from you on your findings."

He is about to respond when the wagon takes a turn, going up an elevated road heading to the palace. The street-side buildings open up a spectacular view of Tu-ne in the distance. He follows the view. Choka smirks. "I guess not all business? Good."

He grins like a kid and says, "I would be happy to give them a report. Reluctantly, I must leave tomorrow evening to get to Atlantis." Tu-ne is behind them now, and Tolen turns back and points at it. "Have you determined when the next eruption will be?"

"As far as we have been able to determine, it will be a few decades until we have to start worrying."

Turning back to the front, he asks, "Why did we ever build so close?"

Laughing, she responds, "A thousand years ago, when Utanor was founded, Tu-ne was inactive. Only in the last two hundred years."

Tolen watches the Hall of Elders fill up. Famous throughout the Empire, the builders, nearly a thousand years ago, decided to make the room spin.

It sits at the top of the governor's palace and has a 360-degree view of the surrounding countryside. He watches the Sun touch the top of Tu-ne, a view only seen from the city two months of the year as the Sun progresses along the horizon.

Opposite the view of Tu-ne is the great ocean of Tes Tira. It is the largest of the oceans and takes many hours to cross from one continent to the other.

The final members of the council find their seats, as do the last of those attending in the audience. As is customary in many Atlantean towns and cities, the audience bleachers are open to the public. Most of the time, folks decide not to attend.

Earlier, Choka advised him that this time was special, with him speaking about the mission to the ice packs. Many of Utanor's top citizens are present.

Choka quiets the chamber and calls the meeting to session. She is also a council member, and since this is a session about science, she is the sponsoring council member.

Todoru Kotan, the senior council member and current master of the council, starts, "Welcome, Shilot Dekarn. We are pleased you could make it today. We would like to ask you to clarify some points on this expedition."

"I would be honored too, my Lord."

Lord Kotan nods down the table to Talos, another member of the council and one of the leading merchants of Utanor. "My Lord, Choka states you are the discoverer of the melting ice caps. Is that true?"

Nodding, "I came about this when reviewing previous ice pack expeditions. The Empire has sent one every few years to determine if the ice pack is advancing."

Meiku, another council member and a fleet captain stationed in Utanor, asks, "Not to see if it was melting, Shilot Dekarn?"

Meiku cut quite the figure with her ocean blue uniform. She is from Atlanta Luxa or Coda, Tolen imagines. Her onyx skin seems to shimmer as the sunset's rays hit her. He is quite taken with her to the point he almost forgot to answer her.

"I am sorry, the sun." He stumbles on his words for a second. "No, honored one, at least not until I correlated the information. I am embarrassed to say this, but it seems the Imperial Academy considered these only an opportunity to study the animals and plants of and near the ice packs. Luckily, they still took measurements and made ice observations."

Mita Torgar, the senior Somena or healer of Utanor, responds, "And you found that the ice is melting and retreating?"

Tolen turns to face Mita. "It's not really retreating, Somena. The ice melting on the ice pack is mostly forming ice lakes."

Choka interrupts, "Tolen, please explain why there is a need for the expeditions."

Meiku nods, "More specifically, why is Utanor funding and manning the expedition?"

Tolen looks at each council member before responding, "While the Academy elders are interested in my paper, they do not consider the implications of an immediate concern."

Lord Kotan asks, "Which are?"

Taking a deep breath, Tolen says, "There is enough water in the ice lakes to raise sea levels, threatening many of the Empire's cities, including Atlantis."

The audience explodes in discussions. Accusations that the Shilots are crazy or just want money are easily heard above the uproar. Kotan looks at Choka, who looks back with pleading eyes. Tolen sighs at that look and knows he is in trouble.

Kotan picks up the leader stone and speaks into it. "Silence." That word echoes around the hall. As the crowd quiets, he puts the stone back down.

"Shilot Dekarn, you believe there is enough water to cause this scenario to come to pass?

Shaking his head, he says, "I am not sure, my Lord. That is why we need to find out."

Choka adds, "I have reviewed his evidence and believe it is a worthwhile cost."

Talos follows up, "And Shilot Dekarn, why have you not used the resources of your home city of Altai? They also have the people and means, correct?"

Tolen nods," The council of elders in Altai has my people studying the impact of the waters on our city and those along the coasts of Tes Falta."

Choka continues for him, "The last expedition in our region of the ice pack was over twenty years ago. We do not know how many ice lakes are in this region, and thus, we are not sure of the danger to us."

Tolen continues excitedly, "The more data I have, the more I can show the Academy that this is a global concern and that all of our cities near the coastlines could be impacted."

Lord Kotan looks at each council member, who gives barely recognizable nods. Then he pronounces, "Have your expedition, and let's see what they find. Does the council agree?"

Each council member verbally agrees with the decision. Tolen slowly lets out his breath when Choka, the final member, states her position.

Lord Kotan nods and then states, "Good. If there are no more questions for Shilot Dekarn, we can let him take a less conspicuous seat." No one speaks, and Kotan motions him to sit near the front of the bleachers.

The meeting continues as other business is discussed. At the conclusion, Lord Kotan ends the session and dismisses the attendees.

Choka comes up to Tolen while beckoning others to attend. One is Shilot Yanis, who will lead the expedition. The other two are military officers. Vailixi fliers Tolen notes.

Choka introduces them. "Shilot Dekarn, I would like for you to meet Lord Kotan. Lord of the Aska Pass, commander of the Flying Dragon squadron and son of Council Elder Kotan."

They greet each other. "It is an honor, my Lord."

Shandar Kotan smiles a warm smile, "The pleasure is mine." He takes the female officer's hand and introduces her. "This lovely lady is my betrothed, Lady Sahama of Moia, and commander of the Tiger Claw squadron."

Tolen bows to her, congratulating the couple.

She smiles, "My Lord, I have heard much of your work. Is it true?"

"I believe so, my Lady, but one must test and confirm with knowledge. Thus, Shilot Yanis and his team will learn for us."

Yanis bows and says, "Yes, master. I will ensure we learn all we can in the allotted time."

Choka says, "Lord Kotan's squadron will shuttle the expedition north."

Tolen bows again, "Thank you, my Lord. And again, congratulations to the two of you. I must say, I imagine it is pretty rare to see two squadron commanders getting married. My good friend from Altai, Risor Tarnor, is the commander of the Falcon Claw squadron, currently stationed near Vortia in Atlanta Suna."

Shandar and Jolna look at each other and raise questioning shoulders. Jolna responds, "I am sorry, my Lord. We do not know Commander Tarnor or the Falcon Claw. I am afraid we are too spread out to see each squadron regularly."

Tolen smiles, "No worries, I understand, as this is the first time Choka, Yanis, and I have met."

Shandar takes Jolna's hand, "We are happy to help out, Lord Dekarn. If you will excuse us, my Lady and I have other matters to attend to before our departure tomorrow morning." Looking at Yanis, "Don't forget six bells, sir."

Tolen, Choka, and Yanis bow to the couple as they leave. The hall is almost empty.

Jolna stands behind Shandar with her arms wrapped around him. They are on his balcony, looking at Tu-ne in the failing light of dusk. The moon is full and already lighting the streams of smoke coming from Tu-ne.

She hugs him closer, "I wish I had more time this trip."

He covers her hands in his and leans back to kiss her on her head. "Me too. But duty calls. We will be together soon enough."

She smiles with her head pressed against his back, then she has a thought, pulls away, and spins him around. "You are not going to escort the Shilot's party, are you?"

A look of concern from her pulling away melts away to amusement. "No, I will have one of my sub-commanders stay near them. I will go for the ride up and see what they initially see."

Satisfied with his answer, she smiles and pulls him back to her. "Think they are correct?" she asks while trying to find a perfect place to rest her chin on his shoulder.

"I hope not." He folds his arms around her. "Imagine Atlantis inundated. Thirty thousand years with nothing really threatening us, and then bam! Ice melts and destroys Atlantis. Sounds like a story the bards use to entertain guests at a party."

She kisses up his neck to his ear and nibbles a little. She gets a pleasant sigh for her efforts. He turns to kiss her and barely touches his lips to hers when she pulls away.

"Speaking of parties. We have one starting soon, and you still need to get ready."

Looking hurt, "I would prefer to continue here with the most gorgeous of women."

He tries to kiss her, and she puts her hand between his and her lips. She purrs, "I think one of us is the guest of honor and the other her companion."

He raises his eyebrows and then starts to lick her hand. She pushes away from him and smells her hand. In mock anger, "Ewwww, I will need to wash again."

He grins, "Right, a bath it is."

Laughing, "I do not think your mother would approve."

He smiles and folds his arms, "Ha, she loves you more than me, I think. Don't worry, she will blame me anyway."

Returning his smile, then forcefully pointing inside the bedroom. "Be that as it may, it is time you get ready."

He loudly sighs in mock regret, "Yes, my Lady."

ATLANTA NADO

The city of Reiche Mesto is the capital of the Tugar people. Nestled on a cliff overlooking the great Tia Moheno, it is one of the furthest human habitations along the river. Less than a week's march south of the closest volcano along the river's path, the volcanoes give the river its name, the river of many fires, and its great fertility.

The city's aeroport is on a hill near the cliff. A narrow ramp, maybe wide enough for ten men to walk shoulder to shoulder, led from the aeroport and farms below to the top of the cliff to the city proper.

Large Aether Air Bow cannons sit near the cliff's edge to defend the city and valley below. The barely discernible blue glow of the Aether shield could be made out around the gun emplacements. The city's shield is up 24x7, a reminder of a world at war.

Indrajit, Zhenjin, and the captain of the Imperial Vimana, Vagir, step down the ramp onto the stone base of the aeroport's landing pads. Across the river, Indrajit can see and hear the mammoths lowing and trumpeting as they move down the river towards the Tes Naldo.

They move away from the ramp to let Tugar men retrieve the cargo of weapons that they brought from Rama. Two crew members armed with Aether bows stand on the ship's quarter deck, monitoring the unloading of the cargo. Other crew members start to direct or help the Tugar with the unloading.

A young man with a princely bearing walks up to them, followed by an entourage.

"My Lord Indrajit, I presume?" Asks the young man.

"Yes, Prince Arawn, is it? May I introduce Captain Agarwal, the master of this beautiful vessel. And lastly, my lieutenant, Zhenjin. He was the War Master of the Elk Riverbend Clan. A clan of the Hu."

Prince Arawn clasps arms with all of them, as is the culture of his people. Looking at Zhen, "An ally of our allies is an ally to us. Well met War Master."

Zhen bows and says, "Your Highness, I am no longer the War Master of my people. I gave that up to follow my Lord Indrajit after he saved my village."

Indrajit nods to the captain, who says he must return to his ship's tasks.

Prince Arawn leads them and his entourage to an Aether wagon waiting for them. The supplies from all three of the Vimana are loaded into larger cargo Aether wagons.

The palace is hewn from the mountain's living stone. The throne room entrance is a massive four-meter-tall stone archway cut from marble. There are great columns every five meters in the hall, ten rows in total. Marble tiles cover the floor, and Aether globes light the hall from pedestals at least six meters high on the columns.

At the far end of the hall is the throne. It is built on a large marble-covered dais. The throne is enormous and not built for humans. In the 'seat' is cut another seat that would fit a human. The look hints at the age of the palace and throne since giants are said to have not been seen for thousands of years. Only a few skeletons or mummies of these creatures are still around, mostly in museums.

In this seat sat Allen, King of the Tugar. While older, he is still a powerful-looking individual, even dressed in a flowing robe and seated.

Indrajit, Arawn, and Zhenjin approach the throne past Tugar soldiers and citizens petitioning the King. To the side, Indrajit notices a group of Greeks outfitted in breastplates with helms removed.

One young man, a strong and powerful-looking man, looks intently at Indrajit. He is not entirely positive, but he believes he is also a blessed hero like himself.

They stop at the base of the dais.

Arawn bows to his father, "Father, I bring you Lord and hero Indrajit of Rama and his lieutenant, a war master of the Hu, Zhenjin, of the Elk Riverbend clan."

The King rises and comes down the dais to them. "Greetings, my Lords, and thank you for escorting the supplies. It has been difficult getting supplies of late. Atlantis advances further upriver and makes short work of our forces without Aether."

Indrajit replies, "Your Majesty, I have brought the weapons and parts for the Air Bows as requested."

The King looks aside to one of his priests, who bows and walks back down the hall. "My priests will put them to good use. The enemy has recently taken a stronghold downriver, and now we can strike back."

The young Greek that Indrajit noticed earlier separates from the crowd and approaches with an older Greek. "Your Majesty," he starts, "maybe the lords from Rama would be able to join us in taking back the stronghold?"

Prince Arawn nods to the newcomer, "Indrajit, this is Demetri of Eros and his lieutenant, Artos."

They all clasp hands as King Allen and Arawn watch them.

Zhenjin tries to act nonchalantly. "Maybe a small diversion would be harmless?" He looks at Indrajit.

Artos looks between Indrajit and Zhenjin and adds some emphasis. "My Lord, it would be nice to have your Vimana port some of our Air Bows. We could move our warriors quicker."

The King agrees, then looks expectantly at Indrajit, "We would welcome any help great Rama could offer."

Indrajit nods, "Yes, your Majesty, we would be honored."

Zhenjin and Artos grin at each other. Zhenjin could barely contain his enthusiasm, "Two of the Gods blessed heroes in the same battle. This will be some fight."

Artos replies, "Almost wonder if we would be spectators."

Demetri laughs and claps Indrajit on the shoulder. Looking back at Artos, "We will try and leave you some. I, for one, relish to see Indrajit in action."

Artos looks over the log to the stronghold. The same stronghold that Rogat had taken weeks earlier.

With the light fading, he could see the large megalithic blocks of the stronghold start to darken. Indrajit, Demetri, Artos, and Zhenjin are near the forest's edge, while the rest of the Companions, Demetri's followers, are back in the woods.

Artos settles between the four of them, saying, "It looks to be well-manned."

Indrajit pops up and then comes back down, "I can't see any Aether weapons on the guards."

Zhenjin replies, "We will know when they come out of the cracks and crevices, like cockroaches."

Demetri looks at Zhenjin, "I take it you don't like Atlantis?"

Zhen looks him in the eye, "No." Then moves up to look over the tree.

Demetri sat there for a few seconds. Zhenjin said nothing further. Demetri speaks to Indrajit, "Talkative person, isn't he?"

Indrajit chuckles, "I learned to deal with it."

Shaking his head, Demetri continues, "Fair enough. I think we can take them. When the other forces get in place, we can move."

Artos looks behind them, "They should be ready soon, and the Air Bows will be..."

Demetri smiles at Indrajit as Artos is talking. He gets a quizzical look in return. Artos notices the look and stops.

"My lord, no, don't..."

Zhenjin comes back down to them and gives them a strange look. Demetri claps a hand on Indrajit's shoulder, gets up, and jumps over the tree. He starts running toward the stronghold.

Shocked, Zhenjin blurts out, "What the... The Gods curse him."

Indrajit jumps up and over the tree. He turns back, "Bring up the men and follow." Then takes off after Demetri.

Zhenjin gets up to look over the top of the tree, shakes his head, and then looks at Artos. Artos shrugs and starts to say something, but Zhenjin puts up a hand to stop him.

Sighing, "No. They are alike. Call up the men."

Indrajit and Demetri bound across the open terrain with the grace of gazelles, their legs moving so quickly that it is hard to see them as they easily cover great distances. Despite their incredible speed, they can maintain this pace for hours without tiring - a testament to the blessings the Gods bestowed upon them. As they run, they pass the halfway point between the dense forest behind them and the towering walls ahead.

Demetri looks at Indrajit, "Can you get to the top of that wall?"

"Seriously?"

"Just checking. Okay, I will take the left side of the battlement and you the right. Okay?"

Nodding, "Okay."

The stronghold's alarm sounds. Meanwhile, arrows start to embed in the dirt around them. Aether blasts from the Air Bows fly overhead, hitting higher levels upon the stronghold's walls, and the Vimana dives, strafing the defenders.

The two split apart, dodging arrows and running close to the wall. Indrajit takes out his dagger and throws it at the wall. It sinks deep in the wall. He turns to Demetri and grins, then jumps onto the dagger and bounds over the wall.

Demetri hoots, seeing Indrajit somersault over the wall. He jumps for the top and catches it with his hands. Then kicks over to land on the battlement seconds behind Indrajit.

Indrajit is already decapitating a surprised archer before he can react. Whirling in the opposite direction, he counters a swordsman's thrust and punches him in the face. Seconds later, two other archers stumble back, staring at stumps that used to hold bows.

Not to be outdone, Demetri kicks one archer hard enough to throw him back toward the entrance to one of the tunnels leading away from the battlement. Troops are already pouring out of both tunnels.

He pulls his Sun Sword out, and it bursts into flames. Lighting the battlement like it is day. Most defenders start to backpedal or run into those coming out of the tunnels behind them. They have no experience with dealing with an Aether-powered weapon like this. It usually means heroes, which means death for those opposing them.

Both heroes cleave their way through the throngs of defenders trapped near the entrances to the tunnels. Those at the rear of the pile up not yet turning to give their less fortunate compatriots a chance to escape death.

Before they enter the tunnels, a cheer comes up from behind. Demetri's Companions arrive. These soldiers work their way past both leaders, giving the two a break.

Artos and Zhenjin come up to the blood-splattered pair.

Artos reports, "The other units are gaining the lower-level parapets. The outer walls are ours."

Zhenjin hands Indrajit his dagger back. "I think you left this. Was hell trying to pry it loose."

Grinning, "Thanks Zhen."

Loud explosions are heard from the tunnel going up to the next level.

Demetri asked Indrajit, "Your Vimana?"

Indrajit shrugged, "I imagine so. Shall we finish this?"

Demetri nods, pulls out his sword again, and says, "Let's, friend Indrajit."

One Month Before

ARCTIC ICEPACK

The ice is like a thousand tiny mirrors reflecting the blinding sunlight, but thankfully, the day has become slightly overcast, softening the harsh glare. The Arctic wind blows fiercely, whipping Indrajit's hair around his coat and freezing it in place. His down-lined coat provided some protection against the biting cold, but he could still feel the icy chill seeping through to his skin.

Since undertaking this trip, they have learned how to survive the hard way. At first, they did not come prepared for this cold. It was almost a disaster, with a few of his men freezing to death. Luckily, their Vimana returned with warmer clothing and camp materials.

Once better prepared, they eventually found the scientists. He and his men had been watching the Atlanteans for half a day. They had identified which ones were the Shilot and which were the helpers or guards. Soon, it would be time to move. Even though it was twenty-four hours of daylight, the large hunting animals would soon be out. They needed to capture these people and get back to their camp.

He split his team into two groups, one on either side of the camp. Indrajit led one group, and his friend Zhenjin led the other.

Indrajit quietly tells his men, "Get ready. Kill the guards, but try not to kill the assistants or scientists." They nod their acknowledgment.

Taking a deep breath, Indrajit turns and rises from cover. Quickly, he finds one of the eight guards and shoots. His men rise around him and start firing at the other guards.

With the commotion from Indrajit's men, Zhenjin and his men also rise. Within seconds, all the guards are dead, along with a few of the assistants.

Indrajit stands atop the snow bank he used as cover while his men and Zhenjin's team move into the camp. The Atlanteans are completely surprised and unarmed. The men move all surviving Atlanteans to the center of the camp. Down on their knees, there are only eight left.

Indrajit approaches them. "Greetings from the Raman Empire. You are all my prisoners now. Be good, little boys and girls, and nothing will happen to you before we get you to Rama. Cooperate, and I am sure there you will be treated well."

The oldest of the prisoners speaks up. "I am Shilot Yanis. What right do you have to attack us, sir?"

The Ramans laugh, all-knowing Atlantean. "Are you serious, Shilot Yanis? We are at war, sir. You are the enemy. We kill the enemy. This is how things work. I think you are valuable, which is why you are still alive. Prove me wrong, and I will quickly kill you and leave you for the snowbears or tigers."

Looking over to Zhenjin, he says, "Zhen, pack up their gear and bring it. I will take them ahead." Nodding in acknowledgment, Zhenjin gets his team moving towards the tents.

Walking next to Shilot Yanis. "Tell me, Shilot Yanis, what is it that you consider so valuable that you came up to this frozen wasteland?"

"We are studying the ice melt." He said, implying that Indrajit was stupid for not seeing the obvious.

Familiar with Mantriks's condescending nature, he plays dumb to gather more intelligence. "Studying the ice? But, sir, it has always been here. It's ice."

"That is where you are wrong, sir. The planet is warming, and ice lakes are growing. Eventually, they will break their ice walls and flood the lands."

Indrajit walks along in silence. He is troubled by Shilot Yanis' words. He is not a wise man; his strengths are in military matters, but something about this didn't sound good. He would take Shilot Yanis and his lot to the Mantriks and let them figure this out.

ALTAI

The sunlight dances off the waters of Tia Yolan in such a way that Risor has a hard time listening to his sister, Rina. Peaceful, he thought. Altai is his home, a small city of around eight thousand Atlanteans and the local tribes that pay homage to the Atlanteans, located a day's trip from the mouth of the great river on the landmass of Alta. Like many other colonies in Alta, this city has been spared the pain of war. The Raman Empire does not consider these outposts of Atlantis worthy targets.

Far away from the battlegrounds, these quiet backwaters of the empire go about their daily lives with little worry of war. Closing his eyes, Risor takes in the sounds and smells of home. The next day, he leaves to return to his base.

Breathing deeply, he concentrates on the sounds and smells, like he will never again smell or hear them. He smiles to himself. Thoughts of the simple life he will leave behind play repeatedly in his mind.

"Are you listening to me, Risor!" cries Rina. She sits up straight on the couch and stares intently at him with a look that dares him to give the wrong answer. His little sister, many years his junior, has grown up a beautiful lady of the House of Tarnor. Yes, his friend, Tolen, is a lucky man. Once he figures it out, that is.

Quickly placing his drink on the table and raising his hands in defense. Risor playfully says, "Yes, my dear sister, I hang on every word!"

"Ha, don't be mean," she quips, returning to a more relaxed posture. "I know you don't care about the stars as much as you do your silly war, but they are important to me!"

"Yes, I know they are," dropping his hands to a more conciliatory gesture, "but I never really paid attention to our teachers and thus am lost when you talk about them."

He gets off the couch, grabs his drink, and walks to the balcony rail. Turning back to Rina, he says, "You and Tolen liked the mysteries, not me."

Joining him, she asks, "You will see him tonight?"

Risor nods and suppresses a smile. A servant enters the room and fills their drinks before bowing and departing. Rina contemplates her drink and then looks at him.

Casually, "May I join you tonight?" Then turns to watch the sun setting. "It is your last night, and even the boring talk of war would be bearable." She turned to him with her most winning smile, "Besides, I can see our friends again before they return."

Ah, the game is on now, Risor merrily thought. "Even boring talk of war?" he purrs as she innocently nods. "Funny, you didn't want to join earlier this week." Unable to hide a grin, "Could it be that Tolen will be there tonight?"

It is worth all the pain and revenge she will inflict on him for cornering her like this. Her look of absolute horror when she realizes he knows her reasons is priceless.

To her credit, she recovers quickly, "Oh, Tolen will be there? How nice." It is a forced performance but almost believable. Risor lets her off the hook, as it would soon be time to go.

"I see. Shall we get ready then?"

The tavern is on a riverside bluff overlooking a little island in the middle of the river. The river is wide, at least four kilometers, with a strong flow. On a clear day, you might glimpse the opposite shore from the tavern. With evening coming, the lights of Altai could be seen up the river about a kilometer away. Occasionally, a Vailixi would come or go, adding to the spectacular view of the night sky.

Risor and Rina joined their friends at a balcony table to enjoy a meal, drinks, and good company. Rina looked excited when they left their residence but visibly deflated upon arrival. Tolen is not there, and Risor has to control a laugh.

Joining them is Rogat, who is back from Atlanta Nado. The other friend is Niko. He had a gloomy look but was ever a loyal friend to Risor. His father also worked for Risor's father.

Once greetings are done and everyone settles, Rogat summarizes the beginning of his story and then begins where he left off. "So, as I was saying, it wasn't long before those archers couldn't stand it and ran."

Risor asked, "Did you take the hold?"

"Yeah, but our casualties were so high, we had to return to base. Another company marched out and took over garrison duties. Those damn Tugar overran them a few weeks later." Then, in a whisper. "No one survived."

It goes quiet around the table, and Rina looks confused. "Rogat, if you had Aether spears and power armor, how could these barbarians defeat you?"

Gently, "Not us, Rina. Our replacements were locals loyal to us. They had no Aether weapons."

Still seeing the confusion on Rina's face, Risor offers, "Only Atlantean citizens may use our weapons. They are too powerful to trust with others."

Niko fell back into his chair with an explosive sigh, "Too bad the Ramans do not believe that. They arm their allies with Aether weapons."

Raising his cup, Risor counters, "Only in the last few years of the war."

Rogat turns to Rina, "Plus, most infantry, like my unit, do not have power armor. Only the Home Guard and other special units do."

Risor chimes in, "Also Vailixi squadrons, like mine. The armor is just very complex and expensive to make. That is why..."

Interrupting Risor, Tolen enters the balcony.

He was wearing the white robes of his office, First Shilot of Altai. "Hello everyone, did I miss something?"

Rina brightens at Tolen's entrance. They get up and greet, then settle back down into their chairs. Tolen sits between Risor and Rina.

Risor turns to Tolen and puts his hand on Tolen's shoulder. "Rogat was just regaling us with one of his stories."

Tolen sighs, "Not the one about the stronghold again, is it?"

Rogat doesn't miss a beat. He toys with his cup, looks up at Tolen, and calmly says, "Why Tolen, you look like you could use a swim."

Laughing, "Peace Rogat, the waters are too cold at this time of year." The rest of the group joins in the laugh.

After the meal, Rina asks, "How is your research coming along, Tolen? You are up north way too much."

Smiling at Rina, "As you might have guessed, it is getting warmer, and the ice sheets are melting. There is a large body of water trapped on the ice sheet. It could present a danger someday if the ice barrier fails."

With a concerned look, Niko asks, "What do you mean, Tolen?"

Everyone looks at Tolen. Rogat speaks first, "So this ice sheet is breaking now?"

Realizing what he said was alarming, Tolen raises his hands and, with a calming gesture, "Not now. In time, it will."

Everyone seems relieved, but Niko is not satisfied. "How much water is there on the ice?"

"It is a series of connected lakes. I am unsure how deep the connections go, but if the barrier fails in this direction, it will send a wall of water down the Tia Yolan, destroying Altai."

Everyone is silent. Eventually, Risor finds his voice, "Tolen, what has the council said about this?"

Tolen's smile disappears as he remembers his last unsuccessful attempt to get the council to act. "The council acknowledges the problem, but since we have lost a few field teams and do not know when this will occur, they will do nothing. We can only monitor."

Risor asks, "We have lost a few teams?"

"Yes, we dropped off a few teams to cover a larger area, and when we went back to pick them up, we couldn't find them. The ice took them."

Shaking her head, Rina looks around the table, "But, if all that water crashes down on Altai, our families are doomed."

She looks for confirmation from Tolen, who nods. "How can they justify this?" She asks.

Tolen toys with his cup for a second before picking it up and slamming it in frustration. Scornfully, "Why, the Shigar party believes this is a local problem of Altai. And, since Altai is a Nalos stronghold, they don't really care. They don't believe this will raise the sea levels, but the evidence states it will."

In a timid voice, Rina asks, "Raise the sea levels?"

Looking embarrassed, Tolen responds, "Yes, Rina. That water is not accounted for in the sea levels today. When released, it will flow into the oceans and add to the sea level."

To prove his point, Tolen selects a bowl, fills it with water almost to the rim, and then puts his hand in it—the water overflows. Everyone silently sits and watches the bowl while the staff cleans the mess. Risor stands and walks to the rail. Peering out at the river.

After the staff leaves, Tolen continues. "Depending on the total volume, even Atlantis will sink."

Niko, ever the worrier, "Atlantis will sink? The Council of Elders will not allow that."

Rina puts her hand on Niko's shoulder to comfort him, and Rogat does the same on his other side. Tolen, trying to be reassuring, "We don't know when that will happen, Niko. That is the problem. The Shigar say they will work on it once the war is over, and the council listens to them."

Risor, seeing the mood at the table disappear, decides it's time to call the evening. He returns to the table, "Regardless, we can not solve the problem tonight, and there is little time before we must go our separate ways again. So, a toast to our friendship."

Raising their glasses, they finish their drinks and get up to leave. Risor looks around at each of them. Rogat is heading back into the fight in Atlanta Nado. Niko accompanies his father to work for the local Altai council. Tolen, with his Shilot, works for Altai and Atlantis. Then Rina follows Tolen into the realm of the Shilot or maybe just after Tolen.

ATLANTA NADO

The rain pours off Demetri's helmet, with his head slightly bowed forward so that the water pours down the sides rather than onto his face. He vainly tries to move his head around to get a decent view of the ravine below, but he can barely see his men around him. His Companions.

Artos, his trusted second, is next to him. They are peering intently into the downpour, trying to discern the enemy. They were told the Atlanteans would come this way. When the scouts reported it, Demetri quickly gathered his Companions to set an ambush.

The Atlanteans are brutally driving the inhabitants up the river valleys. Demetri and his Companions were sent by his king, King Agos, to help their allies, the Tugar. With no Heroes of the Gods amongst the Tugar and few Aether weapons, the Tugar are outmatched by the Atlanteans.

The signal comes, and the enemy is approaching. Bows are pretty much useless, but spears and Spirit Bows would do the trick. Demetri didn't like using Spirit Bows in such weather. They were a gift from Apollo, the Sun God, but they needed sun rays to recharge. Using them now could make them unavailable for later when they are really needed.

Some of his men have Aether shields, but they are limited in their effectiveness, draining each time they are hit. Repelling Aether bursts or fast-flying physical materials drains energy from the shield. Many of his people did not like Aether shields because they did not know when the shield would give out, and people tended to find out in the stickiest of situations. Better to know your weakness and work around it than find out in the middle of a battle that you are vulnerable.

Demetri could hear the Atlanteans complaining. To Artos, "Sounds like they don't like the rain, eh?"

"I am sure they will like it a lot less in a few minutes," Artos said, raising his arm as the signal to fire.

Looking back at Demetri, "My Lord?"

Demetri nods, rises, and, adjusting the grip of his spear, launches it at the leader of the main body of Atlanteans. With God-gifted strength, the spear went through the leader and into the man behind him.

Artos yells, "Now!" rises and launches his spear at another Atlantean. His spear skewers the man but does not pass through him like Demetri's had.

As the surprise is complete, the Atlanteans yell with alarm and pain. With the initial strike, many of them are down. Blasts from the Spirit Bows start to ring out, with a small but growing number of Atlantean Aether spears answering.

While surprised, the Atlanteans are professional and start laying down effective counterfire. They could not see the Greeks above them but could return fire. All of their scouts and the lead contingent are down. The rest are moving back down the ravine to escape the death trap.

Knowing that they could be in trouble if the Atlanteans can get down toward the end of the ravine and organize a counter-strike, Demetri decides to close with the enemy. Pulling his Sun Sword, which starts to glow, he races down the ravine's edge toward the enemy.

While the Atlanteans could not see the Companions unless they fired, they could see the glow from the Sun Sword racing toward them from above. They fire at Demetri, but he is able to deflect all blasts coming his way.

"My Lord, no, wait for us!" Seeing that Demetri would not listen to him, Artos bellows, "Companions, to our Lord!" He gets up and starts to race after Demetri. Those around him also do the same. Some fall, as the Atlanteans now have some targets to fire at.

Having caught up to the Atlanteans still in the ravine, Demetri jumps into their formation. As he lands on one unlucky soul, he whirls his blade, its glow becoming even more potent. With speed enhanced by the Gods, he dashes between the Atlanteans, cutting them down quicker than they could bring their Aether spears to bear on him.

Atlanteans are dropping quickly as Demetri continues his dance of death amongst them. Some of them, trying to get off shots at him, shoot their comrades. He is too quick for them to get a bearing on. Those near him realize their peril and try to get away.

Alarmed calls of "Hero" start to come from the Atlanteans. The soldiers scramble back, screaming and pushing against each other as they desperately attempt to create space between themselves and the Godspawn. They know their only hope is to get some distance to concentrate large amounts of fire on the Hero and hope that they will hit him.

Artos and the rest of the Companions jump down the ravine onto the demoralized enemy. Where before, they were demoralized and frightened, they break in terror as the Hero and his troops are amongst them. Those that could, turn and run, others fell. The much larger Atlantean force is no more.

Decapitating his last foe, Demetri stops to take measure of his surroundings. No Atlantean remains alive. Most of his Companions have run past him to chase down the fleeing foe. Artos, covered in gore, even in the rain, walks up to him.

"One of these days, Lord, you will not be so lucky. King Agos will skin me alive if you die in one of these stunts." Artos said, wiping his face of blood.

"I would think you would be more worried by my mother than our king, my friend," Demetri said with a laugh.

"Aye, either way, I would be better off taking a blast from one of the Atlantean spears."

"Sound recall, Artos. Let us not get too scattered in this downpour," Demetri orders as he picks up one of the dead Atlanteans' Aether spears. He continues, "At least we have more weapons now, and we can give some to the Tugar."

ATLANTIS

It is a beautiful day, if not a sad one. Lena looks at the Vailixi taking off from the aeroport. It gently rises in the air, turns south, and speeds off to some unknown destination. She looks at Tilor Togolan, studying his face.

He is rugged but handsome-looking. He has short dark hair, a chiseled jaw, and dark brown eyes that make her melt. She stares at him, memorizing every detail of his face, broad shoulders, and barrel chest. She reaches for his hand and gently touches him.

"Lena, it is only for two months. Then I will be back. I promise," he said in his deep but tender voice, putting his other hand on top of hers.

"I know, but I always worry." She squeezes his hand fiercely. "I never know when you will not come back."

He then cups her hand in both of his. "I will be fine. We have a good crew, and Risor is a good leader."

She looks at his smiling face, "Will we ever be together, Tilor?"

His smile turns to a frown. "I want to, but I do not know," sighing, he continues, "I am expected to succeed my father when his time comes."

Feeling the loving warmth of his hands slip away with his words. With a tinge of despair and anger, "Tilor, am I a mistress forever? To be cast away when you marry another noble to fulfill your duty?" The momentary satisfaction of making him hurt, as she hurt, is immediately replaced by the guilt of spending their last moments together making him suffer.

Removing her hands from his, she takes his head and looks into his eyes. There is pain there, Lena feels worse now, she knows she caused that pain. "I am sorry Tilor. I know you are trying to work something out for us, but I sometimes feel it will never work out."

He wraps his arms around her, and with their noses touching, he promises her, "I will make you happy." He pulls her in, lifting her slightly so she is on the balls of her feet.

Gently, she felt his lips touch hers. Then the tingle came, as it always does when he kisses her. She moves her hands further back on his head, softly digging her fingers into his scalp while their lips press harder together.

One of his hands moves up her back, pressing her breasts closer to him while the other continues to support her on the balls of her feet. She felt the heat rising in her. The desire for this man is starting to overwhelm her as they kiss passionately.

His tongue touches her lips, pushing into her mouth. A soft moan escapes, but whose she is not sure. She thought only of him and wanted to return to her apartment with him to relive the lovemaking they had shared earlier that morning.

His upper hand moves to the back of her head and firmly grabs her hair, further tilting her back. He separates their kiss, their mouths both partially open, and as she exhales, he inhales. Their lips gently touch as he stares into her eyes. She feels more heat welling up inside her, encompassing her whole body. Those eyes show he wants her, and she is willing to give him everything to keep looking into his eyes.

Touching foreheads, then lowering her back to the ground, he takes her hands into his again. The passion of the moment starts to drain. Looking down, he whispers, "My flight will leave soon."

Not trusting to talk, Lena nods.

"I will be back." Untangling his arms from her and cupping her face in his hands, "By the Gods, we will be together." A tear starts to gather in the corner of his eye. "I love you, Lena."

Tears are starting to overwhelm her, too. She touches his tear as it starts to run down his cheek. He wipes her tears away with his fingers, too. Then he bends down and kisses each eyelid and the tears around them.

ATLANTA NADO

Rogat walks into the barracks at Delin and sees his friends. He walks to them with his bag and throws it at Noko, who lounges on his bed. "Get off my bed, you turd."

"Rogat, the Gods be blessed. You made it in time," cries Migu. "Now, I don't have to be promoted to take your place because you decided to be late."

General laughing around the barracks. The unit is rebuilding, and many in the barracks are not familiar to Rogat. Most are new recruits that he will have to teach to survive the war.

Noko gets off his bunk and sits next to the others. He, Teado, and Migu sit on the next bunk, smiling at Rogat. This is not what Rogat wants, as these guys never really smile. Something is up, and they are waiting to surprise him.

"So, what are you three cut-throats planning?" Rogat said with some trepidation.

Migu speaks up, "Captain Skerios wants to see you. You have been blessed." He starts to smile viciously. The others smile more, if that is possible.

Rogat doesn't like what this means. They have been friends in this unit for the last few years and are the only survivors of the original Piilo members. Their company came from Altai when it was initially formed. The 3rd Alta Faltan Infantry Battalion has a history of hard fighting, winning, and heavy losses.

A company has four Piilo, and each Piilo is further divided into four sections, with a Senior Trooper leading three of the sections and a Troop Leader leading the Piilo. Rogat is a Senior Trooper leading the 1st section, 3rd Piilo of the 3rd Alta Faltan Infantry.

With a threatening look to his three "friends," Rogat leaves the barracks to seek Captain Skerios.

He enters the captain's office and comes to attention with his right fist over his heart. "Senior Trooper Rogat reporting, sir."

"At ease, Rogat." Captain Skerios looks at him with a measuring gaze. "Welcome back, Rogat. Seems like you had a good trip." Rogat nods. The captain continues, "How long have you served the 3rd?"

Relaxing his stance, he said, "Eight years, sir."

"And tough fighting, even leading some."

"Yes, sir. What are you getting at, sir?"

Captain Skerios chuckles, "What you feared the most, my friend, I am promoting you to Troop Leader of the 3rd Piilo." He sits back and watches Rogat.

Feeling like someone ran a sword through his gut, Rogat choked, "But sir, I can't do this. I am just a junior section leader."

"You are the senior section leader now." He picks up a view tablet. "While you were knee-deep in the whores of your hometown, Dogat was knee-deep in his guts. The 2nd section participated in a raid and was ambushed by some Greeks. Their bad luck, the fuckers had a damn Hero with them."

Loss for words, Rogat unconsciously takes a seat. Captain Skerios has an amused look.

"Yes, Rogat, you are now Troop Leader of the 3rd Piilo because you are the senior surviving member of the Piilo. Congrats."

"I was wondering where most of the guys were. No one told me."

"Well, yes, I told them not to. I didn't want you to devise a good excuse not to accept the promotion. We all know how you like just being a trooper. Sorry, no more." He activates the view tablet by putting his hand on it.

"Promotion of Rogat of Altai to Troop Leader of the 3rd Piilo, of the 3rd Alta Faltan. Witnessed by the Gods, promotion granted by Skerios, Commander of the 3rd Alta Faltan. May Poseidon watch over you."

Putting down the view tablet and standing, he offers his hand to Rogat. "There, all done."

Rogat stumbles out of the headquarters to see his three "friends."

"Did he make you a noble?" chortles Migu to the laughs of the others.

"Fuck yall," Rogat responds.

Two Weeks Before

ATLANTA NADO

The new Tugar recruits are quickly learning to use the sword under the experienced eyes of Demetri's Companions. They will soon be needed in the coming campaign.

Sitting in the tent's shade, Demetri watches the recruits go through their drills. He takes another drink of wine. A slave comes forward, fills his cup again, bows, and moves back. Demetri thought these Atlanteans made good slaves. Once captured and the hope that they will be freed dies, they become meek and humble.

"Good news, my Lord. King Agos sends word that he is sending another thousand swordsmen," said Artos, coming into the tent.

"When will they get here?"

"The messenger was sent from the swordsmen. He said they were two days behind him."

Arawn, son of Allen, leader of the Tugar, sat there stroking one of his wolfhounds. "That is good news. Yesterday, we thought we could not counter the enemy's plans to attack the town of Bicas. Now, maybe we can if you agree to use them in such a manner."

While watching the sword exercises in the field, Demetri said, "My Prince, it will be a tight fit to get those men into Bicas before the strike. What, two days from now?" Artos nods. "I think we can count the loss of Bicas and its garrison as done."

He stands up and stretches, "But we might be able to cause the Atlanteans to give it back to us. Their fort at Dedeni will be the staging base. It will probably have few defenders when they strike Bicas. The force we have in Bicas will probably last a day or two. What if we strike Dedeni, plunder their supplies, and kill those there?"

Artos smiles, "They would probably move back to relieve Dedeni and abandon Bicas."

Grinning, Demetri bows, "If we are lucky, we might catch a few of their damned Vailixi on the ground. I would love to skewer a few of their crews, too."

Arawn thoughtfully reconsiders the strategy. "We might get a nice cache of Aether spears, too."

Rogat watches the last of the Vailixi take off and head west. Captain Skerios split off Rogat's Piilo to man the fort at Dedeni, the campaign's staging base. The thinking is that it would be better to let Rogat ease into command of the Piilo and secure the fort than in the midst of what could be a ferocious battle.

Noko, Teado and Migu stand next to him. He got even with them by promoting each to Senior Trooper, leading three of his sections. He led the command section.

Migu, ever the joker of the group, breaks the silence, "Well, they didn't leave us much, did they?"

Nodding, Noko responds, "They are expecting stiff resistance in Bicas. I think I'd rather be here with the wine."

"Okay, it's time to set our watches. Let's keep a strong watch. Something feels wrong. I'm unsure what, but I don't want surprises." Rogat looks at each of the walls, trying to divine what secret dangers are hidden from his sight.

They all salute Rogat half-heartedly and walk back to their units. Rogat sighs, "Guess that is the best discipline I am gonna get from those fools."

The fort sits along the road that bisects the valley lengthwise. The valley slopes gently to the floor, good enough that most enemy forces could not use the ridge as cover to fire into the fort. The only problem is that if the enemy holds the ridges, the defenders cannot get out of the fort on foot without massive casualties. Of course, with Vailixi, that is not that big of a problem.

Rogat walks up onto the sand berm against the wooden stockade. This gives the defenders a chance to fire over the stockade walls. Looking out at the valley, farmers work the fields.

To a nearby guard, "Make sure none of the farmers put a haystack near the stockade."

"Yes, sir. They seem content to keep away from the stockade."

"Yes, it seems so." Rogat wonders aloud. The farmers are creating many haystacks. He looks around the fort and sees haystacks everywhere. Not a farmer but from Altai, a considerable agriculture colony, Rogat is familiar with farming. He doesn't feel right about this.

There are haystacks every twenty to thirty meters. Some are relatively small stacks, and others are very large. Not that he pays much attention, but he does not remember other farmers in the region doing this.

He must remember to question some of the farmers about this practice when he finds time.

ATLANTA SUNA

Lady Kalin Jana, commander of the elite Wave Rider squadron, enters the Falcon Claw squadron's briefing room without the customary knock for permission to enter. Technically, it is a slight to Risor and his squadron but also disrespectful to Commander Varno, who is at the briefing. Risor keeps his temper in check and watches Varno as Jana saunters up to him. Varno seems annoyed but not as angered as Risor and many of his officers. Apparently, this is not the first time Lady Jana has pushed her privilege.

She leans over and softly talks to Varno. He looks unhappy but nods and sits on the table's edge. Lady Jana turns to everyone, puts on an obviously false smile, and says in an upbeat manner, "This is a glorious day for Atlantis and Atlanteans, my brothers and sisters." The room gives polite applause.

"The Gods have given our priests the knowledge of a new weapon, the Hand of Ares, that will destroy the Raman cities in great balls of fire." Stabbing her finger at Risor. "Your squadron will help us unleash this onto our enemy."

Inwardly cringing at the "honor," Risor wonders what hell the Gods gave Lady Jana and the Shigar to visit upon the people of Rama. Unlike Lady Jana, who is extremely vocal in her hatred for the Rama Empire, Risor has no such hatred. Being a follower of Nalos, he, like his party, believes that the war with the Rama Empire should be ended and a return to peace. Over time, Atlantis has grown from an unmatched power that benefited the world to an Empire that demands obedience and tribute from all those below them.

Picking his words carefully, "My Lady Jana, would not this invite retaliation from Rama with their brahmastra weapons? It is said they can destroy armies."

In an annoyingly superior manner, Jana replies, "My Lord, do not worry. The defenses of Atlantis have stopped Rama from ever getting to our great city. They will stop any retaliation. Do you doubt this?"

Varno flashes Risor a warning look. Risor, being Lady Jana's social and military equal, is less worried. Something makes him stop and rethink his reply. In his most gracious tone, he says, "My Lady Jana, I do not doubt the defenses of Atlantis. But no other city in the world has such defenses. How do we protect those citizens?"

Risor catches a hint of anger in Lady Jana's eyes that she cannot control. It took her some time to visibly calm before she could talk. An unemotional tone replaces the upbeat tone. "The priests of Poseidon have found favor in our actions, and the Oracles tell us the Ramans will not destroy our cities with these weapons. So you see, my Lord, there is nothing to worry about. Do you not agree?"

Risor, sensing things could get dangerous for him, decides to fold and be part of this scheme. "Thank you for the additional information, my lady. How can we help your mission succeed?"

The wave tops glisten in the mid-day sun. Risor is mesmerized by the beauty of the scene below his speeding Vailixi, viewed through the forward viewer.

His squadron is on its way to their primary target: the great city of Dwarka, one of the main ports of the Rama Empire. They have never successfully attacked it because it boasts one of the most robust defenses in the world—almost the rival of Atlantis itself in its protection.

His musings are interrupted by Tilor's call out that they are starting their turn north. The attack force rounds the southern tip of the Indian sub-continent, which the neutral Sangam Empire rules.

Sitting back in his seat with his viewer open, Risor calls out. "Have we been detected yet?"

Imshina, the prober responsible for sensing when an enemy has sensed their ship, responds, "No, my Lord. We see no reaction to our force yet."

The second prober also responds, "Sir, we are detecting a large increase in a defensive posture, though."

A minute later, both of them call out at the same time, "We have been detected."

Risor sits forward, "Okay, up to combat altitude. We will see their Vimana soon. Tilor, action stations, if you please."

Tilor starts talking into his glowing dish to contact all the other Vailixi, and the craft rises. The forward portal dims to block the sun's glare as the craft moves northwest toward Dwarka.

Imshina turns to Risor, "My Lord, they are not sallying forth against us. The Vimana are heading north."

Initially shocked, Risor starts to grin. "Good. I guess Lady Jana's plan is working after all." Turning to his communication officer, Dimera, he says, "Dimera, tell command our situation."

Then, to Tilor, "It's time to catch the Ramans in a vice. Tell the squadron to advance at full speed. Let's see which way they turn to defend."

The plan is for a multi-pronged attack on the heartland of the Rama Empire and its allies, the Greeks and Tugar in Europe and the Hu in northern Asia. The idea is to swamp the defenses, so Rama would not consider Lady Jana's particular group more than another squadron-sized attack.

Risor is still leery of the special weapons, the Hand of Ares, that Lady Jana plans to employ. He learned that Atlantis only has a few of them at this time. The strategy seems sound. Atlantis has not tried a general offensive against Rama in a long time. The last time was eight years ago. It was a bad time for the Atlanteans. Rama had outstanding leadership with strong heroes that smashed the Atlanteans enough that after that failed offensive, the war devolved into small strikes back and forth. A war of attrition that Atlantis recently started winning.

Using these weapons will destroy cities and Rama's industrial base. Maybe then, they will sue for peace. The Raman allies, the Greeks of Tes Zeita, the Tugar of Atlantis Nado, and the Hu above the Himalayas in Atlanta Questo are all war-like peoples. Their problem is that they do not have Atlantis or Rama technology. If Rama surrenders, then their allies can be quickly taken apart.

Imshina calls out, "Incoming Vimana."

Risor orders, "Tilor, execute attack plan, Raging Bull."

The Vailixi squadron splits into two groups. One is heading higher and to the left, while the other stays at altitude and goes wide right to vector behind the enemy. Halfway through the Atlantean maneuver, the enemy Vimana try to disperse.

With superior maneuverability, each Vailixi group goes after a single Vimana on the edge of the group. One group dives and strikes, destroying the Vimana with all the Aether fire pumped into it. The group quickly passes below the larger Vimana group, then climbs back to a higher altitude as they move away. The Vailixi move too fast for the Vimana to concentrate their fire.

The other Atlantean group comes from behind the Vimana and tries to take out their target. This aircraft is able to dive below the larger Vimana group, as many of those craft bring their weapons to bear on the Vailixi. The Atlanteans quickly scatter and retreat.

While slower than the Vailixi, the Vimana have larger Aether cannons. They will overwhelm a Vailixi's shields and destroy the craft if given the chance. As one of the Vailixi learned to their detriment, splashing into the ocean below.

The first group turns from their climb and starts diving at another Vimana when a great flash from far inland occurs. All craft lose power and fall toward the ocean.

In total darkness, someone screams in fear due to losing power. They all feel the fear of falling thousands of meters into the ocean below. Fear grips Risor and threatens to overcome his control.

Then, power is restored. It is glitchy at first, but all stations start to glow, and the craft starts to respond. Training takes over as the crew regains control of the craft.

Once the craft stabilizes, a shaken Risor asks, "What happened?"

Tilor turns toward Risor, "Sir, I am not sure. We lost all power and fell a few hundred meters."

"How about everyone else? Milo. How is our ship? Dimera, what of the others?

Tilor, Milo, and Dimera responded rapidly.

Tilor responds, "Everyone is reporting the same thing."

Milo responds, "Small structural damage, but nothing I can not fix."

Dimera responds, "Sir, other strikes are reporting the same."

Risor's attention goes to the forward view portal. A Vimana splashes into the ocean below. Most of the other craft are righting their flight and starting to separate from the interrupted dog fight.

In the distance, landward, a massive mushroom cloud grows. It is growing larger and is very far away.

Risor is mesmerized, "Poseidon protect us, what is that cloud?"

Tilor responds, "Lady Jana's Hand of Ares?"

One of the shielders announces, "My Lord, we can not keep our shields up to full strength. Something is still keeping us from forming a solid shield."

Risor asks Dimera, "Is that the same for the others?"

Dimera takes a few seconds to talk into her glowing dish and then responds, "Yes, sir, it seems the same."

Risor takes a minute to look at the cloud and then at the people around him. "Tilor, let's go home. I'm not sure what happened with the disruption of Aether. But from the looks of that cloud, there has been enough killing today."

ATLANTA QUESTO

Kotan commanded his Flying Dragon squadron to come in low across the Tia Heilun River Valley. Streaks of orange and pink illuminated the faint horizon as the sun began to rise at their backs—precisely as he had planned. Kotan's squadron was on course for their attack against the city of Magno.

The Hu are mostly nomadic people, but they build cities where their old and slaves live. Each sept of the tribe has to offer up warriors to guard the slaves. These cities are far from anything and are usually visited by a sept monthly. The slaves mostly don't try anything because of the distance to anything relatively safe. Also, the Hu are not particularly cruel masters.

New slaves or those of little use are kept in slave pens, but those who prove their usefulness get homes of their own. Those who are valuable and loyal are allowed to marry and have children.

The goal of Kotan's raid today is to open the slave pens and crush the guard force. Atlantean High Command wants the slaves to revolt, destroy the city, and cause issues for the Hu. The more concerned the Hu are with rounding up slaves and rebuilding, the less they will raid Atlantean colonies or allied villages.

Kotan worries. Flying tree top is dangerous but makes it harder for any Hu Aether adept to feel the strike force. The longer it takes the enemy to detect them, the more complete the surprise.

Miko, Kotan's second in the squadron, breaks Kotan's concentration. "My Lord, we are coming up to the jump-off point."

"Thank you, Miko, inform the troopers and proceed."

"Yes, my Lord." Miko breaks the communication.

The sun continues its ascent in the sky, the fading shadows still cover the valley below, concealing the approaching aircraft from casual observers. The aircraft remain hidden from prying eyes, but their distinct whirring sound gives away their presence to anyone paying attention. The people of Hu start to react to the approaching danger.

The city stands tall against the river, its buildings solid and imposing. From the east, Kotan's force begins their attack, swiftly crossing the river and unleashing a barrage of firepower upon the targeted defensive positions and important structures. The air is filled with smoke and dust as explosions rock the city, leaving destruction in their wake.

"Execute the plan," Kotan calls.

Half of the Vailixi roll right and the other half left. Kotan's force heads right and turns back into the defensive fire in a sharp turn. They fly parallel with the walls, firing at the defensive turrets, then head across the river.

Miko's force heads left but climbs the slopes to the ridge top. There, they drop off one hundred armored troopers, who bound out of the access ramps and down the slope to the city's slave pens, located right outside of the walls.

Like the first strike, Kotan's force comes back at the city from across the river. The defenses are already weakened, and the second strike digs deeper into them.

The Flying Dragon squadron did lose one Vailixi on this run. The craft crashes into the city's main temple.

The armored troopers fight in the slave pens with the guards. That is a short fight as the Hu do not have many Aether weapons. The armored troopers make short work of those brave or foolish enough to stand against armored warriors.

The troopers release the slaves and encourage them to take up arms and fight with them. Kotan's force comes back over the slave pens and concentrates their fire on a segment of the city's walls near the pens.

Miko's force flies over the city's western wall, losing two in the defensive fire of that area. While losing two Vailixi, they did manage to smash most of the defensive positions. They cross the river and meet Kotan's force near the other side.

The armored troopers and the freed slaves pour into the city, fighting street to street with the much-reduced city garrison. Those worthies are fighting a losing battle.

The Hu try evacuating many of their people from the eastern gate. The old, infirm, and slaves that have thrown in their lot with the masters take what they can carry. The defenders fight for time to allow out as many as they can.

"Flying Dragon, concentrate fire on the few remaining defensive positions. Commander Altak, keep your people back, along with the majority of the slaves. We want the Hu to flee without butchery if possible."

All concerned acknowledge his orders.

"My Lord, you know High Command will frown upon this decision. They demand we destroy the Hu and might see this as disobeying orders." Miko said across a private channel.

"I will not butcher fleeing civilians or even the troops amongst them. The city is ours. There was never really any doubt." Kotan said, lowering the privacy shield.

"I understand my Lord. I am just reminding you what might happen for your show of mercy. I agree with you, but I wanted to let you know. I am with you no matter what, my Lord."

"Thank you, Miko. I will land my group near the slave pens. Keep your force in the air to ensure we have no surprises."

Miko acknowledges.

ATLANTA NADO

Demetri studies the walls of the fort below him. Dedeni was a Tugar garrison before the Atlanteans' recent offensive. A wooden stake stockade surrounds a few buildings, three of which have solid stone walls and underground strong rooms.

Demetri estimates that the defenders number around one hundred. About a fourth of that is currently manning the walls and gates. It's not really a difficult attack for his men. With over 2500 men with him, the defenders could do little. It didn't hurt that his forces had over 500 Aether weapons.

Artos approaches him, "My Lord, the men and Air Bows are ready to move up."

Nodding, "Prince, I do not think it wise of you to go in the initial assaults. I think it best to remain in the second wave."

Looking at the fort, Arawn responds, "My Lord, you go in the first wave. How would it look for my men to go, but I stay back."

Artos, bowing his head to Prince Arawn, said, "My Prince, Demetri, is protected by the Gods."

Demetri shakes his head and responds, "I understand, but at least stay at the back of the first wave."

A look of relief crosses the prince's face, and with a bow of his head, "I will do as you bid."

"Good, let us get this going. The enemy should have already been engaging the garrison at Bicas. Artos, order the attack."

A horn shatters the quiet of the afternoon. Immediately, men on the top of the ridge stand up around the valley. Flaming arrows fly through the sky. They are too far from the top of the ridge to hit the fort but not too far to hit the smaller stacks of hay stacked along the sides of the valley.

A hundred fires ignite around the valley. Within seconds, they turn smoky as they hit wet grass below the top dry levels, filling the valley with smoke.

The defenders start to shoot at the ridge, but it is too far for any shot to make it. Demetri's men remain on the ridge line, quietly awaiting the order.

Arawn turns to Demetri, "My Lord, I am off. I await your word."

Nodding his head, "Remember my Prince, lead from the back of the men. You are still there with your men but hopefully a little more protected."

Pulling his sword, Arawn salutes and then takes off at a run with his body-guard.

"He is going to get himself killed," Artos sighed.

"He is in the hands of the Gods now. Like all of us. Shall we?"

Artos blows another loud blast from his horn. Men start streaming forward, not yelling or shooting. They run through the smoke to the larger haystacks that are not on fire. They begin to pelt the fort with arrows and the occasional Aether blast.

Large Aether Air Bows move over the ridge top and fire at the fort. They can reach the fort but not see what they are hitting, as the smoke obscures the view. Firing into the general area of the fort, the Air Bows only fire a few shots and then stop. They are not here for the fort.

Demetri and Artos move down the slope toward the fort with the rest of the Companions. Tugar archers pepper the fort. When Demetri sees the fort, flames come from inside the fort and the wall. Aether blasts have blown a few holes through the walls.

Speaking to one of the swordsmen, Demetri said, "How is the enemy?"

"My Lord, their return fire is greatly reduced already. Some of the Air Bow strikes took out their towers and bunkers. I don't think they have many left."

Grinning, Demetri claps the soldier on the shoulder. "Let's go pay them a visit."

Artos blows another loud blast on the horn, and all the troops take up a cry and run forward. Some are carrying ladders, and others large axes.

Demetri leaped the ledge of the destroyed stockade and into the compound. He ducks as an Atlantean sword sails over his head. Rolling away, Demetri comes up and parries the enemy's thrust. Quicker than the opponent, a thrust in and up to open the man's stomach.

Before the man falls, Demetri moves on to the next target. Artos and the others start to stream into the compound through the closest breach, and a general melee near the breach grows.

Demetri dispatches his next opponent with a jumping thrust into the man's chest. With no living enemies near, he takes stock of the battle around him. The enemy is heavily outnumbered and falling back all around the stockade. There is a small force gathering near one of the stone bunkers. Demetri starts heading that way.

The stockade near the main gate explodes. The large Aether blasts are turning this fort into a death trap.

Rogat asks Noko, "How many men do you have left?"

"I am not sure, sixteen, I think."

Teado chimes in, "I have eight. I can't hold the wall, Rogat."

Migu comes up at a run, nearly out of breath. "They are moving in now. I have half my men to hold my area. Sorry, Rogat, I can't hold much. Hundreds are coming from my direction, and those large Aether blasts have put holes in the wall."

Rogat nods. His force is in no better shape. "The one thing about the smoke is it probably keeps those Air Bows from accurate fire."

The sounds of fighting come from all directions as the enemy enters the compound.

Shooting an enemy coming over the closest part of the stockade, Rogat yells, "Fall back to the command center!"

Some troopers nearby start to run for the stone building. Rogat and his friends do the same.

Teado yells as they run, "Did we get word to command?"

"Yes, but they are half an hour away at the quickest."

Migu laughs, "So they can bury us, eh?"

Reaching the entrance to the command center, Rogat unsheathes his sword and lets some troopers by, "Not if I can help it. Everyone in. Down to the store room. We will force them to come to us."

One of the last troopers runs past Rogat into the entrance. Rogat feels a presence, turning to see a Greek swordsman thrusting at him. He is quicker, parries the strike with his Aether spear, and then flicks his sword at the man's exposed throat. The man falls, holding his open throat.

A few Aether blasts near him tell him to get inside. He runs through the entrance and just avoids a blast that sends some splinters into his arm. Troopers pull him inside and slam the reinforced door shut.

"Bar the door. A few Aether blasts, and they will be through it." Heading down to the store room, he takes stock of their situation. Looking at the men around him, most tired and many wounded. "Noko, get me an inventory of what we have."

"Teado, get a barrier built around the stairs. We need something to protect us."

"Migu, contact Captain Skerios and tell him the fort is theirs."

Everyone starts moving around to do what Rogat ordered. Rogat takes an Aether spear and puts it near him. He scabbards his sword, hoping to get a few Aether blasts in first.

Boom, Boom, Boom at the door above. Each time, more dust falls from the ceiling.

Teado looks at Rogat, "I figure another two blasts, and that door is gone."

"Think the barricade is out of sight from up there?"

Teado looks at the door, "Maybe, but it will not be easy."

Noko approaches Rogat, saying, "We have nineteen left that can fight. There is enough water and food for a few days. Most of the Aether spears are at half charge."

"Well, I didn't think we could take the fight to the enemy. We will just have to stay here."

Boom, and the door explodes. Everyone ducks behind the barricade, and many Aether shots ring in the room above them. Then, yelling men charge down the stairs.

"Open fire!" Yells Rogat. Nineteen Aether spears fire into the stairs, hitting bodies or the stone of the stairs. Burnt bodies start falling down the stairs as the screams of the victims fall away.

"Cease fire!" Bellows Rogat. "We need to conserve our Aether power if we are going to get through this."

Yells in the distance tell him the enemy is holding back. The initial surge was a disaster, with the eight visible but Aether-burnt bodies as proof. Rogat looks at those bodies and shakes his head.

"Greeks," he said to no one in particular.

One of the junior troopers, looking scared but still manning his place, asks Rogat. "What do you mean, sir?"

Rogat walks over to the stairs, careful not to get in the line of sight from above. Pointing his Aether spear at one of the bodies, "Oh shit, even better, this one is a Companion."

A few moans from behind him. There are a few soiled pants as well.

Migu comes forward, "Fuck Rogat, this might be the same fucker that got us a few weeks ago."

"Well, let's see the hero get down here through that stairwell and nineteen Aether spears." They both move back behind the barricade.

Demetri takes a drink from his water skin when Artos approaches him.

"My Lord, we have secured the fort. Most of the men have moved back into the fields to await our guests."

"Good, I think they have less than twenty in there."

"Yes sir, but getting them out would be near impossible."

"I don't think we have to, either. We have the armory. Detail Arawn's men to get those weapons home. We can get him out of danger and make him look good to his people."

"King Agos would be proud of you, Demetri," Artos said, clapping a hand on his shoulder.

"I have a good teacher and friend."

One of Demetri's Companions comes up. "My Lord, we are ready to fire the bunker."

Looking at Artos, "Go, get Arawn moving. I need to talk to our new friends."

At the command center's entrance, Demetri looks down the stairwell at his dead men. They were too brash and charged down without thinking.

"Hello down there. Can we talk?" He calls out in passable Atlantean.

"Who wants to talk?" Came from below.

"I am Demetri, son of Delno of Eros. I seek a truce to discuss terms of surrender."

"I think we can let you leave instead of all surrendering. You see, our fort cannot hold your force captive."

Demetri likes this guy, ballsy. "That is good. Okay, how about you come up here, and we can talk? I promise no one will harm you."

"Thank you, but maybe it's best you come down here alone. Unarmed, too, would be nice."

The Companions around him looked on in alarm. "No, my Lord, please do not expose yourself that way," said one of his men.

"Do not worry, I believe all will be fine." Taking off his sword. "Okay, I accept. I will come down unarmed to talk."

Demetri slowly walks down the steps. Slowly, because he had to avoid the bodies and he didn't want to give anyone a reason to shoot.

When he gets to the bottom of the stairs, a large black man stands unarmed in the center of the room. Behind him is a barricade with many soldiers at the ready with Aether spears.

"I am Rogat, commander of this fort."

"Rogat, well met. Your force put up a valiant fight, but we both know the outcome was pre-ordained."

"Yes, it would seem so. So how can I help you today, my Lord?"

"I am prepared to offer you and your men a chance to leave this fort with your arms. You just need to promise you will march toward your territory, not Bica."

"Hmmmm, that's a surprising offer, my Lord. I am sure you are aware that reinforcements will be coming soon."

"Yes, I am aware. Thus the reason we would like to finish this as soon as possible. We have the armory and have taken all the weapons there. No matter how small a force, I prefer not having anyone follow us."

"I understand what you mean, my Lord, but I must decline your offer."

"I see. You realize that no further offer of quarter will be given, and all of you will be killed."

Rogat looks at his men. Some had hard faces, and others were scared out of their minds. Noko, Teado and Migu nod to him.

"Thank you for your offer, my Lord. I appreciate it but must decline it."

"I understand, Rogat." Extending his hand for a shake. "You and your men do Atlantis proud. We will sing your praise when we sing of this victory."

They shake hands, and Demetri starts to leave. He stops at the first step. "May I ask a favor?"

"If I can grant it."

"Can I remove our dead from the stairs? Give them a proper burial?"

"That would also tend to clear the access, but I will grant this to you. Four men only, unarmed."

"Thank you, Rogat." With that, Demetri goes back up the stairs.

The Vailixi speed back toward Dedeni. The smoke around the valley of Dedeni is thick and impenetrable. Demetri watches from the ridge line. His men are scattered all around the valley and in the fort.

The Air Bows and troops are hidden by smoke and cover. The Vailixi speed over the valley unopposed. Demetri is waiting.

They come back for another pass, and of the eight, four slow down and stop on the ridge line near the road to Bica. The other four race to the other side of the valley.

Demetri orders the attack as the four land and start to disgorge their troopers. The Air Bows are near the landed Vailixi and score direct hits quickly. Hundreds of bows and Aether bows rain down on the Atlanteans.

The four remaining Vailixi speed back toward their troubled brothers but are too late. In that short time, the four landed Vailixi are destroyed, and the majority of the men are dead or dying. A few remain in a firefight with the surrounding Greeks.

The four surviving aircraft start strafing the areas around the downed Vailixi. Quickly, the Air Bows begin returning fire, and the fight digresses into a fight of survival for the Atlanteans. Two of the four aircraft are damaged. The men on the ground run up the ridge line and flee for their lives.

Only ten of the eighteen make the ridge line, with the four Vailixi flying after them. The Greeks and Tugar cheer, knowing they have beaten the Atlanteans this day.

Rogat hears the battle and the cheers and knows there are more Atlantean deaths.

"Noko, send word to Captain Skerios that the enemy has beaten back the relief force," Rogat said. He wonders if the Greeks would try to force their way into the bunker.

Teado seems to pick up his thoughts. "Think it is our turn now, Rogat?"

"I don't know. They have us beat, too. It would take reinforcements a day or so to get back here without Vailixi."

Migu walks around the barricade and goes toward the stairs. Everyone is quiet to give Migu a chance to hear what is happening.

"I can't hear anything." He said.

"Let us wait. Migu, keep a watch there." Rogat goes back to the communications node.

"Captain Skerios is on the line for you, Rogat." Said Noko, getting up from the chair.

"Sir, I think they destroyed most of the Vailixi in an ambush."

"Rogat, it is a tough way to start your officer career, eh? Noko told me the situation. I would say stay put and wait. We have heard that some of the Vailixi and troopers survived. A relief force is coming from base with armored troopers. Maybe six hours. We will be there in fifteen."

"Rogat, they are firing the stockade walls," Migu calls out.

"Sir, they are burning down the stockade."

"It looks like they won this day. We will abandon Bica and pull back to base. Strike again another day," the captain said.

"Yes, sir."

ATLANTA SUNA

Jubilation reigns back at the base, with everyone celebrating the successful strikes. There were a few hiccups, one involving the Tugar, which was a disaster, but overall, the news for the Atlantean forces was very encouraging.

This is nothing to Risor, who stands tall before Varno and the Vortia colony governor. He is explaining why he turned his squadron around. This action did not jeopardize any other unit nor allow any mission objectives to be missed. His squadron's mission was a diversion with the secondary mission of attacking any target of opportunity for as long as possible.

He now believes that he did not go unscathed from questioning Lady Jana. She waited until the strike was a success, and her glory became unassailable before acting.

Risor had to give her credit for doing it right.

Varno is not a member of the Shigar party, so Risor doubts the ire is his. On the other hand, the colony governor is a minor member, and of course, Lady Jana is still on base.

"Your orders were to attack anything near the coast. To continue stirring up trouble that would force the Ramans to concentrate on your force vice going after the Wave Riders. This is a dereliction of duty, at the least," yells the governor. "

"My Lord Governor, as I stated in my report, the Vimanas we engaged left after Lady Jana's strike was completed. Also, that strike disrupted our use of the Aether. This was a surprise that no one saw fit to advise would happen." Risor is starting to get annoyed with the governor's questioning. He knows they are going after him because his father is a high-ranking member of Nalos.

"Had we been briefed on this disruption, I would have known we could continue the mission. Since it was not deemed appropriate to inform us, how was I supposed to know that there would not be more disruptions the closer we got to the detonation point?" Standing now and leaning forward over the table.

"Had we continued to attack and further disruptions occurred that disabled my squadron's craft, I would be accused of recklessly endangering our force's welfare."

Varno tries to calm the situation. "Risor, sit! My Lord Governor, I think squadron commander Tarnor's argument makes sense and that we should further investigate the squadron's sensors and logs to confirm the disruption. Commander, you are dismissed."

As Risor left, he could hear the heated argument continue down the hall. He will owe Varno a drink for stopping him from doing something stupid.

In the squadron's lounge, Risor relates the discussion to the officers there. Eventually, the heated emotions subside, and the group changes the subject.

Milo leads the conversation to the Ramans. "Sir, what do you believe the Ramans will do in retaliation?"

"Well, if they do not surrender, then I assume they will strike back with their brahmastras."

One of the junior officers asks, "Where do you think they will strike, sir?"

Tilor responds for Risor. "Lord Tarnor can not tell the future Geiro, and I will not have anyone here starting rumors."

"Peace Tilor" Risor calmly says, "Tilor is right, I do not know. I would imagine they will try to strike Atlantis or another large colony first. If that does not work, which I do not think it will, then they will try to hit softer targets."

"You do not think they will surrender, my Lord?" asks one of the other Vailixi commanders.

"No, I do not." Sighing, "I believe they will need a few more lessons and a few failed missions before giving up. They are proud, and, of course, the Shigar will make unreasonable demands." Risor believes he can safely talk about the Shigar since none of his squadron are openly known as Shigar party members.

"When do you think they will strike, my Lord?"

"Soon."

TES RAMA

The Vailixi cruise at combat altitude, again near the Sangam Empire but still east of the subcontinent. Another run towards Dwarka, this time with three squadrons. This mission is under the leadership of Jamal and not Risor. Risor, still under investigation for returning to base after the previous attack, could not lead this mission.

Taking full advantage of this, Jamal puts Risor's squadron in reserve for the attack. So all the glory, if that is today's fortune, would be his. Risor and Jamal have jostled for leadership since Jamal's squadron, the Sun Darters, arrived at base last year. Their relationship is best described as official.

One of the probers turns to Risor, "My Lord, we have detected Vimana near the eastern coast of Sangam heading towards Atlanta Suna."

Risor nods his head, "Thank you." Turning to Dimera, "Dimera, get me, Jamal, please."

He brings forth his command viewer so it is sitting in front of him. Jamal's face appears in the dish. "Yes, Commander Tarnor?"

Biting his tongue, "My Lord, we have detected Vimana heading towards Atlanta Suna. It seems we are not the only ones raiding today. Shall we inform base?"

Thinking for a moment, Jamal says, "No, do not break protocol. If the Ramans detect our signal, they will know where we are."

Surprised by the answer, Risor responds, "My Lord, if we have seen them, then it's reasonable to assume they have seen us also. They are at a lower altitude and might not be seen by the base probers until it's too late."

Jamal, visibly angered, "You have your orders, commander."

Sighing but accepting the order, "As you wish." He breaks the connection and angrily pushes the viewing disk back to its resting place.

Tilor turns back to Risor, "It is a full squadron-sized force, sir."

Shaking his head and sitting back in his chair, he said, "Yes, but there are the base shielders and the Aether Strikers. Hopefully, Rutan's Vailixi can keep the Vimana from concentrating against the base shields long enough for the ground defenses to drop a few of them."

While a Vailixi has two gunners and two shielders, a base would have dozens. Shielders work together to build a composite shield around the target they are protecting. On a Vailixi, each would cover half the craft. When gunners hit a shield, the power of the shield and the shielder are weakened.

Aether spears work differently for infantry. They use a set amount of Aether in each discharge. Once the stored Aether is exhausted, the Aether spear is no more than a spear or club.

Closing in on the target, they encounter an enemy force of approximately thirty Vimana.

Dimera turns to Risor, "Sir, Lord Jamal is signaling."

Moving the view dish back in front of him, "Put him through."

Jamal's likeness appears in the view dish. "Commander Tarnor, the Sun Darters, and Cloud Warriors will make one pass over this group and then continue forward. Your orders are to engage and destroy the remainder and then join us. Do you understand?"

Risor nods, "Yes, my Lord."

The connection drops, and Risor pushes his dish back to its resting place, thinking, *"Sure, fifteen against thirty is fair."*

Checking the straps on his chair harness, he said, "Reduce speed to three-fourths of the lead squadrons. I want to target those who are left on our first pass."

The lead Vailixi squadrons break off to the left and right, respectively. The Falcon Claw continues straight ahead but slows down. The enemy tries to break formation to meet all three groups but can not turn to meet the flank attacks in time due to their slower maneuverability.

The Atlanteans turn into the flanks of the larger enemy formation. With longer-range Aether weapons, they start firing at the Vimana before they can return fire. Both squadrons concentrate fire on targets with the first shots.

The Falcon Claw is still out of range when both of the other squadrons succeed in destroying seven craft and continue past the enemy. Risor sees that they lost three Vailixi in the exchange.

The Rama formation is utterly disorganized with the first strike. Risor's squadron splits; eight go higher, and the remaining seven lower. Both groups meet up and continue through the enemy formation, losing two squadron craft in the initial pass but destroying five craft in exchange. Once past the Vimana's range, the Atlanteans gain altitude and split again. Both groups turn in their respective directions to come again at the enemy formation as it tries to turn. The Vailixi go further out than the Vimana, again flanking them and reducing the effectiveness of their weapons. Many of the enemy inside the formations do not fire to avoid the risk of hitting their fellows.

Coming out of a dive and seeing many smoking wrecks temporarily floating on the ocean below, Risor smiles. He knows they are going to destroy this force eventually.

Dimera's voice catches Risor's attention. "Sir, Jamal's requesting assistance. They are being overwhelmed."

"Break off towards Dwarka, Tilor."

Tilor initiates the commands to turn the craft towards land and their beleaguered comrades. The forward viewer shows open ocean before them. Risor touches his view console screen, and the forward viewer displays the battle scene. Many smoking wrecks momentarily float on the waves below while the enemy craft grows smaller in the distance.

Risor asks, "What's the damage Tilor?"

"We lost nine, Sir. I believe we knocked out nineteen Vimana."

Imshina says, "Sir, up ahead, there are only eight Vailixi still in the fight and around thirty Vimana."

In the forward viewer, small trails of smoke from sea level become visible. The unmistakable signs of Aether fire appear.

Dimera advises, "Sir, Lord Tironi is hailing us."

Risor touches his view dish, and Lord Tironi appears. The view behind him is smoky.

"Lord Tarnor, thank the Gods! This is Sub-Commander Tironi of the Cloud Warriors. I believe I am the ranking officer." Gritting his teeth. "The commander's craft just went down."

Risor nods, "Lord Tironi, I am taking charge of this mission. Disengage. We are returning to base."

Looking up to Tilor, "Get us out of here."

The forward viewer turns to a rear view. The battle scene is fading, with a few Vailixi catching up. Risor could see Aether strikes toward the sea. He realizes that the Vimana are strafing the wreckage.

Rounding the Sangam coastline back towards Atlanta Suna, Risor considers what is lost. Of the forty-five Vailixi, three full squadrons, the survivors now number fourteen, with one of the damaged ones ditching. Almost three hundred crew members are dead. It will take a while to replace the lost. Atlanta Suna will need another squadron stationed there, just for defensive duty. Until the Aether masters can build new Vailixi and find additional adepts to train, the Atlanta Suna air wing is out of service.

On his way back to base, Risor reviews a replay of the battle. He watches one of his Vailixi pierced by four Aether beams and explode. Then, the faces of that Vailixi's crew display. Sighing and moving the viewer back to its rest position, he says, "Dimera, let command know we are returning and our status." He then chuckles.

Tilor turns around. "Sir?"

"Sorry, I was just thinking. Figures Jamal would royally screw up this, then die to get out of the coming investigation. Now I have to deal with it."

Dimera interrupts their discussion, "Sir, there is no response."

Tilor looks at her, "None?"

"No sir, nothing. No chatter. Nothing. Nothing from Vortia either."

Risor sits up in his chair, "Check all communications and distress channels."

Tilor checks his dish, "We are still too far away to see anything. About an hour."

Thinking for a moment, Risor says, "Any Vailixi in the air?"

Dimera raises a hand for attention. "Sir, I have a fleet vessel on the merchant channel. It is Poseidon's Servant, audio only and a weak signal."

Risor sighs, "If only it were one of the newer merchants with visual communications. Oh well, put him through."

The merchant fleet, which is used for commerce and regional passenger runs, is low on the priority list for Aether augmentation. Most of the merchant fleet is wind-driven surface-only vessels, as they have been for thousands of years. A few have been upgraded to use Aether systems that allow them to go against the wind or, for some, to dive, but they are rare.

Risor pulls the view dish back to him and pulls up the registration of Poseidon's Servant. There is a static sound.

Risor initiates the call, "Poseidon's Servant, this is Commander Tarnor of the Imperial Vailixi Forces, Falcon Claw Squadron. Where are you, and what is your situation? We have been trying to raise Vortia without any luck."

The captain of the Poseidon's Servant responds, "Commander, this be Capn Volck. We are outside of what is left of Vortia's harbor. The city is gone, suh. We be running fruits from the Xuli tribes up north..."

Cutting off Volck, "Captain Volck, this is important. What do you mean 'the city is gone'?"

Volck responds, "Well, Commander, the buildings that remain are all burning. Nothing is standing; even the woods that surround the city are burning. Only Poseidon's temple mount stands tall—a tall pile of rubble, that is." He pauses for a minute. There was a bright flash. There is still a big cloud over the area. I don't see anyone around, either. I tried hailing, but nothing."

Recovering from his shock, Risor said," Stay out of the harbor, Captain. We should be there in a little over an hour. Just wait, if you can?"

"Okay, Commander, we will remain where we are."

This was a brahmastra strike, and Risor is sure of that. It's probably the same thing that hit their base, too. They are still too far away to see destructive clouds, but that should change quickly. The fact that the temple mount remains but the temple is destroyed is disturbing. Once reaching a certain size, each colony creates a temple mount for the gods, especially Poseidon. A room for the Mother Stone would be built inside. The priests would maintain the Mother Stone and use its power to recharge tools of Aether. Larger cities like Atlantis, Vortia, and Altai would have Mother Stones large enough to charge tools of Aether at a distance. This would allow tools to be used in most of the city environs without visiting the priests for recharging.

Risor moves his view dish back to its rest position. "Tilor, how long do you think it will be before we see this cloud?"

"Probably another ten minutes, sir. Should I advise Atlantis?"

Shaking his head in the negative, "No, not yet. Not that I don't doubt our Captain Volck, but I would like to report what I see as well."

ATLANTA SUNA

Through the front viewer, Risor sees the massive cloud that Captain Volck mentioned starting to dissipate. Shortly afterward, the shoreline comes into view.

The crew is stunned, even though they saw pictures of the same thing when Lady Jana hit the Rama cities.

Risor, finding his voice, "Dimera, get me, Lord Tironi, please."

On his personal view screen, Lord Tironi's ashen face appears. "My lord, what has happened?"

Risor sighs, "Death, my Lord. Death is what happened. Lord Tironi, please take your undamaged force to our base to see the status there. Pick up any survivors if you can."

"Yes, my Lord. We will contact you as soon as we get there." The connection is broken, and four Vailixi peel off and start racing north.

Risor has the remaining Vailixi follow him over the beach and the mountains to Vortia. *"Or the remains below the massive mushroom cloud,"* he thought. His Vailixi slows and drops down to near building top level. They split up, looking for survivors.

Risor is mesmerized by the destructive force unleashed. Most of the buildings were three to four stories before the attack. Nearly 20,000 people lived in this city, the jewel of the region. Almost all the buildings in the city are wiped to their foundations or burning and smoking. Nothing looks like it could survive the destruction. Risor has little hope of finding survivors.

Dimera interrupts Risor's gloom, "Sir, Lord Tironi is on the link."

He slowly nods and moves the view screen back in front of him. Tironi comes into view and looks very distraught.

"My Lord, the base has been destroyed. I do not believe there are any survivors here."

Feeling the world's weight on him, Risor unemotionally responds, "That seems to be the same thing here. Do not stay on the ground long. We do not know what poison remains from the brahmastra strike."

"So you believe this was a brahmastra strike, my Lord?"

Absently nodding, "Yes, I think we have seen the answer to Lady Jana's strike. Report back in an hour."

At the base, only a handful survived. Lord Tironi brought those alive to the city so they could be cared for by the city survivors. Of the natives around the base, most had run to the hills before the attack and have not returned. Word from the few that did venture back down to the base to meet the Vailixi rescue parties is that they believed the war of the gods was not for them, and they would not return.

ATLANTA RAMA

Indrajit walks into this father's office, the grime of many days travel still on him. "What has happened, Father?"

Venkat is sitting at his desk, holding his head in his hands. Looking up with tear-filled eyes, he says, "The Atlanteans used a brahmastra or whatever they call their version of it."

"Where, Father?"

"Kalibangan was hit. Then Sagala and others."

Indrajit, in almost a whisper, "Where is Mother?"

Venkat could not control himself any longer. He breaks down into uncontrolled sobbing. He started a few times but could not put words together.

Indrajit goes to his father and hugs him. He waits, giving his father time to compose himself.

Finally, after a few attempts, his father choked out, "In Kalibangan, they killed my poor Sita."

Indrajit feels like a knife has plunged into his chest. He staggers back and then drops next to his father's chair. Together, they cry. "I will kill them. Many of them."

"It will not matter. My Sita is gone."

He holds his father. "We will strike back."

"We have. We destroyed Vortia. There were other colonies in their lands, Atlanta Nado and Atlanta Coda. We tried to hit Atlantis but failed."

Shocked at the number of targets. "What are we doing, Father? We will destroy the world. Between us and them."

"It is up to the Gods now, theirs and ours. Men are just the tools of their anger now. The Elders have revenge in their hearts and listen to nothing else. I have no heart left to argue."

He looks at his father, a strong man of much wisdom who now seems so frail—a heartbroken shadow of what he once was. "I will talk to Kali. She will know what to do."

At the temple, Kalpana, Kali's assistant, escorts Indrajit to Kali's study. Looking up from her desk, Kali says, "The hour is dark, blood flows freely, and the hero returns. How was your mission north?" Kali asks as she slowly gets up. Darshik, her male assistant, moves quickly to help her.

Indrajit's face contorts with anguish as he stares at her. He swallows the lump in his throat and takes a deep breath before moving to embrace her. "My mother was killed in the strike on Kalibangan. Too many of our people are now dead. What is happening?"

Holding him, "I am sorry, Indrajit, it is hard for many now. The world is on fire." He does not let go for a time, and she keeps comforting him. Eventually, he sighs deeply and breaks contact.

Returning to her chair, she watches him. Kali says, "I hear you bring gifts from up north."

Nodding and grateful to think of something different, he says, "Yes. Some of their Shilots are studying the ice melts. They said it would eventually flood the lands. Is that possible?"

Darshik says, "My Lord, it has been suggested that there is enough water to raise the sea levels. It will be good to compare notes with the Atlanteans."

"Well, they are pliant now. I think they understand they will not leave here without permission, and that will depend on how they act."

Kali seems deep in thought. "My hero, do not wander far. I might need you soon. You and your team."

"Of course, I will stay with my father. He grieves deeply over mother. I also need to say my farewells."

ATLANTA SUNA

Risor establishes a recovery site about a mile down the beach from the city for Vailixi landings and casualty collection. There was little Captain Volck and Poseidon's Servant could do, so Risor released them to go where they felt best.

It has been two days since Risor's squadron came to Vortia. The Flying Dragon squadron, coming from Utanor in northern Atlanta Questo, has been sent to relieve the survivors of the strike.

Risor's people have gathered over four hundred survivors between the base and Vortia. Almost all are badly burned. Of the approximately five thousand natives in the region, only a few hundred survived. The majority were in the city at the time of the attack.

While other Flying Dragon Vailixi fly over the city or land further down the beach, one craft lands near Risor. Out comes a few armored troopers carrying large containers. Following them comes the commander of the Flying Dragons, Kotan. While Atlantean, Kotan is a native of Atlanta Questo.

Bowing Kotan says, "Commander Shandar Kotan, leader of the Flying Dragon squadron and Lord of the Aska Pass. At your service."

Risor bows, "My Lord, Commander Risor Tarnor, leader of the Falcon Claw squadron and first son of the Elder of Altai. Praise Poseidon for your arrival."

"We have brought the supplies and tents, as you have requested."

Coming up behind Kotan is a healer, one of the Somena of Aceso, the God of Healing. A few other Somena exit the Vailixi carrying large jars, followed by more armored troopers carrying large containers.

The healer bows to Kotan and Risor. "My Lords, I am Mita Torgar. May your need of her blessing always be slight." Kotan, Risor, and Tilor bow their heads. "My people will get started immediately."

Risor turns to Tilor. "Tilor, please show Master Torgar to the survivors and coordinate with Lord Kotan's people." Turning to Kotan, "My Lord, if you will follow me. I will brief you on the status."

Risor sits at a folding table, looking over a view tablet. The soft glow of the tablet's screen lights up his face while he reads. Finally, he puts his palm on the screen and intones.

"Commander Risor Tarnor of Falcon Claw." He puts down the viewer and goes to another table to pour himself a drink. Kotan enters the tent, and Risor motions him to the drink he just poured while pouring another glass.

Kotan takes the drink and says, "Risor, this is gruesome work. Are you sure these were brahmastra strikes?"

"Yes. I believe this was the work of the brahmastra masters."

They drain their cups and pour another round. When Master Torgar comes in, he wipes his blood-covered hands on a rag.

A pale-faced Torgar finishes wiping his hands and says, in a tight voice, "My Lords, what have we done? Their wounds will not heal. This is not regular fire we are dealing with. This must be the fire of the Gods."

Risor hands the healer a drink. "Master Torgar, can anything be done to ease their passing if they can not be cured?"

Draining his cup, Master Torgar looks at Risor and then droops his head. "We will do what we can. Of the four hundred we have today, only one hundred will survive the next few days. Probably a handful will survive the year."

Toying with his cup, Risor said, "This was a city of over 20,000 a few days ago. A thriving city."

A very angry Kotan asks, "How many more of our cities will go up in fire?"

With a sarcastic smile, Risor responds, "Ask the Shigar. They have brought this on us with their war-mongering ways."

Finishing his cup, Kotan said, "I believe you will have a chance to ask them first. You have to report to Atlantis, right?"

"Please don't remind me." Risor puts down his glass and passes the view tablet to Kotan. "Here is my report. I am sure the Shigar will try to blame me for all of this."

"They are a pestilence on our society."

Nodding at Kotan, Risor lays a hand on the Somena's shoulder. "Master Torgar, please take care of them. I know they will have the best care possible."

Risor and Kotan leave Master Torgar, head in hands, in the tent.

Walking towards Risor's Vailixi, Kotan and Risor walk in silence. Tilor is ahead with some troopers moving containers onto the Vailixi.

Risor could see that Kotan was frustrated and wanted to say something. "Shandar, do you wish to say something?"

Kotan broods momentarily, then asks, "What possessed Lady Jana and the Shigar to start using such evil weapons? Didn't they know that Rama also possesses such things?"

Sighing, Risor responds, "I wish we had met under better circumstances, but that is not our fate. The Gods are playing a foul game with us, I fear. They are using the Shigar as their tool for our destruction. Those who think less of the Gods are becoming the tools of their own downfall, and reluctantly, I think they will take us with them."

They clasp arms in farewell. "Farewell, Risor. Stay safe, and do not associate with these monsters more than necessary. I agree; the Gods will punish them and all around them. We will do what we can for these poor people."

Risor turns and enters the Vailixi. Miko Tsuru, Kotan's lieutenant walks up to Kotan.

"Do you think they will try to blame him, my Lord?" Miko asks.

"They will try Miko, they will try. But they will not succeed. I hear he has strong allies in Nalos and the military."

Risor's surviving force gathers and heads west over the dying city and the mountains beyond. Kotan and Miko watch them until they are beyond the mountains and out of sight.

Miko starts to turn, "Will that be enough?"

ATLANTIS

Risor faces six judges arranged in a half circle in front of him. This is the court of inquiry that he had feared would come. The Shigar members of the military high command try to blame him for the destruction of the Atlanta Sunda colony and the defeat of three squadrons.

Two of the judges are definitely Shigar party members. Lady Tomar is the regional commander of Atlanta Luxa. The other, Lord Delmat, is standing in for his commander for the region of Atlanta Meito. If rumors are true, he is foppish and not too bright.

Of the others, Lord Sutor is a Nalos supporter and friend of the family. It also helps that he was a hero to the Atlanteans for his victories during the Battle of the Nile many years before.

The other three judges are neutral in the sense that they do not let others know their leanings. Risor thought he had an even chance of hanging or walking.

Tension fills the courtroom as Risor's report is read aloud. The crowd eagerly awaits the outcome, their reactions ranging from apprehension to excitement. Lady Tomar sat with an unsettling smirk, seemingly reveling in the drama unfolding before her, while the rest of the panel remained stoic and composed. Murmurs and whispers could be heard throughout the room, some supporting Risor and others questioning his credibility and loyalty.

After the reading, Lord Sutor pounds his gavel and asks, "Lord Tarnor, you admit that you ordered the retreat upon your arrival at the scene?"

"Yes my Lord. When I arrived, Lord Tironi advised me of their situation. Between our forces, we were outnumbered nearly two to one. Include the remaining Vimana we left behind, which would be closer to 3-1 odds. I determined that the mission to attack the city of Dwarka could not be accomplished. That to stay could destroy our entire force."

Lady Tomar said, "Admit it, Lord Tarnor. You are a coward!"

"My Lady Tomar, do you think you could have overcome those numbers?"

Sputtering, "You dare question me!?!" She stands up, points at him, and growls, "I have commanded our forces way before you were born, and you dare compare yourself to me?"

Before she could continue yelling at him, Lord Sutor calmly responds, "My Lady Tomar, I think you mistake our Lord Tarnor's question. I do not believe he was questioning your skill but was stating what I consider an obvious point."

He stops talking to adjust how he is seated. With the wind taken out of her argument, Lady Tomar sits back down. Throwing angry glances at both Risor and Sutor.

Lord Sutor, not even glancing her way. "Thirteen effective Vailixi and one damaged against thirty Vimana would be an unlikely victory that would probably be of historic proportions. Also one that I would not attempt, if I had an opportunity to avoid the battle."

He gets up, adjusts his uniform, and then plants both hands on the table, leaning forward and staring into the audience. "Since I am the only one to have succeeded in a battle of similar scale, I can tell you that I did that because I had no option. We had men on the ground, and if we had left, we would have left thousands to the mercy of the Ramans. Where I succeeded, many have failed. Even battles more evenly matched. I believe you, Lady Tomar, had to retreat from a battle of closer odds than what Lord Tarnor found himself against." And with that, he sits back down as everyone waits.

Continuing, "While I do not believe Lord Tarnor failed in his duties, I will agree that an investigation into the matter should continue. Not at this trial, with the current information. We should question all strike force members and review the logs. Then we can make a decision. Lord Tarnor, do you agree?"

Barely containing his excitement, Risor says, "Yes, Lord Sutor. I will abide by your wisdom."

Lord Delmat blurts out, "My Lord Sutor, it seems you protect this coward."

With authority, Sutor responds, "Delmat, are you questioning me?"

Realizing his precarious position, "Never would I do that, my Lord. I was just..."

Interrupting Delmat dismissively, "I didn't think so. So it is settled. Lord Tarnor, you will await our decision in Altai."

With that, he stands up along with most of the other judges. Lady Tomar remains seated while Lord Delmat partially rises but then notices Lady Tomar and returns to his seat.

Risor bows, "Yes, my lord." He waits a minute for most of the judges to depart. Eventually, Lady Tomar and Delmat also depart. The crowd has a mixed reaction, as is expected with Shigar and Nalos supporters.

Risor turns and walks to the exit. At the end of the crowd benches, he spies Lady Jana near the exit. She is waiting for him. Mentally sighing, he moves forward, knowing she will have something ill to say.

As he nears her, he looks straight ahead. She states, "Well, you survived again. It seems I have underestimated you."

He is taken off guard by her openness. "I didn't know we were enemies, Lady Jana. I will remember that for the next time we meet." He continues to walk past her.

"You would do well to remember that. For I will not underestimate you again."

Risor bows his head slightly as he walks out the door.

Back in his quarters, Risor is packing when Tilor comes in.

"So they didn't have you executed yet, eh sir?"

Grinning, "No, my friend, not today. Not that they didn't try, though."

Packing away his uniform, Risor fingers the command emblem he always wore: a golden trident with wings, claws, and a star over it. This symbol of office for all Vailixi squadron commanders cannot be worn anymore, at least not until the investigation is over. He explains what happened at the trial to his friend and second.

"Back to Altai, is it?" Tilor sits in the only chair in the room.

"Yes, Lord Sutor ordered that. It's probably a good thing. I think the Shigar smelled blood and would keep trying to push me to something," pausing. "What news of our people?"

"The Shilot are working on our craft, and the crew has also been awarded rest. I will go back home, too, but I will probably stay in Atlantis for a while."

"To see Lena?" Risor asks.

"Yes, who knows how long before I can see her again." Tilor produces a bottle of wine, "Care to have a drink, sir?"

"I have no glasses."

"When did we ever need that?" they both laugh.

"What else have you heard, my friend?"

Uncorking the bottle, "Well, it seems that we have struck a few more cities of the Ramans. They have retaliated against the northern Atlanta Nado colonies and our allies there. I have heard that some of the strongholds have been blasted so bad that the heat turned the walls to glass." Taking a swig of the bottle and passing it to Risor. "This is not how we should fight."

Risor also takes a swig and passes the bottle back. "No, it is not. Things will change, my friend. They will change for the worst, I am afraid."

Suddenly, the air raid alarm starts. Since the squadron is deactivated, they have nowhere to go, so they go to the window and look around. Most people are picking up the pace of their movement, with some windows and shops being closed, but for the most part, the citizens of Atlantis carry on.

"Seems like no one is worried, eh, sir?" Tilor continues, taking another drink from the bottle. "Think we will be able to finish this?" Both return to what they were doing inside the room.

"Atlantis has never been breached, while our homes and poor Vortia only have a handful of shielders. I think we will be fine since Atlantis is guarded by many shielders and two full Vailixi squadrons."

Tilor passes Risor the bottle when a bright flash bursts through the window. The surprise makes Risor lose his grip and drop the bottle. This flash resembles what they saw near the Raman coast when Lady Jana struck for the first time. The bottle shatters on the floor right after the loud boom of the explosion reaches them. People in the streets start to scream and run.

"Apparently, this is not a normal raid," a grinning Tilor offers. He looks down at the floor. "What a waste."

"Sorry about that. I was kind of shocked to see that flash. I thought the defenses would stop anything like that well before the shields were hit. I guess one of the Ramans got close enough to fire a brahmastra at the shields or something."

Returning to the window, they see the top of a mushroom cloud rising over the distant mountains. Similar to the clouds they saw over Rama and Vortia.

"Not sure, Sir, but it did scare the locals. I bet some heads will be rolling for the Ramans getting this close."

"I wonder how large the strike force was?" Risor pauses while he calculates what size force could get this close to Atlantis and strike the shields with a brahmastra. "I bet at least three squadrons were involved in the attack, maybe more."

"Think so? That seems to be pretty large to get this far without notice."

"True. It would be hard to hide if they all went together, but if they moved in groups via different paths and linked up close to Atlantis, that might work."

"Or even struck from different directions to draw off the defenders," Tilor offers, nodding. He looks out the window and then at Risor. "Don't go admiring their work that much. They will probably succeed in breaching soon if they keep at it. Or run out of Vimana."

"Yes, that is true. I heard from one of the other officers that they have had three attempts since Lady Jana's attack. From the people's reaction, I don't think they have been this successful before." Pausing for a second. "Luckily, I will be out of here tomorrow."

"Yes sir, you seem to be a magnet for Shigar anger. Getting you away from here will be good until our squadron is ready to ship out." He heads toward the door.

"Safe trip, sir." Sticking his hand out.

They grasp each other at the elbow. "You too, my friend. You might want to consider getting Lena out to another colony or something, just in case the Ramans get lucky."

"Hmmm, that might not be a bad idea."

The next morning, Risor makes his way to the aeroport. Talk of the raid is everywhere. The enemy did fire a brahmastra, but the shields held, and the strike scorched a mountain valley to the north before the Vimana were beaten off. Atlantis is safe once again.

Atlantis is the world's greatest city, with people from all over the world selling, buying, and mingling. The city is at the gateway between the Tes Atlan and the tranquil sea of Tes Zeita. The imperial section of the city is located on the opposite side of the city proper, from the military district and aeroport. Not open to the public except on festival days of the Gods, the great central island is where the major temples of the Gods reside and, of course, the imperial palace. The outer rings have most of the government offices and noble mansions.

Risor's family, the Tarnor, has a small mansion on the third ring, but it is usually not a place Risor likes to go unless other family members are in the city. It is far from the base, and only the servants live there. He could also not be there without being invited and attending parties that are always going on. The city nobles live for parties and take offense easily at perceived slights. Sometimes, it is interesting to participate in, but not this time with the events of the last few days.

There is talk of canceling the aeroport's passenger service and pressing these Vailixi into the war effort since making a Vailixi is still complex. To create such a craft, many builders using Aether must work together. They would build the craft from bronze and iron around a smaller version of a Mother Stone and then, using Aether, meld the metals together. Many conduits lead to the crew stations on a military version but less so on the civilian craft.

Another reason the passenger service remains is that the wealthy of the empire have grown accustomed to using it to travel quickly between colonies and Atlantis. More nobles now live in their home regions and commute to Atlantis a few times a year to attend business and pleasure. So, the empire would need to be in dire straights for the nobility and wealthy to give up such a privilege.

ONE WEEK BEFORE

ATLANTIS

She runs her fingers through his chest hair, admiring the hard muscles under the hair. This is their last night in Atlantis before they leave.

"Lena, do not worry. It is only temporary," Tilor whispers and then nibbles her ear. "Until things calm down between Rama and us."

Not falling for the distraction, "I don't understand. Atlantis is the most protected city in the world. Why should we leave?"

"Yes, it is well protected, but the war has taken a bad turn, like yesterday's attack. I'm afraid Rama will find a way to break through Atlantis' shields, and I don't want you here when they do. I can't forget Vortia."

He rolls on top of her. Sliding his hands under her arms and behind her head to run his fingers through her hair. She loves the feel of his hands gently massaging her head. She loses herself looking into those dark brown eyes. Missing what he is saying, she quickly kisses him.

"Tell me again, my love."

Chuckling, he kisses her again. A soft kiss, then another, stronger. She feels his breathing getting harder. She feels herself stirring as well. Grabbing his head, she pulls him closer, a deeper passionate kiss. He bites her lip.

Later, the moonlight filters through the curtains, highlighting her breasts in the surrounding darkness. He gently blows the sweat that beads on her chest and neck.

Exhausted but satisfied, she remembers he was telling her something before they started. Giggling at the thought, "Honey, what were you trying to tell me before you lost your concentration?"

He stops blowing and gives her a quizzical look. Then he smiles, "I forgot. You completely blew my mind." They kiss, but just a soft, quick one, without the promise of more.

"Do we have to leave tomorrow?"

"Oh, now I remember." Rolling off her to her side. "One of the people in my squadron, Geiro, has family there. You will stay with them. His sister is very nice and has a few young children."

Tears stream down her cheeks as she clings to him, not wanting to let go. He gently strokes her hair and whispers comforting words. "I promise I'll come back for you," he said, his voice full of determination. She tries to believe him, but deep down, she can't shake off the feeling that this could be their last embrace. As he holds her in his arms, she drifts into a restless sleep filled with worries and doubts about their future together.

Days later, they arrive at the village of Dumon tu Mare. It was a long trip with little time for them to be intimate. This added to Lena's sense of wrongness on this trip. She is irritable, and the wagon's bumpy ride did not help.

They crest a hill, and the sea opens before them. The sea breeze carries a briny odor, like fish and seaweed drying on the shoreline. Lena feels the salt of the sea is thick on her tongue.

Below them is a small dock for fishing boats and twenty small homes around a central square. A small fort stands on the hill overlooking the village, with a central watch tower rising above the low walls.

Riding into the village, Tilor stops and asks for directions to Geiro's family. They stop out front of a single-story home with flowers planted around the front door.

Tilor's visit is brief. He stays for the night as Lena meets Kala and her two children, Gurio and Kara. The next morning, he swaps the wagon for a horse with the garrison commander.

He comes to her with his horse saddled and waiting. "Lena, please do not look so sad."

"I feel like I will not see you again." She feels even worse, heart aching, tears welling up. Lena can not stop feeling that this is the last time they will see each other.

"Please, honey, it is not goodbye. I will be back. You will see."

Looking into his eyes, she sees that he is tearing up now, too. She feels bad. She didn't want to leave this way, but it seems to be the norm for them when he goes away to war. "You promise?" she says, trying to laugh it away.

He looks miserable. She feels miserable. She wipes away some tears with her hand. Tilor cups her face in his hands and wipes away her tears using his thumbs. Even though his eyes are glassy, he gives her a sad smile that tugs at her heart. She feels more miserable seeing him so sad, and her tears come freely.

He kisses a tear that runs past her nose to her mouth. He continues to kiss up her cheek and nose to her eyes. Lena sniffles and cries a little. Throwing her arms around him, he holds her fiercely.

"I promise, sniffles. You are my everything, and I have no life without you." Whispering to her.

They stand there for hours, but only a minute or two passes. Lena memorizes his feel, smell, warm breath on her shoulder, the wind, the sounds, everything. The moment is burned into her memory.

"I must go now, Lena." He pulls apart and gives her a long but soft kiss, gently touching her lips. He ends the kiss with a kiss on her nose and then forehead. "I love you, Lena. I will return."

Her tears come as he quickly turns and mounts the horse. He looks down at her, tears freely flowing down his face as well. He looks at Kala, who is in the doorway. "Thank you, Kala, for taking her in. Please take care of each other."

Lena comes to his side and touches his leg. He looks down at her. "Someday, we will be together, my love. Please understand that I am worried for you, which is why you are here. I will return." With that, he moves the horse forward. Slowly at first while next to her.

She could barely see him through the tears. Kala comes to her and hugs her. "He will be back, Lena. Gerio speaks so highly of Tilor."

They stand there as Tilor moves the horse to a trot and then over the hill. Once out of sight, Lena cries harder.

They stand in the street, hugging each other. Letting Lena get her cry out. Kala is also tearing up.

Eventually, little Kara comes up to them. "Why are you crying, mommy?"

Gurio stands in the doorway with a quizzical look on his face.

Both of the ladies start laughing and cleaning their eyes. "Uncle Tilor had to leave, and Auntie Lena was upset because he left."

Gurio runs past Kara and up to his mom, "Oh, like you do when daddy goes fishing in bad weather?"

"Yes, exactly like that," Kala said.

Lena, glad for the change, "When will Fortos be back?"

Hugging her two children, Kala looks back, "Usually, they stay out a week or longer. It depends on what they are after and how the fishing is."

Kala offers Lena a hand, "Come, let me teach you how to make baskets. It will take your mind off him. Works for me."

They enter the house with a last sniffle, rub of the eyes, and a short laugh.

ATLANTA NADO

Rogat looks at the almost complete fort his men are building. The Tes Naldo is a peaceful backdrop to the hilltop fort. A tranquil seaside village is an excellent way to rebuild and rest his people.

They received their replacements. Recruits brought them back up to strength, but it is an untried unit. With only twenty survivors from the Dedeni disaster, Rogat has a lot of training to do.

The Tugar and Greeks started raiding this area to keep the Atlanteans off-balance. The 3rd Alta Faltan was sent to this region to deter the raids.

As Rogat and his patrol march past a small farm, a young boy stands by the fenced entrance, his eyes wide with curiosity as he watches the soldiers approach. In the nearby field, a young girl and a woman work under the hot sun, their dresses stained with sweat and dirt. The farmhouse is quaint but well-maintained, with colorful flowers blooming in its garden. The boy's gaze follows the soldiers as though they are creatures from another world. This must be an unusual sight for him - the fort is an hour north, and the military rarely venture into this area.

But today, they come to this quiet corner of the countryside, disrupting the peaceful routine of the farm. The sounds of marching boots and clanking weapons fill the air, a stark contrast to the usual sounds of nature that surround the farmstead.

Giving a friendly smile, Rogat says. "Hello, child, what's your name?" He slows his walk.

"Telko, sir."

"Well, well met, Telko. My name is Rogat." He slows down as the patrol continues. They are in the safe zone, with other patrols out in the area.

"You are an Atlantean?" Telko asks. His sister comes closer, and the woman in the field walks toward them.

"Yes, I am from Altai, from far off Alta."

"Does everyone look like you from Altai?" Telko asks.

Chuckling, "No, my family is originally from Atlanta Coda. Far to the south of here." Rogat smiles as the young girl comes up to stand behind her brother. "Hello there, what is your name?"

"I am Mila, his big sister." She said.

"Well, you do look like a young lady. It is a pleasure to meet you, Mila. I am Rogat."

"She isn't a lady. She is a sister," Telko said.

Mila rolls her eyes, "Yes I am a lady, you just don't know."

Laughing at them, Rogat smiles as the woman from the field approaches them. A beautiful woman with long blond hair, her deep blue eyes held laughter and sadness. Rogat is taken with her. "My lady, I am Senior Trooper Rogat at your service," he says with a slight bow.

With a quick laugh, "My lady? I am no fancy lady, soldier. My name is Yalana, and these are my kids and my farm. What is your business here?"

Surprised by her directness, "I am sorry and meant no offense, ma'am. I just thought I would say hi to your son while we were marching by."

Telko tugs on his mother's apron, "He is from Atla, mommy."

Before Rogat could correct him, Mila said. "It is Altai, dimwit."

Before Telko replies, Yalana says, "That is enough, the two of you."

Rogat tries to suppress a laugh. Yalana gives him a look that makes him burst out laughing and makes him feel the need to explain himself. "I am sorry, Yalana. It is nice to know that families are the same worldwide. I have a brother and sister, and we also used to do this."

She smiles, "Yes, I guess it is. So, how long will your people stay here in Tar Deg?"

"We are here to chase out the Tugar."

She gives him a piercing look, "Well, we have no love for the Tugar and their friends, but if you don't stay long, I would thank you not to come near my family or farm anymore."

Rogat is taken aback by that. "May I ask why?"

She softens a little, "No offense, Rogat, but they have spies everywhere, and while I appreciate you taking the time to talk to my children, I do not want to earn their attention."

Understanding dawning, "Oh, I am sorry, ma'am. It's a shame. I would have loved to talk to you more."

"Well, maybe a little if you stay a while or successfully clear them out." Then, looking at the kids, "It's time to finish your chores before sundown. Well met, Rogat."

They stare at each other for a moment. Rogat sees interest and concern but is excited by the interest. "It was a pleasure to meet all of you. I do hope to see you again."

The walk back to the fort is pleasant. Rogat has known women before and considers himself pretty experienced, but he has never felt as excited as he feels now, especially about being told to leave.

When he enters the fort, the sun has set. He thinks it is a beautiful sunset. He walks past Noko, who looks like he is about to say something.

Rogat beat him to it. "Fuck you." Which earns him a laugh as he continues walking.

ATLANTA QUESTO

Shandar leans on the rail, wine cup in hand, and looks at Tu-ne. The gently smoking volcano rises significantly above its neighbors, ringing the plain below. Occasionally snow-capped, the locals revere it.

The rooftops of the city of Utanor, his ancestral home, cover the immediate surroundings of the Kotan city palace. Having a third-story balcony is the privilege of the leaders of the city. Which is what Shandar's father is, a city leader on the Council of Elders.

After Vortia and a trip to Atlantis, he just returned to the city with most of his squadron. What he saw in Vortia disturbs him, and what he saw of the Shigar in Atlantis scares him even more.

"I always find this a tranquil place to reflect on my problems," his father, Todoru Kotan, said, walking up behind him.

"I am afraid it does little to ease my mind, Father."

"Ah, Vortia was disturbing, was it?"

Nodding, "Yes, how could we and Rama do such things? That might happen here as well." He turns toward his father.

"The Shigar are going crazy in Atlantis. They stir the citizens to more war and rejoice in the destruction of the cities of Rama." Getting angry, "They do not care that Vortia and other cities of ours are destroyed."

Yelling, "They wouldn't care if that happened here or to Moia!"

Putting up his hands, Todoru soothingly said. "Peace, Shandar, the enemy is not here."

Trying to calm down. "I wonder who the real enemy is, Father."

His father puts his hand on Shandar's shoulder. Looking him in the eye, "This is a question that the Council has discussed recently. I think it is time I bring you to the Council for your view of things."

The Council of Elders meets the next day, and Todoru brings Shandar. The Hall of the Elders is on a cliff overlooking the bay below them with Tu-ne behind them.

Only a colony of Atlantis for one thousand years, Utanor is one of the newest outposts of the Atlantean civilization. Because it is so new, the Shigar and Nalos have not established themselves here or in Moia.

Moia is a little older at one thousand eight hundred years. Further south along the coast of Tes Tira, a bustling maritime hub. Especially now with Vortia reduced to rubble.

Todoru sits at the Council table while Shandar stands near the door until called.

Shandar strides to the center of the Council table to the Speaker's seat. He stands at attention, awaiting permission to sit.

His father intones, "Welcome Shandar Kotan of House Kotan, Commander of the Flying Dragon Squadron and Lord of the Aska Pass. The Council of Elders of Utanor bid you sit and tell us your tale."

Bowing to Tes Tira in the east and Tu-ne in the west, Shandar sits and then begins. "Weeks ago, I was ordered to Vortia to assist in a humanitarian mission. We linked up with the remnants of the local squadrons, led by Risor of House Tarnor from Altai."

"A Brahmastra weapon destroyed Vortia. We have little doubt of this. The Ramans destroyed Vortia in retaliation for the strikes on their home cities. We continue to trade strikes on each other, but we are more successful in our strikes."

One of the elders asks, "Kotan, how do you know this?"

"I was ordered to Atlantis with those that survived past a week. There were only one hundred at that time. When there, I was briefed on the situation by Command."

He looks at all the elders. "The Shigar have control over the military at this point. They are ordering more attacks against the remaining Rama cities. Attacks against villages and centers not protected by Raman forces. They are ordering a massacre."

Talos, one of the oldest elders and one who comes from Atlantis, clears his throat. "Commander, Rama is our enemy, is it not? What is different now than before in our attacks?"

"Honored Elder, we never really struck at non-military targets in the past. Now, Command is asking for us to leave none alive. This is not our way but the Shigar's thinking."

Another elder asks, "Does the Emperor condone this?"

Shandar turns to her, "From what I was told, the Emperor has not been seen in the last month or so. And Nalos supporters are being targeted. Why, even Lord Tranor was on trial for cowardice and losing Vortia. He was not even the commander of the strike he was on and was not present when Vortia was struck. It is madness."

Todoru says, "We should try to talk to the prime minister. Find out what is going on. If they are openly attacking Nalos, then they must feel they have a clear advantage. It is just a matter of time before they go after all that do not bow to them."

Talos nods, "Commander, keep your squadron intact. I fear we might have need of them before long. Todoru, we should summon Dilon and Shinriki as well. We need to take stock of what we have."

ATLANTA NADO

The sun touches the peaks behind the fort, illuminating the sky in a fiery red as darkness settles over the fort. Turning to see the shadows of night swallowing the village and coasts of Tes Naldo, only the distant horizons of the sea remain lit with the last rays. Below, the village is peaceful. Even those in the fort are settling in for the night.

The last patrol, just lighting torches, passes the village. Teado's section is coming back from a two-day sweep up the river.

His sight settles on the farmstead of Yalana and her kids. The lights inside the home are lit. He wonders what they are doing. Rogat could not get the fiercely independent woman out of his mind.

He imagines her in his arms, stroking her hair.

Then, the sounds of fighting reach Rogat. He thinks Teado's section must be caught in an ambush. The sounds of Aether fire mix with screams of the dying and orders being called out.

The villagers stay in their homes, and a few lights go out. Rogat turns to yell an order when the door at Yalana's opens. There, she stands with a weapon in hand.

"To arms!" Calls Rogat. Men come running out of the barracks. One more look at Yalana's farm, and he sees the door closed. Good, she went back in, he thought.

In the courtyard of the fort. "Noko, double the guard and keep the rest of your men ready." One of his men comes running with his weapons.

"Migu, take your men to the village. Set a perimeter if you can, but watch your back. I will take my team down the road, cut across the stream, and try to take them from the rear."

Migu's section and Rogat's head out the gate. Migu's force heads down the road to the village while Rogat's team heads down the river road past Yalana's farm.

Fighting continues where Teado's section seems to have set a perimeter and is stalling the ambush. Good, Rogat thought, they can keep them busy while we come up behind them.

Migu's force will be close enough to support them and protect the village. Honestly, Rogat did not know how many villagers sympathized with the Tugar or were allies with them. Hopefully, Migu will keep an eye on the village and the enemy to his front.

As Rogat's force comes even with Yalana's farm, the door opens, and Yalana and her kids are in the doorway.

"Get back inside, woman!" Yells Rogat, slowing to make sure she listens. He waves his men forward. "It is not safe. Stay inside."

Telko recognizes Rogat and waves while Yalana tries to close the door. They should be safe, he thought. He rushes to get back in the lead of his men.

The fighting continues unabated as Rogat's team makes the river. He stops the men and tries to peer into the dark of dusk to see if anyone is waiting for him on the other side. His men spread out around him.

"No one fires unless you have a valid target. We don't want to give ourselves away."

A minute passes and Rogat thinks he sees something but is unsure. He keeps staring at the object, hoping it will reveal itself, but nothing happens.

He readies to lead his men across the ford when one of his men shoots his Aether spear. Rogat turns to yell at the man when he hears the scream of the man's target.

Diving to take cover, Rogat feels the wind of the arrow fly past his head, where he was a second before. The whistle of more arrows is heard as he hits the ground. Luckily, most of his men make it to the ground as well.

Return fire from his side starts to pick up, mixed with the cries of those who did not get under cover quickly enough.

Many of the enemy come out of cover to better shoot their targets. They also, in turn, become better targets. While the Atlanteans have more firepower, the fading light hid the Tugar arrows, making them hard to dodge.

The firefight goes on for a while. Then, a roar comes from further back where Teado's force is holding out. Rogat hopes that doesn't mean their force is decimated.

Eventually, a battle cry mixes with Aether blasts. The firing from the opposite riverbank lessens. Rogat can see some of the enemy withdrawing.

"Keep up your fire. Our boys are taking them from behind!" Rogat's team fires more, not so much taking aim as firing for effect in the immediate area.

They see the Aether blasts through the woods now. The enemy seems to be in a total rout.

"Ahem, sound 'Disengage.' Marcon, take your team back a ways towards the fort. I will take my team across the ford."

Later, they discover that among the enemy dead are a few of the local villagers. Rogat hopes that it is all of those sympathetic.

THE DAY BEFORE

ALTAI

"Risor, a courier just delivered this." Said his father, entering Risor's room. Risor has been in Altai for a week, awaiting the tribunal's judgment. Taking the letter from his father and looking up at him.

"Well, at least it wasn't accompanied by a squad of soldiers. I guess I will have the dignity of leaving my home on my own."

Both mother and sister arrive in the doorway. While opening the letter, his father places a hand on his shoulder.

Scanning the document, Risor says nothing to the assembled family. Just staring at the letter.

"Well?" Rina demands. They all look anxious, with mother and sister coming to stand next to them.

In a near whisper. "I have to go back to Atlantis."

All three of them—father, mother, and sister—start talking simultaneously, declaring they will fight this.

"Write Lord Sutor.."

"I will go with you.."

"It's not fair!"

Risor could not hold it in anymore. He starts laughing, and all three stop mid-sentence, staring at him like he had lost his mind.

"You should see yourselves."

Looks of shock turn to false anger as his mother and sister start beating him, and his father starts laughing.

Risor continues laughing and trying to deflect the punches. "I am sorry, I could not help myself. You all just looked so serious."

With one last punch to the stomach and a gratifying grunt from Rogat, Rina said. "Of course, it is serious."

"Yes, little sister, you are right. The tribunal has declared me innocent." With a deep breath. "I am to report back with the squadron early next week."

His father. "Will you still be in command?"

"I do not know, Father. The letter does not specify." Handing the letter to his father.

"Well, we have you for a few more days at least," his mother says, then hugs him.

"Yes, Mother, a little more time."

OVER THE NORTHERN ICE

The Vimana continue north over Tes Tira, east of the Raman Empire. They travel south of Rama out into Tes Rama, then turn east to cross the southern half of the isolated landmass south of Atlanta Suna, called Atlanta Isla. Once out into Tes Tira, they turn north. Their goal is the massive northern ice shelf.

This mission is the last hope of the Raman Empire. They know they are losing and will soon not have the strength to fight the Atlanteans anymore.

The Atlantean version of the Brahmastra has destroyed many of their cities. Rama no longer has the means to stop these attacks. Many Vimana have been destroyed, along with most of the industry used to build new ones. Many argue to sue for peace with Atlantis, even though that would mean the destruction of the Raman way of life.

Already, many of the Raman allies have fallen or turned and joined the Atlanteans. Only the Greeks, the Tugar, and Hu remain. Many of the smaller allies have been lost. Even Sangam will no longer be a supportive neutral. So great is their fear of the Atlantean weapons of destruction that they refuse to even talk to Rama.

It has been a losing cause for most of the last decade. The Ramans never thought they would be able to defeat the Atlanteans. It has always been hoped that they would be able to hurt Atlantis enough to have a cease-fire and let their internal divisions tear them apart.

The fight between the Shigar and the Nalos is well-known to the Ramans. The plan was to contact the Nalos party and support them as much as possible. Reluctantly, the Ramans learned that most Atlanteans hated someone becoming as powerful as them more than they hated each other.

This mission is conceived in desperation because the Ramans could not pierce Atlantis' defenses, and that is the key city. Atlantis, being what it is, is a very paranoid nation that keeps most of its force and ability to generate new weapons of Aether, right around Atlantis. This protects the assets and ensures no rival Atlantean group grows strong enough to challenge the Emperor. Ten thousand years ago, the Emperor's family did that exact same thing to the royal families of the principalities of Atlantis.

Converting the principalities into an empire, the imperial family took Atlantis and beat the Princes into submission—a short but bloody struggle for supremacy.

After twenty-six hours in the air, the Vimana reached the northern ice shelf. The massive walls of ice tower a mile above the ocean and are said to be even higher in some places. As the Vimana gains altitude, the wall is shrouded in rain clouds. The waves dash against the ice wall far below. They reach the top of the ice wall and begin the next phase of their mission by hugging the ice terrain.

After an hour, five of the Vimana break off and head west while the remaining ten continue north. After another ten hours, the Vimana move north and then south, effectively crossing the northern ice shelf to the smaller landmass of Alta.

Over the last few years, the Ramans discovered the Atlanteans were exploring the ice shelves. A few of these expeditions were captured, revealing the status of the ice shelves. What the last captured explorers told them was the nature of the great ice lakes and how that concerned the Atlanteans.

The Raman leadership decided that they would try to use the ice in this last-ditch effort, even though this would affect more than just the Atlanteans. Considering that the Raman Empire is near annihilation, the cost to everyone is considered worth it. If successful, some Raman people will survive, and the Raman culture will continue. If the Atlanteans defeated them, the chance of the Raman culture to continue would be greatly reduced.

As the craft reached the massive ice lake of the northern ice shelf, the remaining Vimana split into two groups of five each. One group heads to the southeast and another south. The three groups will synchronize their attacks to ensure little to no warning. Total surprise is required for this attack to be successful.

Like the first group that remains north of Tes Naldo, the group going to the southeast arrives at their destination and waits for the specified time.

The third group reaches its target above the Tia Yolan, an ice lake near the ice's edge and above a great lake at the base.

At the allotted time, they act. Each group is above an area where the ice barrier is the thinnest between the ice wall and the ice lakes. They rise higher into the air, with three defenders spreading out into a defensive pattern for the two specialists bearing Vimana. The last hope of the Raman Empire plays out.

Indrajit, the last Raman hero, walks out onto the observation deck. A blast of arctic wind hits him and whips his cloak wildly. He looks into the cloud-shrouded darkness, looking for movement, anything to give away an enemy they do not wish to see. His goal is to protect Kali, the mantrik aboard this Vimana.

Satisfied, he calls back through the doorway. "Darshik, it is safe, bring Kali out."

Draped in dark robes, Darshik and Kalpana come out to assist Kali. Being physically frail, Indrajit believes Kali will fly away if not adequately supported. He also moves to help her, but she shoos him away.

"I have been in stronger winds than this warrior, Indrajit. Fear not. I will complete my task."

Kali's dark robes whip around her fiercely, causing Indrajit not to believe her words.

Darshik produces a heavy bow and gives it to Kali. She handles it as if it is nothing. Both Darshik's producing the bow and Kali's handling of the bow amaze Indrajit. Where did it come from, and how could she hold it? Magic is definitely something he is not used to.

Kali starts to chant and seems to gain strength and stature in the chanting. Kalpana comes forward, produces an arrow, and reverently hands it to Kali.

Kali's chanting grows louder, which Indrajit does not see how. The wind makes hearing anything not within a foot or two almost impossible. Yet here is this frail old woman holding a bow about the same weight as she, chanting louder than the wind is howling and seems to become stronger by the second.

She notches the arrow and draws back in one fluid motion that Indrajit thought impossible. Her chanting seems to be all around him. She hits an incredibly undulating note and lets loose. The arrow flies faster than a standard arrow and shoots out into the dark.

Even Indrajit's superior eyesight could not keep track of the arrow as it sails out of sight.

In a commanding voice, Kali calls out, "Close your eyes now!"

An involuntary urge comes over them to close their eyes as a flash engulfs them, followed by a loud, booming explosion. The Vimana falters for a moment, and a massive heat wave strikes those on the observation deck.

The clouds disappear, replaced by a massive wall of steam and a giant mushroom cloud rising into the air.

Kali said, "It is done." Then turns and goes back into the vessel. Dishrak and Kalpana follow, leaving Indrajit alone to hear the loud cracking noises in the distance.

The top of the ice wall is engulfed by a cloud of steam, making visibility high on the ice wall impossible. The Vimana moves closer to the ice wall to see the results. As they listen, a massive crack is heard. Then another and another.

Suddenly, the Vimana is hit with ice and water from a massive spout erupting before it. The Vimana swerves away to safety, and more spouts erupt. Quickly, half the ice wall falls away, and a great sheet of water flows through the crack. The flow hits the lake below, and a massive wave twenty meters high pushes out in all directions.

Indrajit holds on to the rail in total shock at what he is witnessing.

When the wave hits the debris dam holding back most of the lake, it explodes in spectacular fashion. The wave and the debris create a raging wall of destruction that wipes out everything before it. Now twice the size of the original river flow, trees, boulders, animals—everything fails to withstand the force unleashed. The power is so great that even hills seem to dissolve before the torrent. The Tia Yolan River valley would be forever changed.

The Vimana follows for a while, the crew mesmerized by the power of the flood. What isn't destroyed by the roiling mass of debris at the front of the flood has to contend with the unyielding power of torrents of water flowing downstream. The crew is so amazed by the power they unleashed they don't realize how far down the river they have gone. They quickly turn back to avoid detection because they are nearing areas patrolled by the Atlanteans.

All three missions are a success. It is just a matter of time before they see what effect the breaching of the ice lakes will have. The goal is to raise the sea levels and sink the coastlines.

This will affect the great Raman city of Dwarka, but it is a price they have to pay. When they left their base, the Ramans had already started to evacuate Dwarka. They also notified their allies to move away from the coasts and riverbanks.

The Vimana turned around to take the long flight home.

THE WALL OF DESTRUCTION

ALTAI

Risor awakens to the tolling of the bells and yelling coming from the streets below. Racing to the hallway, he meets other family members and servants. Everyone demands to know what is happening, with servants charging off in all directions to try and get some answers. Rosan orders everyone back to dress and prepare a few changes of clothes.

Maybe the Ramans have finally decided to strike the Atlantean colonies on this side of the world. Risor quickly dresses and goes down to the courtyard below. Servants are hustling back and forth, and his father is directing actions. A small stack of bags grows in the courtyard.

"What is going on, Father?" asks Risor.

"We do not know yet, but the order is to evacuate to the hills."

In moments, an officer of the Home Guard comes through the front gate with one of the servants sent to find out what is going on.

"My Lords, Sub-commander Ruland." He bows. We are ordering an evacuation of the city. A great flood is coming from the north, and it will be here in one to two hours. Please gather what you can easily carry and head out the Morning Gate to the hills."

Risor asks, "What about the aeroport? We can use Vailixi to shuttle people to the hills."

The officer responds, "The collection point at the aeroport is already swamped with people. The gate will be the quickest way to the hills."

Turning to Rosan, "Councilman Tarnor, Councilman Zailor advises the council to meet at Sun's Farewell Bluff as soon as possible. We will maintain that as our headquarters until the crisis is over."

They thank the officer, and he departs.

"Flood, eh?" Risor remembers what Tolen had said months before. "Father, if this is related to what Tolen told us before, it could be very bad."

"Yes, he told us too. We need to get everyone moving."

Within fifteen minutes, the family, servants, with baggage are on the move. While not running, especially since it is still a long distance, the group moves quickly along with hundreds of other fleeing residents.

Within the city proper, the streets are well-lit, and it is easy to see dropped items that someone before them had second thoughts about taking. The roads are strewn with debris from those fleeing. Luckily for the Tarnors, their home opens onto one of the main thoroughfares, and they quickly exit the city gate.

Hundreds are on the road to the hills with all manner of wagons or animals as beasts of burden. Risor would not mind having one of the Aether wagons that would allow them to run along the side of the road, a few feet off the ground. It couldn't stay on the road with all the people, but they could use it as long as the ground near the road is flat.

With only starlight, the occasional torch, or Aether light to light their way, it is pretty scary for those fleeing. It is a quarter-moon night and not very bright. They move on in silence so they can hear when the flood nears. The silence is broken by the whirl of Vailixi occasionally flying overhead with their Aether lights beaming along the road. The light shows all of the discarded belongings thrown to the sides of the road.

Apparently, many people feared not making it, so they threw their belongings away to move quickly.

Risor believes they are halfway to the hills when, up ahead, an animal bellows, and then an Aether spear shoots the beast.

Many of the animals near Risor's family are skittish. Risor thinks this means the flood is close. He had heard Tolen say that animals have a sense, like those who control the use of Aether to detect when danger is coming.

When they get to where the beast was killed, they see a group trying to remove it from the road.

"Citizens, leave it. It is to one side, and there is little time. Pick up your gear and move on," Rosan said to the crowd.

The people didn't need much convincing, they drop their holds on the beast and move on.

"Father, the beast will still block any larger wagons coming up the road," Rina tells her father. She seems in a state of shock since leaving their home.

"Honey, any wagon that big will not move quickly with all these people in the way. If it did, it would more than likely run people over." When she said nothing, he added, "Better that one wagon be left than many people harmed in the driver's attempt to reach safety."

Again no response.

A few minutes later, a Vailixi comes down the road to where the Tarnors are, and through the use of Aether, the commander's voice is heard by all in the area. "Citizens, please move quicker! The flood will arrive in approximately thirty minutes, and it will come almost to the foothills."

Then, the Vailixi moves off further down the road back towards the city.

Risor and many people around him did the same mental calculations and thought they were close to thirty minutes from getting into the foothills. Like most people, Risor and his family decide the time estimate is cutting it too close.

Rosan beat Risor to it. "Everyone drop anything heavy, less food and clothing. We need to move quicker! If your load is too much, distribute it amongst the others."

After a few exchanges of foodstuffs and clothes, the group starts jogging. Most of the people around them do the same.

One family still tries to carry a large statue, but it seems they will never make it. Risor stops next to them. "Citizens, I know this must be valuable to your family, but you will never make it to the foothills with that before the flood arrives."

"Can you please help us? I can pay you." Said the patriarch of the family.

"Sorry, not worth my life." Risor turns and jogs to catch up to his family.

Further along, Risor stops for a second, his heartbeat softly pounding in his ears, his breathing quickly returning to normal. After a few seconds, he starts to hear a distant rumble. His father stops next to him, breathing harder than he. "Father, do you hear that?"

Another person who stops near them answers before Rosan can. "The Gods! It is almost here." Then he takes off running.

Turning to the dark figures back down the road, Risor bellows, "Run! Run now! It is getting closer, drop what you can and run!" Following his advice, they run. They quickly catch up to their family, and Risor grabs his sister by the hand to pull her after him.

She is tiring, and he can see she is contemplating giving up. "No, you don't, we are almost there!"

He stops for a second next to one of the older servants, who is also starting to stagger. She is almost like a mother to him, and he bends down and lets her get on his back. With a hold on Rina's hand, he continues to move forward.

The sound turns from a rumble to a distant roar, getting loud enough that he can hear it over his heart pounding. Rina even starts to move more quickly as she hears it. Others, further back, begin to scream, curse, cry, or all three. Many more people start to run past Risor since his burden slows him. The rest of his family is ahead, with Rosan pulling Risor's mother.

Many older people start to fall or sit down, giving up. They know the uphill part is coming, and they do not have the strength to go on.

A Vailixi tries to land further down the road and is instantly mobbed, with everyone trying to get on board to save themselves. The crew tries to fight off the people to establish order, but they are overwhelmed as people's survival instincts clearly take over.

One crew member is thrown out of the craft, sees the crowd mobbing the Vailixi, and runs up the road toward the hills. Risor hopes he makes it and pities the terrified civilians and the remaining crew that can not get out.

Risor and family make it to Sun's Farewell Bluff. The place is a swarm of activity. One of the Falcon Claw Vailixi is being used for its external lights and communications. He learns that all other Vailixi are tracking the flood or over the fleeing citizens, trying to hurry them along.

Looking back toward the city, he sees its lights and that the Morning Gate is now closed. If they are lucky, the flood will not top the ten-meter walls. If the city survives, they will have plenty of supplies inside the granaries to hold the population over until a new crop can be grown. He thinks they can also count on supplies from Atlantis or other colonies for added safety.

Looking down the road he just left, he sees that the line of people went almost halfway to the city. He thinks many will not make it, as he notes the swarmed Vailixi. He hopes they can close the access ramp and ride out the flood in the water-tight craft.

"Sir, thank the Gods you are alive!" Said Timur, one of his sub-commanders in the Falcon Claw squadron. His family also lives in Altai.

"Timur, where are our Vailixi?"

"They had left by the time I got back to the base. I was with my parents."

Concerned, Risor asks, "Is your family safe?"

"Yes, sir, I brought them to the refuge and then made my way here." Looking back at the city. "Think the city will survive the flood, sir?"

Risor also turns to the city and a feeling of foreboding washes over him. "If it does not breach the walls, we can live off the stored foods." Looking upriver, Risor sees Vailixi lights. "Look, some of our Vailixi return."

One of the soldiers tending a fire behind Risor comes up and follows Risor's pointing arm. "No, sir. They are tracking the flood."

Completely shocked, "Poseidon protect us."

Looking back down at the people on the road, Risor wills them to hurry up. The Vailixi flying over the stream of people keep moving around the road, illuminating one group and then another. The roar of the flood is almost deafening. People around Risor yell to be heard. The Vailixi, following the flood, are almost to the road, and Risor sees their Aether lights illuminating debris in the flood.

It looks different from what Risor imagines a flood would look like. He thought it would be a wall of water crashing down on everything. It actually has a deceptively slow look—a wall of destruction that pushes everything before it until the front of the flood is a roiling mass of debris.

With the first rays of sunlight outlining the mountains behind them, Risor sees that the front of the flood is a wall of tumbling trees and boulders, among other things. This wall slams into the fleeing people like they are not even there. One second, people are running for their lives, and the next, a flood of debris.

The mobbed Vailixi is there, and then the next second, swallowed by that wall of destruction, lost from sight. Risor could not see the Vailixi's external Aether lights shining through the water. The flood must have pushed the Vailixi downstream.

A hush falls over the crowd on the bluff, their eyes wide and mouths agape as they bear witness to the incredible might of millions of tons of water cascading through the river valley below. The sound of rushing water fills the air, drowning out all other noises with its magnificent force.

In the distance, the once-bustling city of Altai disappears into darkness as lights flicker and go out one by one. From this vantage point, the observers can also hear the telltale sounds of destruction: explosions, crumbling buildings, and ripping sounds like buildings torn from their foundations. It is a scene unlike anything they have ever experienced, both awe-inspiring and terrifying at the same time.

The early dawn starts lighting up the doomed city, with the first rays of the sun hitting the floodscape below. The water continues to rise, flooding into the lower foothills below the bluff. The early light of day shows that the city will not survive this. Already, most buildings are no longer visible above the water. The city is not being destroyed but wiped out. Altai and her three thousand years of history, gone in less than one hour.

ATLANTA NADO

"Rogat!" Someone yells, along with banging. He is instantly awake and trying to figure out what is going on. "Enter," Rogat yells. He then makes out an alarm bell peeling in the background. He jumps to his feet and reaches for his short sword. He notices the trooper at the door.

"Sir, command reports a tidal wave bearing down on us."

Naked from the waist up and barefoot, Rogat passes the trooper. Taking the stairs two at a time, he bounds up to the ground level and heads toward the command bunker. Troopers are running everywhere.

"Rogat, what should we do with the villagers?" Calls out Teado, trying to muster his men.

"Bring them to the fort or get them moving for the hills. Safer here unless the wave is too high."

Teado nods and gets his men moving for the gate. Rogat sees Migu walking the ramparts and urging his men to be vigilant. Noko's men are starting to form up, too, but Noko is not present.

Rogat reaches the stairs of the bunker when he meets Noko coming up from below. "Rogat, command expects a fifty-meter wall to hit our coast in two hours."

Rogat stops on the third stair. Fifty meters high? He turns around and runs for the rampart, facing the sea. Noko is a few steps behind him, and Migu runs around the ramparts toward them.

They all get to the rampart at the same time. Rogat yells to no one in particular, "How high is the fort's base from the sea?"

One of the troopers stationed at that part of the wall answers first. "About seventy meters, sir."

Migu nods, "Give or take. Why?"

Noko responds, "Command said the wave is about fifty meters."

Rogat looks up and down the drop before him. "That is cutting it close."

Looking at the distant hills, Migu asks. "Should we evacuate to the hills?"

The trooper asks, "Can we make it, sir?"

Rogat looks back toward the hills. The men could make it, but could the villagers? Rogat is not sure. "We will have to take our chances. I am not sure we are safe here. We are screwed if we guess wrong."

Noko, looking over the wall. "Yes, we might not get it bad, but probably enough to flood the fort and go down the bunkers."

Rogat decides. "Right. Noko, send a runner to tell Teado's men to get the villagers moving to the twins." He points to a set of distant hills across the river ravine from the village. It's about three kilometers distant. "Tell them we have about two hours to evacuate. Take supplies and what animals we can move quickly. This area might not survive, but we will need something until help arrives."

Looking at Migu, he continues, "Make sure we take as many supplies as possible and start heading there now. Noko, take your men to the outlying farms, get what we can, and move them to the twins."

Rogat heads back toward the command bunker. Everyone starts moving. The command section takes over the fort wall watch.

At the communication station, Rogat orders. "Get me command."

Within a minute, Captain Skerios' image is before him. In the background are people running back and forth with tons of conversations. "Rogat, we have a shit storm coming our way. A Vailixi patrol over the Tes Naldo received a distress call from a merchant ship. The ship stopped communicating before they could get too much from them."

Guessing, Rogat interrupts, "Swamped over, I bet."

"Aye, most likely. Anyway, the patrol went forth to investigate and saw the wave. Going further north to the ice, they saw it was breached. The mother of all waterfalls is pouring out."

Breathing a sigh, Rogat believes he guessed right about evacuating the fort. "I am ordering an evacuation to the hills. What is the rest of the company doing?"

The captain looks at him. "Dying, most likely. We are trying to get out what and who we can, but it is a fair distance to anything safe. Part of the unit is evacuating to set up security. The rest will march up the valley, along with all the people who can leave that quickly."

Looking around, the captain continues. "I'm sorry, Rogat, but I think your people will be on their own and probably for quite some time. I will tell the others where you will be. Maybe you can all link up. Try to take your communication unit."

Rogat shook his head. "It is too heavy, sir. I can not move it safely without risking those who carry it, and I will not order that."

Grabbing a map and turning to the table, Rogat quickly studies the region. Then, stabbing a finger at a point on the map, he turns to talk to the captain's image, "We will stay here if not that bad or head inland to Tar Deg. Can you pass that information along to Atlantis too?"

"Understood. Atlantis will eventually respond, but who knows how this will affect everyone else. Good luck, Rogat. May the Gods protect you and Poseidon keep you."

ALTAI

Despite the desperate search for survivors in the aftermath of the devastating flood, the efforts prove fruitless. The Vailixi, determined to aid those in need, followed the fast-moving waters for several miles, scanning the debris strewn about for any sign of life.

Risor takes his turn to search for survivors. He isn't necessary to perform the scout mission, as he is a commander and not one of the specialists who operate the Vailixi, but Risor needs to do something. He became the senior Vailixi commander since the local commander died on the Vailixi that was swept away, attempting to pick up survivors.

Risor's craft flies past the doomed city. There is no indication of the original riverbanks or city remaining. Most trees along the river valley below the foothills have been uprooted or are now underwater. The raging river extends from the foothills, where the survivors are, to the foothills of the western bank, almost twelve kilometers wide. Sweeping the far bank, they find a few survivors.

The city of Altai was approximately eighty kilometers from the delta of the great river. Risor notices that most of the delta's trees are gone as the flood pours into the gulf, and the debris disperses over a large area. Performing low sweeps over the now-disappearing delta, they find no survivors.

They see the occasional body but can tell there is no life. The water flow out of the great river drives massive plumes of muddied water deep into the Gulf of Tes Falta. No fishing in these waters for some time to come, he thought. It will take time for the silt to resettle to the sea floor.

Further out, they find partial building structures, furniture, and other items belonging to Altai floating in the Tes Falta. Risor has the Vailixi head toward the islands to see the situation.

The first island they encounter is nothing but sand and almost entirely underwater. It used to be a forested island about a kilometer long. Risor surmises that a massive tsunami rolled across the Tes Falta when the flood waters plowed into the gulf. They must check the other colonies around the Tes Falta to see if they are okay. Some of those colonies are near the shore.

ATLANTA NADO

Rogat's heart pounds as he races up the hill. The thunderous sound of the oncoming water grows in intensity as Rogat scrambles up the hill, little Telko tucked tightly to his chest and his other arm full of meager belongings. Yalana and Mila are struggling beside him. Each is weighed down by a bag of their family's possessions. The others from the village and most of Rogat's section stagger and stumble behind them.

Those at the top of the hill are running down to help those still struggling up the hill. In the distance, Rogat hears faint screams from below as the waters rage well below them, cascading over the land like an unstoppable force of nature.

Rogat knows that all those left behind are already doomed or dead. Some villagers insisted on getting all their belongings out. Rogat left them to their fate—no sense dying with the fools.

Noko is at the top of the hill, yelling encouragement. Rogat could not make out what he was yelling but knew the gestures from how he talked to his troopers when trying to motivate them.

Sparing a quick look behind him, he sees that it is not a massive wall of water but a wall of destruction. The front of the oncoming water is blackish with trees, bodies, and other things roiling forth. It is only three to five meters high and already at the base of the hill.

With an extra surge, he makes the crown of the hill. Putting down little Telko, who runs to his mom, Rogat drops his gear and stands panting, watching the water creep up the hill.

Migu comes up beside him. Between pants, "Think it will get up here?"

Rogat looks back to see the distance between them and the next incline. "Pray to the Gods that it doesn't. I am unsure we can make it that far before it crests this hill."

Picking up her bag and urging the kids forward, Yalana looks at Rogat and says, "We should be moving." Then she turns and heads for the next incline.

Rogat, Noko, Migu, and Teado stand watching her leave. Other villagers and even some of the troopers follow her.

"She's too smart for you, boss. Just give it up," says Migu. They all laugh, pick up their stuff, and start after the others.

Demetri peers out of the cave toward the Atlantean city of Delin. Or what remains of it. It was a relatively large city of some 40,000 souls. Now, most of it has been washed away. The plain that feeds the city lies submerged below a meter of water in many places. Large piles of debris from the tsunami dot the plain as haystacks during harvest time. Many of these piles are burning brightly in the gathering darkness.

The Ramans told King Agos, and he got word to Demetri's raiding party about Rama's plan to flood the Atlanteans. Demetri decided to lead his men on a scouting mission instead of a raid. They made their way to the mountains, near the city of Delin, and waited.

The Atlanteans were warned of the coming danger and attempted to flee their doom. Demetri's men watched as thousands streamed out of the city in the mid-day sun. The problem was that most fled over the five miles of plain up the road that would eventually wind its way into the surrounding mountains.

When the tsunami came, the force of the water pushed the water higher up the plain. Funneled by the surrounding mountains, the water pushed further and higher. Not many were able to make it into the mountains. Those who fled directly to the surrounding mountains had a better chance.

Prince Arawn, standing next to Demetri, interrupts his thoughts. "My Lord, should we start our return trip? The enemy is no more. Even the survivors are scattered and offer no threat."

"It has been hours since the flood receded, and still no Atlantean rescue attempt."

Artos, standing on the other side, looks at Demetri. "We don't have the power to ambush any rescue attempt."

"Oh, I know, but if there has been no attempt to come and see what happened to one of their larger cities, then maybe the Ramans did it." Demetri smiles. The thought that Atlantis has been destroyed or so disrupted that they could not come to the aid of their own is very pleasing.

Understanding hits both Arawn and Artos.

A smile starts to split Artos' grizzled face, "You think their lack of response is because they have their own problems?"

"Yes, Atlantis should have been hit by now."

Arawn adds, "Should we chase down some of the soldiers that survived and see what they know?"

Shaking his head, Demetri replies. "No, I imagine most of them have little clue. Those Vailixi that left before the flood hit probably had most of the command staff."

Turning back toward the cave path to where his men waited. "Besides, I think we know from the lack of rescue response."

ALTAI

Risor returns to Sun's Farewell Bluff and finds that large tents have been erected, one for the military and the other for the council. One Vailixi still sits to the side as the communications terminal for the new command center.

Inside the council tent, Risor tells the council, "We have found no further survivors. Also, the flood caused a tsunami when it reached the sea. We checked out a few small islands near the delta, and they were wiped clean of their trees and are mostly underwater."

Tonda, one of the council members, asks, "Underwater?"

Tolen rises to stand like Risor. "I believe the sea levels will continue to rise as the flood continues. The amount of water flowing down Tai Yolan has not dropped in the eight hours since it hit Altai."

Risor continues, "We should probably check the other colonies and warn Atlantis. If the sea levels rise, it will affect them as well. Correct, Tolen?"

Nodding, "Yes, we have a report from the team that flew north. They have reported the ice barrier has been massively breached. I fear this will drain a significant volume from the ice lake."

Another council member, Stolar, asks, "Shilot Dekarn, how long will this flow?" Many council members nod their agreement.

"I am sorry, Councilman Stolar, we can not tell from what we know. As I have previously reported, the ice lake is made up of interconnected smaller lakes. How deep these interconnections go is unknown. I do believe the flood will continue for a few weeks."

The tent erupts in general arguing over the implications of Tolen's statement. Geiro, one of Risor's officers, comes into the tent. Tolen sees him and waves him over. He tries to get the crowd to quiet.

Geiro says, "My Vailixi was sent north to investigate the reason for the flood." Pausing, Geiro looks at Risor, who nods in encouragement. "We found two massive breaches. The one flowing into the Tia Yolan and another, a few hundred kilometers east, flowing into the Tes Atlan."

Tolen continues, "Thank you, Geiro. The bottom line is that the ice lakes are massive, and the sea level will rise. Atlantis needs to be warned."

Risor's father, Rosan, asks, "Tolen, what will this mean to us in trying to re-establish our homes in Altai?"

Tolen looks at Rosan and then the rest of the council. "From the information I have, I would say we will have to abandon Altai where it is."

The tent explodes in loud voices while Tolen waits. Rosan slowly gains control of the crowd.

"Continue, Shilot Dekarn."

Tolen bows to Rosan, "Thank you, my Lord. With the river flowing for at least a few weeks at or near the current flow rate, the people will need a place to stay."

He pauses to think. Everyone remains quiet and awaits him to continue. "These foothills are not conducive to farming without irrigation. When the flood subsides, the land will be so saturated that it will need at least a few months to dry out. Lastly, all of the buildings will need to be rebuilt."

Risor's communication officer, Dimera, enters the tent and approaches Risor. She whispers to him. Risor calls everyone's attention. "My Lords, Tolen, I am sorry for the interruption."

He nods to Dimera to talk. "We have received warnings from Atlantis. They expect a massive wave within the hour and are trying to evacuate the capital. Also, some of our colonies along the Tes Naldo have been wiped out, and there are only a few survivors."

Stunned, Zailor asks, "What about the other colonies south of us? Like Neptius?"

Dimera shakes her head, "We have talked to Sumtori, who reported being hit by a large wave. We have not heard anything from the other colonies."

The tent is silent as they realize the implications of what was just revealed. Risor puts his hand on Dimera's shoulder, then stands tall, "It seems we are on our own. Tolen, please continue."

Nodding towards Risor, Tolen said, "The city of Altai is not salvageable. We might wish to rebuild in the future, but I would ask you to reconsider this idea."

Councilman Tonda asks, "Why Shilot Dekarn?"

"If the ice barrier broke once, it will do so again. What we see today will be the first of a few of these events. As the world warms, the ice will continue to melt."

Tonda asks, "So where would you believe it best to rebuild?"

"The flow of the flood, along with the debris, will cause a massive disruption to the fishing grounds in Tes Falta. It will take years to rebuild, if ever. The migratory animal patterns will change. Living near the coast is not wise until the ice shelf is no longer a threat. We should probably find a sheltered valley to live in."

Rosan speaks up, "Thank you Tolen. Lord Fordo, what is the status of our supplies, the people, and military strength?"

Fordo moves to stand at the council table. He is the military commander in Altai. "My Lords, we do not have an exact count of survivors. Many have continued deeper into the foothills. We currently number 1200 here."

Pausing for questions, then, "There are a few homesteads where we can acquire animal stock and supplies near here. I have about 200 effective troopers with Aether spears and some armor. We can protect ourselves but not recharge the spears—the same with the other Aether tools. Master Itarus was not one of the survivors. Also, we did not get the Mother Stone away from Altai."

Councilman Stolar asks, "Lord Fordo, the Mother Stone was securely bound in the temple. I am sure it will survive, and we can recover it after the floods recede."

Tolen interjects, "Sir, the power of the flood might have swept the entire city off its foundations. There is a chance the Mother Stone is gone along with the temple."

Tonda responds, "Atlantis can send us another Mother Stone and a new Master." Many people around the table nod in agreement.

Risor states, "Council, remember Atlantis has a tidal wave coming. With rising sea levels, we have no idea if Atlantis will survive their coming ordeal."

Rosan turns to Ulta, the chief of the Suda. The Suda are the Atlanteans' local ally, living south of the city along the river. "My friend, what of your people?"

Ulta has a harrowed look to him, "Of the Suda, only fifty survived. Many of our fishermen were out at sea when the flood struck. It is the mating season of the Tuli. I am afraid they are lost with those we lost getting here."

After many declaring their support for the Suda, Rosan speaks up. "Enough discussion at this point. We need answers. I propose the following. Lord Fordo will be in overall command of our military." Turning to Fordo. "We need to have all the food and tools gathered and inventoried. Make sure they are guarded. You might need to go to these homesteads and retrieve the resources there. Risor, you will command the Vailixi as senior flier. You will report to Lord Fordo. My fellow councilmen, do you agree?" All agreed.

Continuing, "We need to send Shilot Dekarn north to inspect the breaches to get a better estimate on how long the flood will flow. Provide one Vailixi to his service." Risor and Fordo nod.

"We also need some Vailixi to go and report on all the other colonies to see if we can pick up any survivors or get supplies."

Maps After the Wall of Destruction

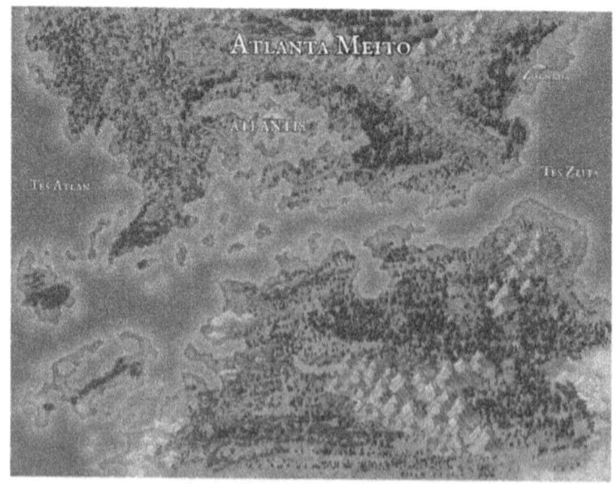

Atlantis after the Wall

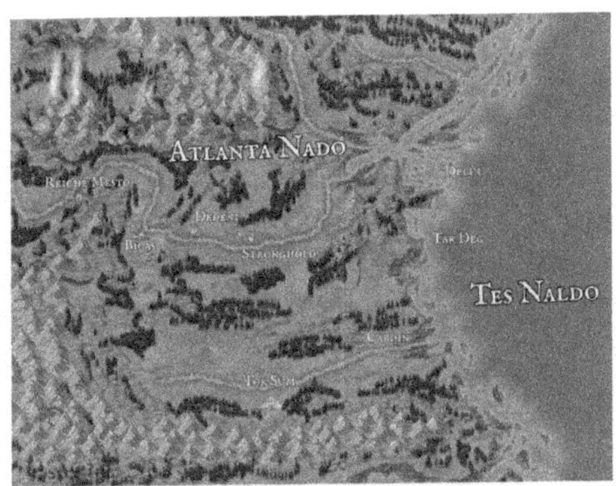

Atlanta Nado after the Wall

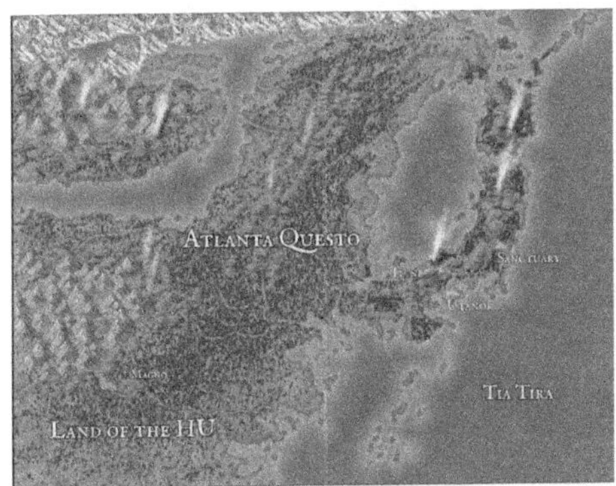

Atlanta Questo after the Wall

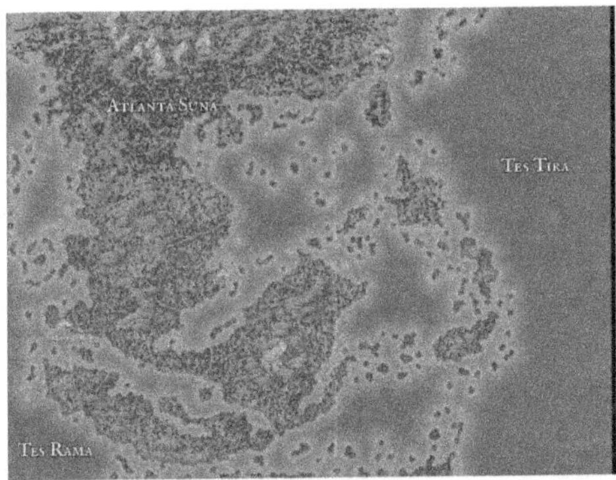

Atlanta Suna after the Wall

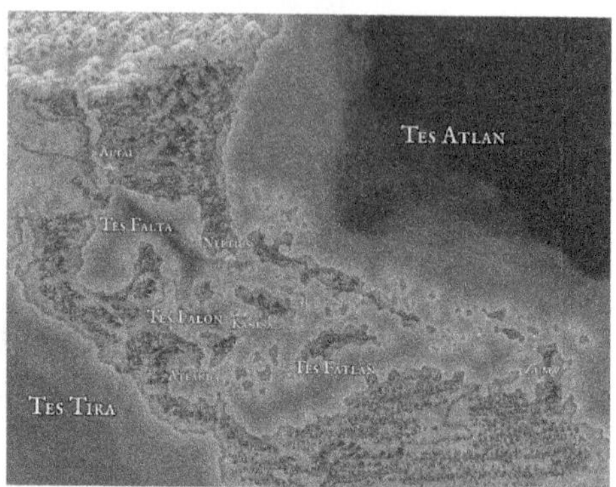

Alta after the Wall

THE DAY AFTER

ATLANTA QUESTO

Shandar and Miko walk into the Utanor Council chamber, having been summoned. The council is present along with Commander Dilon of the Utanor defense force. Standing along the wall behind Shandar's father is Shinriki, the local Awane tribe leader.

Shandar bows, "My Lords?"

Todoru says, "My son, terrible tidings, Atlantis was hit with a great wave that destroyed parts of the city. Atlantis is to be abandoned."

Shandar and Miko stand, mouths agape. They are not prepared for this message.

Recovering first, Shandar speaks, "What are our orders?"

Talos responds, "Well, the High Command believes Rama somehow caused this. They are requesting that the majority of our force be sent to participate in a revenge attack."

Commander Dilon says, "Your squadron, my Lord, and most of my armored troopers. Moia's squadron and troopers too."

Shandar and Miko look at each other. Miko responds, "My Lords, that would leave us open like Vortia was."

Talos nods, "Yes, it would seem so. What do you think we should do?"

Shandar responds. "I think we should not leave ourselves so open. Many homesteads are between here and Moia. Plus, the Hu is still a concern. We need our force to survive." Dilon nods in agreement.

Shinriki comes toward the table. "You mean to disobey Atlantis?"

"I do not think Rama will await our return before attacking, and our families and homes are important to us."

Many council members nod. Talos smiles, "As it should be, Lord Kotan. We and the council of Moia are in agreement with you. We will send nothing and inform Atlantis that the Hu is attacking, and we can not send anything."

Todoru spoke, "Commander Dilon, you and Shandar should go and prepare plans to defend Utanor and Moia. We should coordinate between the cities to meet the threats that come. Atlantis might visit us to take by force what we will not give. Also, we need to make sure the Hu and Rama do not strike."

Dilon motions for Shandar and Miko to follow. Shinriki follows, "I will join your talks, as my people can help." Dilon nods and continues to the exit.

TES ZEITA

Lena worries. The last word they received was Atlantis, and many of the colonies along the Tes Naldo were hit with a tsunami. Their village expects rising sea levels but not much compared to what hit Atlantis.

The strait blocks most of the tsunami's power. So far, there has been only a one-meter rise and no tsunami.

The village of Dumon tu Mare is lucky compared to what is happening elsewhere, as reported via Imperial News Network (INN). Lena worries if Tilor is in Atlantis or back home in Atlanda. Wherever he is, is he safe?

It is early morning, and the sea rises above the average high tide mark. Lena sits near her window and watches the soldiers measure the rising seas. Some of their neighbors are already moving stuff to higher ground. No one is sure how high it will rise, but they believe there is a chance that it will come high enough to enter the homes.

Kala and Lena await moving things until they can see what is happening. They do not have the strength to move any of the big things and have already packed everything they could quickly move. The community decides to set up in the garrison's stockade until they determine where the rising waters stop.

Lena hears a soft knock at her door. "Lena are you up?" asks Kala.

Kala comes through the door and goes to Lena. "I'm worried about Fortos. Will the rising seas cause his ship a problem?"

"I don't think so, Kala. They might not even notice until they get back."

Sighing, Kala leans her head against Lena's shoulder.

"It's not knowing that drives me crazy. Atlantis and many of the other colonies are gone. What is happening to us?"

Patting Kala's cheek. "It is what Tilor was worried about and caused him to bring me her. I hope he is okay. I wonder if I will ever see him again."

"Oh, Lena, I am so sorry. I am so wrapped up in my worries I forgot about yours."

"I know. You have to worry about the children, too. But that is okay. I believe Tilor will come back to me."

Sighing, she continues, "Although I fear it might be a while before I see him again."

"And Fortos will come back to us, too!" Kala exclaims as tears well up.

Crying, they both start to laugh and hug.

That afternoon, the village's fishing fleet returns to a half-swamped fishing pier. The pier is barely above the waves, and most of the surrounding land is underwater. The men bring their catch to shore but are unsure what to do with their fishing boats. They know the water will continue to rise, but how far?

ALTAI

Risor wakes up feeling stiff from the previous day's events. Rina and his parents are still asleep in the tent they are assigned. Rank has its privilege, to a degree. Most refugees sleep in larger tent structures that house thirty or forty people.

This is fine in late summer, but Risor knows that none of these will provide proper warmth come winter. They will need to build permanent structures.

The survivors gather in tent farms around two homesteads closest to Sun's Farewell Bluff. Many have military experience, so the tents are ordered, and the "camp" is organized. They split the people between these two homesteads.

The bluff is still the base of operations, with the road between the camps and the bluff being regularly patrolled. Not that they expect any problems, but with the flooding, many animals that generally keep their distance might be more stressed, hungry, or aggressive than cautious.

After cleaning up, Risor makes his way to the bluff to get a status on what the communications team has heard. Atlantis was hit badly by the tsunami. The military is still functioning there, but most of the civilians are dead or missing. The city had a population somewhere above one hundred thousand souls, but from the initial reports, it seems that less than forty thousand have potentially survived. Risor shivers just thinking of all the destruction and death around the city.

Back on the bluff, Risor walks up to the table that Milo is near. Food is on the table, and if Milo is there, it must be good enough. Milo is Risor's squadron scrounger and could come up with stuff that amazes Risor. As long as he is scrounging for Risor, he didn't ask where Milo got the stuff.

"Good morning, Milo."

"Good morning, sir." Milo hands Risor a cup of quat.

Smelling and sipping the hot liquid, Risor sighs with contentment. "At least we still have quat. Do you have any news?"

Milo hands Risor a view tablet. "Just got this in. The second section talks about the status of Atlantis. The tsunami wiped out a lot of buildings, and the current death and missing tally is around 82,000. The waterfront is still under a few inches of water."

Scanning the data, Risor says to no one in particular, "Looks like they will abandon Atlantis. That isn't good."

Then, in a loud and surprised voice, "Whoa, what is this?!" Spilling his cup of quat. He locks eyes with Fordo.

To Fordo, "Atlantis believes the Ramans did this to the ice shelves."

A general uproar ensues. Many people crowd around Risor and Fordo. Councilmen Stolar and Zailor are also there.

Fordo asks, "Is there anything else on that part of the report?"

Scanning the rest of the report, "Yes sir, there is a report that a science team on the ice saw some massive fireballs where the Tes Naldo was breached. High command believes that the three breaches are no coincidence. They are preparing a strike against Rama." Handing the view tablet to Fordo.

Fordo reads for a minute while the crowd talks amongst themselves. "They order us to send all Vailixi and as many ground troops as they can carry to Atlantis. To participate in the raid."

The crowd quiets. No one moves.

Councilman Stolar breaks the silence, "That would leave us defenseless."

Further back in the crowd, someone yells, "This is a Shigar trick. They don't care about us."

Using his command voice, Fordo says, "That is enough of that kind of talk."

The two councilmen look at each other, and then Zailor says, "Lord Fordo, could you please send runners to bring the full council together? We need to discuss how we will respond to this order."

Fordo turns to the councilmen, "Councilman Zailor, we need to follow the orders of Atlantis and trust in the Emperor." Turning to Risor, "Commander, prepare your people. We will send five craft plus 100 troopers."

Stolar and Zailor move to confront Fordo. Stolar starts, "Lord Fordo, you will await the leave of the Council. Is that understood? We need to discuss what our response will be." Shaking his head, "This changes so many things."

Fordo turns red, indignant that Stolar is ordering him around.

Risor, realizing this could get out of hand, points to two guards, "Guardsmen, please go get the remaining councilmen and advise them that they need to come immediately."

As the guardsmen take off at a run, Risor turns to Fordo, who is livid. "My Lord Fordo, if we strip most of our strength, we can not check the other colonies. Who knows how long it will be before Atlantis allows our forces to return? We might be those other colonies only chance of survival."

Fordo visibly tries to calm down. "Call the council then. Lord Tarnor, remember your position."

Fordo turns and marches down the bluff with some troops in tow. He could be seen giving orders to his men, which those on the top of the bluff did not hear.

Risor does not know of Fordo being a Shigar member, but Fordo didn't seem to have Altai's interests as his top concern. The Council of Altai is mostly Nalos supporters, as are many who live in Altai. Lord Fordo has only been in Altai for the first year of his six-year tour.

Thinking that a showdown is in the making, Risor walks to the Vailixi with Milo following him, sensing his boss's angst. Most of the flyers are his people or Nalos supporters, so Risor is pretty sure he has the backing of the Vailixi crews. Dimera comes out of the access ramp to meet them.

"Risor, I mean, sir, what was that all about?" She asks.

Risor looks around to make sure he is not overheard. He motions Dimera to wait. "Milo, it would be best if you stay here for a while. I know you have just come off duty, but I think Dimera will need some help."

Milo briefly studies Risor and then shrugs, "No problem, sir. I can crash here as long as Dimera can tolerate my snoring."

Rolling her eyes, "Sir, do you believe there will be trouble?"

"I am unsure, but the council will not agree to send that much. Lord Fordo will probably force the issue. We might need some air support depending on how things go down." Both Milo and Dimera look surprised.

Risor continues, "Altai and Atlantis are gone, and who knows what comes next? We need to determine what is best for our families more than for the Shigar of Atlantis."

Nodding his head, Milo agrees. Dimera seems to think about it for a few seconds and then says, "I am with you, sir."

Putting his hands on Dimera and Milo's shoulders, he said, "Thank you, my friends. Okay, recall Falcon Claw to take up stations on the far bank. If we need them, I want them to come in with shields up, hover over the bluff, and target troopers. Do not shoot unless ordered."

Risor, his father, and most of the council are drinking quat on the bluff near one of the cooking fires. Functionaries wander back and forth, with a few military members going in and out of the command tent.

Councilman Zailor said, "We should ignore the order."

"We can not just ignore it, can we? What will the repercussions be if we do?" asks Councilman Stolar.

"My friends, I do not have any intention of disobeying the order, but we will question it. I will craft a response to the high command and the Emperor." Rosan assures everyone.

"That will not be necessary, Lord Tarnor. I have presented orders that will be carried out. This is strictly a military matter and not for the Council of Altai," Said Fordo, coming into the circle of leaders with about twenty men at his back. The troopers spread out, surrounding the council and even disarming the troopers guarding the path.

When they go to the Vailixi to take that over, they run into the shields. Running into shields is not fun. The power of the shields causes the lead trooper to be blown back about two meters into the other four troopers behind him.

"Lower the shields," demands Lord Fordo of Risor.

"I will not." Risor counters. "This is an abuse of power, and I will not be a party to it." Turning to the Vailixi. "Milo now!"

Turning back to Fordo. "Lord Fordo, I am relieving you of command. Troopers, please take Lord Fordo into custody." None of the troopers that remain armed move to comply, leading to a big smile on Lord Fordo's face.

"My Lord Tarnor. You are hereby arrested, as is the crew of the Vailixi." One of the troopers comes to hold onto Risor's arm.

Rosan walks to where Risor and Fordo are. "Lord Fordo, what is the meaning of this? The military is subservient to the Council, and this is not what the Council ordered."

Squaring up before Rosan, "Altai is still a colony of Atlantis, and the Emperor is our leader. He has commanded that we provide all possible support to the offensive against the Ramans, and I will ensure we comply." Stabbing a finger at

Rosan, "Your son has attempted mutiny. By our laws, I can have him executed now. I will withhold this if the Vailixi crew lowers their shields and surrenders. Then I will take all of them to Atlantis for judgment."

Both Rosan and Risor know that would be a death sentence. Luckily, at that time, four Vailixi came over the bluff with weapons pointing at the troopers. The council and other people on the bluff move away from Lord Fordo, Risor, and the troopers for Fordo. The other troopers pick up their Aether spears and aim them at the troopers with Fordo. Some of Fordo's men drop their spears. The number of armed troopers for and against is roughly the same. The difference is the four Vailixi hovering nearby.

Fordo's shoulders sag. He sighs and signals his troops to surrender.

"Men, lower your weapons. Lord Tarnor, in the interest of preventing bloodshed, I surrender. I am sure the Emperor would exonerate me once the tale is told."

Rosan tells Fordo, "The old ways are done for Jolta. It is the council that needs to decide whether to keep to the old path or start a new one."

Looking at Risor, "You are in command of our forces. Have Lord Fordo and his men confined to the cellar of the Rizat Homestead." Nodding to his father, Risor gestures to one of the loyal guards to escort them. One of the Vailixi follows the prisoners.

The council members sit around the table in the Council tent. Attendants provide drink and food. Risor stands to the side of his father.

After everyone is served, Rosan begins. "My friends, as we have discussed many times, we have a decision to make. It seems we need to decide if we will follow those in control of Atlantis now or follow our own path."

"Rosan, you know you are talking treason. This will involve everyone here, too," said Stolar, getting a refill from an attendant. "Not only us but the people who follow us must also decide."

"The people will follow us. They believe that we are looking after their best interests," Rosan said, clapping a hand on Stolar's shoulder. "Atlantis is gone, the high command, or let's call it what it is, the Shigar, continue to fight a dead fight and probably will not try to rebuild until the war ends. We have seen Rama's resilience and know that this continued war could take a very long time. Do we bow to the Shigar? We don't even know if the Emperor is still alive. The old ways, the blessing of the Gods, of Poseidon, is gone. What we have today is what we have."

Councilman Ordo said, "It is time to build a new life for those that have survived. We can not count on assistance, and the other remote colonies must be checked for survivors."

The council members nod their heads in agreement. Stolar said, "I have no love for the Shigar and their warmongering ways, but I don't think we should abandon Atlantis yet. We should try to work with them. We do not have the masters of Aether to rebuild our city with the tools and comforts it once had. We need Atlantis if that capability exists. Many of our people will die without it."

Looking from member to member, he continues, "If the Empire continues, I'd rather fight the Shigar in politics than fight the wilds without Aether and the tools of our empire."

One of the troopers who escorted Fordo and his men to the homestead approaches Risor and whispers to him.

Rosan arches an eyebrow in Risor's direction, and Risor nods in response. Then Rosan says, "Councilman Stolar speaks with wisdom. So let us do both. I propose we send one Vailixi and advise the high command that we are currently attempting rescue operations of the remote colonies and Neptius. We can send more once our operations are complete and the people are cared for. We will also ask for another Mother Stone and Shuma to work on it. The priests can keep our Aether tools operational. What say the council?"

"What of Lord Fordo and the troopers that backed him?" from Councilman Zailor.

Councilman Stolar responds, "Why not remove them from the active defense force and use them only if we are in danger? We can secure the Aether spears in the communication's Vailixi and have them available if necessary."

Rosan said, "Agreed. We also should start looking for a place to rebuild. Shilot Dekarn stated we should consider a sheltered mountain valley further north. I propose we use one of the Vailixi to go north with some of the farmers and members of the Suda to search for a suitable spot."

Risor says, "My Lords, should we not keep Lord Fordo and his men out of sight until the Vailixi departs to Atlantis? I know which team I will send to Atlantis. Also, I know of some troopers who might sympathize with Lord Fordo. I suggest we send them to Atlantis. The detained men, with Lord Fordo, number about twenty-five, are being held in one of the barns. Lieutenant Skola, Lord Fordo's second, is with us and has identified another twenty that are most likely with Lord Fordo." He stops to ask one of the troopers to get Lieutenant Skola.

Smiling, he continues, "With your permission, I believe I have a plan." There are nods of approval from many in the group, so he continues, "I will keep Lord Fordo and his men in the barn. Lieutenant Skola will assign an officer and those men she believes are Lord Fordo's to join the team returning to Atlantis. I know the crew I will assign as well. This should remove most of those who sympathize more with Atlantis than Altai. We will tell them that Lord Fordo went on a mission and will return in a week or two."

Looking around for questions, "That will leave us seven Vailixi and about one hundred and fifty troopers. One Vailixi will take the survey team north. Two Vailixi will go to pick up survivors in Sumtori. I will take two Vailixi to Neptius and the other colonies, and one will remain for the protection of our people. We will announce all rescue missions before the Atlantis team departs to allow them to honestly report our use of the aircraft. This should happen today, as keeping Lord Fordo's detention secret will be harder the longer we wait. How does that sound, my Lords?"

There is a general discussion with a few minor changes to the plan. When Lieutenant Skola arrives, she is made aware of the plan, and those involved leave to have the teams prepare.

Councilman Ordo, one of the merchant class representatives, asks, "What of Lord Fordo after the Atlantis mission leaves?"

There are looks of frustration and helplessness among these leaders. They know they will have a hard time trusting Lord Fordo and his men. They need unity of purpose in the people to give the survivors a chance to rebuild and move on with their lives. Many guilty looks and starts, then stops to speak from those assembled, saying what most think the best option would be. That is to execute them.

Luckily, Councilman Ordo saves them from speaking of such a cold solution, "I was thinking, we need to see how our neighbors are doing. We have the Nataku to the east and the Shonat to the west of the great river. What if we send Lord Fordo with his men to visit one or both of these people to see how they are doing and if they will help us? We send them via foot, so they will be out of our way for at least a week or two, maybe more. If they complete their mission and return, we can trust them more. Plus, the relationship with Atlantis will be known."

Rosan bows to Ordo, "Ordo, that is brilliant. We will need to send more than just Lord Fordo and his men. I do not think they have the skills to survive in the wild, and we can not afford to give them too much food. I think we should send some of the Suda as well."

Ordo grins back at Rosan. "Thank you, and I volunteer to go with them. I believe we really do need to send an emissary, and sending a member of this council will make it a real mission. Plus, I would like to see how my friends, the Nataku, are surviving this catastrophe. There are a few other merchantmen who would also like to go. A few relationship things, if you will."

Stolar says, "I agree with him and believe we should provide Ordo with a communications ring. Commander, I understand those have a limited range, but it should have the range from the Nataku villages to here, should they not?"

Risor thought, "Yes, my Lord, I believe they have the range and would not be a danger if Lord Fordo were to betray us unless Atlantean Vailixi comes this way."

ATLANTA QUESTO

Shandar returns to his family's home when a guard comes running up the street.

"My Lord, please wait."

Shandar stops and waits for the guard to approach. While waiting for the guard to make the last 20 meters, he notices that Miko is about one hundred meters behind him.

Shandar thought this couldn't be good.

Out of breath, "My Lord, Moia calls for help. The Atlanteans are there. Commander Dilon has orders for your squadron."

Shandar nods and follows the guard back down the street. Miko stops and awaits them to get even before falling in. The streets are not busy this late in the evening, but they still dodge those about.

Breathlessly, Miko asks, "You heard?"

"Yes, assemble the squadron. I'm going to Commander Dilon's headquarters to get our orders. Have the squadron ready to fly when I get there."

"Yes, sir." Miko peels off down another street to head toward the aeroport district. Shandar could hear Miko's bellow behind him as Miko rallies the squadron from their quarters or entertainment.

They arrive at the headquarters out of breath.

"Reporting as ordered, sir." Shandar gasps out.

"I am sorry about the rush, Shandar. Moia reported that an Atlantean squadron had arrived and secured most of the council in their council room. Commander Sahama reports that her squadron has orders to pack up and be ready to leave. She has not been able to get in touch with the council."

"What do we know of the Atlantean force?"

Dilon sighs, "I am afraid not much. We believe a full squadron arrived and probably with at least 50 armored troopers."

"Okay, then I will depart immediately and figure out what I can from what we find there." Shandar starts to leave.

"Commander, try not to kill if you can help it. I imagine us destroying Vailixi and killing troops will paint a target on our backs for Atlantis."

"I am sorry, sir, but I believe it is too late." With that, Shandar leaves the command center.

Dilon, shaking his head, yells after Shandar. "Nobuma will join you with some of our armored troopers."

Nobuma nods and starts to run to his barracks to gather his men.

Dilon yells at his back. "Take 20 with you, Nobuma." The running man raises an arm.

Walking back into the command center. "Now to our defenses."

Shandar watches the landscape flow by quickly below his Flying Dragon squadron. They are almost within range of Moia.

"My Lord, contact with Commander Sahama." States his communication officer.

"Put her through."

A beautiful face appears—a face that Shandar knows well. It is Jolna Sahama, daughter of the Elder Councilman of Moia, Jolodar Sahama.

"Jolna, are you okay? What is the situation?"

"Shandar, I was worried I would never see you again."

They stare at each other momentarily, then realize others are listening. Shandar lowers the privacy field. "A few of my squadron are at Tainen's Ridge about an hour south. The rest of us are in the barracks. I could sneak out to the priest's quarters and use this communications unit. Most of the Marauding Bear squadron is on the ground, and Commander Folstan is with the Council. They brought…"

Worry eating him, he interrupts Jolna. "My love, are you safe?"

She pauses, smiles sadly, and touches his image before her. "We must do what we must. Rikar brought about 50 armored troopers with him. Half are around the barracks, keeping us prisoners, while the others are split guarding the Vailixi or at the council. I will have Lee Na contact you to assist in your strike."

A tear runs down Shandar's face. He is so proud of her strength and how she calms him down. She is the foundation of his life, and he dreads losing her. He will kill all of them to protect her. "Jolna, stay in the priest's quarters. Your part is played. I will work with Lee Na, and we will rid Moia of Rikar and his bastards."

She nods, and then the connection is broken. Shandar is confused. Dropping the private field and looking at his communications officer, "What happened?"

"It just dropped, Sir." The man said.

"Bring her back!" Shandar demands. He feels the knot in his stomach tighten.

The officer turns and tries to continue to raise Jolna again after a few tries. "Sir, I can not. She is not responding."

Miko broke into Shandar's personal hell. "Sir, I believe she was discovered. Your orders."

Shandar freezes with fear.

"Sir, your orders," Miko asks again, louder and more forceful.

Pulling Shandar back from the abyss, he looks at Miko. Miko nods back. "Full speed ahead. We attack now and hope to catch them on the ground before they fully realize what is happening."

Miko nods, turns around, and starts relaying orders. Shandar comes entirely back to his senses, realizing that his love's predicament could mean her death if they hesitate. The Vailixi under him jumps forward to maximum speed, forcing Shandar back into this seat.

Calling up a map of Moia on his viewer and projecting it to the main screens of his squadron's Vailixi, Shandar highlights the aeroport, the barracks, the temple, and the council chamber.

Quickly deciding how he would strike things. "Pod 1 and 2, hit the aeroport and try to take out any Vailixi of the Marauding Bear squadron. Shoot for damage, not destruction. We might need to scavenge what we can from them. Pod 3 and 4 take out the air cover. I will take the barracks to free our people. Lt. Nobuma, I will drop you off at the barracks."

Shandar turns on a private channel to Nobuma. "Lt., I would like three of your people to stay on board. I wish to drop them off at the temple complex and look for Command Sahama."

Nobuma responds, "I understand, sir. I will give you my best. Senior Trooper Suna will lead them."

"Thank you, Nobuma."

"We will get her back, my Lord. Don't worry."

The Vailixi speeds at treetop level, cruising at maximum speed, and is not worried about ground-based listeners. Shandar knows that if Jolna has been discovered, there is a good chance that those who discovered her are questioning her at the priest's quarters. They are not yet reporting their findings but are trying to determine who she was talking to.

This gives them a short window before the enemy figures out there might be a force inbound.

Shandar surprises himself. Thinking of the Atlanteans as enemies, and Commander Rikar Folstan embodies that enemy. He knew of Rikar, a pompous ass that is equally brave and stupid. His Marauding Bears have had more victories than most but also some devastating defeats. Shandar hopes to use that against him this time.

"Sir, I have detected the patrolling craft, only two." Came across the link.

"Roger that, Delvon. All pods proceed with missions."

With that, the Vailixi scatter. The six craft, going after the defensive patrol, rise to meet them head-on. Six on two should be no issue.

"All defending Moia units, this is Commander Kotan of the Flying Dragon squadron from Utanor. Stand down and do not interfere or join our forces. We have come to drive off the Atlanteans and free your council." Broadcast across all local channels.

Shandar's craft and two wingmen drive toward the barracks area. Most of those outside the barracks are gathered in a few defensive locations pointed toward the barracks. He imagines they are Atlanteans keeping the Moians confined to their barracks.

Shooting erupts between the barracks and the defensive positions as Shandar makes his run.

"Fire on the outside positions." He prioritizes targets for his pod.

All three Vailixi fire their heavy Aether weapons at the three positions. Luckily, the armored troopers are still in those positions and not trying to advance on the barracks. Direct hits on all three positions in their first pass.

The Vailixi swoop a few blocks from the barracks and drop off Lt. Nobuma's armored troopers. Those worthies bound off towards the barracks.

"Good hunting, Lt," Shandar said via their communications unit.

"Thank you, sir. Once we dispatch those at the barracks, we will move towards the council. We will have the freed troopers move to the aeroport."

"Agreed." With that, the Vailixi head towards the temple complex.

"My Lord, the skies are ours."

Another Vailixi reports, "My Lord, the aeroport and majority of the Tiger's Claw squadron are freed. A few enemy troopers are resisting but retreating from the city."

"My Lord Kotan, this is Lee Na, second to Lady Sahama. I have six Vailixi with me, and we should be over Moia in 10 minutes."

"Good to hear from you, Lee Na. Meet up with my defensive patrol in case Atlantis sends more forces."

"Yes, my Lord will do."

Shandar's Vailixi lands near the temple, and Senior Trooper Suna leads his men out. Shandar is in one of the Vailixi's lighter armor suits. It's the same style as the armored troopers but not as heavily armored.

"Miko, you have it. Cover the skies around the council chambers for Lt. Nobuma. After we search here, we will move that way."

The group of four burst into the grand public hall of the temple, their feet pounding against the marble floors. Huddled against the walls, a few terrified citizens watch as they pass. A priest appears from the far end of the hall, from the inner sanctum, his white robes billowing behind him. He sees them and runs toward them.

Shandar removes his helmet. "Shuma, do you know Lady Sahama, and did she enter the temple? I am Commander Kotan of Utanor. I believe she is in trouble."

The Shuma nods his head. "Yes, my Lord, she is held by Lord Shuta and two troopers in Poseidon's Well." He starts to turn back toward the rear of the hall. "Follow me."

Shandar and his team quickly follow the priest. Lord Shuta is Moia's local ground commander. Shandar didn't think he was a Shigar follower. Hopefully, that means she is not in any imminent danger.

They quietly navigate the dark halls of the priest's domain in the temple. They are going down to the lowest levels of the temple to Poseidon's Well. The deep well is the core of each temple and is where the Shuma pray to Poseidon.

Upon reaching the well, they hear voices over the deep rumble coming from the well. Shandar can not make out the voices but can tell they are coming from behind a door on the other side of the well.

He asks the priest, "Shuma, can you knock on the door and announce yourself? Step back, and we will rush in after they open the door."

The priest nods and moves to the door. Shandar and his men stand to the side. The priest knocks and calls to the men inside.

Jolna calls out for help but is cut off midstream. Shandar's heart skips a beat, and anger wells up in him. The door opens outward, and a trooper steps out. Two Aether blasts take him and the door out of the way. One trooper and Shandar rush into the room.

The other guard is out of his armor, as is Lord Shuta. The other guard is shot, and Shuta freezes. Shandar rushes to Jolna as the other two enter. The trooper has Shuta on his knees and an armored hand on his shoulder. He isn't going anywhere.

Shandar throws his helmet and gloves off to hold Jolna. She is bleeding from her nose and mouth with a red welt on her face. Shandar fumbles to free her and holds back the tears.

"My love, are you hurt anywhere else?"

"No, I am fine. It will heal." Shandar touches her bruised face.

Unbinding her, he lifts her and then, shaking with fury, turns to Shuta. "You bastard, I should kill you here."

Licking his lips, Shuta said, "You are all traitors. The Emperor will punish you severely for your betrayal."

The trooper squeezes Shuta's shoulder and gets the wince he desires. Shandar takes a step toward Shuta.

"My Lord, no, not in the Lord's sanctum," begged the priest.

A familiar hand takes his arm, and Shandar feels the fury leave him. Jolna said, "Shandar, he will pay, not here."

Shandar takes a deep breath and takes control of himself. "Let's get him out of here. We have to get to the council chambers. Shuma, I am sorry, but we must leave this mess to you and yours." He nods his head in the direction of the dead soldiers. He bows to the priest, and then they leave, Shuta in tow.

In the plaza in front of the temple, people start to gather. The sounds of fighting seem less, and Vailixi are circling in the air.

Shuta yells, "People, these people rebel against the Emperor. Help me."

Shandar draws his short sword and grabs and spins Shuta around. Then with a strong upward lunge, runs Shuta through. The others are shocked but do nothing to stop him. Shuta drops to the street and shudders once.

"Atlantis betrays us. It is time to chart our own course." Shouts Jolna.

The five pick up the pace out of the plaza, leaving a stunned crowd in their wake.

They round the corner to the plaza in front of the government house, where the council chambers are located. Lt. Nobuma's men guard a few men on their knees. A crowd has gathered around the armored troopers and their prisoners. Behind the crowd, the government house smokes from some of the windows on the left wing.

Shandar and the team walk up to Lt. Nobuma, who is talking to one of the council members.

Jolna gasps, "Father!" and runs through the crowd.

Shandar follows her path and sees some healers looking after a few people, and Jolodar is over there with bandages around his head and arm.

"Trooper, please go with Commander Sahama." Shandar orders one of the soldiers.

Then, turning to Lt. Nobuma. "Lieutenant, what transpired?"

"My Lord, we had a small fight with some of the scum. We secured the council chambers and had a room-to-room fight with the last few of them. I lost a few good men." He adds that last in a tight voice.

"Kotan, I should have known you were involved." Spits out Rikar. "I should have destroyed Utanor first, then come here."

One of the troopers standing next to Shandar jams the butt of his Aether spear into Rikar's stomach. He is rewarded with a painful grunt on Rika's behalf.

"Why, you low-born scum, I will..." This time the butt is smashed into Rikar's face.

"Trooper, that is enough." Senior Trooper Suna orders.

The trooper turns to Suna, "What? He deserved it."

"That is enough, Trooper. I think you taught him a lesson." Shandar orders, wearing a cruel smile, while Rikar spits a few teeth.

Rikar stares at the trooper who struck him with fury in his eyes. He is about to fire off a retort when Shandar says, "Commander Folstan, I would remind you that you are a prisoner now, and I will not always be around to save you if you open your mouth."

Rikar realizes the precariousness of his situation and thinks better than saying anything further. He still has fury in his eyes. Shandar sighs, "So, Commander, why did you do this? What did we do to deserve Atlantis turning on us?"

"Turning on you? I came here to get Commander Sahama's squadron to come with me. We were going to go to Utanor as well. The council shows their treachery, and I acted." He spits blood from his mouth and gives the trooper an evil look. "You will release me and follow my orders if you know what is good for you. If you do quickly, you might even be allowed to retire as a noble."

Shandar is about to respond when an Aether blast blows Rikar's head off his shoulders and continues into the prisoner next to him. Shandar is shocked and turns to see Jolna with an Aether spear leveled in her hands.

Lt Nobuma is behind her with his helmet off and a look of shock and fear on his face.

"That bastard tortured my father. The pig deserved death." Jolna said in a way that brokered no dispute.

The prisoners look afraid and try to edge away from the woman with fire in her eyes.

Shandar walks to Jolna with hands open and to his sides. He stands between her and the rest of the prisoners. They have to defuse the situation. He didn't want a massacre of the prisoners on their hands.

"Okay, Jolna, you had your revenge. Give the trooper back his Aether spear. Enough blood has been spilled this day."

She aims the spear at another prisoner. "All of these bastards were responsible for the deaths of our people. They should pay."

"Jolna, please put down the Aether spear. Those responsible will pay, but I imagine not all did."

Still, with death in her eyes, she glares at Shandar. He is wondering if she is about to shoot someone else or even attack him.

"Jolna, stop this insanity this instance. I order you to put that weapon down. Now!" Yells her father, Jolodar, from behind her.

That instantly took the fight out of her. She drops the weapon and goes to her father. Shandar lets out an explosive breath.

"Lt. Please get the prisoners down to the barracks."

"Yes, my Lord. Oh, and we caught these two," pointing at two technicians, "passing the situation to Atlantis."

Shaking his head, "Well, with the death of Commander Folstan, I guess there is no going back now."

ALTAI

In the early afternoon, all the teams prepare for their missions. Lieutenant Skola organizes ground teams to salvage what they can from remote homesteads. Risor sees off the mission to Atlantis. Sub-Commander Moza is likable and would probably be loyal to Altai, but his family lives in Luxa, and he is very worried about them. Having him lead the Altai mission would allow him to see his family.

"Moza, we wish you and the team luck. I hope your family is okay, my friend." Risor said as he clasped his elbow. "You need not return when the high command releases the Vailixi back to us. If they can have someone else assigned, that would be great. If not, it is probably okay for the others to return without a commander."

"Thank you, my Lord, we will do our best. When do you think you and the others will come?"

"I am not sure. We need to gather all survivors and get them settled in as much as possible before leaving. With the death of many of our Aether masters and the destruction of most of the tools we had in Altai, the Vailixi are probably the best bet to help rebuild."

"I understand, my Lord. I will do my best to convey that and will update you on how things are going there. Farewell, my Lord." And with that, Moza turns and goes up the ramp into the ship. Risor watches as the Vailixi rises approximately one hundred meters in the air. Then, it shoots forward to the east. Within a minute, it is out of sight.

Two Days After

ALTAI

Early the next morning, Risor enters the Council tent to brief the remaining Altai leaders.

"Councilman Ordo's party left last night and reported good progress through the hills."

Zailor asks, "What of Lord Fordo and the others? Did they go easily, and how are they armed?"

Risor, seeing concern on Zailor's face, "Lord Fordo seems to accept the situation. Nevertheless, we only gave them a few Aether spears and no armor. We believe things will go well." Zailor looks relieved at this last pronouncement.

"To continue, Tolen's Ice Pack team reports that the break above the Tia Yolan is still pouring out. He believes this will continue for some time."

The council starts arguing about what this means. Rosan said, "People, as Tolen told us, it means we must abandon Altai."

Frustrated, Stolar replies, "Yes, Rosan, but where would we go?"

Risor interrupts, trying to defuse the frayed nerves and tempers. After all, their city and nation are destroyed, the majority of their neighbors dead, their belief in their Gods sorely tested, and their lives turned upside down.

"Councilmen, please, we are sending a mission north to look for a suitable location. Chief Ulta is leading them, and they are leaving within the hour."

This mollifies Councilman Stolar. The others also quiet down.

Risor continues, "Moza arrived at Atlantis. Large portions of the city are flooded. The survivors are moving to the town of Zornada down the coast on higher ground near the Zoloten mountains to the north."

Councilman Tonda asks, "What bout the palace and Temple of Poseidon? Are they destroyed?" He ends quietly, like he could not stand the thought.

"No, Councilman, Moza reported the destruction wasted most of the third and second rings but did not reach the inner ring. The palace and Temple stand undisturbed. But they are also abandoned, as most of the city was not that lucky."

Heads nod, and the council waits for Risor to continue. Risor lifted the view tablet again and said, "Moza reports meeting Lord Tironi of the Cloud Warrior squadron, who was with me in Atlanta Sunda. Lord Tironi told him the Emperor was alive, but the Shigar were in full control. The Shuma no longer seem to have much say. Since the tsunami, the Emperor has seen very few. Prince Neppori is the most visible Imperial member, and of course, he is a Shigar party member."

There is a general murmur as the implications sink in. Risor continues, "Additionally, the Council of Elders has been disbanded, as has the Hall of Commons. It seems most of our fellow Nalos party leaders in Atlantis died in the tsunami."

Stolar groans, "I don't think I would like to live under those conditions." Hesitant heads nod around the table as Stolar mentions what many are thinking.

Zailor asks, "Funny how our Nalos brothers and sisters all died, but Shigar remains strong."

"Do you think we can get to the Emperor? Or what of the non-aligned nobles?" Rosan asks.

"Bah, the Emperor is probably dead. He wasn't a good Emperor, but he did like to show HE was doing stuff. If no one has seen him, then he is dead or incapacitated. Either way, he is no longer in charge of things. Also, I bet the non-aligned lords are all dead, back at their colonies or following the biggest wave." Stolar said.

Zailor grunts, "You could be forgiven if you thought the Shigar planned the tsunami to force a coup and remove or silence their opponents."

Rosan smiles, "If they didn't plan it, it sure seems they quickly grasped the opportunity they had before them. I'll give them credit for boldly acting."

Tonda, looking thoughtful, "I seem to remember reading that the first Emperor, Julna, also took advantage of a natural disaster when he seized Atlantis all those years ago."

Risor offers, "Seems the Shigar also like history then."

The council continues as Lieutenant Skola enters the tent and talks to Risor. Sighing, Risor softly announces, "Sub-commander Naga reports that the Sumtori colony is destroyed. They have found many bodies, and the communications system has been destroyed."

Risor has Skola relate the rest of the story to the council. The rescue Vailixi completed a few passes over the area but had seen no signs of survivors. The town was built on a hillside of a river valley as it met the sea. The buildings near the riverside are gone, but some of the buildings that were built up the hill remain. The water seemed to get to the height of the highest homes but didn't have the force to destroy them. There is a chance of survivors, but they probably fled into the hills.

Risor orders, "Mara, please have Naga return to resupply and pick up some troopers to help search for the survivors. Assign twenty-five troopers for him."

"Father, councilmen, I will depart now. I have tarried too long and if something happened to the Sumtori survivors, I want to ensure we avoid that with the other colonies."

Neptius is the oldest city west of Tes Atlan. It was established 15,000 years ago as an Atlantean outpost in the continent of Alta. It is larger than Altai and older by about 12,000 years.

Long ages ago, when the Atlanteans only had sailing ships, Neptius was their first overseas colony. In its early days, a way station and small trading outpost for meeting the local tribes. There was little need for Atlantis to expand in those days, as they came in peace as explorers and teachers. From there, they discovered the rest of Alta. Ages later, when they started to desire power, they founded other colonies. Not content to just trade with the natives, they started to demand fealty from them. Unlike the continent of Atlanta, there were no large kingdoms in Alta to contend with.

Risor's Vailixi flies due east, crossing the peninsula to the Tes Atlan side, and then turns south. The Tes Atlan coast is wiped clean from the tsunami coming from the north. Half the beaches that used to grace the shoreline are gone or covered in debris.

Near the tip of the peninsula, three straits meet to separate the mainland from two large islands. Where the three straits converge, Neptius was founded.

The city boasts a large lighthouse, the largest in the world, for incoming ships. The tower is larger than the city's temple mounts, of which Neptius has three: one for Poseidon, another for Zeus, and the last for Athena.

Smaller ships would sail to Neptius from the other Alta colonies, including Altai. Then, larger Aether-enabled ships would take the freight to Atlantis or ports on the other side of the world. Aether-enabled ships have been in use for the last thousand years and rarely ever sink due to the use of Aether. This method of transport almost ensures no loss of life would occur for trans-oceanic crossings.

The closer they get to Neptius, the more Risor worries. They have not received any communications from anyone at Neptius, not even Aether-enabled ships. This does not bode well for the people of Neptius. When the Vailixi reaches the northern end of the northern strait, Risor knows what happened. The strait is not quite a strait anymore.

The small sea of Tes Falta connects to Tes Atlan through these straits, and a tiny strait to the southwest connects to Tes Falon. With the flooded Tia Yolan and the force of water it sends into Tes Falta, it pours out these narrow channels at a much higher pressure than normal. The northern end of this strait is just a sample of what the high-pressure flow can do to land. What is normally a twenty-kilometer strait is now nearly one hundred kilometers wide. The flow out of Tes Falta is eating away at the peninsula and the islands.

Near Neptius, Risor sees two temples still standing but cannot see the last one or the lighthouse. The power of the water, pouring through the straits, turns the water nearly black. Half of the city has already disappeared below these black waters. Much of the rest of the city is smashed, apparently from the tsunami, with almost no buildings undamaged.

Even as Risor and team fly over the city, some buildings finally surrender to the powerful currents that engulf them. Falling apart, the pieces disappear beneath the waters, to be carried away on the strong current.

Large stones from the two surviving temple mounts are tumbling away as the torrent eats away at their foundations. It is only a matter of time, maybe just hours before the temples of Poseidon and Athena are completely destroyed and join the temple of Zeus beneath the waves. The temple mount to Poseidon still has an active Mother Stone as the blue lights of Aether show through the damaged entrance.

The Mother Stone would have been a blessing to retrieve, but it would require a few of his people to go in there to retrieve it. Reluctantly, the temple mount doesn't look very stable, with one side already being eaten away by the water. With the debris near the entrance, it could also be underwater, making the task of removal even more difficult. No, Risor thought, his people must get a Mother Stone somewhere else. Better that than risk lives on a chance.

Risor is unsure but believes Neptius had over six hundred large buildings and covered a few acres. Now, there are only a few dozen left, and debris is strewn through the streets around them, or they are partially destroyed. They come to the aeroport, where two Vailixi are smashed against a retention wall. Neither looks flyable. One is at the edge of the water. The other is on dry land for the moment.

Risor points to the one that is still safely on dry land. "Let's land and see if we can get anything useful from that Vailixi."

Dimera nods, "The other one looks like it will go any minute."

"Yes, we will only check the one against the wall. Milo, let's go." As the Vailixi lands, Risor and Milo leave the command deck.

The sound of the water is deafening. Creaks and snapping of structures sound from nearby buildings are constantly heard. They walk to the damaged craft when the smell of rotting corpses hits them. The Vailixi is on its side, with its top facing the wall against which it is pushed. The access ramp is partially open, and as they get closer to it, they see an arm wedged under the ramp. It seems that the birds and other scavengers have not found this site yet.

The slightly open access ramp forms a nice barricade to the entry with the wall. It seems the only way for them to gain access or at least to see inside is to climb the access ramp to enter from the top.

Milo, putting a hand to cover his nose and mouth, "Damn, you know what that smell is, right?"

Risor takes his jacket off and ties it around his nose and mouth to try to block the smell. "All too well. We need to see if we can find anything useful in there."

Once Risor is confident the "mask" would block some of the smell, he moves closer to the ramp. "Milo, give me a boost."

Milo, looking like he was going to get sick, "Um, that smell is bad. I don't think there is just one body here."

"Ya, probably the crew never got out."

As Risor put his foot in Milo's clasped hands and sprung up. He grasps the edge and then pulls himself up. The smell really hits him, and a flock of ravens speeds past him, surprising him enough that he almost loses his handhold on the ramp. Once the flock flees, he sees what they are about. The Vailixi is filled with bodies, three to four deep. All with bloated black faces and bodies. Children and adults.

Risor falls back down, gasping for air while puking his guts out. From the top of the wall, a few ravens angrily caw at the humans for interrupting their feast. A few braver or hungrier ones fly back into the doomed Vailixi. Once he could control his retching, "The Gods help us. They tried to use it to escape. Maybe thirty or forty men, women, and children. I think..." He starts to retch again, seeing their faces.

"Never mind, sir, I think I know what happened."

Milo stands up and looks back at the Vailixi. Without turning, "Should we fire the insides?"

When Risor returns to a semblance of normality, "That isn't a bad idea. Not so much for the dead. Animals need to eat, too. But the explosion might get any survivors to pop their heads up."

They return to their ship and communicate the plan to the other Vailixi, who is still doing circles above the doomed city. Risor's Vailixi moves off a safe distance and fires. The downed Vailixi explodes into a big fireball, with one of the shots going inside. A fireball rises, and the Vailixi move off further inland to hopefully see any survivors who might have noticed the explosion.

After another hour of circling, Risor decides that if there are any survivors, they have probably moved far inland already, and he has other cities to check out. While they are moving off, Risor watches the dying city recede in the distance. Risor imagines the Gods want to show him that Neptius is truly dead.

The forward view portal displays Neptius' receding remains. Before it is out of view, they could see the Mother Stone's light blink a few times. Then, the remnants of the temple mount of Poseidon slide under the waves, forever out of sight.

Moving south, the team is sullen. Losing Altai is bad and understandable since it is along the river from which the flood burst forth, but Neptius is far away and across the gulf. That a tsunami came from their river to wipe out a city almost a thousand kilometers away awes them.

Their next destination is Kanesa. This city is a huge agricultural center with lush lands along Tes Falon. This sea is the outlet for the smaller strait from Tes Falta and has a large outlet to Tes Fatlan and Tes Atlan.

Kanesa boasts large plantations along the coast and massive fishing fleets harvesting the bounty of Tes Falon. This sea is perfect for harvesting nature's bounty. A major storm rarely comes here because it is far from the Tes Atlan currents.

Crossing the central ridge line of the island of Kanesa, Risor and the team thought to see the plantations of the southern lowlands curving southeast towards Kanesa. Instead, they see that the coastline is moved miles inland closer to the foothills of the southern side of the island's spine. Much of what used to be the coastline is gone or wiped clean. The tsunami hit here as well.

The tsunami wiped large swaths of forest and beach dunes clear or deposited massive debris. Seawater, a little more than ankle deep, is coming into the former fields or lapping at the foundations of the plantation buildings. Many of the buildings are stripped to their foundations from the tsunami, further adding to the feeling of loss. As more water pours from the ice lakes, this will rise, engulfing the fields and buildings.

The team is looking at another doomed colony.

Continuing along the coastline at a slower speed, the team looks for survivors. Now that they know what to expect in Kanesa, they figure if anyone survived from the plantations, they would need rescuing as well. At every plantation, the Vailixi slows down, calls out via external speakers, circles the main area a few times, and then moves on.

Kanesa is built on a long, narrow peninsula that is probably ten kilometers wide at its widest and two kilometers at its narrowest. Between the second and third plantations, they see that the sea has severed the peninsula. There are almost no trees standing in this area.

Risor surmises that the tsunami probably rolled through here, scraped the land clean, and made a channel at the lowest point. The rising waters are not just rising but also flowing strongly out towards the channel to Tes Fatlan and Tes Atlan. The result is the sea is constantly eating away at the land adjacent to it.

They find no survivors in the first four plantations when they see smoke coming from the fifth. They are pleasantly surprised there are a few people around a fire made from building beams and furniture.

Risor orders his Vailixi to land while the other remains airborne. Once landed, the people approached the Vailixi, "Hello, I am Lord Tarnor of Altai; we are here to rescue you."

"Thank the Gods. I am Zulti of Kanesa, foreman for the Digota family's plantation. We were worried that this tsunami would affect everyone. When will the others come to help rebuild our homes?" Zulti said with a look of hope on his face and the faces of the other seven survivors.

"I am sorry, Foreman Zulti, but there will be no others coming to help you rebuild. The flood has destroyed Neptius and Altai, and it is possible that Kanesa has shared their fate."

It takes a minute for that to sink in as the smile of relief is slowly replaced by a look of disbelief. "You are joking, my lord, that can not be. Neptius was a great city that stood for thousands of years. It can't be gone."

"I'm sorry, Foreman, but it's true. The great ice sheet in the far north of Altai had a massive ice lake almost the size of Tes Falta. The Raman Empire struck the barrier holding back the water, and it continued to flood down the Tia Yolan. We are checking the fate of each of the colonies."

He gives them a few minutes to consider what he said while some of his teams walk around the plantation buildings to see what can be salvaged. As the sun is setting, Risor decides it is a good place to rest for the night.

"Dimera, please ask Altai what the status of the flood is. We should probably stay here for the night. We don't want another wave hitting us." She nods and heads back to the Vailixi.

Speaking to the Vailixi, who is still in the air via his wrist communicator, Risor says, "Nelo, take your team and do a quick fly-by of Kanesa. Let's get an idea of what we have to do tomorrow."

While Nelo's Vailixi heads south, Zulti asks Risor, "My Lord, do you plan to stay here tonight? Is it safe? What if we have another tsunami?"

"These buildings are on a hill and were not affected by the initial tsunami or the rising seas yet. I think we are safe to stay here for the night. We will need to gather the salvageable items from these buildings to take back to Altai. Tomorrow, we will send you to Altai."

"We are leaving? Can't we rebuild this place? It – is – our – home." It seems that Zulti is heading for a breakdown. One of the other survivors, a young lady, bends down and starts crying and rocking back and forth. An older lady goes to her as another old man plops down where he is and stares at his feet. Zulti stumbles backwards.

Risor shouts, "YES! You are leaving." Startling the survivors and the crew. He takes a deep breath and then more softly, "Yes, the waters are rising, and we do not know how far they will rise. Already to the north, we saw that the sea had cut a path between a few plantations north of here. It is only a few hundred feet wide and very shallow but will grow as the flows continue. Other cuts will probably occur as well. I am sorry, but our world is changing."

The young lady who is crying looks up at Risor and asks, "If Altai is destroyed, where will we go?"

The old lady holding her tells the young lady, "There there, Mistress Eliina, we will go back to Atlantis with your relatives when we get a chance."

Zulti notices Risor's look and tries to explain. "My Lord, this is Eliina Digota, daughter of Zeron Digota, master of this plantation."

Whispering to Risor, "Her father and mother were at the main manor with most of the workers when the tsunami hit. Our mistress was going to have a party with her friends tomorrow, so we came to set up the summer house for the event. The manor was wiped away by the tsunami, and we do not believe there are any survivors."

"I see. My Lady, I am so sorry for you and your people's losses, but Atlantis has also suffered the same fate. The emperor lives, and there are many survivors, but Atlantis has been abandoned." Risor tells them.

This is too much for them, and they all start wailing. Milo approaches Risor and quietly says, "Maybe a little less honesty would have been best right now, sir."

Shaking his head, he said, "Yes, but the truth would have been learned soon enough. Keep an eye on them. I am going to see what Dimera has found out." With that, Risor walks away.

Inside the Vailixi, Dimera updates Risor. "Sir, there is no increase in flooding, so we should be pretty safe on this hilltop. Altai will send an alert if anything happens, and I will sleep inside the Vailixi tonight." Risor nods.

Rubbing his temples, he said, "Everything has changed."

Dimera comes over to him and puts a hand on his shoulder. "We still have our families and each other."

Smiling at her and placing his hand on her hand, "Thank you, Dimera. I don't know what to do without you and the others."

Staring into her eyes, he realizes it is the first time he really sees her. She looks like she is thinking of something, too. She blushes, blinks, and then sighs.

He quickly asks, "Was there anything else from Altai?"

She doesn't respond for a few seconds with that thoughtful look on her face. Before Risor could ask what she was thinking, "The council would like to update you on the other developments." Risor nods and sits in his command chair. "Patch me through."

When the connection is made, Councilman Stolar appears on the view screen, "Ah, Commander, it is good to see you are well. Sad news on Neptius."

"Thank you, Councilman. What else is happening with the other missions?"

"Ah yes, the team we sent to Sumtori finally found a few survivors, and they are returning to Altai tonight. They were getting ready to come back and refit when they found twenty people coming back to the colony. The survivors were actually camping in the hills above the town when the tsunami struck."

"That would be another four thousand lost souls then," Risor said, starting to feel the despair that Foreman Zulti and his companions felt. So many lost.

"Councilman, please tell Mara, I mean Lieutenant Skola, to send that team here tomorrow morning if they get in early enough. Grab a few people and a healer to help these survivors. They are in shock. The workers can help salvage what we have found. We might get lucky on some of the other plantations that were not built near the beaches."

"Of course, Commander. Also, Ordo and Fordo report they are making decent time on their mission but still many days out." Risor nods as Stolar continues, "Shilot Dekarn has returned from his survey of the ice shelves and headed off to help Chief Ulta's survey mission up north."

"Thank you, Councilman. What of Moza? Any word from him?"

"I'm sorry, but I have nothing from Moza. That is pretty much it, Commander. Are there any other items?"

"Where are Lieutenant Skola and my father? No offense, my Lord, but I was expecting my father." Risor said rather sheepishly.

Stolar smiles and says, "No worries, Risor. I understand your concern. Rosan and your family are fine. Some of the children are performing a play, and Rosan and Lieutenant Skola went to watch. The people are trying to do things to get our situation off everyone's mind. Giving the kids a play to work on for the adults has kept most of them occupied. Some are even smiling. It's not working for everyone yet, but it's a start."

"I see. That is a great idea. I think a few people here could use something like that as well. Have a good night, my Lord."

After the connection is broken, Risor establishes a link with Sub-commander Nelo. "Nelo, what is your status."

"My Lord, we have seen a few campfires along the way, but the town is dark and mostly destroyed. We are returning to your location now, but it looks like we will have some more survivors."

"Good news! Thank you, Nelo. I will tell Foreman Zulti and the other survivors. Maybe that will help them feel better."

It did help them. They are still shocked by the news and recent events, but the knowledge that others they might know are alive comforted them.

As Risor's team and the survivors are having breakfast in the morning, the other Vailixi arrives. Sub-commander Naga brought five troopers, a healer, and a few workers. They decide to use this plantation as a base until they have searched the Kanesa region. Risor's two Vailixi would continue the search while Naga would head back north to check if anything was usable from the plantations that had already been searched. Naga's second Vailixi would take Zulti's group back to Altai and then return. The troopers, healers, and workers would remain at the Digota's plantation, gathering supplies and handling any survivors that were brought there.

THREE DAYS AFTER

ATLANTA QUESTO

Jolna's Vailixi dives and strafes the Hu forces in front of the eastern gate of Moia. She thinks they will soon break through. Moia has lost part of its strength fighting Atlantis in the last few days. Their raids are taking their toll.

"Lee Na, take pods four and five and help Niwa against the Vimana. We can't let them support the Hu."

"Yes, my Lady. Will the Flying Dragons get here in time?" Lee Na asks as his four Vailixi head further east to battle the enemy's supporting Vimana.

Jolna's Vailixi makes a sharp turn to come back and strafe again. "I don't know. They should be coming." She turns to her comm person. "Get me control."

Within seconds, she has them. "Commander, we are a little busy here with the walls being stormed. What can we do for you?"

"Is Utanor sending aid? Are the Flying Dragons coming?" She demands.

"Yes, my Lady, they are coming. They report they should be in comm range in about fifteen minutes."

A minute later, her father joins the conversation and says, "Jolna, try to down one of the Vimana but not destroy it. We need to talk to them. We must tell them we are no longer part of Atlantis and want peace."

"That is very difficult, and they might not listen."

"We can not survive many more days. We will need to evacuate to Utanor as it is. If Atlantis and Rama with the Hu continue to attack us, we will not survive."

She knows the truth in his words. Even though they kept most of the Marauding Bear Vailixi, they still have losses with the daily battles. Utanor helps, but her Tiger's Claw usually takes the brunt of the attacks since Shandar's squadron stays in Utanor until they know where the attack will come.

"I will try, Father."

"We are counting on you. I do not trust the Hu to take that message. We might have to evacuate the city if we can not stop them."

On another frequency, she hears, "Tiger Claw, this is Flying Dragon. We are almost there. What is the situation."

Talking to her father. "Father, Shandar is almost here. I will try to do as you ask. Tiger's Claw out."

Switching back to Shandar's frequency. "Shandar, there are about ten Vimana east of the valley. We are mostly holding them there. A few others and I are at Moia supporting the defenders. The Hu have a large force and are attempting to take the walls."

"It is so good to hear your voice, Jolna. Okay, we have all twelve of my squadron with about 100 armored troopers. I assume the Hu are not armored as usual?"

"Yes, no armored soldiers detected, nor any heroes."

"Thank Poseidon for that. Okay, we will drop off our troopers on the ridge to the north, then do one pass up along the walls. Then we will head off to take out the Vimana."

Jolna knows they will win this day. She briefs Shandar on what her father wants.

Shandar is standing in the cargo bay of his Vailixi talking to Lt. Nobuma, who will lead the ground assault.

"Poseidon watch over you. Hit them hard and watch for any downed Vailixi. Jolna is doing ground support."

"I will, my Lord. Good hunting." With that, Lt. Nobuma bounds away after his troopers. They have a ten-minute run and would slam into the enemy's unprotected rear. Shandar figures he would give them five minutes before striking. Closing the bay door, he walks back up to the command deck.

The Flying Dragon squadron leaps into the air and shoots forward low over the terrain.

"Line them up against the wall, people. We need to give the defenders some breathing space. Hit them with everything we can."

The Vailixi come in three waves and shoot up the Hu infantry and horsemen. Luckily, they destroy the Hu's ram. Finishing their run, Jolna's four craft bank back to start a new one.

"Tiger's Claw, they are all yours now. Good luck, and don't get shot down. Our ground force should be hitting their rear in about three minutes."

"Thank you, Shandar. See you after the battle, my love."

Chuckling, "I thought so. You start these little wars to give me an excuse to come down here to see you."

"Ha, you flatter yourself, my Lord." She pauses. "Be careful, Shandar."

"We will." The Flying Dragons zoom over the distant ridge line to find the Vimana.

It didn't take long. They see the tell-tale signs of Aether weapons discharging. Closer to the battle, Shandar announces himself and takes over command of the dogfight.

There are only four Vimana and three Vailixi remaining in the fight. The twelve craft of the Flying Dragons come in at full speed.

"Okay, team, we are going to fly through the fight. Aim to disable the craft, not destroy it. We need one of the alive." Shandar orders.

All acknowledge and fly through the fight. All four Vimana are shot down, two in explosions and the other two in crashed landings.

Shandar's craft circles above the area of one of the crashes. The wreckage is scattered over a large area.

"The Gods are fickle. Miko, what does the other crash site look like? This one is a wreck."

"While beat up, it is still in one piece."

"Great, land an armored team and see if we can capture the crew. Try not to kill them. We need them to take a message back to Rama."

"Yes, my Lord. You really think that will work?"

"It is worth a try. Jolodar is right. We can't last much longer at this rate."

"Lee Na, lead the rest back to Commander Sahama."

Only three Vailixi remain in the area. Shandar lands his craft near Miko's while the last patrols above them to ensure no surprises occur.

Miko's team captures seven of the crew. The other four are killed in a short firefight. Shandar, in his shipboard armor, walks over to where the prisoners are held.

"Good going, Miko. So, any of you speak Atlantean?" Shandar asks the prisoners as he takes off his helmet.

They are on the ground with arms tied behind their backs. One looks up with a split lip, spits out some blood, and says, "I do."

"Say, my Lord, Raman. You address Lord Shandar Kotan, Commander of the Flying Dragons and Lord of the Aska Pass." Miko said while mildly hitting the Raman's back with the butt of his Aether spear.

Shandar raises his hand for Miko to stop. "Peace, Miko."

Then, looking at the Raman. "Your name, Sir."

"I am called Karanvir of great Dwarka."

"You are not the captain of this craft, correct?"

"Yes, your people killed our captain."

"I am sorry. Karanvir of Dwarka, if we release you and your men, will you promise not to bring violence against our people until you return to your lands?"

Karanvir and a few others look up with hope and suspicion warring across their faces. The others look fearfully at their comrades and then at Shandar. They speak amongst themselves so those who did not understand Atlantean would know the offer.

"My Lord, we accept your offer and conditions," Karanvir said.

"Good. Miko, release them."

While his men unbind the prisoners, Shandar brings water out for them. He waits until all have been released and have their fill of water.

"Karanvir, I have a message I want you to take back to your people. Do you think this craft can fly again?" He points to the Vimana.

Looking critically at his craft, he said, "I am not sure, my Lord Kotan. We need to go through her and check the damage."

The Ramans are allowed into their craft and start checking the systems. Karanvir comes back out of the craft with a smile on his face.

"My Lord, I think we can fly her again. Do we have your leave to go?"

"First my message, and then you may go. My people have broken away from Atlantis. They wish to make war on everyone, and we have had enough. The people of Moia and Utanor wish peace with Rama. We will no longer attack any Rama lands or forces if Rama does not attack us."

"Those are generous and good words, my Lord. I can not promise that my people will believe you or agree to your pledge, but I will deliver it."

"And the Hu as well. We would have peace with them."

"That, my Lord, I am not sure. We are allies but do not control them."

"I see. Thank you, Karanvir of Dwarka. You now may depart. May your Gods watch over your flight back." Shandar bows and then leaves with his people.

Karanvir stands watching as the Vailixi take off. All three Vailixi head into the east to join the fight.

Shandar and Jolna stand on the balcony of her father's home. The battle had been won hours before, resulting in the Hu retreating with heavy losses. Shandar could see the people streaming out of the northern gate from the balcony. They are heading to Utanor, leaving behind the city's smoking ruins forever.

The battle had been won, but the truth is that the citizens of Moia are drained. The daily attacks significantly reduce the defenders' strength. Jolna's squadron is barely able to keep a force in the air. Supplies are running low as the croplands have been destroyed or trampled.

Soon, the seas will rise, and parts of the city and surrounding farmlands will be inundated. The city can not survive long. The weakened population of Moia has little hope of saving their city without additional fighting. With the constant attacks, there is no hope.

"What will become of us, Shandar?" Asks Jolna, wrapping her arms around him and leaning her head against his shoulder.

"I am not sure. I think we will have to abandon Utanor as well." Covering her hands with his and leaning his head into hers. "The world is changing, and we can not count on the old ways."

"Do you think the Ramans will give us peace?"

"I do not know. We had ten years of fighting and then the destruction of the last few weeks. I believe there is a lot of hate on both sides. And Atlantis is still not done."

"We are not going to make it, are we?" She pulls him tighter.

"We will." Disentangling himself from her embrace, he turns towards her and cups her face in his hands. Staring deeply into her eyes, he says, "You must not lose hope, my love. You are my strength. I need you."

Her sad smile pains him that he can not make her feel better. She is the stronger spirit of the two. Shandar knows this and is okay with it. The problem is when she is down, she really beats herself up.

Running his fingers through her hair. "I love you, Jolna. When we get to where we are going, I want to marry you."

This initially shocks her, but a smile replaces it, and her eyes sparkle. She laughs. "You always know how to make me feel better. I guess there is a silver lining, isn't there?"

She pulls him into a fierce hug, and he grunts. It is so strong. "It has to take us losing our homes to finally have a chance to be together."

He smiles, happy that she seems past the funk she was starting to slip into. He needs her strength now, just as Moia and Utanor need her strength. "I will make you happy, Jolna."

"You always do, my love." The fierce hug subsides and becomes a more gentle snuggle of her face into his chest.

As they look on, clouds are gathering far in the north. The late afternoon sun shines bright against those clouds and over the few smoke streams rising above the city. Vailixi speed north, carrying citizens unable to walk out of the city. It would be weeks before all the citizens arrive in Utanor.

Weeks of possible attacks against Utanor and maybe attacks against the fleeing citizens of Moia, too. They will have to protect both the city and the people. Are they up to it? This is the question no one is asking, but everyone is thinking.

They know their lives will become more difficult. They still have the Mother Stones but only a few priests. Some sided with Atlantis and were either killed in the uprising of Moia or left. Their ability to make Aether and recharge their tools is limited.

To add to this concern, they cannot make more Aether Spears, Aether-powered armor, or Vailixi. Atlantis will be able to continue building forces, while each loss for Utanor and Moia will further deplete their forces.

Shandar knows the end of Utanor and Moia is near. They will have to leave most of their way of life and live more like the tribes around them. Will those tribes let them do that? That is the question.

ALTA FALTA

Nelo marks off the locations where they saw fires yesterday so they could go there first. While Nelo checks these fires, Risor will head straight for Kanesa. When Risor reaches Kanesa, Nelo advises they have found another eighteen survivors. He is taking them back to Digotas.

Kanesa's port is in a long, sheltered bay. It is one of the few areas along this peninsula that could be called mountainous. High cliffs follow the bay from the mouth to where it opens into a high-sloped valley, where the port city of Kanesa stands. With a ten-foot seawall separating the waterfront from the town proper, there is enough protection for normal storm surges—just not enough for a tsunami.

The seawall is breached in two locations, and most of the town behind it is gone. Additionally, it looks like the tsunami funneled up the inlet and went over the seawall. The few remaining buildings are little more than skeletons of what they used to be. In some areas, piles of debris, partial homes, or structures remain mostly intact but separated from their foundations. Only a few homes in the hills above the town survived.

They see many survivors coming out of these homes. Over a hundred people seem to be coming out and running toward the area where the Vailixi is landing. A few troopers with Aether spears amongst the survivors lend a semblance of order. This is good, Risor thinks, as it will make things easier when evacuating the people.

An older man comes forth, wearing the robes of a councilman, to stand at the base of the Vailixi access ramp as Risor walks down.

"Welcome, Commander. Thank the God's help has arrived. I am Councilman Zalnur, reluctantly the only surviving Council member."

The people are tired and beaten, but hope lights their eyes—hope that the Vailixi means they can rebuild, that the Empire has not forgotten them.

"It is good to see all of you. I am Commander Tarnor from Altai." The crowd cheers. Risor let them calm down before continuing, "I am sorry, but we bring sad news. The world has changed. The Ramans caused a great flood in the north."

From the crowd, "What does that mean?"

Risor looks down and then up. "Altai, Neptius, and Sumtori have been destroyed as far as we know. Even Atlantis has been abandoned. The peninsula you live on is slowly deteriorating due to wave action. We have come to evacuate you to Altai. We are trying to build a new city there."

Many people start to speak at once. Finally, Councilman Zalnur quiets them and asks, "Why should we go to Altai? Why not come here or let us be?"

"Citizens, I understand your desires and concerns. The truth is the Empire might be dead. We are all survivors of a major catastrophe that may signal the end of our Empire. I see you have Aether spears and, I assume, some Aether tools. Did you rescue your Mother Stone? Or do you have masters to maintain them?"

Councilman Zalnur said, "No, we could not. Our temple mount has been destroyed, and the priests died with it. We are hoping that we can get replacements."

"No, my Lord, we also lost ours, and Atlantis has not agreed to send us new priests or a new Mother Stone. If they send something, I believe it will be after they have rebuilt Atlantis, which will take some time. So your people, like mine, are on our own." Risor looks around to see if it is registering in their minds.

"Like I said, your peninsula is disappearing beneath the waves, and it will probably continue to do so for some time. Our Master Shilot told us the flood could continue for weeks, which means the sea level would rise at least a few more meters. The current flood coming from the Tes Falta into the Tes Falon will continue to erode your land."

Risor looks at the people instead of the leaders. "Altai still has over one thousand survivors, and we plan on rebuilding a town further away from the riverbanks to ensure additional flooding does not harm us. We can bring you all there as well. Together, we can rebuild a life."

"Commander, I am sorry, but we will stay here," states Councilman Zalnur, with some of his troopers starting to look edgy. Risor thought they would do something foolish if he didn't extricate his people. Right now, the Vailixi are probably looking awfully valuable to them. He needs to get out of there before his vulnerability becomes apparent.

"My Lord Zalnur, I understand your position. We will give you and your people time to consider the idea. My team will continue looking for survivors and return tomorrow to see what you have decided." Risor turns back into the Vailixi with the rest of his team before Zalnur can counter the statement.

When he returns, Risor believes he must show more deterrence tomorrow to ensure the people do not try something. Once they realize they are on their own, the desperation of their situation will hit home hard.

As the Vailixi gains altitude, Risor sees the crowd gather around Zalnur. This isn't going to be good, he thought. The team moves south to continue looking. Risor reports the situation to Altai and requests additional troops be sent back with the returning Vailixi.

That evening, with an additional twenty troopers in full combat armor and all four Vailixi present, Risor makes his plan. They have an additional forty-six survivors that will go back to Altai. Risor asks the survivors if they want to go to Kanesa, and they all say no. Zalnur is a known bully, and no one wants to live with his dictates. Their story makes Risor believe many of those there might not wish to stay either.

ATLANTA NADO

Rogat's gaze sweeps over the lush valley below. Behind him, the weary survivors of Delin, Tar Deg, and other towns in the region trudge on, their feet heavy with exhaustion. The Greeks and Tugar have mercilessly swept through the land, leaving a trail of destruction and despair in their wake. Their army grows closer each day, driving the refugees onward like a pack of hunted animals. And yet, despite their desperate situation, help from Atlantis has yet to arrive, adding to the sense of hopelessness that pervades the weary refugees. As Rogat takes in the scene before him, he can't help but wonder how much more the survivors can endure before they are completely broken.

In the peaceful valley below him is one of the last allies the Atlanteans have in this region.

"Rogat, I think we can get everyone into the stockade by nightfall." Said Migu.

Teado's men are already at the stockade, while Noko's men cover the rear.

"Good. We must get everyone to safety before the damn Greeks find us again." Rogat leans heavily on his Aether spear. A weapon that is almost out of Aether.

Yalana, with her kids in tow, approaches Rogat. "Can we stop here tonight?"

"I'm hungry." Complains Telko.

Rogat tussles his hair. "Tonight, you can eat your fill, Telko. We will be behind strong walls with a good fire and lots of food." Telko smiles.

Migu points them down to the village. "Think the Calcannut have a bloody priest? Or anything to resupply our Aether spears?" Migu mutters.

"Careful, my friend, Poseidon might not take kindly to your cursing his priests. We need all the help we can get."

Migu said, starting to move down the hill, "Poseidon and the Gods have already left us, Rogat. As has Atlantis."

Rogat stares at his friend's back. If he has lost hope, what about the rest of his men? Or the civilians? Rogat worries that his force will melt away when the next battle comes.

Looking to the sky. "Poseidon, show us a sign. Send us help."

Demetri looks down at the village. "What is the name of this place again? Cadin? And the tribe are called the Conuts?"

Sighing, Artos said. "Cardin and the people are called the Calcannut. The Gods grace you with speed and strength but no memory of names."

Smiling at his friend and second. "They graced me with you, friend Artos. I have no need for such things when I have you."

"Great, I am a glorified scribe to a death-seeking fool," Artos says in mock despair.

Laughing at Artos, Demetri responds. "Death seeking?"

Shaking his head, Artos ignores the comment. "Shall we attack tonight, my Lord?"

"No, the men are still streaming in. Set a good watch, and we can rest tonight. We will encircle them tomorrow and then let the fun begin."

TES ZEITA

Lena awakes to the fort's alarm bells. She sits up and sees Fortos, Kala, and the kids also sitting up. The kids are frightened by the cries of alarm.

"Stay here." Orders Fortos as he leaves the tent.

Kala looks at Lena with worried eyes. Lena tells her, "Let's start packing our clothes up." Kala nods, and they put their belongings into travel bags and get the kids to do the same.

The tent flap is whipped open, and Fortos ducks back inside. "Hurry, gather what you can. The Greeks are attacking by sea. Kala, Lena, I need you to gather the kids and go further inland as quickly as possible."

Kala squeaks, "What are you going to do?"

"I need to help the garrison. Since the cavalry left, there are not many soldiers left." With that, he gathers the children and gives them a big hug. Kissing them on their heads, he nods to Kala. "Come here, Kala."

Crying, she goes to him and joins the family hug. Kissing her, he releases the hug and starts to leave the tent. When he gets even with Lena, he looks at her and tells her, "Lena, help Kala, ya?"

When he leaves the tent, Kala slumps down crying. The kids look like they are about to cry, too. Lena realizes that they will get nowhere, crying and knowing the Greeks will make slaves of them. "Kala, cry later. Now, we must gather what we can and leave."

They leave the tent to the sounds of steel on steel and the cries of men in pain and battle lust, coming from the walls where the Atlanteans defend.

Lena, Kala, and the kids, along with many other civilians, run toward the inland gate. They are all trying to escape the enemy.

"Hurry, the enemy surrounds the fort and will cut off your flight." Yells one of the soldiers. Lena sees him by the light of a burning building. He is waving a torch in one hand and a sword in another near the gate.

Old and young, everyone runs toward the gate and freedom. Then, the worst thing imaginable happens. Large armed figures start to burst through the gate as screams turn the soldier. He drops the torch and rushes to the gate as a large warrior armed with a shield and sword cuts down an unarmed man. He grabs the woman who is running with the man, punches her in the face, and throws her to the ground. The woman lay there, apparently stunned or knocked unconscious.

The warrior turns to meet the Atlantean soldier. The soldier fights bravely but seems overmatched. Within seconds, the enemy dispatches the valiant soldier, slamming his shield into the soldier's face and then skewering him with his sword. The dying soldier drops his weapon and slides off the warrior's sword.

Lena watches in horror as more Greek warriors come through the gate. The few defenders who try to stem the tide are quickly cut down. Kala pulls at Lena.

"Lena, we need to hide. Back to the tent."

Finally, registering what Kala is saying and watching the children slump to the ground in terror, Lena counters. "No, not the tent. We must find another place to hide."

They gather the kids and run toward one of the nearby barracks buildings. Out of the darkness between the buildings comes one of the enemy warriors. His sword is dripping, and he turns and looks at Lena. She sees the rage in his eyes, and her legs go watery. She might be able to outrun this monster but realizes that if she did that, she would leave the kids to their fate.

"Run! Run!" She says as they change direction and try to escape this vision of evil. The warrior starts to give chase. Lena's group passes an older couple that is too slow to outpace the warrior. The enemy barely slows at the couple. Instead, he splits the couple. Pushing the woman to the ground, he does a backhanded swing of his sword that nearly decapitates the older man.

Lena is frozen in place, watching what this guy is doing. He walks over to the woman, who is begging for mercy. Lena is sure he will punch her in the face like the man at the gate, but instead, he stares at her for a moment and then starts hacking into her.

Fighting is erupting all around Lena and her group. The warrior and his total savagery still transfix her. He staggers back, blade dripping, and wipes his arm across his face. Turning to look at Lena, he starts moving forward when he is struck.

The warrior is slammed sideways by a smaller man. One that is not armored. One of the villagers gives a good account of himself before he is killed.

"Fortos!" yells Kala. She moves forward to help her man when Lena grabs her arm.

"No, we must go now. Fortos is buying us time." Lena yells at Kala, who is fighting her armhold.

Fortos parries the warrior's blows, but it looks like a losing battle. He gives ground, then loses his balance. Kala breaks free of Lena's hold and moves toward her husband.

Lena grabs the kids and starts to turn and flee when a shield slams her in the face. She falls, and the last thing she sees before the darkness takes her is

Fortos being run through by the giant warrior. Kala is halfway there, and the kids huddle together near Lena, looking up behind her in fear.

ALTAI

Risor is alone in the Vailixi, talking to his father via his viewer. The rest of the crew are outside, relaxing.

"Father, I believe some people there would leave if given a chance. From what Zulti and the others say, Zalnur is a pompous ass and might be bullying them into being quiet."

"Risor, I understand what you are saying, but what can we do?"

"With the additional armored troopers, I will confront him, disarm his troopers, and ask the people who would like to come."

Rosan takes a minute, "I don't think we would like to do that, Risor. If we rejoin Atlantis, that would not look good for us."

Giving his father a look of sympathy, "Father, we both know we will not rejoin. Kanesa is doomed. We should tell Atlantis about them, but the town is doomed. If some people want to leave, we should help them."

Rosan turns to talk to others Risor could not see through the connection, "Okay, Risor, we approve. Try to get out of there without anyone getting hurt."

"Of course, Father. See you soon. Give my love to Mother and Rina."

FOUR DAYS AFTER

ATLANTA NADO

"My Lord, my Lord, come immediately." Yells a soldier running into the command tent. The guards block his further access to the tent.

Artos calls. "Let him pass."

Demetri and Arawn lean over a table with a crude map of the valley before them. A few block objects are on the valley's eastern end, with more in the hills further east.

Catching his breath, the soldier said. "My Lords, Vailixi have entered the valley."

"Damn them. How many, man?" Arawn said.

"Three, my Lord."

Demetri grabs his sword and runs out of the tent faster than most could react. Artos, already knowing his leader, straps on his sword and heads toward the door when Demetri passes him.

Demetri calls back. "Artos, get the men moving, and for the love of the Gods, bring up the Air Bows."

Artos changes direction back into the camp, calling out for the men. Arawn and his lieutenants exit the tent, calling for their men to organize. Most of their forces are still in the hills far from the valley.

Demetri runs up the road toward the valley rim. He stays close to the tree line in case one of the Vailixi reconnoiters the surrounding areas. He wants to see what they are doing before ordering the attack.

When he reaches the top, he sees what he fears the most. The Atlanteans are leaving. The refugees gather around the Vailixi, loading into them.

There are too many to go on one flight, so he has to set up his people quickly before they take them all. Artos and Arawn come up behind him, out of breath. At the bottom of the rise, he sees the Air Bows being pulled by teams.

"We need to get our people up and around the rim quickly. They are evacuating the Atlanteans, and we need to stop them."

Arawn looks at Demetri. "My Lord, why stop them? Destroy the Vailixi, yes, but why care if they get away? They are away from here."

Demetri smiles and claps Arawn on the shoulder. "Young prince, if we destroy them and take the village with them. We can get their weapons and hopefully get more called in before they realize it's a trap."

Artos adds. "My Lord Arawn, we can get the Air Bows in place and destroy the Vailixi, then await the next batch looking for this group."

Smiling, Demetri said. "My Prince, get your men around the left side of the rim. Do not move in until I fire first. And try to have some go all the way around to block the other road."

Arawn nods and calls his men. Looking at Artos, Demetri continues. "Artos, take your company along the right side rim. I will get the Air Bows set up around here."

"Chief Doena, thank you for your hospitality. We should have our people out of here by the end of the week." Sub-Commander Moza said.

"Thank you, Sub-Commander. We appreciate the supplies and are happy to help our friends from Atlantis."

Moza smiles and turns to Rogat. "Troop Leader Rogat, how long will it take for the first load to be complete?"

"About an hour, and we will have all three Vailixi loaded, sir."

The chief interrupts, "Sub-Commander, I will leave you to your preparations." He turns and walks back to the Elder's meeting house.

Moza turns back to Rogat. "Troop Leader, you are from Altai. Is that not correct?"

"Yes, sir. The 3rd Alta Faltan comes from there."

"I was part of the Falcon Claw squadron, and many came from Altai. In fact, the squadron commander is Risor Tarnor. Do you know of him?"

"Yes, sir. He is a friend of mine. The nobility didn't separate themselves from the rest of us in Altai."

"No, I can see that. Lord Tarnor is a man of the people."

"When did you leave them, sir? Do you know what happened to Altai?"

Moza hesitates to answer, then sighs. "You will know soon enough. The city was destroyed. A flood from the north destroyed the city. Many got away, but not all."

With a slight stagger at the news, Rogat quietly asks, "Did Risor and his family survive?"

"Yes, they did. I left when Atlantis called for reinforcements. Rama apparently caused the flooding. I left the day after the flood."

A sad smile crosses Rogat's face. At least his friend is safe. He didn't think Moza would know about his family. They are unimportant in the greater scheme of things, just to Rogat. That his friend lives is good. If he ever leaves this place, he will return to Altai and learn of his family's fate.

"To Arms! To Arms!" A frightened call comes from the wall. "The enemy is on the ridge."

Rogat looks to the rim near the eastern road. There is movement there. "Damn them. Couldn't they give us peace for a few days?"

Moza follows Rogat's gaze. "I can get our Vailixi in the air and strike them." He turns to leave, but Rogat stops him.

"Sir, they have Air Bows, see?" He points at an Airbow coming into view on the top of the ridge. "Better push the people onto the Vailixi and get up and out before they are fully set up." Looking around the rim of the valley.

"Noko, get your men to the eastern wall, Teado you to the south, and Migu, your men to the north." Rogat bellows. Everyone starts moving. "Marcon, get those people moving quickly into the Vailixi."

Chief Doena comes out of the Elder's house. He walks to where Rogat and Moza are. "How many?"

Rogat looks at the chief, "I think a hundred, maybe more, plus some Air Bows. But I don't think they have the western road yet."

The chief looks worried, "A hundred and Air Bows? We can not stop that. Nor can we get all the people out of the village in time before those Air Bows destroy our village."

Moza interrupts. "He is right, Troop Leader. There is a fortress about an hour away from here. We checked in with them when we were searching for you. We will drop off the first batch there and return."

Rogat nods. "Okay, and we will get the rest moving up the western road before it closes. Chief, will you and your people join us?"

The chief shakes his head in the negative. "I am sorry, Troop Leader, but we will stay and say you forced us to help you. I have too many old here, and this is our home."

Both Moza and Rogat nod, knowing that is not a guarantee but not willing to take the time to argue. These people are allies, not Atlanteans. Chances are the Greeks would let them live as nominal allies. It's not the best arrangement, and Rogat could always find himself fighting these people someday, but it's not one he can genuinely deal with at the moment.

Moza said, "I will come back along the line of the road, and we will pick up those we can."

Rogat nods. Moza heads to his Vailixi, calling orders to his men. Rogat bows to the chief. "Thank you, Chief Doena. I hope they will believe your story."

Rogat looks around and sees his men and the scared people. "Trooper Ahem, sound retreat."

Trooper Ahem nods and blows the signal. Everyone starts to look at Rogat. Noko, Teado and Migu run back to Rogat.

"Marcon, get those people loaded. Men get the others moving to the western road." His friends get close. "We are leaving to save the village. Every other man to me and the western gate. As we get the civilians out the gate, get the rest of your men moving too." They acknowledge and start to head back to their men.

"Men, we need a delaying action. But not too long. Those Air Bows will tear apart the village if we stay for a fight."

Demetri and his men are trying to wrestle the Air Bow into a firing position when one of his men cries out. "My Lord, the Vailixi are leaving."

Demetri leaves the Air Bow and steps toward the rim. The three Vailixi are flying west. Massive smoke columns are rising from the village, blocking the view. "Clever one, this captain is."

"I am sorry, my Lord?" Said one of the soldiers watching the valley.

Demetri waves him away. He is trying to discern movement in the smoke. He sees sentries on the walls, but not too many. The smoke would hide his targets well, but he still has a general idea of where to fire.

It looks like there is movement west of the village, but he can not make it out. He turns back to his men.

"You there, run after Artos and tell him to look to the western ridge. The enemy might try to flee." He turns to another soldier and tells him the same for Prince Arawn. He then continues to help set up the Air Bow.

Once he has the Air Bow in place and the other two are nearing the top of the ridge, Demetri walks back to the ridge. He can still see a few men on the walls.

Looking to the west of the village, he is sure people are fleeing. Hopefully, Artos and Arawn would see that and move in.

Then he sees the men on the walls disappear. They are fleeing. He pulls his sword. "Men, to me. Forget the Air Bow for now. We hit the walls."

Men drop the lines for the Air Bows, start to strap on shields, and draw swords. Many do not know what is happening, but their Lord calls them.

"Forward, men. Quickly now, but don't run and break your necks." Demetri says, then starts down the road at a quick pace. About fifty men are following him.

Twenty minutes later, when they near the walls, Demetri slows the pace. He strains to hear what is going on inside. It is too quiet. There is the noise of the fires and animals braying. They are probably scared by the smoke. He doesn't hear much more.

They get to the gate, and Demetri orders a few men over the walls to open it. The men scramble over the low walls with some rope they brought. Within a few minutes, the gate swings open.

He and his men walk through the gate and spread out. The village is empty. A soldier runs up to Demetri. "My Lord, we have found the villagers. They were locked in the Elder's meeting house."

"At least they are not butchered. Take me there."

Walking there, he orders troops to check the western road. A few of his men surround a group of men, women, and children. Many are old. One old man stands between two of Demetri's soldiers.

"My Lord, Chief Doena, leader of the Calcannut people. This is their village of Cardin."

The old man speaks first. "My Lord, it is good to see you. We were placed under arrest when your forces came."

"How many were there, and where did they go."

"They were the survivors of Delin, my Lord. Maybe 100 soldiers and about 500 civilians. The Vailixi took many of the old and will come back for the others. Along the road, they will meet."

"Thank you for your information, Chief. Why do you give it so freely?" Demetri asks out of curiosity.

"Atlantis is dying, my Lord. The Vailixi officer said they would not return for some time. A new power shift is coming, and my people want to live where we are." Chief Doena said with a shrug.

Demetri nods. "I understand, Chief. Who leads the infantry? What is he like?"

The chief looks at him, trying to judge him, Demetri thought. "His name is Rogat. Born and raised in far-off Alta, he is as black as the night he is, as those from Atlanta Luxa seem to be. An honorable man."

"I know this man. Yes, he is honorable. I met him before. A worthy opponent." With a nod to the chief, Demetri starts to jog to the west. "Men to me."

When they exit through the western gate, Artos joins him. Demetri looks to his left and sees Prince Arawn's men are still high on the hill but also coming down.

Artos calls as he nears. "It is too thick on the ridge. We could not cut off the escape, my Lord."

"Yes, it seems our old friend from Dedeni is leading our enemy."

Artos grins, "A worthy opponent then."

"Yes, take your men and bring up the Air Bows."

Addressing one of the men with him, he said, "You, stay here and await Prince Arawn. Tell him to bring his men up behind us. An easy pace will do. I do not think we will catch them on the road, not with the Vailixi returning."

"Where do you think they will go, my Lord?" Asks the man.

"There is a stronghold of the enemy on the other side of the mountains to the northwest. I think they still hold that. Probably there. If not, it is time we take that place."

Demetri and his men start a light jog up the hill on the western road.

They jog for an hour. Many are exhausted but all driven along by fear. Many keep looking back down the road they came. The smoke lessened over the last hour, so they knew the enemy knew the subterfuge they attempted.

"Okay, the break is over. Everyone, keep moving. Move to live, people," Rogat calls out. The soldiers start everyone moving. He looks over at Yalana. She is okay, but Mila and Telko look tired.

Telko is holding his legs and whining. "My legs hurt. Can we rest more?"

Yalana looks at Rogat. He shakes his head. Sighing, she turns to her son. "I am sorry, Telko, but we need to keep moving. The bad guys are still following us, and we can not wait too long."

Telko whimpers. Rogat looks around and notices a few other children and adults are sluggishly getting up. Noko and Migu join Rogat.

"Rogat, we will not be able to jog to Tor Sum with the people already sore," said Noko.

Migu adds quietly, "Nor walk. We should move on without them if we want any chance of surviving this."

Noko and Rogat stare at Migu. Migu, usually the group jester, nails the situation in the most cut-and-dry way possible. Rogat considers that. Not that he wants to abandon anyone, but the chances of keeping most alive might require the sacrifice of a few.

He is about to answer when a trooper from Teado's section comes running up to them. "Sir, Senior Trooper Teado advised me to inform you there is a river crossing about three kilometers ahead. The river runs deep and is not easily forded for some distance in either direction." Stopping to suck in a deep breath.

Rogat smiles. "Go ahead, trooper." The man leans on his Aether spear.

"Sir, he assumes we need a place to hold them up and is fortifying the opposite bank."

Patting the man on his shoulder. "Thank you, trooper. Take it easy heading back." Looking at one of his section's troopers. "Devin, run ahead and tell Teado to proceed."

Rogat goes to Telko and picks him up. "Come Telko, we can relax soon." He calls out loud to the civilians who are still slowly getting up.

"Citizens, we have a river ahead of us in a few kilometers. We are building a defensive position there. It will provide some protection from the enemy and give the Vailixi a chance to pick you all up. Please move quickly. Move to live!"

This news gives everyone more energy.

A short time later, Rogat walks across the stone bridge with the last refugees. He hands Telko to another trooper, who takes him across the barrier.

The Vailixi returns and starts loading some civilians further down the road. All civilians move to where the Vailixi has landed. This will be the Atlantean's stand. Moza joins Rogat at the barrier they are building.

Moza, Teado, Migu, and Noko stand with him. Teado grins, "Looks like the Greeks will have to fight their way across now."

Rogat smiles. "Yes. Good call, Teado. If only these other two knuckleheads could be as resourceful." Pointing at Migu and Noko. They all smile at each other.

Moza interrupts. "Troop Leader, I will take another ninety to Tor Sum. They are making preparations. Should I bring a few of their troopers when I return?"

Rogat thought about it for a minute. "No, it would be nice, but I imagine those troopers will be needed there too. We will fight this line as long as we can. Just get the civilians out of here."

Moza nods and jogs back.

Noko turns back down the road they came. "Well, if I were not such a knucklehead, I would probably fell a few trees a distance down the road with some of them burning. That should them take longer to get those Air Bows in range."

"Okay, maybe half a knucklehead. Sounds good. Get your team moving on it." Rogat said. Noko turns back to the defensive position and calls forth his men. They jog back down the road.

Rogat looks at Migu, who looks hurt. "Well, don't look at me. I am fine with being a knucklehead if it keeps me alive." The three laugh.

"Migu, get some of your people to fell a few trees closer to this side of the river. Why not make it hard for them to see us."

Migu nods and gets his men moving. Teado and Rogat move into the defensive position they are constructing, mainly consisting of fallen trees that are soaked wet and mounds of dirt. On the defender's side of the barrier, the wood is dry.

Teado looks at his men's creation and smiles. "Ya, not much, but it shouldn't catch fire without too many Aether bursts and should give us some cover."

"It looks good, Teado. I think we should put some decent-sized logs on the bridge itself. That should slow a charge, and we might be able to light them up. Soak those on that far side so they will stay an obstruction. Keep this side dry so we can fire them if need be."

Teado nods. "I will get my men on it."

"No, your men already did a lot. Keep them building a second wall behind the first. I will get my men to fell some trees and lay them across the bridge." Rogat calls out to Marcon to get the men on it.

Rogat walks toward the civilian gathering point. Some are helping Teado's force build the walls. Yalana is sitting with her children. Rogat heads in her direction when some of the other civilians call out.

"My Lord, will we be safe?" "Can you hold them?" "When will the Vailixi be back?"

Rogat raises his hands for silence. "You are safe now. We can not hold them for a long time, but it should be enough time for the Vailixi to get all of you out of here. Relax now, conserve your energy. If you feel you can help, my men would appreciate your assistance."

Mollified, the refugees return to their misery. Rogat makes his way to Yalana. Telko is already asleep, and Mila is about to fall asleep.

"Rogat, will you be able to take a Vailixi?" She asks with concern in her eyes.

He stares into her eyes, "I don't know, but I want you to promise me you will get on the next Vailixi to arrive. You and your children." Caressing her face, she smiles and allows him to continue. He stares at the skin he is touching, then looks back into her eyes and takes his hand to tilt her chin so she is face to face. "I care for you, Yalana. I guess I always have since we met. Seems like a lifetime ago. I can't handle you being here, in danger."

She grabs both sides of his face and pulls him down quickly into a short, sharp kiss. She pushes his head back to where it was. "And I care for you. Don't get yourself killed doing anything stupid, or I will not forgive you!" She lets go and turns back to her children.

Rogat is stunned and surprised by the quickness of the encounter. He looks at her, her back to him, then at the other civilians. Most find something else to look at. A few smiling, knowing smiles. If a man could blush.

Turning back to the barrier, Migu is standing there with a stupid grin. Rogat groans when he sees him. Of all the people, why Migu? He will not hear the end of this.

Walking past Migu, Rogat heads back to the wall. Migu locks in step beside him. Neither saying anything but Rogat dreading what is coming. They stop at the wall to look beyond.

"It's good to be the king," Migu said as he continued past the wall onto the bridge. Acting like he forgot something, he turns and continues. "Oh, and in case you were curious, Noko reports the lead elements in the distance. We will fire the logs."

Rogat shakes his head. "One-day Migu. I will forget we are friends." Teado comes up and claps Rogat on the shoulder.

"He does have a way about him, doesn't he?" Said Teado, not hearing the exchange but seeing the exasperation on Rogat and the self-satisfied look on Migu. He then looks at where some of the men are packing mud. "You there, pack it tighter." Then he moves off.

In the distance, where Noko's men have built the first barrier, fire and smoke grow. His men are running back before the oncoming Greeks. Migu's men stay where they are and make small fires to light their barrier when the time comes. A few smaller fires add to the smoke.

Most of their men are on Rogat's side of the river, with just a few remaining to light the last fires. When they all make it over to the Atlantean side, there is a great blanket of smoke in the distance where the first fires were set.

Teado stands next to Rogat. "You know, we probably should have fired the forests too. The river would have stopped it from getting to this side, but the forest would have caused them all sorts of issues."

Rogat nods. "I really do not like destroying the forests, but maybe that would have been a good idea."

Migu comes over. "Rogat, the Vailixi are here. I imagine you would want to say goodbye," with the most innocent expressions.

Teado looks at Rogat. Before he can say anything, Rogat raises a finger. "Not a word." Turning to Migu, nothing would come out. He sighs and moves back to where the civilians are.

Migu, not to miss an opportunity. "Don't worry, Rogat, we will not start the fight without you."

Rogat finds Yalana with her kids. "You need to go now. The enemy comes."

"There are so many others that should go before us."

"No, go to safety. I need to know you are safe. Please, for me." He begs.

Starring into her eyes, he sees the fight still there. His eyes water with the frustration of trying to get her out of there and not cooperating. "Please go now."

Finally, the fire leaves her eyes. "Okay, we will go."

Touching his cheek. "Don't do anything stupid."

"What would I do?" A relieved smile breaks across his face. He feels all the stress of the last few days lifted—momentarily, at least. Then he turns to where Moza is directing others onto the Vailixi. "Sub-commander, please ensure she and her kids get on this craft."

Moza looks at her and him and then nods his head. He directs her to get into line.

She looks back at him, concern in her eyes. "I'm serious. Please be careful."

Smiling, "We will stay as long as we have to."

Looking at the kids, he says, "Take care of your mother." Then he turns and trots back to the line.

As he nears the wall they made, the smoke thickens across the river. There is no sight of the enemy yet. Behind him, Rogat hears the Vailixi take off, and the few soldiers detailed to protect the remaining civilians are already herding those who remain further down the road. There is no sense chancing they can get an Air Bow into range, where a lucky shot might take down their lifeline.

Migu, Teado, and Noko watch Rogat's approach. Migu has a stupid grin, Teado has a knowing and approving smile, and Noko has a curious look. Of course, Migu breaks the silence. He leans against Teado's shoulder and acts like a love-swoon person. "I wub you, Rogat, mwah mwah."

Teado shoves him off, laughing, while Rogat shakes his head. He gets up next to Migu, who looks up at Rogat, teasingly batting his eyes. Rogat raises a hand in a choking motion to Migu. "If I didn't need every sword right now, I would seriously consider throttling you to death."

Migu laughs, "You would miss me too much."

Teado puts his hand on Rogat's shoulder. "We will get you back to her."

Migu says, "Ya, but will we get back too."

Rogat smiles, "I am seriously thinking of leaving you and letting the Greeks suffer with you for a while."

Logs lay burning across the road as Demetri's men move along the forest edge to scout ahead.

"He is a pesky one, isn't he, my Lord?" Artos asks.

Demetri stood with arms crossed, fifty meters from the first crackling flames. The weak breeze causes the smoke to linger, potentially hindering their attack. "This may pose a challenge," Demetri's voice cut through the tension. It seems our opponent is not eager for battle."

Prince Arawn stands a little behind Demetri and Artos. "I would imagine something about being outnumbered four to one, without Air Bows and fighting a hero, would have something to do with it."

Demetri nods, "I bet this first barrier is outside Air Bow range for wherever they are, too."

Artos grunts the affirmative, "Probably built a barrier across the bridge, on the other side. That is what I would do."

One of the guards closer to the fire calls out, "My Lords, the scouts return."

"Moment of truth, it seems." Said Artos. The others nod.

The scouts jog up to the leaders, bow, and report, "My Lords, the river is still around two kilometers away. They have set a few barriers to block the Air Bows. We can easily move the men off the road but not the Air Bows."

Demetri nods. This Rogat is clever. By the time the fires die, the enemy would probably have all their people evacuated. If he attacks, they probably can not cross the bridge without heavy losses, and the enemy probably will still get all their people evacuated.

He decides. "Okay, my Prince, if you bring up the Air Bows when you can safely move the burning logs out of the way. I will take my Companions up to harass the enemy. Mind the forests catching from these fires. I do not fancy a forest fire to my back."

Everyone starts moving. Then Demetri turns, "My Prince, also set up the Air Bows now. Continue doing this as you clear the road. In case those Vailixi decide to attack us."

"We will not be able to see the enemy, my lord." Said Arawn.

"They will not be able to see where the shots are coming from either. Getting shot at might scare them away. Also, you might want to have a few scouts climb some trees to pass aiming instructions. We might get lucky."

Demetri can hear the river when the enemy starts firing on his men. They passed two burning barriers, and another lay in front. The smoke is thick and hanging in the air.

Aether blasts coming out of the clouds of smoke force him and his men to their bellies. They crawl forward to see where the enemy is making their stand. Some of his men start firing their Spirit Bows in the general direction of the Aether blasts. Regrettably, that tells the enemy where someone is, and then large numbers of blasts hit the unlucky souls.

"Stop firing until we can get near the river's edge," Artos shouts. Demetri nods, still slithering forward.

When Demetri sees the river, he also can see the enemy's position. They have a high barrier across the bridge and along the river's edge. There is no way they will be able to rush the barrier. There are logs across the bridge that will trip up his men.

"The Gods curse this man. What was his name again?" Artos said.

"Ro something. And yes, I think we will lose him again."

In the distance, they hear the whirling of nearby Vailixi. Demetri points at one of his men. "Go back and tell Prince Arawn that Vailixi might be coming. Have the Air Bows ready."

The soldier starts running back at a crouch.

Rogat crouches behind a large rock, surveying the river's far bank. The haze from the burning logs makes this task more difficult. He sees enemy soldiers cautiously peek their heads out from behind the cover of trees and bushes. Relief washes over him as he realizes one wait is over, and another begins. It looks like they are settling in. A small grin forms, knowing they will not challenge the bridge today.

The whirl of the incoming Vailixi tells him that he will have most of the civilians out today and before the Greeks attempt the bridge. One more run and all the civilians will be gone. After that, it will be just soldiers; if needed, they can run back and get picked up along the way. Most of his men are well-rested, if not pumped full of adrenalin.

A brief exchange of fire kills one of his men and wounds two others. Rogat thinks they killed about six or seven of the enemy in the exchange. Overall, it was a good deal, but he could not sustain these losses long, being outnumbered.

"Teado, take charge. I am going to talk to the Sub-Commander," Rogat said. Teado nods, as do Noko and Migu. It's all business now that the enemy is near.

Rogat runs back to the Vailixi and the civilians boarding. Moza directs the civilians onto the craft. He sees Rogat and starts to walk toward him.

"How is everyone settling in at the stronghold?" Rogat asks.

"Good, we have plenty of room and supplies for now. After this run, we should be able to get the rest and then take one last run to pick up all the soldiers. Should we strafe the far side?"

"No, I need you to get those civilians to safety. I do not know how far along they are in dismantling our barriers and would hate to have a lucky shot take down one of your Vailixi."

"Can't say that I disagree with your logic. And I don't relish the idea of one of my craft going down on that side of the river. Don't imagine they would be treated well."

"I am not sure. The Greeks are pretty honorable, but it depends on how much you hurt them before they get a hold of you. No, best to evacuate us."

"Agree. Oh, your lady friend and her children are safe and sound. I told the base commander to ensure she is protected."

"Thank you, Sub-Commander. I imagine you will have to return to Atlantis after helping us?"

"Yes, we will. Hold out there, and we will let Atlantis know we have one foothold here, or they might plan an evacuation."

"Home, not for me, but a welcome sight that would be."

"I understand. I, too, wish to return to Luxa and my family."

One of Moza's men calls for him. It is time to go. Twenty-nine civilians remain standing around looking at the Vailixi.

"Farewell, Rogat. We will be back soon."

Rogat returns to the barrier.

"Well, I should go say hi to our friend again. Maybe they will surrender." Demetri said to Artos.

"I rather doubt it. You might get shot for your troubles, too. Maybe we should just open up on them."

"No, the road is blocked for us, and the tree line seems rather dry over here. I imagine all that Aether fire would start a forest fire."

"So what do we do, my Lord?"

"I will mention the stronghold to see if I can get a reaction out of him. If I do, then we sit back and wait for the fires to die down. If I do not, we may attack and try to get them." Demetri said as he slithers closer to the road.

Calling out in his loudest command voice, "Don't shoot. I want to talk to the commander of the Atlantean forces."

Nothing for a minute. Then, "Okay, everyone hold fire."

He hears a few acknowledgments. "Okay, come out where we can see you."

Demetri takes a deep breath, prays to his patron God, Apollo, for his safety, and then stands up. He waits a minute, every fiber of his being ready to jump for cover at the first flash of Aether. But nothing happens. He can hear only the sound of the river rushing and the burning of logs.

He walks past the last burning log to the foot of the stone bridge. The bridge is covered in logs. Definitely, no one would cross that bridge at any speed without concentrating on his footing. Of course, that would mean they would not see the Aether blasts coming their way.

He waits a few minutes, and no one comes out. So, he starts to negotiate his way across the bridge. Halfway across, a voice calls out, "That is far enough."

Looking at the barrier in front of him, he sees Rogat rise tall above the barrier. There is still a five-meter expanse between Rogat and Demetri. A part in the barrier allows Rogat to slide sideways between logs.

Rogat walks to within two meters of Demetri. Demetri figures he could probably close the distance and strike at Rogat, but could he actually kill him before being blasted by many Aether weapons? He is not sure. It is not his intent, anyway.

"We meet again, friend ???" Demetri trails off.

"Rogat. Troop Leader Rogat of the 3rd Alta Faltan, my Lord Demetri, Son of Delno of Eros."

"Ah, you are much better at remembering names than I. Well met, as I said. You have led us on a merry chase, Troop Leader Rogat of the 3rd Alta Faltan. I commend you, but you know you can not hold this position for too long, right?"

"We seem to meet when you have the advantage, my Lord."

Demetri grins. "Part of being blessed by the Gods, friend Rogat. I can call you my friend, can I not?"

Rogat shakes his head in mirthless amusement. "Normally, one would not try to kill one's friends."

Shrugging his shoulders, throwing his arms wide, and grinning even wider, he said, "Of course not, but this is war." Like that should answer everything. "You are my enemy but a good one. I have enjoyed the chase. I consider you a good person and a friend. One I might have to kill, but still, it would be my duty.

"I see. I assume you wanted to tell me something?"

"Ah, yes, well, I was going to ask if you wish to surrender to prevent your small force from being killed."

Putting his chin between his fingers, Rogat gives it a moment to think. "No, I didn't contemplate that. I think we have the better position and, as you know, the Vailixi."

"Yes, but do you believe that stronghold two days away will really stop us?" Demetri says, concentrating on Rogat's face. There! His eyes widen slightly, and a quick tick before the veteran recovers his emotions. "It will just delay the inevitable retreat again or destruction of your command and the death of the civilians."

"Delays are good, usually means there is time for reinforcements to arrive. You might find yourself fighting a much larger force with many Vailixi," said Rogat, crossing his arms.

"A worthy battle that would be, friend Rogat. Tell you what I am gonna do. We will give you until tomorrow morning. Your men don't fire on us, and we will not fire on you. We will not attempt to cross the bridge either. As you can imagine, we will bring up our Air Bows when possible. We will attack and destroy you if you are still here tomorrow."

"Generous, my Lord, why?"

"Like I said, you are my friend." Throwing his hands wide again with a big smile. "And we will meet again at the stronghold. Maybe I will gather more force. In case you find these reinforcements. I rather doubt it. From what I have seen and heard, Atlantis has other worries. They are abandoning you, friend Rogat." Looking at the barrier, at those he knows could hear him. "Atlantis has withdrawn from this region, and you are left to fend for yourselves. Surrender, and we will let you live. Fight, and well, I am sorry, but you will die."

ALTA FALTA

The following morning, all four Vailixi and the twenty armored troopers head to Kanesa. The rest start to prepare the camp for departure. The rescue of the Kanesa colony is coming to an end. When they arrive, Risor's Vailixi lands and the troopers come out and position themselves around the back of the craft. Risor, also in armor, comes out and stays near the ship. The other three Vailixi take up positions around the landing area about fifty meters off the ground.

Zalnur comes out with his fourteen troopers. As militia, his troopers don't have armor and have less training than the regular unit that Risor has at his disposal. Behind the troopers, the survivors gather.

Risor starts, "Lord Zalnur, people of Kanesa, we have come for your answer. Will you leave with us or stay to find your own way?"

Zalnur looks at all the troopers and says, "This is less cordial than I was expecting from you, Lord Tarnor. You ask us to come, but you seem geared for war."

"Yes, my Lord, this is true. To be honest, some of your men gave me pause yesterday. Would I be able to leave peacefully today if I came as I did yesterday? We want no fight from you and yours and will leave if that is your decision."

Lord Zalnur said, "I think you can help us more before you leave. We believe it would be fair if you left one of your Vailixi and a team to train our people to use it. That would give us a better chance of surviving. We will stay but would like your assistance."

"The people of Kanesa, we accept that you wish to live here and will leave you to your desires. I am sorry, but we also have limited supplies and cannot assist you. If you stay, you are on your own. Like Atlantis, if we have secured our future, we will come again to see if you need help, but we will not help before then."

"Lord Tarnor, you will leave us without an ability to defend ourselves?" Zalnur asks.

"My Lord, you have your men with Aether spears, and as long as they use them wisely, you can keep a strong defense to fend off most. We have started to make normal spears to augment our force because, like you, we have no way of recharging them."

Risor continues, "We are leaving you as we found you. If any of you would like to join us, you are welcome to come. This offer is only for now. We will not be back in the near future. Although, we will send word to Atlantis that you are here and need further assistance. If or when they come, we do not know."

Zalnur looks angry, but he knows he can do little since he is outgunned. Finally, he said, "We have very little food for all of us. Leave us a Vailixi to let us salvage what we can from the other plantations."

"No, Lord Zalnur, we have scavenged through all the plantations, but the food remains in the fields. The sea has cut a channel blocking your path north. The bridge is out to the south, going to the next plantation, but most southern ones are already wiped out. Of course, the rising waters could make these observations false in short order."

No one seems to move forward, but Risor can see a few faces turning the choice over in their minds. Risor calls out, "Time to make a decision. We leave now." With that, he turns to make his way back inside when a few people call out.

Turning back, he sees that some people want to go, but Zalnur and his troopers are trying to stop them. Risor decides it is time to act on his plan. He calls his troopers to action. The Aether spear does have the means to stun a victim, not only kill, and at that moment, his troopers fire on the Kanesa troopers. Most of Kanesa's troopers go down in the first strike, and the rest give up without a fight. It doesn't hurt that the Vailixi in the air activate their Aether spears, making an evil hissing noise as the weapons energize. That is incredibly nerve-racking if you are on the receiving end of the spear.

"What is the meaning of this, Lord Tarnor? Atlantis will hear about this," screams Zalnur.

"My Lord, you will not stop any of these citizens from deciding to go if they wish." To the people, "Go get your things; we can not carry a lot, and all major items will need to be left to benefit those staying. You will be taken care of in Altai. Only small family heirlooms should be brought."

Of the hundred and thirty-nine people that survive in Kanesa, sixty-one want to go. Risor does not like leaving the rest but decides that he has no choice unless they are willing to force seventy-eight people to leave. That is a lot of disgruntled people if he forcefully takes them. It isn't worth it. So, each Vailixi takes their fair share of the people, and the Altans leave the colony of Kanesa to its fortunes.

FIVE DAYS AFTER

ATLANTA NADO

Rogat has Teado take his men down the road early in the morning. They aim to meet the Vailixi way down the road and ensure the Greeks do not hear them. To create cover for Teado's men, many of those remaining at the bridge are walking back and forth with torches.

For Moza's Vailixi to see Teado's men, Teado will have to light torches, too. If the Greeks see those fires, they will know that the Atlanteans are abandoning the bridge. Rogat is not ready for them to know that.

The fires on the Greek side of the bridge have already died down a few hours before. Rogat is sure that the Greeks have brought up the Air Bows and have them in place to start destroying his wall in the morning.

Rogat hopes Demetri will be a man of his word and not attack until dawn. He doesn't want to take chances, so they created this elaborate ruse. Teado will go about four to five kilometers down the road and wait for the Vailixi. They will wait until Rogat's force catches up. Then, they will airlift the whole unit.

Before leaving, they will fire the bridge's and wall's logs to make a massive fire. A bunch of logs are scattered behind the wall to slow down the Greeks further. While the Air Bows can destroy the wall and create an opening for the men, getting the Air Bows past the bridge will not be safe until the fires are much smaller.

Judging dawn a few hours away, Rogat orders the firing. Migu's men move off down the road while Rogat's and Noko's remain to keep up the ruse. It would do no good if the Greeks didn't see men still around the wall when the fires are lit. The Atlanteans figure the fires will burn for a few hours, and the wet logs will throw off a lot of smoke to add to the mess.

An hour into the burn, Rogat quietly orders all the remaining men to form up, drop the torches, and jog down the road. They need to get much further down the road before the Greeks react. This will not be pretty if it is a running battle. At least not until the Vailixi get involved, but that damn hero could even screw that up for the Atlanteans.

ALTAI

The day after the return from Kanesa, the Altai council decides on a river valley as the new home. Five of the seven Vailixi are used to airlift workers, equipment, and supplies to the new valley. The idea is to build long houses like those used by many local tribes and then start moving the people. Building before moving will keep most people in relative comfort in Altai while the new site is under construction. The people of Altai still have Aether tools to construct these structures quickly and with limited manpower.

Altai reports the situation of the Kanesa colony to Atlantis.

"My Lord Tolloc, as you can see, the Kanesians were a little upset when we made them let people go," reported Rosan.

Lord Tolloc is the First Minister of the Empire and has the Emperor's ear. He is also a leader of the Shigar party and is not very friendly to the Tarnor family or the Nalos party.

"Yes, Rosan, I see that. Well, we will investigate if they accuse your son. It might not be much of a problem."

"Thank you, my Lord. Will Atlantis be able to spare a Mother Stone for us and Kanesa? As well as the priests to maintain them? It would greatly speed up the rebuilding of our colonies." Rosan said.

Looking slightly annoyed, then sighing, "I am sorry, my Lord, we can not spare any Mother Stone at this time. Between the rebuilding of Atlantis and repairing Luxa, it is taking all we have left. Surely you understand the importance of these two cities over some of our remote colonies?"

"Yes, Lord Tolloc, we understand and will make do with what we can until we can receive help from Atlantis. How is the Imperial family, my Lord?"

"The Imperial family is fine. The Emperor does wonder why Altai has not sent more of the Vailixi to supplement the defenses of Atlantis. I assured him it was no slight to the throne that you and your council believe they are needed to help Altai survive." With a severe look, he said, "I do not know if I can keep saying that for long, Rosan. Eventually, he might order you and the council to come here and explain yourselves to him directly. That would really be a shame."

The threat is understood. "First Minister, should we abandon our colonies on this side of the Tes Atlan and return to Atlantis? This would ensure the Vailixi and troopers are available for reassignment quicker. They would have to ferry all the people to Atlantis first."

A look of disdain comes over Lord Tolloc's face as he considers the disruption that a large number of additional Nalos supporters in Atlantis would cause. "No, I do not believe that is necessary, Rosan. I will work on the Emperor. The colonies of Altai and Kanesa are important to the Empire. We do not wish to abandon them."

Fidgeting in his chair, "You shall have your time. Another three days should suffice. Since we have destroyed the Rama, we can take apart their allies at a more leisurely pace."

"Thank you, First Minister. What of the news of our other colonies, have they suffered as we have?"

"Some have and some haven't. I am sorry, Lord Tarnor, matters of state await me. Please file your report on the status of rebuilding Altai. Your people need not worry about Kanesa any longer. We will send support and then deal directly with them." He then vanishes from the viewing screen.

Stolar is near Rosan during the exchange and speaks up once he is sure the connection has been broken. "Rosan, that was a dangerous game you just played. What if the First Minister said he wanted us to return to Atlantis? We would have to return."

"My friend, I did not believe Tolloc would want us back. Had I believed so, I would never have offered it." He starts to chuckle, "The ploy worked. The thought was so repugnant to him that he gave us another three days."

Risor, listening from a discreet distance, says, "Father, three days is not much time. It might take that much time to build out the longhouses."

Stolar adds, "We can move up the schedule to move people over and have some of the younger ones start walking with some of the troopers and supplies. But, the question is still, will we rebel against Atlantis?" He scans all those in the Vailixi.

"This is not a game. They still have about twenty to thirty Vailixi, from what Moza told us. And they still have Mother Stone to recharge, whereas we do not." He continues.

Rosan finally stands up and walks to the middle of the deck, putting his hand on his son's shoulder and then turning to Stolar. "Yes, my friend, I think we understand the situation. On the other side of the issue, if we stay with the

Empire, there is a very good chance that we will be replaced or killed, and the Nalos party and its ideals will be but a memory."

ATLANTIS

Tolloc gets out of the command chair, thanks the communication officer, who leaves and then turns to talk to Lady Jana.

Jana beats him, "Was it a good call, First Minister?"

"I know you were listening. What do you think?"

A predatory smile that made Tolloc shiver, "I think you gave them too much time. We should go and get the things we need and throw the Nalos leaders in prison."

A little shocked but recovering quickly, "Lady Jana, you are a great soldier, but you should leave diplomacy to those who understand it. The military's actions are what caused Utanor and Moia to rebel."

A flash of anger, "First Minister, they were ready to rebel before we arrived. We were following orders."

Angry because he has gone through this conversation with so many Shigar military members, "Yes, yes, following orders of the military. Had you fools not tried to force Moia to give up their source of Aether, they might still be with us. Of course, they would not give in to a demand so quickly after the disaster."

"They attacked.."

Anger rising, "That is enough. I will not listen to this nonsense from a mere squadron commander. No matter how highly regarded you are."

Tolloc turns and leaves the command deck while Jana seethes with anger. Quietly to his back, "One day, you will know my anger."

The Atlantis command tent is in the middle of the newly established military base, outside the new city environs. Jana enters the tent where Lady Tomar sits at the table reading a view tablet. Lord Dentam lounges in a chair, chatting with some others. A few servants are walking around. Jana plops down in a chair across from Lady Tomar.

Barely looking up, "So, what is it, Commander?"

Having the anger turn to frustration, "The First Minister has given those vermin in Altai another three days to send their Vailixi and troopers. He is such a coward. He wouldn't stand against them."

Dentam leaves his group and comes over to take a seat near Jana.

Lady Tomar puts down the view tablet and matter-of-factly says, "If we get the Vailixi and troopers peacefully, then it matters little that it took another three days."

Not satisfied to leave it lie. Jana said, "Something is up. I do not trust them."

Lord Dentam interrupts, "My Lady, do you believe they will rebel like Moia and Utanor?"

Looking at Dentam in approval for his thinking, "I do not believe they dare to consider such an act."

Sighing at the line of thinking, Lady Tomar said, "You are imagining things."

Undeterred, Dentam backs his part-time lover, "Commander Folstan was a fool. He should have waited until your squadron was in the vicinity before trying to take charge. Those damn rebels were ready for him. The results would have differed if we had two full squadrons."

Considering the idea, Lady Jana absentmindedly said, "Yes, my squadron could have turned the battle."

Starting to get annoyed, Lady Tomar quips, "Nonsense. They were prepared, and you would have been torn to shreds, too. If Altai is planning the same, then we will send your WaveRiders. They have less force."

Lady Jana smiles, happy with the conversation's turn. "Then I will find a way to take care of that galling Risor. He deserves a painful death."

ALTA CIETO

Risor sets off for the remaining colonies. Next on the list is Atlanda, south of Kanesa, on a peninsula off Alta Falta.

Atlanda is an agricultural town with significant trade. Many fruits are grown in the area, and the natives come from around the region to trade. Many tribes from the deep south, in the mountains, come there to trade their metals, precious stones, and other exotics for Atlantean cookware and clothing. Many Atlantean traders would ply the Tes Fatlan to meet natives from around the region. Meanwhile, large caravans of metals and other items would usually travel up the isthmus to Atlanda and trade there.

This time, Risor's team will travel south before they turn to follow the coast in an easterly direction. Heading directly south from what used to be Altai takes them over the mouth of the Tia Yolan. The delta at the mouth of the river used to be pretty well-defined. It is known for excellent hunting in the swamps and savanna inland.

It has been five days since the flood, and the shoreline is no longer defined. The river used to be navigable, if not a little fast running. After five days of massive flooding, it is still a raging torrent, kilometers wider than before. The delta is no longer an easily navigable river mouth with large tracts of marsh to buffer between Tes Falta and Tia Yolan. What land that used to define the delta has been washed away. Large tracts of land behind the old shoreline and beach dunes are now underwater.

Flying over this disappearing landscape, Risor wonders what the new world will look like. So much flat land near the shore is susceptible to flooding or being washed away.

"The world is changing," he says to no one in particular.

Milo turns to him, "We have fought the Ramans for many years, and they have not taken us down. One week of flooding and our civilization hangs in the balance. Crazy, sir."

"I remember Tolen once telling me how the beach dunes and marshes protect the shoreline from eroding."

"Really, how do they do that?" Milo asks.

"I can't remember. I was not really listening. I was more interested in my wine and the serving lady. But I seem to remember something about it anchoring the shore somehow."

Dimera says, "Sir, you can ask him when we return."

"Yes, if we get some quiet time. You know, it has been so crazy over the last week I have not been able to talk to my mother or sister. Or really, even my father. Having a little time to see how they are doing will be nice."

Milo looks up from his viewer. "Doesn't Tilor live in Atlanda, sir?"

"You're right, he does. It will be good to see him again."

Dimera said, "Sir, you know he is alive?" Quickly adding, "I hope so too, but we have not heard from Atlanda since the initial messages."

"Yes, Dimera, you are right, but something tells me our wily sub-commander will have cheated death yet again. I am sure there is a reason they have not contacted us since."

They continued for an hour. Risor is still amazed that the waters are roiling and very brown. The fishing will be bad for quite some time, at least until the waters settle. Tolen said most fish have died or left the area due to the stirred-up mud.

Another hour gets them to an area where there should be land, but it was still open water. After a few more minutes, they see something in the distance.

Milo said, "Sir, there are trees in the distance. We should be overland by now. I'm not sure why our maps show differently from what we see. Someone has screwed up the maps."

"I don't think that is the problem, Milo. I think the lands have flooded. Slow her down so we can get a better look."

Milo does a few things on his viewer and then reports, "Quarter speed, sir."

The crew can see debris in the water, knocked down trees, trapped trees, decomposing animal bodies, and other junk stuck amongst the tree stumps. It looks like the land is under two meters of water.

They are nearing the "trees" they saw and could see the water going into the forest with large piles of debris at the edges of the forest. This went on for another hour with the occasional dry hill or range of hills above the swamped land below.

Dimera asks, "Sir, do you think Atlanda is the same way? If I recall, it is near sea level."

"It might be Dimera. Only part of the town is at sea level, and there are hills around it, too. However, if I remember correctly, the government buildings and temple are near the shore. That might be the reason Tilor and Atlanda have not contacted us. City communications hubs are too big to be carried around easily."

Milo said, "Sir, we are getting to the foothills. Shall we speed up to make Atlanda before it gets dark?"

"Yes, Milo, please go to half-speed. I want to ensure the recorders get a good view for Tolen to review in the future."

As they speed up, they turn southeast to cut across the foothills. They leave the foothills but don't see the kilometers of mangrove swamps they expect. Instead, the land quickly falls away to water. Clear evidence that the tsunami hit hard in this area. After almost an hour, they see swamped land again, but it is on the peninsula of Atlanda. This didn't bode well.

Atlanda, being on the southeastern side of the peninsula, would still be approximately forty minutes away. Ten minutes after crossing the "shoreline," the land continued to look like a giant broom swept it clean, and pushed all the debris up in the foothills. Occasional hills or ranges of hills would be above sea level and usually crowded with animals.

Risor said, "Poor animals. They think they are safe, but the sea levels will continue to rise, and either their refuge will sink, or they will eat all the food and then have to move on."

Milo agrees, "Yes, sir, I don't think it will be pretty when they start fighting for the last scraps of food or want water."

They are coming up on Atlanda from the north. Risor wants to see if anyone is caught on dry hills further up the coast. They go about fifty kilometers north and see a great channel carved out of the land between Tes Falon and Tes Fatlan. The land is low and soft enough that it washed away a large section of land when the tsunami hit. They slow down to take a better look at it. They can see that the sea continues to erode the channel's sides.

Risor whistles in awe of the power of the Gods, "If the flood keeps going, this channel will continue to widen."

Dimera said, "Sir, our maps show the same elevation for a good twenty kilometers north and fifteen south of this location."

"Thank you, Dimera. Let's hope that Atlanda is better off."

Risor worries that most of the land of this peninsula is already flooded, with only the hills dry. Many of the hills of this peninsula also look like they are affected by the tsunami. His hope for Atlanda and his friend is starting to dim.

Milo breaks his thoughts, "Coming up on Atlanda, sir."

Pointing at a column of smoke. "Doesn't look good."

"Well, the good thing is that hills surround Atlanda," Risor said.

The Vailixi come to Atlanda from the northern side and see that the smoke column comprises many individual columns. Atlanda was on fire.

The crew sees many buildings smoldering. Apparently, the tsunami did make it through a pass in the hills and struck the colony. Circling the colony, Risor's team could see that the pass seemed to funnel the waters to a natural dam in the past. It appears that the water eventually burst through the dam, more likely soft dirt and not rock.

When the water burst through the barrier, it seemed to have shot through the gap, as a jet, into the town proper. Those buildings in the jet's path were scraped clean down to the foundation. In some places, not even the foundation survived. The water cut a groove into the ground beneath the foundations and rooted them out. To add to the doomed town's miseries, the rising sea level is swamping those remaining waterside buildings. Eighty percent of the town is destroyed or inundated by the sea.

With a few exceptions, those buildings not in the jet's path and above sea level seem to have survived untouched by the calamity. A few burnt-out buildings are on the surrounding hillsides. They suspect that accidental fires caused the burning that could not be put out because of the greater destruction in the town.

"Anyone see any survivors?" Risor asks. There are no signs of activity anywhere.

No one answers. They are all concentrating on their view screens to see if anything shows up, but nothing does.

"Make a few wide circles at a higher altitude to see if we can see anything around the area or give people a chance to see us," Risor orders.

On the second pass over the southern side, they notice a stack of supplies and equipment near the road heading southwest along the coast. This is a road through the hills, so there is a chance that survivors went that way.

Risor orders, "Land near that building with the supplies. Let's see what we can find there."

After landing, the team investigates the pile and determines the survivors made it. There are a lot of supplies, a few Aether tools, and spears.

Milo picks up an Aether spear and looks at Risor. It's not good that someone left a fully charged Aether spear."

"Could be that they could not carry more items. Lots of supplies, too."

"Yes, sir, but an Aether spear can protect you more than supplies." Milo persists.

Dimera walks over and chimes in, "I remember Tilor mentioning Atlanda deals with the natives more than most other colonies. Most of the people knew how to use the tools of the natives." Risor signals her to continue. "Well, they would have more native weapons like we had in Altai. For trading or for the trappers when they go into the wilderness. Those weapons would last longer than an Aether spear, which is only good for as long as the charge remains and then is just a weakly built club."

Milo and Risor both catch her point. Milo said, "Yes, I see if you are limited on what you can carry. Why carry these? Maybe two to three for protection against big predators or a tribe that doesn't like you, but outfit everyone else with a weapon that will last."

Risor agrees, "Sounds like a good theory. One I think we will need to consider for Altai. In fact, I wonder how many spears and other items we missed from the abandoned places. Okay, let's load up these supplies and check the surviving buildings near us for more materials."

While half his team starts loading the supplies, Milo leads another group to the nearby buildings. Risor goes inside the closest building to look around.

It is a smithy with lots of tools still on the walls. There are hammers of bronze, iron, and Skor, an alloy the Atlanteans discovered a few thousand years ago. The bronze and iron hammers are probably for trade with the natives, while the Skor hammers would be for the people of Atlanda. Risor notes that they should take all the hammers, but he wonders if they could take the smelter. Altai did not save an Aether-enabled smelter; having one would allow them to make more potent tools than they could without until it ran out of power.

Continuing to look around, Risor notes a few view tablets and goes to investigate. One view tablet is on the top of the table as if it was recently left there. The others are neatly placed on a shelf; their labels identify them about smithy topics. All of the view tablets have a full Aether charge, so they can be useful for some time.

Dimera comes into the smithy and up to Risor. "What is this?" she points at the view tablet on the table.

"I am not sure. Let's see." He turns on the tablet.

Tilor's face appears. "To those that find this, I am Sub-Commander To-golan of the Falcon Claw squadron and the senior survivor of Atlanda. We were struck by a tsunami coming from the northern side of the peninsula with little warning. Most of the citizens were killed or went missing in the initial flooding. Those that remain number eighty-four with many injured. We are trying to reach higher ground as the lands around Atlanda are flooding. We will stay on or near the road for some time to see if someone comes for us. We pray to the Gods that you find us soon. We took what supplies we could carry but do not have enough for an extended time." Then, the screen goes blank.

Dimera hugs Risor, "He's alive!"

Shocked but also happy, Risor hugs her back. After what seems embarrassingly long and, at the same time, regrettably short, they separate.

Blushing, "I'm sorry, sir, I..."

Trying to smooth things over, Risor starts, "No, I didn't mean ... It was the moment. I enjoyed it..."

"Sir, you in here?" Milo interrupts and enters as Risor and Dimera step back. Dimera is still blushing, and Risor also feels the heat rising in his face.

Dimera scopes up an armload of view tablets from the shelf and walks to the door. Passing Milo, she said, "We found Tilor, he is okay." She continues out the door.

Milo stares after her, giving Risor time to use a breathing exercise to calm down when Milo turns back.

"That is great news. Sir, we are ready to leave." Said Milo.

Slapping a hand on Milo's shoulder, "Let's go get our friend."

Reporting to Altai, Risor tells his father, "We will soon go after Tilor and the survivors, but I think we should send another team here to scavenge as much as possible while we can."

"That sounds reasonable. I will ask Lieutenant Skola to provide one Vailixi to make the run there. They will take what we can."

"Father, tell them to go through houses as well. There might be workshops and such in the courtyards that contain some tools we could take. Also, Tilor reported wounded survivors, so could we please have a healer sent as well?"

"Good point, Son. How bad is the town?"

"The peninsula is sinking. The town is pretty much destroyed, with only buildings built in the hills overlooking the town surviving. With the rising sea levels, I don't expect this place to stay viable. It seems a lot of the hills are more dirt and less rock, too, so the waters will probably take them if they continue for a while. Scavenge and abandon it."

"Makes sense. Okay, we will send word when we know which Vailixi will come your way."

"Thank you, Father. See you when we get back."

Later, Risor's crew follows the road, and after an hour, they come upon the refugees. The Vailixi lands near the refugees, and all the crew come out. Tilor comes to the front of the refugee crowd as the crew exits.

The crew rushes Tilor, and many comments are said at once. "Tilor, it's good to see you!"

"I can't believe it."

"Knew you were lucky."

"We got your message."

Laughing, Tilor responds, "I am so glad to see you all."

Things get back to a more serious nature. Risor looks at the crowd and says, "How are your injured and the rest of you?"

"We have no healers, sir. The wounded are in the wagons. The rest? They're mostly shocked and tired," Replies Tilor.

"Okay, I think the best thing to do is get those injured into the Vailixi so that I can get them back to Altai." Then, speaking louder for all the refugees to hear. "The Empire is hurting. I will not lie to you. The people of Altai are trying to gather all who can come to Altai. Atlantis was also hit by a tsunami and has been abandoned. They do not have the resources to help us at this time."

Some in the crowd cry. Others stand in shock.

Turning back to Tilor, "Do you have enough food and weapons to defend yourself? This might take a few trips to get everyone back to Altai."

"Yes, sir, we can turn around and head back to Atlanda."

Clapping Tilor on the shoulder, "Good, Let's get your injured loaded and as many of the old as we can. Then you can turn your party around. It is really good to see you again, my friend."

ALTAI

Risor enters the Council's tent, and his father comes to him. Most of the council is there.

Hugging Risor, "It's good to see you, Son. Are Tilor and the rest of the Atlandeans okay?"

"Our healers are looking after some of the injured and old we brought with us. The rest are heading back to Atlanda to await our return. Mara brought me up to date on New Altai. I figure I need a few more trips to Atlanda."

Councilman Ordo came up to them, "Welcome back, Risor."

"Thank you, Sir. What happened? And where is Fordo?"

Smiling, Ordo said, "With the new deadline, we had to cut short the trip. Another Vailixi came and got us. He and some of his men took a group of 600 out today. They are walking to New Altai. The rest are scattered here and there."

Looking relieved, "Good, glad that is settled. Any issues with them?"

Rosan answers, "No, they seem on board with the situation."

Mara comes into the Council tent." Council, Sub-Commander Naga has reported an attack by Aether weapons at Zuma. He picked up some survivors that reported armored troopers chasing them. Some militia were killed in the incident."

Councilman Ordo, "Is this Atlantis?"

Councilman Stolar asks, "Does Rama have armored troopers?"

Mara turns to Stolar, "No, Rama does not use armored troopers. It was definitely Atlantean."

Risor wants to talk more to Naga, "When will they return?"

Mara replied, "In a few hours, sir."

Rosan, sitting down, said, "This is not good news."

Risor looks at all the council, "No, it is not. So, what is the status of the move?"

Councilman Stolar responds, "We have five long houses completed with another seven within this week. We can house about 2000 people in them."

Nodding, Risor asks further, "How about feeding the people? We can not grow crops because Atlantis will find it."

Rosan speaks slightly louder, "Tolen, please tell Risor?"

Tolen is in the back of the tent reading a view tablet. He stops and looks up bemused, "Sir? Oh, hello, Risor."

Councilman Ordo, "Shilot Dekarn, could you explain about your groundless growing?"

Catching interest in a subject he likes, "Oh, yes, we are building a lot of groundless growing houses around New Altai. They grow food vertically instead of using the ground."

Risor, trying to imagine what magic this is, says, "How is this possible, and when did you come up with it?

Standing and coming to the table, "The Empire has done this for quite some time. Many remote stations are in inhospitable places, and always using Vailixi to send them food is expensive, so we built these systems. Mostly, they run without Aether, so perfect for what we need."

He did not quite understand but accepted his friend's explanation. He said, "Good, so how will we get water?"

The discussion continues into the night.

Six Days After

ATLANTA QUESTO

"By all we cherish, why did you attack them?" Yells Shandar.

Niwa has his head down. Everyone in the Utanor council chamber is silent. "They fired on us and killed Sheena. We lost it. I have no excuse, sir. They are Atlanteans, and we are at war."

Shandar stood near the Speaker's seat where Niwa sat. Anger rose, and he drew his sword into an overhead strike.

"No, Shandar, no!" Yells Todoru, Shandar's father.

Shandar hesitates. He takes a deep breath and then lowers the sword. Looking around, he sees the horror on everyone's faces as they realize he is going to kill Niwa—a comrade and another flyer.

Fighting to keep control of his anger, Shandar said. "You killed the innocent people of Zuma. You killed others who did nothing to us. And you killed them for supplies."

Looking at the rest of the people in the chamber. "What separates us from the Shigar if we take what we want and damn the consequences?" Pointing the sword at Niwa's head. "You have disgraced us and might have started a war between us and the colonies of Alta." Again, looking at everyone in the chamber. "I know the commander of the Falcon Claw, whose family rules Altai. He is an honorable man. They are also Nalos supporters. That means they are not our enemy. We will not act against any other colony." He puts his sword back in its scabbard and leaves the chamber.

Through the chamber's western-facing windows, Tu-ne ominously bellows smoke. As Shandar departs, the volcano starts to bellow an even larger amount of smoke and loud grumbling issues from Tu-ne's direction.

Jolodar, former leader of Moia and now a member of Utanor's council, said, "It seems even the Gods are not happy with our actions."

Talos, one of Utanor's council members, responds, "The Gods are not happy with much of our actions lately. I am afraid, Jolodar, your people are seeking refuge in another place they must flee from. If not for the same reason, the Gods will make us flee."

Dilon, now overall commander of the Utanor ground forces, responds. "My Lords, we have already started moving some of our supplies to a new location further north. Some of our people are building infrastructure and setting the place up for us."

Todoru nods, "Commander, when can we start moving people in that direction? I have heard from our Shilots that Tu-ne might not give us the luxury of moving when we want. Come to think of it, neither might Atlantis."

"We can start moving people in a week. Before then is possible, but they might not have enough accommodations or infrastructure."

Jolodar says, "Commander, if Tu-ne blows, how will we get my people to our sanctuary?"

"We can use Vailixi. It's not as efficient, but we should be able to complete the movement in a few days. We are still communicating with them and could tell them to hold up and build a camp. We would evacuate them from that location. They could build up defensive positions in case the Hu show up."

Another council member, Meiku, asks, "Why do the Gods make Tu-ne wake? What have we done?"

Choka, senior shilot of Utanor, raises her hand. "My Lords, from the reports of what happened last week, we believe the earth is reacting. The weight of the water released in the Rama attacks has disturbed the balance of our planet. We are getting more earth shakes, and the oceans are rising. Tu-ne is not the only volcano going active. Others around Atlanta Questo, and I imagine the world is going active."

Meiku asks, "Shilot Choka, so the Gods are not causing this?"

"I am not sure if they are affecting it, my Lord. They might have the power to mitigate the effects but choose not to, or they might be strengthening them."

Commander Dilon adds, "We also have two Mother Stones. Ours and the one from Moia. We will deliver the Moia stone to the new sanctuary in the next few days. By the way, we have not named our new sanctuary yet."

Everyone looks at each other, not sure what to say.

Shinriki, the local tribal chief of the tribe loyal to Utanor and considered part of the people of Utanor, speaks up. "Why not call it Sanctuary."

"You are always a voice of reason, Shinriki. I think that is a good name," replies Todoru.

Heads nod around the chamber.

Shandar is staring at Tu-ne but not looking at the volcano or the rising clouds of ash. He is still upset with Niwa for murdering the people of Zuma and himself for getting angry enough to strike him down in the middle of the council chamber without a trial.

He hears footsteps and then looks back to see Jolna coming toward him. Her presence lightens his mood.

Looking back at Tu-ne, he thinks about how Utanor must be evacuated, too. Once that volcano blows, it will probably destroy Utanor or make it unlivable. They probably could not clean up the city and defend it from Atlantis. Luckily, Atlantis has not started any attacks against Utanor.

They concentrated on Moia and seemed content to let things go for a while. Shandar thought they might be striking someone else at the moment, and Utanor would feel their sting soon enough.

He feels her hands run up his shoulder blades, squeezing and massaging his shoulders, a tingle at her touch. She kisses between his shoulder blades, then up to his neck.

"Feeling better?" she asks.

"Yes, with you here."

The sun is setting, with a slight reddish glow surrounding it from the ash cloud. Tu-ne's top also glows slightly red, with the ash continuing to bellow forth.

Turning to her, he pulls her in close. He runs his hand up her back and into her hair, opening his fingers and gently massaging her head while they kiss.

Pulling back slightly, he touches his nose to hers and then moves to kiss her nose and then her eyes. "I want you," he says.

She smiles devilishly, licking her lips and staring intently into his eyes. She brings her hands to his face, cupping his face. He drops his hands to her waist, pulling her in closer. His breathing quickens, and she starts to breathe harder, too. The glow of the sunset flashes in her eyes and adds to the mischievous look she gives him. He wants her so much. Leaning in, he kisses her again and scoops her up, planning to take her to their bed.

She stops him, putting a hand to his mouth with a mischievous smile. "Your father asks that we join your family for dinner soon."

Removing the hand, she quickly kisses him and makes him put her back on the floor, moving away. He watches her walk back to the room, trying to recover his composure. "Couldn't you have just told me that instead of driving me crazy?"

Shaking his head and adjusting his clothes, he said, "I will never understand women." He walks back into the room, taking off his shirt. He sighs. "What did the council say after I left?"

He admires her naked body as she decides which dress to wear. Not turning, "We will speed up the schedule for moving to Sanctuary. Oh, that is the name we decided for our new home. Do you like this one?" Holding up a blue dress.

"I like you better as you are now."

Smiling at the compliment. "Hmmm, so the blue dress?"

Sighing again, "As a second choice. Yes." He selects a new shirt. "We will not attack any more colonies, right?"

"No, we do have the supplies from Moia. Father is worried about Atlantis sympathizers causing problems. We think there were still some in Moia when we left. The council agreed to strengthen guards around supplies."

"Hmmm, we might want to strengthen the guard around military targets and the council, too. They might want to disrupt command, especially around an attack."

"You think they will keep after us?" She asks after putting on her dress. They adjust each other's clothing.

"I don't think Atlantis forgives or forgets. Reluctantly, my love, we are fighting for our lives." He looks into her eyes, then takes her chin and tilts her head back.

"With you, I will take on Atlantis alone." Then kisses her.

After the kiss, she pulls his head back down. "Don't do anything stupid that will get you in a position where it is just you."

ALTAI

That morning, Risor comes out of the tent stretching. Many tents around them have people sharing communal fires or going about their business. His mother,

Miana, and sister, Rina, are tending a fire near the tent. Rina notices Risor exiting the tent and runs up to him.

Giving him a big hug, she said," You're finally awake."

Laughing, "It is good to see you too." Still holding Rina, Risor looks up and smiles at his mother, who is slowly approaching them. "Mother." He extends his arm, and they all hug in a group, "I have missed both of you so much."

Miana pulls away some and fusses over Risor's shirt, "Risor, you look so tired."

They break the hug, and Rina puts a kettle on the fire. Miana looks up at Risor. He cups her face in both hands, "You too, Mother. Don't work so hard."

Tearing up, "I have not slept well since... Since it happened."

Giving her another hug, "It's okay, we are all together and safe. It is a new beginning, and we have to be strong. Once we settle into our new home, life will get better."

Miana breaks off the hug, gives a weak smile, and then goes to sit and help with the tea. Risor stares at them both, then joins them at the fire. Rina gives him a cup of tea while his mother makes him a bowl of soup.

Finishing his soup, "Rina, how is Tolen? Have you had a chance to talk to him lately?"

She looks at him with narrowed eyes, wondering if he is teasing her, but then she decides he is not: "I talked to him yesterday. He has spent so much time in New Altai that I don't get a chance to see him often."

Handing the bowl back to his mother, he said, "You two should probably catch one of the Vailixi up there today. I believe Father will go soon, too."

Putting the bowl and spoon in a wash bucket, his mother asks, "When will you come, Risor? I would really like to have our family together." Wringing hands and looking distant.

He looks worriedly at his mother, then Rina. Rina shrugs. He responds, "Soon, Mother, but there is still a lot of work here, and I am the leader of the military. I have to make sure all is well. Soon, we will all be together once the move is complete."

He finishes the tea and then hugs them both. Miana heads into the tent. Risor turns to leave, and Rina catches his arm. "Risor, Mother is not well. She cries all the time. Between you and Father being gone and all that has happened. I don't think she is taking it well."

Sighing, "I have heard that many amongst us are the same. I think it is very hard for them to accept. How are you, Rina?"

"I am fine. I worry and feel better when you or Father are here, but I understand you can not always be here."

Smiling at her, "Soon we will settle in, and then the fun of trying to learn how to live like our friends, the Suda, will be our job. We will be the students."

Looking nervous, Rina asks, "Will we be okay? I hear many say we do not have enough food, medicine, or Aether. Can we live like the Suda?"

Slightly taken back by the desperation in her eyes, "It will be hard, but I think we will learn how to live. We just need to work hard."

Looking slightly placated, "Will we have enough food through winter?"

Grinning, he quips, "If you don't eat like me."

"Me! You are the pig. Gulping down food quicker than can be placed."

With a glint in his eye, he tries to look serious. "You know, Tolen probably wouldn't like a wife who eats more than him."

A flare of anger in her eyes, "I .. Do .. Not .. Eat that much!

Laughing, he hugs her. "I love you little sister, never change."

Stomping her foot, "Uhhhhha, you make me sooooo mad."

Laughing, he walks away as she loses her "anger" and smiles after him. Then her look turns to horror as she realizes he knows about Tolen.

"You knew!?!?!"

Risor enters the Council tent with his father. Subcommande Naga is retelling the tale of how they found Zuma.

After Naga's report, Risor announces to the council, "I will take a Vailixi to a trading post near Zuma. To see if we can find any other survivors. I will go with Naga since his team knows the area."

Councilman Stollar asks, "Risor, do you think Atlantis attacked Zuma?"

"I believe so, Councilman. Mara informed me of the conversation with the First Minister. I believe there will be a surprise three days from now."

Councilman Ordo asks, "Can we ask Subcommander Moza what is going on? Some first-hand information would be invaluable."

Shaking his head, Risor said, "No, I do not believe that is prudent. I am sure Atlantis monitors his communications, and anything we say to him might endanger him and us."

Smiling, Rosan states, "Unless we feed false information."

Everyone looks at Rosan. He gets up and walks to the food table. Everyone in the tent is quiet and waiting for his further explanation.

Taking a drink, "We believe we can complete the evacuation tomorrow. If we leave some supplies and animals behind." Others nod in agreement. "It will make it a little harder, but we should have enough food for our people."

Mara walks into the tent with a view tablet. She stops and waits to be noticed.

Risor asks, "Father, you talked about false information. What did you have in mind."

"Tomorrow night, we have to report to Lord Tolloc. I suggest we tell him we will complete all operations the day after, and our forces will depart for Atlantis." Pausing in thought. "Risor can talk to Subcommande Moza, as well. Tell him he will be happy to see Moza and the others when they arrive. The Shigar will pick this up, reinforcing what Risor tells Lord Tolloc. We should complete our operations when Risor talks to Tolloc. In case they do not buy our subterfuge."

Subcommande Naga, "If they attacked Zuma, why have they not visited us? At least for intelligence?"

Councilman Tonda, "That is the problem. Could it be a rogue Atlantean element that attacked Zuma?"

Risor responds, "That does make sense. Another colony, realizing they are on their own and looking for supplies from others not strong enough to stop them."

Mara says, "That would explain why we have not been visited. They know we are the major base in the area. Should we inform Atlantis? It might help some other defenseless colony."

Nodding in agreement, Risor states, "This is good. Tell them and see if they corroborate the story. If they are surprised, we know we have a rogue element to worry about. If they know about it, they might provide us with additional information."

Putting his drink down, Rosan states, "Agree. I will tell them that you reported in from Zuma."

ALTA CIETO

Zuma is about four to five hours away from Atlanda. The basin is much further into the Tes Atlan, with hills on both sides. Zuma resides on the western side of the basin. The colony was founded to trade with the natives of the coasts and river systems.

While there are no large kingdoms, the region's people are numerous. They live in built-up areas around the rivers in settlements of three to four hundred. The bounty of this region is legendary and highly desirable to the Atlanteans.

Where Atlanda is mostly for mineral wealth, Zuma is for spices, herbs, exotic plants, and animals.

Risor is tempted to follow the coast to see the damage the flooding has done, but in the interest of time, decides a more direct route would be prudent. After flying for almost two hours, the land came into view. Like other coasts, this one is partially swamped, with the hills dry and the lowlands swamped under a few meters of water.

Like many Atlantean cities, Zuma is built in a protected river or coastal valley. Usually, this would offer protection from land assault and destructive storms, but in this case, the tsunami that hit this region proved to be its undoing.

The valley is steep and narrow, and the bay is shallow but with a wide mouth. It funnels up the bay and into the valley. Since this tsunami was caused by a flood and the water kept flowing in, the tsunami was not that high but constant. The destructiveness was caused by the quantity of water in the tsunami and not the height of it.

The team reasons that the front of the tsunami crashed into the lower town and destroyed the buildings, and the quantity of water kept pushing the water level in the bay higher and higher. While not destroying the upper parts of town with a destructive wave, the general chaotic force of rising water levels did the trick. The destruction of the town of Zuma was pretty complete.

Had Risor not experienced the destruction of so many vestiges of power of Atlantis over the last week, he probably would have been awe-struck by the wall of destruction that leveled Zuma. As is, he unemotionally orders a sweep of the town in ever-widening circles to see if survivors can be found. His team acts on those orders in a similarly unemotional manner. Everyone is numb from the destruction and death they encountered over the last week.

Very few buildings survived the tsunami, and of those that did, half were destroyed by fire. There seems to be the local militia building next to one of the roads that lead over the ridge line of the hills behind Zuma. It is smoking, and there are a few bodies around it. Aether blast marks score the side of buildings in that area.

Turning to Sub-commander Naga, "So this is what you found?"

"Yes sir, we were going to stop and bury the dead but wasn't sure if those that did this would be back."

Nodding, Risor said, "That's probably a smart move. Okay, let's get to the trading post."

They fly over the trading post—just three mud huts in a small opening near the river. The Vailixi circles the opening, trying to give the crew a view of the clearing from all angles.

Risor orders, "Keep circling the clearing, Ledo. Something doesn't feel right."

Sub-commander Ledo Naga answers, "Yes, sir."

One of the probers reports, "Sir, look at the building there." She points at the front viewer, to the one building. Two bodies are poking out of a doorway of the hut, looking like a man and a woman.

Risor sighs, "Not again."

Naga responds, "Do you think it is the rebels that Atlantis mentioned to the council, sir? The ones that hit Zuma?"

Risor looks back at the viewer, "No, I believe this is the locals getting back at us for how they have been treated. The Nataku said pretty much the same thing."

The prober asks, "Why do you think that, sir?"

"No Aether spear shots evident. I would assume if our rebels were at it, they would have shot the place up. Like Zuma."

Sub-commander Naga turns, "Nowhere to land here, sir. There is a place a little ways away. Probably about a two-hour walk."

Starting to unbuckle from the command chair, Risor said, "Let's drop there." Pressing a button on the command chair, Risor spoke, "Troopers, prepare for a hike." Then, back at Naga. "Ledo, after you drop us off, keep an eye out for our rebel friends or natives coming to the trading post. They might have scouts out and noticed our arrival."

Risor and the troopers are all armored and move up a jungle path. All are speaking through their suit communications with face masks down. Spread out about two meters apart with Risor, number three in the order.

Trooper Montazla is in the lead. "Sir, we are near the trading post." He calls for a halt and takes a knee.

Straining to hear any sounds that are not natural. Hearing nothing, Risor orders, "Okay, let's see if someone is waiting. Ledo, where are you?"

Ledo responds, "We are about five kilometers south of you. No activity."

"Understood. Keep circling."

The animal sounds continue while the men stay still. Nothing seems to be out there, not with the animals chattering away.

Risor orders, "Okay, let's move in."

They all start moving forward. The clearing is just around the bend, and as Trooper Montazla moves into the clearing, he moves off to the right. Eventually, two troopers move to the left and two to the right. Risor stays at the mouth of the trail.

When all are in position, they level their Aether spears and move towards the huts. Risor stays in his position.

Trooper Onta, leading the two that went right, said, "Hut on the right, clear."

Trooper Montazla, leading the two that went left, said, "Hut on the left, clear."

Risor starts to walk to the center of the three huts. It doesn't look like anyone is waiting for them. One of the men, Trooper Monda, comes around the hut on the left, heading to the center. Risor stops him and points back down the trail. "Stay here and watch back up the trail."

Risor is returning to the huts' center when he hears Trooper Onta say, "Poseidon help us."

Instantly alert, crouching and moving into the center. He sees Troopers Onta and Zario standing at the third hut's door. He calls to them, "What is it? Onta, what do you see? Everyone stay alert."

In an emotionless voice, Trooper Onta says, "It's okay, sir, I found our citizens."

Risor and Montazla move toward Onta's position. Inside is a mass of buzzing flies covering the bodies of approximately twenty people. The bodies are bloated, having been killed days ago.

Risor calls the Vailixi, "Ledo, we have about twenty dead in this building. Looks like they were from Zuma."

Moving back a little, Onta said, "Lucky we are all in suits. The smell would kill by itself."

Looking around, Trooper Montazla replies, "Looks like the natives don't want to deal with Atlanteans anymore, eh, sir?"

Risor has seen enough, "So it seems, Trooper. Team, bring over all the broken wood from the other buildings. Let's give them a burial pry. Destroy the other buildings."

Heads nod, and the troopers go about their work. Risor stands looking at the dead and the flies.

Naga reports, "Nothing over here, sir, gonna destroy the place?"

"Yes. With the place destroyed, none of our people will stay here to be the next target."

Two troopers bring busted-up wooden table or chair pieces and throw them into the hut of death. Flies buzz around, angered by the disturbance. Aether spear shots start destroying the other huts. Risor lowers his spear and shoots into the hut. The others do the same. The hut goes up in flames as the roof falls in, and the wood catches.

The flies rise in a massive cloud that slowly streams up in what Risor thinks is a vaguely human shape and then disperses.

The team moves back down the trail with the huts burning behind them. "Ledo, we are heading back to the clearing. Time to go home."

"Yes sir, will see you there."

SEVEN DAYS AFTER

ALTAI

The next day, Risor walks with his family to the landing field. There is a line of people waiting for their flight to New Altai. An orderly line boards one of the two Vailixi sitting on the ground. A security force member directs Risor and his family to the second Vailixi. Trooper Montazla is stationed at the second Vailixi to guide people where to sit.

Risor breaks away from his family and goes up to Montazla.

"Trooper Montazla, good to see you. So you are a loadmaster as well, eh?"

Montazla shrugs, "Yes, sir, I should have pretended I was asleep when they came looking for volunteers."

Risor chuckles, "Well, Trooper, you should have known you don't volunteer for anything."

Chuckling with Risor, he then grins, "Momentary insanity, sir. I hear we will walk out together."

"Good to hear that. Always good to have professionals protecting us. "

Standing a little taller at the compliment, "Thank you, sir. I believe Onta and Zario will, but Monda just left on that Vailixi." The first Vailixi banks and heads north.

"Glad to have you all on my team again. Well, guess it's time to let you get to work. You have my family on this one."

Looking at Risor's family, "Will take good care of them, sir."

Risor turns back to his family as Montazla starts signaling those at the front of the line to head into the waiting Vailixi.

Risor talks to his family. "Father, all seems to be in order."

"Yes, good luck with Atlantis tonight. Report to us to let us know how it went." They embrace.

"Yes, Father, will do. I believe Tilor will lead the last trip. I will pass it on to him. No sense waking you up for nothing special." Looking around at family and the area around them. Risor sighs and then exclaims, "Guess this is the last day we are Atlanteans, isn't it?"

Miana and Rina come and embrace both Rosan and Risor. Rosan then says, "Time to start a new life."

Risor looks at his mom. She seems so tired. "Mother, I love you. I expect when I arrive, it will be smaller but comfortable with you there."

Looking up at him, nervously wringing her hands. "Risor, take care. Be careful of wild animals." She starts tearing up, "And make sure you eat well."

With a soft chuckle, he embraces her in a big bear hug. "I will be fine, Mother. I have done this before."

Jabbing him in the side, Rina accuses, "When? You don't know the first thing about camping."

Luckily, his father comes to his aid, "He will have Suda and troopers with him."

"Thank you, Father. Okay, time to go. Rina, you too, be careful. Don't walk around daydreaming about Tolen and walk off a cliff or something."

They all laugh at Rina's discomfort. She punches Risor in the ribs, and he hugs her. Montazla comes up to them. They are the last ones.

"Sir, I'm sorry, but it's time."

"Thank you, trooper."

A final hug for all, and they take their stuff to the Vailixi—a lump forms in his throat.

Risor yells, "See you in a few weeks."

They turn and wave, then turn back. The ramp goes up, and Montazla comes over beside Risor. The Vailixi takes off, slowly turns, and then speeds away north. Within seconds, it is out of sight behind the trees. The distinct whirling sound is lost in the sound of the raging river close by.

Montazla remarks, "They will be fine, sir."

"Yes, I agree. When is the next set of Vailixi due?"

"About an hour, sir."

Risor heads up to the headquarters on the bluff. Or what remained of it. The bluff used to have a Vailixi, a council tent, and a military headquarters tent. Now, there is only the military headquarters tent. A few councilmen are still there, but most have already left.

Councilman Stolar looks up and heads to Risor. "Hello, Risor. Did your family get off okay?"

Grinning, "Yes, sir, tears at a minimum."

"I'm glad to hear it, son. It's always tough to leave loved ones for extended periods, isn't it?"

"Yes, I would agree. When will you be leaving, sir?" Risor asks.

"My Vailixi should be here pretty soon. Figure it's more comfortable to sit up here than down there with all the noise and questions I would have to listen to."

"Avoiding one's work, are we, sir?" with a pleasant smile.

"Just last-minute worries and annoyances, thank you."

Risor laughs. "Understood, sir. Well, if you excuse me, I better ensure we know what is going on in each of the last Vailixi." Stolar and Risor shake hands.

"Have a safe trip, Risor. We will need you on the other side."

"Thank you, sir, you too." Risor walks off to the officer in charge.

"Lieutenant, what is our plan?" Risor asks.

"Sir, Lieutenant Toman, I will be your second on our walkout."

"Pleasure to meet you, Lieutenant. I am rather informal when it comes to addressing my people when we are not in front of senior officers. Actually, I guess we will not be in front of any senior officers anymore, so what is your first name? I am Risor." Extending his hand.

Grasping his hand, "I am Neda, sir. I'm not sure I can call you Risor, sir. Just doesn't sound right."

"Fair enough, Neda, it will come when it does. So what are our plans."

"We have the cargo lists for each Vailixi, with most of the supplies already being arranged and positioned. The last Vailixi will take off after your communications with Atlantis."

"Sounds good. How many are walking out with us?"

"Us two, ten troopers in armor, four Suda trackers, eight volunteers, and four trappers. Total twenty-eight, sir."

"The volunteers? What are we looking at? Everyone has to be able to keep up and handle the walk."

"Six of them are teenagers that wish to become hunters, four boys and two girls. The other two are a married couple of cooks. They are smoking the last of the meat and wanted to walk out."

"These cooks young enough?"

"Good shape, sir, no problems there, I believe."

"Good, I know a few of the troopers from the runs to Zuma and Kanesa. I would like to send the kids, Trooper Onta with a few troopers, and some of the trappers or Suda ahead about twenty kilometers. Let them set up a camp. My call to Atlantis will be around midnight, and I want to leave this area right after finishing. If Atlantis sends someone to challenge our decision, I want this place deserted."

"Yes, sir, I will get Trooper Onta on it immediately." Saluting and turning.

"Neda, ensure he knows we should not have a fire after midnight. If he has to cook, do it early and extinguish the flame. If they do come, they will see the fire from far away. Set up off the road but near it and set a sentry on the road to guide us in."

"Yes, sir."

"Oh, and Neda, could we have those that remain do one last sweep of the area to ensure we have not overlooked anything we want to take? This tent should be taken down and put on one of the Vailixi."

"Yes, sir."

The next few hours are uneventful as Vailixi land, pick up their cargo and depart. Through the communications ring, Risor learns that the third walking group has caught up to the second but is still two days behind the first. These groups had left days before to alleviate the number of loads the Vailixi would need to perform.

The second to last Vailixi takes off, and the remaining people put the smoked meat into the cargo hold of the last one. The hold is stuffed with the last remaining items they identified to go.

"I think I am going to be hungry the entire flight," Tilor said.

Dimera laughs, "I think we can snatch a few on the way up."

Risor looks at them and says, "Sure, but I would not eat them now. If you stuff yourself on them now, you might be sick of the smell."

"What I would give for a nice cold beer right now," Tilor said.

"Soon, my friend, soon. Another hour or so for the link to Atlantis, and then you can be on your way."

"Are you okay with forty-plus days of walking, sir?" Dimera asks with a concerned look.

"What is with you people thinking I can't handle myself?" Risor said.

Milo laughs, "You are a weak, spoiled, rich guy. sir."

Neda looks uncomfortable with the teasing of a superior officer and noble, but Trooper Montazla laughs, "Sir, with all due respect, you are definitely not someone who is used to extended hikes."

Tilting his head and looking wounded, "You too, Montazla? Here I was just saying such great things about you."

They are sitting around a good bonfire as they chat. With a half-moon out, Risor and Neda think they will have no problems reaching the camp. Everyone is enjoying the hot meal that the cooks, Jonda and Rana, made.

Risor gets up and turns to Tilor, "Time to perform. Wish me luck." Dimera also gets up and follows him. She will set up the communications link for Risor.

Risor and Dimera squeeze through the overflowing hold to the command deck. Back down the passageway, they can see the bonfire's glow and hear laughter. Risor moves to his command seat when Dimera touches him on the shoulder.

"Our world is changing, isn't it? This is our last night being Atlanteans, right?"

Risor notices she is lovely to look at. It surprises him like a shroud has been lifted from his eyes. Taking her hands in both of his.

"Yes. We are passing a line that we cannot cross back from. We will start a new life tonight."

Nervously, he drops her hand and goes to his command seat. She follows him to his seat, and as he looks up at her, she surprises him with a hard kiss and then hugs him.

Dropping the embrace, she says, "Good luck Risor."

She rushes to her position without a second look back. Completely ignoring him, she busily starts the process of establishing the call. Risor just stares after her in shocked silence over what just happened.

Turning her head but not looking at him, Dimera announces. "Link established with Lord Tolloc."

Trying to gather his wits, "Thank you, Dimera." Taking a deep breath, then looking at the dish. "My Lord Tolloc, thank you for seeing me."

The face of Lord Tolloc comes on the viewing screen. Risor can tell that he is also in a Vailixi. "Commander Tarnor, it is good to see you are finally back at base. How did your missions of mercy go?"

He looks slightly annoyed. Risor surmises, "My Lord, we have just returned from a trading outpost near the ruins of Zuma. There was nothing but death there. It seems the natives no longer show loyalty to us. They left twenty-plus bodies to prove it." Bowing his head, he says, "May the Gods protect them."

Barely bowing his head, "Yes, the Gods take them."

Pausing, Lord Tolloc looks away from the screen. "Commander, when can the majority of your force be reassigned to Atlantis? And how many?"

"My Lord, I believe I can send five of the Vailixi tomorrow with about one hundred troopers."

Smiling, "Commander, that leaves you two Vailixi and eighty troopers. What on earth would you need such a strong force for?"

"My Lord, it is my understanding we have a rebellion that has already struck Zuma. Without a Mother Stone or much Aether, we leave this colony to fend for itself."

"Yes, I saw the report about Zuma earlier today. That is sad news. You can understand the rebuilding of Atlantis is primary."

"Yes, my Lord, how long will our forces be needed? If it will be long term, there are family members who should be moved."

"Thank you, Commander. Yes, please provide a plan to transport them back to Atlantis."

"Who shall I coordinate the move of the civilians with, my Lord?"

"You may talk to your Sub-Commander Moza for coordination."

Acting like he is taking notes. Risor asks, "Shall I come with those being reassigned or continue to lead the forces here?"

"I will leave that to Lady Tomar. She heads the operations against the Ramans."

"Thank you, my Lord. I will talk to her."

A distracted Lord Tolloc nods his head and then breaks the connection.

A smiling Dimera observes, "I think that went very well. Do you think he bought it?"

Stretching as the tension seeps away, "I hope so. I thought I put up a decent enough fight. Reluctantly, we have another call to make." Sighing, "Let's start the fun one, eh? Please get Lady Tomar on the link."

NEW ATLANTIS

Sitting in the command tent in New Atlantis. Lady Tomar is talking to two other commanders when a junior officer comes up to whisper something to her. Sitting in a chair, off to the side, reading a view tablet, Jana watches the transaction.

Lady Tomar gets up, dips her head, and "Gentlemen, excuse me. I have some distasteful business to attend to." The others stand and bow since she is the senior officer.

Jana perks up. Lady Tomar nods to her as she leaves the tent. Lady Jana follows.

Entering the command deck, Lady Tomar sits in the command chair. Jana stands on the other side of her viewer to avoid being seen.

Looking around at the officers on the command deck, Lady Tomar barks, "Out." Once they have all left, she activates the viewer screen, and Risor comes into view.

He speaks first, "My Lady Tomar."

Not bothering to hide her disdain, "Tarnor, I heard you survived. Where are my forces?"

Lady Jana starts pacing back and forth, obviously angry. Will she be a problem, Lady Tomar thinks to herself.

Risor interrupts her thoughts, "My Lady, I have just advised Lord Tolloc that they will be departing in the morning."

A rising anger in her voice, "Lord Tolloc? Who told you to talk to him? You are still part of the military, are you not, Commander?"

"My Lady, I am sorry, but I was away on a mission. The council talked to Lord Tolloc and told me to contact him."

"Very well, so why are you bothering me?"

"My Lady, I would like to know if you wish me to return with the forces tomorrow or to remain here to coordinate the transport of the reassigned forces' dependents."

I don't care what you do, she thought. Then an evil thought came to her, "You may stay Commander. I have no use for cowards. You may complete the task, resign your commission, and stay with the rest of your lot."

Jana's eyes light up.

He responds in a measured, monotone voice, "My Lady, I will stay and complete your orders, but I will return with the last group to resume my duties."

Enjoying his obvious pain, "As you wish, you can resign there or resign here. I care not. You are through, sir." She breaks the connection.

An excited Jana says, "That was beautiful, my Lady. If he comes, I will kill him."

Not paying attention to Jana, Lady Tomar continues staring at the viewer. "Commander, how many Vailixi can you get in the air?"

Taken aback by the question and tone. "I.. Can get...three in the air today. A few more in a day or two. Why? Do you think they will do something?"

"I have a feeling that went too well. You should try to get as many troopers and trackers as you can and go there."

Still looking unsure. "Yes, my Lady." She pauses and says, "I will get things moving now."

She starts to leave the command deck, but Lady Tomar stops her. "Lady Kalin, realize you are probably walking into a trap or will find they have run away."

Jana nods and smiles a feral grin.

ALTAI

The view screen went blank. Dimera returned her headset to the console and got up. She came up behind his seat and put her hands on his shoulders. "Well, that went even better, didn't it?"

Bringing his hands up to hers, he says, "You know, I really wish I would be there to see her face when she realizes what we are up to." He smiles at the thought of Lady Tomar's rage when she realizes she was deceived. "It was almost too much for me not to laugh in her face."

They both start laughing. Dimera comes around the chair and kisses him. "I think she will go into fits."

Smiling, "I hope she chokes in those fits. Oh well, guess we will never know."

Getting a little more solemn, Dimera said, "It is done, isn't it? We have broken away."

"Yes, baby, are you okay?"

"Yes. What will become of us?"

Holding her tight. Risor says, "We will live. We will love, grow old, and have lots of kids."

She hugs him harder. They sit there for a minute or two in silence, holding each other. Finally, she lets go, "Please be safe, Risor. Come back to me."

Risor exits the Vailixi, thinking of what just transpired with Dimera. He sees everyone sitting around the fire. They look up at him. He decides he will need to think about what happened later. Saying aloud, "Alright, everyone, it's time for a walk."

They say their goodbyes, put out the fire, and move the last items into the Vailixi or backpacks. Tilor comes up to Risor. "Sir, guess you will finally learn how to be an outdoor person, eh?"

Rolling his eyes, he said, "Thanks, Tilor. I am sure I will do well. Oh, and have Dimera tell you what transpired. You can relay that to the council. I am sure you will get a laugh out of some of it."

"Yes sir, will do. A good laugh, you say? Okay, that will make the trip north interesting."

"Glad to be your entertainment, my friend."

"Ha, I would love to see you handle a full month of living off the land. Should make for some good laughs."

Clapping Tilor on the shoulder, "Yes, I am sure you would be disappointed. See you in a month, my friend."

"You too, sir. Be careful."

Tilor turns and walks up the access ramp. At the top, he turns and waves goodbye.

"Okay, everyone, let's get started," Risor said.

The team gathers its gear as the Vailixi rises and turns north. Its external lights blink, and then it shoots forward and quickly disappears into the night.

The troopers keep their external lights off while they walk north along the road in silence. There is always a chance that the Atlanteans would have a force already on the way. About two hours later, after a leisurely stroll in silence, one of the troopers turns to Risor, "Sir, the camp is just ahead."

"Thank you, trooper."

A figure walks out of the forest up ahead and turns on his lights. "We have been waiting for you. Have a good meal and a dry, warm place to sleep."

Risor said, "Glad to hear that, could use the bed."

EIGHT DAYS AFTER

ATLANTA NADO

Noko raises his hand for the patrol to stop. Rogat freezes next to him. Straining to hear what Noko hears, he isn't successful. He could only hear the river ahead.

Then he realizes it. There are no other natural sounds except the river and wind in the trees, no animals, and something is in the trees ahead.

The river is three miles from the path up to the stronghold. The stronghold overlooks the only pass over the mountains for a good week in either direction.

Rogat has twenty men with him. He went out with Noko's team because he felt something would happen and wanted to see what it was for himself. It has been three days since coming to the stronghold, and the Greeks should have reached here by now.

The patrol waits on the road, all members down on one knee or prone. Nothing moves before them, but they all feel like someone is watching them. Rogat figures they have stopped out of range of the enemy, whoever they are, or they would have started firing by now.

"Can anyone see anything?" He asks.

Pretty much everyone responds negatively. "Noko, what did you see?"

"Didn't see, but you hear it? No forest sounds."

"Yes, I noticed that. No shooting either. Okay, let's start moving back. Keep an eye out." The patrol gets up and starts slowly moving back. No one turns around.

Over ten minutes, they move back about fifty meters. Then Rogat hears drums. He put his hand up for a stop. There is a darting figure to the left, about 5 meters into the trees, but only for a moment and a distance down the road toward the river.

"Does anybody see movement on the left?" A few positive responses.

One of the troopers. "There was one on the right, too."

Another. "And I can hear drums in the distance." Others confirm that.

"Okay, let us get out of here. Noko, take a group back ten and wait for us to leapfrog you." Then, they start their withdrawal from the river area.

When Rogat turns with his men, he uses his communication ring and advises the stronghold, Tor Sum, of what is happening. One other patrol reports contact as well. Considering this, Rogat orders all patrols back to the stronghold. Apparently, the Greeks and Tugar are coming in from different directions.

Looking back, he sees men coming out of the woods close to the river and a column on the other side of the river. It's way too much for him to deal with now.

They increase the pace to a jog.

That evening, Rogat, in the fading light upon the ramparts, could see the Greeks setting up field works to enclose the stronghold. They were barely in range of the stronghold's Aether Strikers, so the power and accuracy of his side's weapons would be limited.

Nofolin, commander of Tor Sum, walks up next to him, looking up at the stars starting to appear. "Commander, nice night, I think. Too bad the Greeks will ruin it."

"Oh, I imagine they will not start shooting until the morning at the earliest. They will build their field works first. Their leader is a confident fucker. He will take his time."

"Maybe we should use that time to move the civilians out the other end of the pass. We can get most of our people out and lightly man the stronghold. We can even leave most of the horses to give them a better chance to escape once we are all gone."

Rogat didn't answer for a while, turning over the idea in his head. He thought a few hundred old, young civilians and animals would be slow going. How would he get them away without Demetri and his Greek and Tugar warriors chasing him down? Once his Aether spears were used up, it would be swords against their Aether weapons.

"Where would we go, Commander?" Rogat eventually asks.

"Ah, yes, that is the problem. It would be a month or two before we can get south of the mountains near Tes Zeita. Maybe the Greeks and Tugar would be happy to let us go as they would own Atlanta Nado."

As if on queue, Rogat's three misfits show up. Noko looks at the two commanders. "Who would own all of Atlanta Nado?"

Rogat answers. "Do any of you three think the Greeks would stop chasing us if we abandon this stronghold and slip away?"

All three seem to turn over the idea as Rogat and Nofolin look on. Migu looks over the walls at the barely discernible soldiers going about their work well below.

Still looking over the wall, Migu said, "He does seem to have a fondness for you, Rogat. I would imagine he would continue chasing us until he has 'sadly' spiked your head."

Noko nods, "I agree. I think he wants you and those with you destroyed as a personal challenge."

Teado adds, "I think we are the last force in Atlanta Nado, and his taking us out would give him a claim to victory that would be diminished if we escaped."

Nofolin grunts, "So this force needs to be destroyed or paraded in front of their people to show his value?"

Rogat adds, "Maybe not show his value but cement his legend."

Migu smiles. "He does seem to enjoy this too. I imagine without us, he would have to go find another reason to fight."

Nodding, Nofolin states, "Well, we have at least six months of food and water with the valley behind us. And as long as we hold the pass's gate, they cannot get to the other side."

Teado asks, "Commander Nofolin, I have heard some of the locals talk about mountain passes at the back of the valley. Where would they take us, and are they guarded?"

"They are guarded and, in some places, are dangerous, cliff-side paths only wide enough for one person. The enemy will not come that way. The few soldiers with Aether weapons we have guarding those passes would keep a large force at bay for a long time."

Rogat considers. "Maybe we should send a small force to see where they come out and if it is clear. That might be a better direction to fall back to than directly out the other side of the pass."

Nofolin nods. "Long and treacherous the paths are, but they come out on both the north and south side of the mountains."

Migu laughs, "Well, maybe I should..."

Thinking, Nofolin interrupts, "Pardon, Senior Trooper. There are a few hidden valleys that could sustain this many people for a while."

All the men look at him and then at each other.

Teado starts. "We could get the civilians moving that way."

Noko nods. "If we need, we can make it look like they went down the southern pass instead of back through the valley."

Nofolin, catching on. "We could then destroy the mountain paths to block any followers."

Rogat claps his hands. "I guess Demetri will just have to wait to have my head on a spike. Migu, get some men and map out the specifics. Nofolin, if you have any troopers that know the way, please have them go with Migu."

Everyone starts moving.

ALTAI

They woke to a beautiful day and a cold breakfast. Risor stretches, splashes water on his face, and receives a cup of quat from Neda.

"Thank you, Neda, how is everyone?"

"All fine, sir. After you and the rest finish their meal, we can get started."

"Great, how far do you think we will get each day."

Neda chuckles, "Well, Lieutenant Togolan told me to take it easy on you. So we are expecting around fifteen kilometers a day." Tilting his head, "Depends on the terrain once we leave the road."

Risor shakes his head. "I will get Tilor for that. Fair enough on the assessment. Let's get going in thirty minutes."

"Yes, sir."

A few hours into their march, they crest a hill and see storm clouds in the far northwest.

Risor asks, "Neda, will that come our way?"

Looking at the clouds, "No, sir. That has been forming over the last few days after the flood. I am told that the weather is changing closer to the ice sheets because of all the water, and it will worsen over time."

"Ahh. This is good from an air cover perspective but will be harder on us."

"Yes, sir, my understanding is our last few days out from New Altai will probably be in the rain."

Sighing, "So we have that to look forward to, eh?"

Grinning, "Yes, sir."

They travel about twenty kilometers that day before stopping to camp. The idea is to stop early enough to start a campfire before it becomes dark enough to see it from a distance. Jonda and Rana take over the cooking duties, with everyone helping out. They only cook briefly to make warm meat broth, smoked meat, and hard bread.

After eating, Risor uses the time to communicate with New Altai. Luckily for him, Mara answers the call.

Communication rings are not as good as a Vailixi's viewing dish, but they produce a small image over the top of the ring. They are also limited by distance and the amount of power they store.

"Hello Mara, how are things there?"

"Hello sir, all Vailixi have been secured and covered. Everyone is getting settled into their new home. We have heard from the other walk-out groups, and they have all met up about fifty kilometers north of the turn in the road. The path they were on was washed out, so they are looking for an alternative."

"That isn't good. They have about eight hundred-plus animals and carts, right? That has to make them easy to see from the air."

"The council decided we can use all seven Vailixi one last time to get as much as we could out of there. We pulled out an additional two hundred plus some of the wagons."

"How did they look from the air?"

"Lieutenant Togolan did some high-speed passes over them and believes they will be fine as long as someone is not below quarter speed."

"That is not good. Mara tells the walker group to break up further. Maybe a few groups walking in parallel but separated by a few kilometers. If the Atlanteans come looking for us, they will go slowly over the area near Altai and along the road. We need to break up that group to get them moving out of the area quicker."

"Yes, sir, I will advise the council and the walk-out groups ahead of you."

"What else do we have going on?" Risor asks.

"We have had Atlantis trying to contact us a few times, but nothing else yet."

"I bet they will visit tomorrow morning. Then they will find us gone. Please make sure everyone is aware and takes special precautions. I think we will stay in the forest, near the road, for the rest of our trip. It's a shame it will make things slower going."

Smiling, Mara asks, "So how do you feel today, after your march?"

"Why is everybody wanting to see me suffer? Did I give you offense, Mara?"

She starts laughing, "No sir, but it is a running bet to see if and when you will be overwhelmed. Personally, I give you one week."

Risor notices her turning red, "Why Mara, you are blushing."

"It is kind of strange to tease my superior officer but fun."

Sighing, "I guess I will need to prove you all wrong. So what is the bet about? It's not like we have money anymore."

Mara smiles, "Taking over chores for a few days. Care to help me win my bet?"

"Ha, I think I will be fine the entire trip. Maybe I should put in my bet to complete the entire trip."

If a smile can get wider, "Shall I put you in for that, sir?"

"Yes, please do. I will never hear the end of this if I lose, but to have all of you being my personal slaves sounds like a good idea. By the way, how many people are betting against me?"

"Twenty-two, sir. Including your sister." Mara starts laughing at Risor's jaw-dropping.

"Even Rina?" Eyes rolling as head droops in the betrayal. "My sister, too?"

"Sorry, sir, it seems not many people believe you are in shape enough to complete this."

Looking to the sky, "Poseidon, give me strength. Okay, enough of this fun. I will contact you tomorrow night when we settle down to see if you have more information on the Atlanteans."

"Yes, sir, good luck. Remember, you still need to last six more days."

Risor shakes his head and is glad Trooper Onta is coming over to give him something else to do. He bows his head in mock submission to the image of Mara. He breaks the connection with her grin and the twinkle in her eye, somehow seeming to last longer than the connection, as if she wills him to endure that image a few seconds more.

Nine Days After

ALTAI

A few hours after midnight, they hear a Vailixi flying overhead for a short period of time. The guards on duty wake Risor to let him know. Those on guard duty and Risor listen to the Vailixi fly on without stopping. It seems they are following the road in their search.

One of the guards said, "We gave them the slip, right sir?"

"Let's hope so, trooper. Keep an eye on the road, too. They might have dropped off a ground patrol as well." Risor said. "Make sure we keep all noise to a minimum until daylight, when we can see someone coming up the road from a distance."

"Yes, sir."

Returning to the camp, Risor goes further into the woods to contact New Altai.

"Hello, Risor," said Councilman Ordo.

"Good morning, sir. You are up early."

"Right now, we have a council member on duty every evening to ensure we can react to anything as soon as it happens."

"That is good to hear. We have just seen an unidentified Vailixi fly over our position from west to east. No idea if it has gone further north or will turn north. We do not believe they saw us, but we do not know for sure. Could you relay to Fordo's group to let them know to be vigilant?"

"Will do Risor. Will also make sure the town is secure."

"Thank you, sir, we would...." Risor could hear excited chatter from his team. "Something is going on, sir. I will be back in a minute."

He quickly moves back to the campsite as Neda approaches him. "Sir, there is a ground patrol coming up the road. They are still far away but have their armor lights on."

"Okay, let's move the team further back into the forest as quietly as possible. All troopers to the rear, as their armor could give us away with a light reflection." Neda nods and moves off with loud whispers.

Re-establishing communications, "Councilman, we have a ground patrol moving up the road. I will talk to you later, but make sure Fordo's group also knows there are ground patrols. We do not know the strength as of now. Risor out." Risor breaks the connection and moves back into the campsite. Most of the team is already moving deeper into the woods with most of the gear.

"Keep quiet!" Risor hisses as two of the young team members make a lot of noise, their travel bags scraping against bushes. They freeze but then are motioned on by Neda.

One of the Suda approaches Risor. "My Lord, do you want us to move up towards the road to get a better look at them?"

"No, their armor units have pretty good detection capabilities. They might pick you up. Let's stay back a ways and try to see what we can. We don't want to be seen."

"Yes, my Lord." The Suda goes back to his fellow tribal members. They spread out on the roadside of the camp and move off into the forest at a quick but silent pace.

Risor moves back to Neda, "Neda if we are detected, we have to kill all of them as quickly as possible if there are only a few. If there is a large group, we must run hard and fast to avoid them. Understood?" Neda nods as they both turn to watch the road.

Whispering, "Damn hard to see in this twilight and through the bush, sir." Neda said.

"True, but that makes it harder for them too."

Straining to see, Risor notices the light from the armor suits showing up almost directly in front of the camp. The patrol stops where the team goes off the road, and Risor can see at least ten armored troopers. They search the area but do not enter the woods. Maybe there are some signs, or the Vailixi saw something that this patrol will check out.

Risor finds himself holding his breath and squeezing his weapon very tight until his knuckles ache. It seems like forever while they mill around on the road. He is praying to every god that they will not enter the woods.

It seems that at least one of the gods answered his prayers as the patrol falls in and begins to move off further down the road. Risor can finally breathe and is glad for the opportunity, as cramps and anxiety are starting to take their toll.

He has never been in a situation like this outside of a Vailixi and doesn't like the feeling of being hunted.

Once they are down the road, Risor moves forward to the Suda and asks them to split up, two to follow the patrol and two to go the southern way to see if anyone else is coming up the trail.

As the Suda move off, the team reassembles in the campsite. Risor tells them, "Okay, we need to get moving soon. Let's wait for the Suda to return and start moving north. Reluctantly, we will not be able to use the road."

A big, burly, red-haired, bearded trapper approaches Risor, "Suh, my name be Rindoma Talido, but they call me Rinni. Can I suggest a plan?" He waits, and Risor nods to proceed.

"Well now, we going into our territory. I suggest we grab a quick bite and then start moving north as fast as we can." The other trappers nod in agreement.

Risor looks at the group, "We shouldn't wait for the Suda to return, Rinni?"

Smiling, "Well no suh, they find us when they want. But we need to get north a dem troopers fore they cut in the woods. Once in da woods they harder to see. So we can't move quick either."

Neda taps Risor on the shoulder, "Sir, we should hurry to the turn-off before they do. We don't know how well the path is hidden. It might be difficult for an airborne search but easy to see on the ground."

Risor looks at the ground for a second, "How far are we from the turn-off?"

Another trapper, shorter than Rinni by a full head, stands forth, "Jordon, my Lords." Bowing to Risor and Neda. "We are about twelve kilometers south of the turn."

Rinni adds, "Suh, dem troopers will probably bed down for the night a little further up the way."

"Well, we are all awake now, eh? Let's eat something quickly and then head out. Rinni, we will need to give them a wide berth. They are probably nervous in unfamiliar territory and do not know where we are, so they will probably have a good guard up," Risor said.

Neda replies, "Sir, once Rinni and his boys finish their meal, they can head out and start making a path for us. We can finish up and leave after we have eaten. Gorak's Suda will find us easily enough."

"Okay, that sounds like a plan. Everyone should be ready to move out in about thirty minutes. Rinni, you can take your team to start trailblazing whenever you are ready."

Risor takes out the communications ring to initiate an audio-only call to ensure no light emanates. They have already changed communication links, so they should be safe, but maybe they need to change again.

"Ordo here."

"Hello, sir. It was a patrol heading north, ten troopers. We will break camp and start moving north. We aim to reach the turn-off before they do so we can ensure it looks clean," Risor said.

"Risor, good to hear your voice," Rosan said across the link.

"Father, guess they woke you up? We are good. I have the Suda trackers following the patrol, and the trappers will blaze a trail through the woods for us."

"Risor, Fordo reports the Vailixi came towards them just a few minutes ago. He believes they were not detected." Rosan reports.

"Father, we will try to make the cut-off before the Atlanteans do. Further hide it if we have to." Pausing for a second, Risor continues, "Are all walking groups accounted for? I seem to remember they had to detour. Have they turned back north yet? Or hooked up with Fordo?"

A few minutes pause. "They have not linked up with Fordo yet but are heading north off the road. They also have a communications ring and are aware of the situation."

Risor feels better knowing that all loose ends are covered. "Good news. Okay, we will soon start heading north. If we encounter any issues, I will further relay them. If not, I do not plan further communications until we have settled down for the night."

"Okay, Risor, good luck to your team," Rosan said.

Risor thought for a second, "Father, what are the council's orders if the Atlanteans find the turn-off and start following it?"

Again a few minute pause, "Risor, if you believe they will find the path north or have an opportunity to take them out where it doesn't look like Altan did it, then you have our permission."

"Did anyone tell Atlantis about the Nataku breaking away from our alliance?"

Ordo responds, "Yes, Risor, we did mention this. They said there are similar incidents from other native allies. What are you thinking?"

"If we have an opportunity to surprise the patrol, we will destroy it and try to make it look like a native group attacking them."

Neda and many of Risor's team look at him. Rinni starts to laugh.

Rosan said, "Risor if you believe you can do that, that sounds good. Realize, though, that it will be dangerous and could backfire as well. Only do it if you believe you have complete surprise."

"Understood, Father, Risor out."

"Sir, are you actually thinking we should attack the patrol?" Neda asks as everyone closes in to hear what Risor is thinking.

"Yes, if we can. It needs to look like the natives did it, though. We can use an Aether weapon or two since the possibility that natives have taken a few is valid."

Rana, the cook's wife, says, "Sir, will that get us all killed?" She doesn't look happy.

"Rana, I do not intend to have any of us killed. It might happen that some of us will pay the price. I can not guarantee our safety, but I can guarantee that if Atlantis finds us, they will try to kill many of us, if not all of us." Risor looks at the team, one at a time, to assess their reaction.

Some are nodding their heads. Others look frightened of the prospect. He needs to galvanize those he can and ensure those who can not do this are, at least, not in the way.

He continues, "If we can catch them sleeping or out of their armor, we have a chance to take them out quickly before they can inform the Vailixi of their plight. We could make it look like the natives did it out of revenge for the flooding."

One of the teenage boys, "My Lord, we are not fighters. We don't even have weapons, sir."

"Take it easy, son. No one is asking you to fight. It will be up to the troopers, trappers, and Suda to fight. They are all experienced and can handle themselves. Even I don't want to go up against armored troopers because I know they know more than me. If we are involved, we will do our part in a non-violent way. Scouting or playing a diversion." Risor tries to say it calmly enough for the kids to relax. Reluctantly, it didn't work very well.

Rinni jumps in, "It's okay, boy. We take care of them well." His fellow trappers start laughing.

Neda adds, "Okay, gents. I think you have had your breakfast. It's time to blaze that trail."

"No problem, sir." Jordon makes a bow.

Three Vailixi are on the ground around the aeroport previously used by the refugees. Troopers and scouts move around the aeroport environments and through the former camp area. Jana and Dentam are standing around a pile of trash left by the Altai people. One of the troopers runs up to Jana.

"My Lady, there is no one here nor much of import. From what Senior Tracker Hardont said, it seems they left over a day ago."

Jana loses her cool. She pumps her hands in the air as those around her cringe from the outburst. "Curse the Gods! The cowards ran. Burn everything!"

Looking at all the things they could use, like the buildings for lodging, Dentam suggests, "My Lady, we could use here as a base. The houses and things could be comfortable."

The trooper pauses and awaits Jana's response. She goes up to Dentam and backhands him. He falls to the ground.

Staring down at the fallen Dentam, "I would rather freeze to death than sleep where those cowards slept." Looking at the trooper. "Move before I have your guts for a sacrifice." Terrified, the trooper takes off running.

She turns back to Dentam. "If you ever question me again in front of others, I will kill you where you stand. Do I make myself clear?"

Dentam gets up, looking scared, "Yes, my Lady, I meant no offense."

Taking a deep breath, "After they fire those buildings, have one Vailixi follow the road north, then set a watch. The other is to go to the other side of the river and set a watch there. They will maintain contact with us here."

"Yes, my Lady." He turns and takes off running.

Watching him run and gather a group of men, she swore under her breath, "You bastard, where did you go?"

She turns and heads to the closest Vailixi.

As the trappers load their packs, two of the Suda return. Gorak and his partner followed the patrol. They come straight to Risor and Neda.

"My Lords, the patrol stopped about two kilometers north of us. They are camped right on the road, and the Vailixi landed." Gorak and his partner both grin wickedly.

Rinni smiles behind Gorak as he comes up and catches the tail end of the news. "Suh, it sounds like you getting yer fight ya want."

Even Neda smiles. Risor quickly tries to visualize how they are laid out.

"Thank you, Gorak. Can you show me the layout?" he says, pointing to the ground.

Gorak bends down to start drawing. One of the troopers turns on his external light for better viewing. This makes Risor a little nervous that they are using a light that could be seen from a distance. Of course, with the Vailixi grounded and the patrol settled down, there probably isn't much to worry about.

Gorak completes his drawing and looks up at Neda, "Sir, they have two troopers on guard. The rest were starting to bed down when we left." He looks at Risor, "Four of the crew of the Vailixi are also sleeping with the troopers. I think there are more than that in a Vailixi, correct?" Risor nods as Gorak continues, "Most troopers have removed their armor, at least partially, and the Vailixi crew are in uniforms only."

Risor says, "We must get into the Vailixi before we are discovered. If they get off a message before we can silence them, reinforcements will come quickly."

Neda asks, "Sir, do you believe they have more Vailixi in the area that could quickly get here or maybe just this one."

Risor purses his lips, "If it were my mission, I would have wanted more than one Vailixi. If a whole city went silent and had as much force as we had, they would suspect a larger force took us out, or we turned."

Rinni asks, "How do they know we turned?"

Risor looks at Rinni, "Not that they really know we turned, but it seems some of the colonies near the Raman Empire have turned against Atlantis. So they might deduce that we either were slaughtered by stronger forces or we turned."

Heads nod from the assembled group. One of the teenagers raises his hand. "My Lord, if they suspect either of those, then they probably have more Vailixi in the area, correct?"

Risor smiles at the boy and says, "Yes, that is what I think. If they get off a message, we might have a large number of Vailixi in the area with hundreds of troopers scouring the forests for us."

Gorak frowns, "That will make it difficult. Troopers on watch are armored, and that will require Aether spears. Aether spears are not quiet. The others will wake up as soon as we fire, or at least the troopers will." Many of the troopers and Neda nod in agreement. The reason is that troopers are trained to wake and rise with Aether spears at the ready at the first sound of battle.

Neda looks at Risor with worry, "Sir, this will be risky. Getting to them before they can get off a message will be difficult. Is there a way to disable the Vailixi from outside?"

Risor thinks, "Gorak, how close are they camping to the Vailixi access ramp?"

Gorak looks at his partner, and they converse in their language. "It is almost in the middle of the group. Maybe one body length away from the ramp."

Risor smiles and says, "The Gods smile on us. They do not have their shields up, and if they turned them on, they would fry some of those troopers."

One of the young ones asks, "Maybe their shielders are sleeping outside the Vailixi, right?"

Risor smiles, "It's possible, but all crew members who can use Aether can activate the shields or the communications link. They just might not be as good as the people assigned those jobs. Any of them can deflect a few Aether spear shots and activate the communications."

At this time, the other Suda walk into the campsite. They report no other patrol or contacts behind the team. Neda is quiet and studying Gorak's dirt diagram while the returning scouts give their report. Now that they finished, he said, "Sir, since we need to make this look like natives attacked, that will make things difficult without many Aether spears."

Risor smiles, "Actually, we don't have to minimize our Aether spear usage. In fact, we should overuse and make sure we hit all over the place. Rinni and Gorak's teams can use bow, while our troopers will take out the two sentries and the Vailixi."

Looking at Gorak, Risor said, "Gorak, I need you and your men to do the most difficult job. After you fire a few arrows into the sleepers, I need you and your men to take two Aether spears and go into the Vailixi and kill whoever is there. We can disable the shield and the Vailixi, but you must fight it out with the two crew members still in the ship."

Gorak looks quizzical, "Yes, my Lord, but why us?"

Risor smiles, "Thank you, Sub-chief, you will make your tribe proud. I need you because you are dressed as natives. There are recording systems on the Vailixi that will not be disabled. We can destroy the external ones but not the internal ones without giving away our game."

Risor turns to Rinni. "Rinni's trappers can move around the sleepers to kill them, and the teens can come in and pick up supplies and Aether spears. The troopers must stay in the woods so they are not seen."

Looks of recognition play across almost everyone. Neda smiles and says, "So we disable the Vailixi, kill everyone, and steal what we can quickly. No armor?"

Risor sighs, "No, reluctantly. I believe if we take armor, that might also give us away. It will be heavy and seem not worth the effort unless there are those who know how to use it. That would mark us for Altans."

Looking at the hills to the east, dawn is not far off. Risor says, "Okay if there are no more questions, let's get moving. We have to hit them before they are moving around."

Risor watches at the sleeping camp. He and three of the troopers are near the Vailixi. They see the forward guard sitting on the ground with his helmet off and Aether spear on the ground beside him. He looks like he is fighting to stay awake. The rear guard is seated on a box of supplies near the snoring camp with his mask open. He is also fighting to stay awake.

Risor signals the archers of the group to take out the two sentries. The troopers would blast the external cameras and some of the sleeping troopers. Looking in the dark across the road, Risor could barely make out some bodies closing in on the sleeping camp. Neda has led a small group that will hit from the other side of the camp.

Raising his hand, he looks at the troopers, Suda, and trackers with him.

"Now!" Risor hisses. Suddenly, the silence is filled with the thrmpp of arrows taking the two sentries out, arrows sprouting from their unguarded faces.

Multiple arrows go into the bodies of the sleeping victims. Seconds later, Aether blasts strike the sides of the Vailixi and the bodies of the few rising enemies.

After three quick volleys of arrows into the bodies, Gorak and his party rush the Vailixi access ramp. A few Aether blasts hit the Vailixi and those in the camp. Rinni and his trackers are steps behind Gorak's Suda. While the Suda rush the access ramp, Rinni's men move amongst the dead, slitting throats to ensure no survivors.

Risor turns to the kids and cooks, "Go, get all the supplies you can carry. Rinni, after..." He is interrupted by some yelling and a scream inside the Vailixi. All look at the Vailixi. Gorak and his men come out.

"Both are dead. I do not think they got any message off." He tells Risor.

"Okay, everyone back to the woods. Let's get out of here."

TEN DAYS AFTER

ATLANTA QUESTO

The priest finishes his prayers to Poseidon. He hopes he is doing the right thing, as this is what his God wants him to do.

He picks up the dagger and hides it in his robes.

Already done making peace with himself, he stands, fixes his robes, and looks around his room. There is little of a personal nature in his room, liking sparse accommodations. It makes him feel closer to his God. He fixes the chair's position one last time. A smile creeps in as he thinks of the absurdity of his concern.

Nearing the inner sanctum of Poseidon's temple, Poseidon's Well, he greets the guards. He is a priest who is generally in attendance at the Mother Stone. Its brilliant blue radiance spills out of the room off from the Well. A warm blue pulsing that always calms the priest. He feels incredibly calm this time. He knows that Poseidon has blessed this task before him.

Looking around, he notes the three other attending priests. As usual, he greets each in turn and then moves off to the Mother Stone's room. It is a normal practice for priests to link with the Mother Stone to check its well-being. Any variation in the strength of the stone would be cause for concern.

The priest enters the room and closes the door behind him. It is not unheard of, but the door is usually left open. The other priests in the Well look at the door and at each other. Something doesn't feel right, each thought.

The older priest gets up from his position at the Well and walks to the door. He knocks and then enters. The priest is on his knees, praying at the Mother Stone.

"What troubles you, Joto?" Said the older priest.

"I believe Poseidon has talked to me."

"Really, that is great news. But what good or bad does it portend for us?"

"Bad portents, I am afraid," the priest says as he gets up to face the other priest. You see, it described the destruction of this temple."

"Great Poseidon, No. When?" asks the alarmed priest.

"Now," Joto pulls the knife and lunges at the older priest. He catches him in the chest as the other man cries out in alarm. Joto moves beyond the older priest and barricades the door. The others are beating on the door.

Joto turns back to the Mother Stone and starts to pull more energy into it.

The old priest, not dead yet, asks. "Why, Joto, why are you doing this?" Coughing up blood.

"Why? Because Poseidon told me to. I am his instrument of punishment for Utanor and Moia rebelling against Atlantis."

There is a blast at the door. Joto starts to erect an Aether shield at the door. Another blast, and the door disintegrates against the shield.

The trooper calls out. "Shuma, what are you doing?"

The old priest turns his head toward the trooper. "Kill him. He will destroy the temple and the city."

The two troopers start blasting away at the shield with their Aether spears. One trooper turns to the other priests. "Hurry, evacuate the temple and surrounding areas and get more troopers down here."

Joto continues to draw power into the Mother Stone to the point where its glow starts to hurt the eye. Joto can feel that the blasts of Aether are weakening the shield.

The old priest, still hanging on, asks. "Joto, you will be responsible for the deaths of thousands of innocents."

"I told you, Poseidon told me to do this. I will be rewarded for what I do."

"How are you sure you understood what Poseidon was saying?" The older priest asks in a near whisper. Joto can barely hear him over the Aether blast and the soft hum growing in noise with the ever-brightening Mother Stone.

Joto hesitates to consider the message. At that moment, the shield is beaten down, and the trooper shoots at Joto's back.

Hitting him square in the back, Joto goes flying. The old priest sees that Joto releases the power built up, and the Mother Stone starts to throb brightly.

The trooper knows he is dead one second after the Mother Stone starts to throb. The Mother Stone expands, and the brightness is all the trooper can see. Then nothing.

Shandar exits the Vailixi with a stunned look. Fires are raging on the hills near the center of the city. A massive black cloud funnels upward above the destruction. The government complex at the top of the hill is leveled. Below that, most of the mansions of the nobles are covered in smoke and fire but look leveled as well. Further down the hill, the temple to Poseidon is gone, as is most of the merchant district. The people are trying to fight the fires down in the commons district below the merchants.

Jolna runs to him. Soot streaks her face. "Shandar, they're dead! All of them." She laments.

"Who?" a ball of fear starts to gnaw at his stomach. He fears the worst. She falls into his arms, crying and babbling incoherently about different people. "Jolna, calm down. What happened?"

She continues to cry uncontrollably when Lee Na runs up to them.

"Sir, I am sorry." He said.

"Lee Na, tell me what happened. I can't get her to make sense."

"I am sorry, sir, but Poseidon's Temple was destroyed, and the blast took out a large area surrounding the temple complex." He stops to let that sink in.

Shandar realizes what he is saying. "My family?"

"I'm sorry, sir. We haven't been able to get near your home yet. The flames are still too much."

Stunned, "What happened?"

Jolna tries again to talk but can not. He holds her close to him, letting her bury her face in his chest. He looks at Lee Na, "Her father?"

"Is alive, as are some of the other council members who were in the council chamber. Its strong structure withheld the blast. We were able to land and rescue a few people around there, but the flames from below forced us to leave."

"Blast," Recognition dawning. "The Gods, the Mother Stone?"

"Yes, my Lord."

"Where are the council members now?" Shandar asks as Jolna continues to sob into his chest. She is quieting down, so he imagines she will be back soon. He is hoping she will recover quickly before the idea that his family might be gone overwhelms him. Subsuming his feelings to his duty, he realizes he might be the new Lord of Utanor.

Lee Na points to the aeroport. "We moved all survivors to the squadron's office for now."

Nodding to Lee Na, he lifts Jolna's face to look up at him. "Hey, I need you. Are you with me?"

"Yes, I am fine. But your family."

He kisses her forehead and then places his forehead against hers. "There will be time for that." A slight tremor in his voice, choking up with emotion. "I can't do anything for them now. I can do something for our people."

She nods, wipes her face, and looks at him expectantly. She is his strength and usually the stronger of the two. She is close to his family, and he knows she greatly cares for them. She believes they are gone, which does not bode well.

He pushes away further thoughts of his family. It is time to act and see what can be done, especially if this was not an accident.

Miko, Shandar's second, walks toward them from his Vailixi. Shandar yells to him, "Get the squadron in the air. I'm not sure if this is a precursor to an attack, but we can't be caught on the ground." He looks to Lee Na. "Get your craft in the air, too. Miko will lead."

Lee Na nods, looks at Jolna one last time, and then runs to his Vailixi, yelling for the crews to muster. Most of their crews are standing in shock, staring at the fires burning in the city.

Shandar walks Jolna to the squadron's office to see her father, Jolodar, and the other surviving council. In the distance, the squadron shoots into the air. Shinriki comes jogging up with a few of his warriors.

"My Lord, the Awane are here to help your people. I have sent most of my people to help with the fires. Some of my warriors are patrolling the surrounding hills." he reports.

Shandar bows, "My thanks, Chief. I'm going now to talk to the surviving council. Come with me."

Shinriki and his warriors fall in step behind Shandar and Jolna. Walking, they pass some of the hangars that Vailixi normally parks in. Since the blast destroyed the healing center, they are now acting as temporary field hospitals. From what Shandar sees, there are not many Priests of Aceso, the God of Healing, present.

Shandar lets out a sigh when he sees Mita Torgar, the head priest of Aceso, and his friend. Mita notices him and waves him over.

"Mita, I guess your temple was destroyed too. How did you survive?"

In a sad voice, "My Lord, I was in the council chambers when the explosion occurred. I believe only I and my two attendants are left." He looks sadly at the crowds of people in pain. Here and there, move the few volunteers and his people, trying to comfort them. "I am afraid we will lose many of them before the night is through. We have nothing really to ease their suffering."

Jolna speaks up. "Shandar, we have priests and medicines with our people." Shandar inwardly smiles. The need to act and help brought his love out of her funk.

Shinriki nods and turns to one of his men. In their language, he tells him to head back and bring their healers and medicine. The man starts off at a run.

Shandar yells. "Stop." The man stops and looks back, unsure what to do. Shandar turns to the gathered group. He uses his communications ring to call Miko. "Miko, get me two Vailixi down here. One will take an Awane to their village, bringing medicine and healers back. The other will pick up Jolna and go to the refugees of Moia. They will bring back medicine and priests of Aceso."

He looks at Jolna, who is about to protest. "Jolna, I need you to go and get the medicine. They might not like the idea of giving up lots of their medicine and priests. You are one of their leaders. Take three Vailixi with you."

She nods—a look of determination in her eyes.

The two Vailixi land, one being Jolna's Vailixi. Jolna hugs him and then runs to her craft. The Awane warrior follows. Shandar's party continues to the squadron office.

In the office, they met Jolodar and the other council members who survived. Ground force commander Dilon is also there. Some of them are bandaged up, showing that they did not completely escape the violence of the explosion. Shandar explains what he did to get medicine while they retell the tale of the explosion.

Dilon said, "So until we can get the fires under control, we have to operate on the assumption that we lost our Mother Stone and all the priests of Poseidon."

"Can we still harvest Aether?" Asks Talos, one of the council members. Many people start to speak at once. Concern for the tools that use Aether, how will the healing work, and what about the military? Too many questions.

Choka, the senior Shilot or scientist of Utanor, raises her one good arm for silence. In obvious pain, "We have Moia's Mother Stone with no senior priests of Poseidon. Those from Moia are not senior enough to produce all the Aether we need. We can produce enough Aether in a week to charge one Vailixi."

Silence. Shandar and Dilon completely understand the implications of her statement. They can not defend Utanor for more than a few attacks unless they get a lot of time to recharge the Aether cells on the Vailixi.

Shandar is about to mention this when the ground starts to shake, and a deep rumbling surrounds them. Cracks in the walls and ceiling are heard and seen about the same time. Everyone starts screaming or shouting. Many stumble into the walls or fall to the ground as they try to run for the door. Eventually, they scramble on all fours for passage outside. The building is a single-story structure, but being shaken like it is is very unnerving.

Shandar makes it out just in time to see that Tu-ne, the active volcano seen from Utanor, blows its top. The mountain is still distant, but that is not very comforting when the upper portion erupts upwards in fire.

The ground stops shaking minutes after it starts. The squadron's office and most buildings at the aeroport are still standing. Looking back into the city, Shandar sees that many of the buildings not destroyed in the blast are flattened now.

Meiku, one of the elder council members from Moia, cries out. "Poseidon, what have we done to deserve your anger?!?"

Choka, standing next to Shandar, quietly said, "It is not the Gods that did this."

Shandar looks at her. "Shilot, what do you mean?"

"I believe the Aether blast caused the quake we felt that made Tu-ne erupt. The power of Aether is a force of the world. The overload and explosion must have set off other powers."

Meiku staggers up. "You say the Gods are not angry? What madness is this? You know more than the priests?"

Meiku looks slightly crazed. Shandar has had enough; he is worried this will get violent. He puts his hand on Meiku's chest to hold him from Choka.

"That is enough, Meiku. There are powers at play that we do not know about, but we know we must survive this."

He fully imposes himself between the two. Dilon, seeing what Shandar is doing, gets up and walks up to them. He also stands beside Shandar. Meiku still looks daggers at Choka but knows he cannot challenge these two. He backs off.

Shandar takes this as a sign that he needs to instill order and decides it is time to claim his father's leadership role. "People, it is time for us to abandon Utanor and go to Sanctuary."

Dilon turns and salutes Shandar. "Yes, my Lord Kotan. The military acknowledges you as the leader and will obey." Shandar, sharing a look of appreciation to Dilon, returns the salute, and Dilon moves away with some soldiers.

Jolodar walks up to Shandar. "I am sorry for your loss, my Lord." Then, turning to all. "I agree with Commander Dilon. It is time for a single leader during these terrible times. I say the council should confirm Lord Kotan as Lord of Sanctuary."

Choka agrees.

Talos agrees.

Shinriki agrees.

Meiku looks Shandar in the eye. "I also agree but think we need to appease the Gods."

Shandar approves. "How do you propose we do that, Meiku? We don't have any priests of Poseidon around to tell us. Should we do it now or in Sanctuary?"

Meiku is about to answer when Jolodar interrupts. "In Sanctuary, my Lord. We all declare you Lord of Sanctuary. A blessing for your leadership should be done there."

Meiku agrees, as do all the others.

Shandar nods. "Then abandon Utanor to Tu-ne and Atlantis. May the Gods bless this decision."

ALTA

Jana's hatred for Risor and his people threatens to consume her. She stands there, looking at her people moving amongst the campsite's dead. One of her remaining Vailixi flew north along the road.

Lord Dentam comes up to her, "My Lady, from the marks, it seems there were a lot of wild shots. Some natives or rogues from Altai probably got the spears. They took all the Aether spears, which were not damaged."

Shaking her head, "This was an attack by those cowards."

"My Lady, the arrows? The badly aimed blast marks? Do you think they are that clever?"

"Of course they are. They are cowards, not idiots. That bastard, Risor, would know not to challenge us directly."

One of the trackers, Hardont, and a trooper approach them. She turns to them, ignoring whatever response Dentam is going to make. They bow to her.

Hardont speaks first, "My Lady, there are blasts on some of the trees to the right side of the road. Also, there are armored footprints on the left side."

The trooper bows again, "Also, my Lady, the internal cameras show locals attacking the crew. They look like Suda. The local allies of Altai."

Beside Jana, Dentam challenges the trooper. "I am sure you are an expert in these things."

In powered armor and able to crush the skull of the man insulting him, the trooper gives the lord a flash of anger. This quickly fades as the trooper uses a subservient tone,

"My Lord, I was stationed here and worked with the Suda. These people look like Suda warriors."

Dentam is about to say something when Jana decides to end this. "Enough! Trooper, thank you. I believe you. And you, too, Senior Scout. Altai has rebelled against us."

Turning away toward her Vailixi. "Bury them. I need to report this to Atlantis."

Seated in her chair, Jana sits inside her Vailixi. She is waiting to establish communications with her mentor and leader, Lady Tomar.

Lady Tomar's visage comes onto the view screen. "My Lady, Altai has rebelled. They have wiped out a patrol and Vailixi."

Lady Tomar sighs, saying, "I was hoping I was wrong. We can only afford to send a few more Vailixi and about 100 troopers."

Jana asks, "Will you tell the Emperor?"

"Yes, things are falling apart. Expect your forces tomorrow." She shuffles some papers. "Oh, and Lady Kalin, do not fail me."

TWELVE DAYS AFTER

ATLANTA NADO

Yalana winces as another explosion rocks the stronghold's walls. Rogat gets out of his seat and walks to her. Putting his arm around her, "Yalana, are you okay?"

She looks back at the children. They are sleeping peacefully. Luckily, the Greeks are still targeting the lower walls that block free passage between both sides of the pass. The kids got used to it, but Yalana has not.

"We are trapped, are we not? They will not stop until we are dead or prisoners." She states. There is fear in her question.

He wraps her in his arms, giving her a big hug that crushes her against him. "Like I said, honey, we must move everyone along the mountain paths. You will need to go soon."

"I don't want to leave you again." She whispers.

Only in the last two days have they consummated their relationship. There was no priest to give a proper invocation to the Gods, but Rogat figures it was still good enough. Mila and Telko were happy, and so seemed Yalana.

The Greeks had not fired on them for most of the first two days. More of their numbers joined the camps over the last two days. Once Rogat and Yalana had made love, the Greeks had to go and spoil everything by starting their bombardment.

Since then, Yalana has become unnerved. Rogat figures she worries about her kids and herself, but now that she has shared her bed with Rogat, she has to worry about him. And he tends to be where the trouble is greatest.

"Yalana, I need you and the kids to go. We will follow but must ensure the Greeks can not follow us. We have a pretty good plan for blocking them."

She pushes away and then looks at him with fire in her eyes. "You had a plan to get away from them before, but they found us."

"Uh, honey, we just had a plan to get away from them. They knew where we were going. That is different."

"How is that different? They didn't stop." She is tearing up with frustration.

Rogat gives her a little space as he tries to devise a different path to logic. She is stressed out and does not want to hear logic.

Boom! Another explosion against the wall. She jumps in surprise and throws a punch at him.

He catches her punch and pulls her struggling form against him. This time, he gives her room to punch him in the chest with her hands. She is not strong enough to hurt him, and as long as he doesn't give her enough room to hit his face or private parts easily, he figures he would give her a chance to wear herself out.

She took the chance with gusto. She didn't wind down for a good five minutes. Silently giving thanks to all the gods, he was starting to get sore from the pummeling.

As luck would have it, Migu walks in during the pummeling. "Rogat, we need... Oh, sorry." He turns around as Yalana stops hitting Rogat. Rogat turns to see Migu rocking on his heels, waiting to be told it is okay to turn back around.

Sighing, he knows he will hear about this later. "Migu, why are you here?" Yalana untangles herself from his arms and moves to check on the children.

Migu looks hesitatingly at her and him, then quickly moves to him. Whispering, "Another force has appeared on the southern side. Commander No-folin is requesting your presence."

Cursing the Gods, Rogat grabs his sword. "I will meet you outside." Migu nods and leaves.

Turning to Yalana, "Honey, start packing up. We will probably move everyone today to the mountain passes."

He finishes buckling on his sword and turns to leave. Then stops and turns back. "I love you, Yalana. And I will do everything possible to make you safe and return to you."

Not looking at him, she nods.

He waits a few seconds and sees she will not look at him. He shrugs and heads out the door. Migu is waiting a short distance away. Rogat heads to the ramparts, and Migu falls in step beside him.

Migu said. "So that is what love is all about? Think I will stick to whores."

Without thinking, Rogat turns quickly and punches Migu in the mouth. Migu hits the wall and slumps on the ground. A bloody mouth with a missing tooth smiles back at Rogat.

Rogat is shocked he hit his friend, but then. "You have no idea how good that felt."

Spitting out blood. "You're right, it fucking hurt!"

Offering a hand to help him up, which Migu took. "I told you one of these days."

"Ya, but today? With the enemy cornering us, you had to get sensitive on me today?" They both start laughing and then continue on the way to the rampart.

At the rampart's top, Rogat meets with Nofolin and his friends. Below to the south, a smaller army than what is now gathered north of the pass is starting to set up.

"I don't think the gate will last long," Teado said, looking at Migu. What happened to you?"

Migu spits out a little blood. "Don't ask."

Noko opens his mouth when Rogat turns to Migu.

"So we have five choke points before the first valley?"

"Yes, but I would move past that to the second valley. Another four choke points and a cave system need to be negotiated. We can block off the cave system to keep them out."

Nofolin smiles, "Well, what are we waiting for?"

Thinking of Yalana and how unsettled she is now. "How large is the second valley? Comfortable for us? Is the valley away from the cave?"

They all look at him like he is crazy. Quickly, recognition of who Rogat is asking for comes to Migu. "Yes, there are still two choke points between the cave and the valley."

"Good, okay, Teado and Noko, get your men moving the civilians towards the mountain pass. Don't give them much rest until you get them to the first valley."

Migu speaks up, "Rogat, that is a far distance."

"I understand, but I don't think we will have more than a week to move. I imagine there will be an assault at the end of the week. I have heard that the priests of the Greeks and Tugar could communicate over distances."

Noko asks, "Like our communications rings?"

"I am unsure but don't want to take a chance. I imagine we will start getting pounded once they get their Air Bows in position and behind some protection."

They all turn to go. Rogat looks between the two groups. The southern force continues to prepare their field works while the northern force continues to pound the pass's gate.

Turning quickly, "Nofolin, could you order smoking bales to be thrown over the walls on both sides? We need to keep up a steady stream. Let's get the pass covered in smoke to hide our movement. And it will give them something to worry about."

Nofolin nods and follows the others down.

ALTA

The team beds down around a few trees. Most have already fallen asleep. A few of the troopers are in their armor and standing watch. Risor checks the watch and then decides to report to New Altai. Getting under some low-lying branches, he uses the communications ring. Tilor's face appears.

"Sir, good to see you. What is your status?"

Risor said, "We are heading southeast towards the foothills. We will probably continue that way into the foothills. Then turn north. If the Gods will it."

"Let it be so. You have everyone worried. The other groups report hearing quite a few Vailixi. We have not heard anything here, but we are already limiting the groups that leave the city."

Nodding his head, Risor agrees, "Good. We had three or four Vailixi searching for us today. They dropped at least two groups of troopers. Maybe the same group, but I doubt it."

Chuckling, "Wow, you must have pissed them off."

Taking up the chuckle, too, "I think that is an understatement. Maybe I did piss Lady Tomar off when I said goodbye."

"Did you give her a kiss? Looks like the old bag wants a memento of your skin."

Realizing that he had not laughed in days, Risor calms down. The tension melts away, "Maybe I didn't think she had it in for us that bad. Anyway, we will try to lead them away from New Altai."

"Good luck, sir. When do you think you will communicate again?"

"Not sure, but probably in a few days. I need to conserve this ring's power."

They finish their talk, and Risor goes back to the sleeping camp. Luckily, there were no further flybys that night.

Jana sits at a table reading a view tablet while others move around the tent. A map on the table with soldier and Vailixi markers is circled, as are Altai and the road area where the attack took place. Other smaller circles are further north and east of the attack.

The whirling sounds of a Vailixi are heard and then stop. Afterward, Lord Dentam comes into the tent.

Sitting next to Jana, Lord Dentam says, "My Lady, that was the last of them. All teams have returned."

"So, no further findings?" She gets up and studies the map.

Looking between the map and her, Dentam gets up and points to the circle north of the road. "We found some equipment here but could not find where they went afterward."

"They backtracked. Did you look back along the path?"

"Yes, my Lady, but still nothing. They must have backtracked quite a ways."

Sighing, "Obviously, you idiot. Tomorrow, take a force up there and search all the way back here if you must. Another force will search north of there. I will take one Vailixi and follow the eastern contact."

THIRTEEN DAYS AFTER

TES ZEITA

Lena didn't know what to make of Kala's submission to Gainor. He is kind compared to many of the other Greek warriors on this island. It has been nearly two weeks since their capture and Kala's loss of Fortos. She and the kids took it hard.

She has tried her best to keep the kids and Kala going. In a sense, Lena is happy that Gainor made Kala smile. Many of the other village women and those captured from elsewhere also submitted to the Greeks. For the most part, even the assholes did not force themselves on the women. Their leader, Deros, is an honorable man.

Reluctantly, he also has his eye on Lena. Lena knows that her life will be much easier if she submits to Deros. Those who do not have a guardian tend to have more slave work. It is still not as bad as the men or non-Atlanteans. The Greeks give Atlantean slaves easier work in case they could get a ransom for them. War is war, but money is money.

They are at the Greek raiding camp. The Greeks are generally not big city people. There are cities, but mostly, these are only a few thousand people. Most of the Greeks live in villages.

Many villages would gather to raid. The men would set up a raiding camp away from the villages. Here, they assemble and head out. If an enemy follows them back, they will hit the raiding camp, not the homes of the raiders.

Usually, the raiders stay at the camp for a few days to weeks after they return. If no one hits them, they disperse with their loot and slaves.

Gainor leaves the hut, turning back with a smile at Kala. She is fixing her clothes before the kids come back in. Lena had entered a few minutes earlier and caught them still enjoying their moment. She shoos him away so the kids can come in and eat. Again, Gainor, being a nice guy, wants the kids to like him, so they try being discreet—to a point.

"Honestly, Kala, can't you go to his place? It would be easier for the kids." Lena reprimands her.

"You don't like him, do you? You think I am terrible." Kala starts to get teary-eyed.

"No, Kala. In another place and time, yes, maybe. But I understand your pain. It is not easy."

"Deros would make it easier for you if you smiled for him."

More angrily than she wants. "Never!" She tries to calm herself, especially since Kala recoils visibly and they both can hear the kids approaching the entrance. "Tilor is still alive, and I have not given up yet."

"I have no such hope." Sniffling, Kala tries to hide her face.

As the kids enter the hut, Lena puts a bunch of dishes into the kid's arms before they can see their mother. "Go wash these."

After some sour looks and a momentary complaint, they leave. Lena turns to Kala, who is wiping her eyes. "I am sorry, Kala. We must do what we must. You have Gainor, but I still have Tilor, and I will be his."

Looking up at Lena with slightly red eyes, "You are right. There is still hope, even if it is small. I will do what I can with Gainor to protect you."

Lena goes to Kala and hugs her. "We will do what we can to protect each other and the kids."

ALTA

Trekking through the forest's underbrush was hot and hard work. Risor could see the glint of the sun hitting the river through the trees. He looked forward to a cool drink and a dunk in the water. Rinni and his team, scouting ahead, were already enjoying the coolness of the river when the whirl of a Vailixi could be heard in the distance.

Neda yells, "Rinni, get back further into the woods."

Trooper Onta turns to the kids, "Everyone down." Everyone listens and drops immediately.

The Vailixi hovers over the river a little downstream of where Rinni's group is hiding. Risor and Neda make their way to where Rinni's trackers are waiting. They watch together as troopers and scouts jump down the approximately one meter into the water. They all start moving further down the river, away from where Risor's team is located.

Once the Vailixi and the patrol leave the area, Risor stands up and says, "Rinni, do you think they can see our tracks?"

Grinning back at Risor, "Nah, Gorak and hem boys ar good at covering ar tracks."

Another tracker, Jordon said, "Sir, that is a ford. Look how the water only went to their knees. We can cross there."

Nodding in agreement, Risor replies, "Good catch, Jordon. Okay, we wait a little longer to make sure they disappear."

Over the next few hours, Risor's team silently waits for the enemy to move away from the river's ford. One of Gorak's scouts was detailed to follow the enemy to see where they went.

When he returns, he reports, "My Lord, they continued south. Over an hour away by now."

Relieved, Risor responds," Okay, let's cross. Montazla, you take your section over first and set up a perimeter on the far bank."

Pointing at Onta. "Onta, you stay here and set up a defensive perimeter on this side. Once everyone else is across, your troopers can quickly move across."

Montazla, right hand over heart, nods. "Yes, sir. Okay, gents, let's move out." He and his four troopers move into the river.

Neda tells everyone else, "Everyone, stay down until they are across."

Montazla and his troopers quickly wade across. At the same time, Onta's troopers spread out around the remaining team members and got into good defensive positions.

Onta opens his mask and softly says, "Sir, they are ready."

Montazla's team starts getting into positions on the far side of the river.

Risor looks to Neda. "Okay, Neda, you and Rinni lead across the kids and cooks. Gorak's people and I will come across when you are across."

"Okay, Sir."

Neda's team is about halfway across when they hear the whirl of a Vailixi. Everyone freezes.

Those in the river are clearly scared. Risor yells to them. "Act normal. Wave to them. Do not run." Turning to Onta, "Get your men ready to fire on the Vailixi. Tell Montazla to do the same. On my order. Stay down until we are ready."

Risor, Gorak, the Suda, and Onta's troopers line the bank under cover. They have enough Aether spears for all to use. Montazla does the same. Rinni removes his cloak and gives it to Neda, who is wearing a partial uniform. The whirling gets louder as a Vailixi comes towards them from downstream.

Neda and the team stop crossing, turn towards the Vailixi and wave. The Vailixi moves close to Neda's team, drops its nose up/down once, then slowly turns away and starts to head away.

Risor knows they know who the team is, "They made us, FIRE! Neda RUN!"

Risor, the troopers, and the Suda open fire with Aether spears. Montazla's troopers do the same. Neda and the team start struggling towards the far shore.

The Vailixi takes enough blasts close up that one of her engine pods explodes. Being turned away from Risor's team, it can not return fire, and since it is damaged, it can not turn or speed away. The wounded craft drifts to Risor's riverbank, about 100 meters downstream. There, it roughly lands.

Yelling at all of those with him, "Okay, let's move across as fast as you can. Fire as you cross. Onta, tell Montazla to get Neda and Rinni's men the extra Aether spears. I bet they have troopers in there."

As Risor's people break cover and start firing at the crashed Vailixi, the access ramp opens, and eight armored troopers come out with some of the crew.

One of the kids goes down, thrown backward by a blast.

Two enemy troopers also go down under a barrage of fire from Risor's people. Then, one of Onta's troopers goes down—another from Montazla's side, then a tracker.

Jana, feeling a massive headache coming on, feels the gash along her forehead from the crash. Dentam is on her viewer. Aether blasts come from the hold below with screams of pain.

Yelling and angry, she jabs a finger at the viewer, "Recover your damn people and get over here now!"

"Yes, my Lady, it will take some time. I will dispatch a Vailixi immediately."

"Hurry, you fool, they will get away." Pointing at the communications officer. "You stay and guide in the help. The rest of you come with me."

Coming out of the Vailixi access ramp, Jana is almost hit by a blast. Five of her troopers and two of her crew are already down. Another trooper is firing, but his arm has been blasted away. In the river, floating by her Vailixi is a teenage body. Another one, an older man, is upstream of them but floating down.

In the distance, she can see the enemy. Aether blasts come from the far bank, and a group of armored troopers and unarmored men are crossing the ford.

One of the unarmored men turns and fires his Aether spear at Jana. The blast causes Jana to move to the side. She recognizes who it is—Risor—and her anger blooms.

"You! You bastard, I will kill you, Risor!" Without regard for her safety, she moves forward, shooting at Risor, but it is not very accurate.

One of her troopers grabs her and pulls her down to cover. He lifts his mask to speak directly to Jana. "My Lady, I beg you, be careful. We are outnumbered and need your leadership."

In a murderous rage, "I will kill him." She shrugs off the trooper's attempt to keep her undercover and is thrown off balance as a few blasts hit near her.

The trooper pleads, "Please, my Lady, we must wait until we get reinforcements."

Her force is further reduced as two troopers and another member of her Vailixi crew go down. They can not win, and she sees that now.

Calming herself, "You are right. We will wait."

All surviving members of Risor's team squat under the banks rise on the far side—all of those who lived. An Aether blast explodes a tree near one of Rinni's men. The man gets thrown into the group of huddled kids, and Rinni cries out in pain. One of the troopers checks the downed man and shakes his head in the negative. Rinni is holding his face where splinters from the exploded tree peppered his face.

Risor looks at the dead tracker, then back at the ford. Those troopers remain in the ford. Their armor is too heavy for the current to move them downstream. The two kids, one Suda and one tracker, that were killed in the river had already moved downstream.

"Let's get out of here. Gorak, get your people out front and get us a trail away from here."

Gorak and his men move out quickly, with the kids and cooks following. Rinni's team moves next, with the troopers bringing up the rear. A few shots continue from the other side.

One of the troopers said, "Sir, we should move back. They are still firing."

"You are right trooper. Let's go."

They start moving further back into the woods, and the enemy fire stops with Jana yelling again.

"The Gods curse you, Risor. I will hunt you down and kill you! You hear me. You can not hide. I will find you and kill you and your family. All of you!" Some last Aether blasts.

Neda looks at Risor, "Sir, do you know that person?"

Sighing, Risor nods, "More than I wish. That is Lady Kalin of the Wind Riders. She is a vicious lady apparently sent here to stop us."

With face mask up, Trooper Montazla chuckles, "Seems she has a special place in her heart for you." The other troopers start laughing at that.

Risor joins in, feeling relieved but tired, "You have no idea."

Soft rays of sunlight filter through the dense canopy, barely reaching the forest floor. The trees tower over them like ancient guardians, protecting them from death above as the group trudges wearily through the underbrush. Exhaustion is plain on their weary faces, evident that the mad dash to get away from the river has taken a toll.

Neda approaches Risor, "Sir, we need to start hiding our tracks."

A patched-up Rinni chimes in, "Even Lordy Neda can track us with the mess we made." Many in the team give a tired laugh.

Risor turns to Gorak, "Gorak, what are you thinking?"

Rubbing the stubble on his chin, he said, "I think we should turn east towards the mountains. Go slowly with care of our trail. Find a place to rest and let the enemy calm down."

Trooper Onta says, "Yes sir, we have stung them twice, and you have your special lady waiting to embrace ya."

Cracking a smile, Risor asks, "Neda, what about you?"

"I think the mountains are best, too. They know we are a small group, so I don't think they will invest too much time in us."

Rinni starts shaking his head in the negative, "I think day chase us good. We be da only link to de rest and they needs to ask us where. Plus his lordships lady love." He has a big smile on his face.

Risor grins, "Ask us? I am sure it will not be so polite, Rinni."

Rinni's smile turns into an evil smirk," Oh, I dinna say how they ask. Whoeva dey catch get a good beatin."

Gorak interrupts the banter, "My Lord, I think we should go back about half an hour and then cut east from there."

Trooper Montazla says, "Sir, the power suits are running pretty low after the fight. Most of our Aether spears are fairly well drained, too."

Not wanting to hear this part, Risor asks, "What are we sitting at, with the suits and spears?"

Onta responds, "Most suits are about twenty percent, and the spears are closer to ten percent."

Gorak states, "My Lord, I know the suits are a great equalizer, but it is very hard to conceal their passage because of the weight. We can move quicker and easier without any power suits remaining."

Nodding his head in agreement, Rinni states, "Suh we get rid of da suits, we can make some cloaks from river weeds or such to betta hide us."

With an exasperated look of unbelief, Neda nearly yells, "Why didn't you offer that before?"

Shrugging, "Wit doze big shiny suits, whats da use?"

Smiling, Risor stops the discussion. "Okay, Gorak, Rinni, let's get a trail back to the river further east of the ford. We will find a place to drop the suits, make some cloaks and spears, then move out."

Jana is standing next to Dentam while looking at the dead and wounded. The remaining crew is repairing the damaged Vailixi. Another Vailixi has landed behind the crashed Vailixi. Troopers are all over the place. Another Vailixi is whirling in the air above the ford. Quite a few troopers are heading out over the ford.

After speaking to one of the crew members, Dentam reports, "My Lady, the crew report that this Vailixi will not fly again without some serious repairs."

Breathing deeply in a calming exercise, Jana replies, "Yet another thing to tear out of Risor's flesh when I capture him. When will the others get here?"

Checking his view tablet, "I believe we have another hour or two before they make it here. Would not it be best to return to Altai and use that as a base?"

Wondering how stupid she is to make Dentam her lover, "Think man, it's an hour away. If we find these bastards, getting reinforcements could take that long." Her voice rose with anger. "Had I more men, I would have pressed forward. Now, those skulking bastards could be hiding anywhere."

"Yes, my Lady, I am sorry. I was not thinking. I will have the men clear back this brush to allow more Vailixi to land."

Jana turns from him with a dismissive hand wave and starts to the second Vailixi.

✦

THREE WEEKS AFTER

TES ZEITA

It seems Lena sighs for the thousandth time. Deros had come calling again and again, but she politely refused him. This time, he left visibly angered. Gainor, Kala, and the kids are all giving her frightened looks. This slave's refusal of his advances is testing Deros's polite and calm demeanor.

She knows he could rape her any time he chooses, and there is nothing she can do. He will not have her heart and mind, but there is little she can do to stop him from taking her body. Even Kala, being protected by Gainor, is still enslaved and could be raped by others. It depends on Gainor's strength and sword arm to keep the others in line.

"Lena, you tread dangerous ground now. Deros is not the only one looking at you. Horca and his men were asking about you. If Deros gives his permission, they will not treat you nicely," Gainor said in a semi-whisper, hoping the kids would not fully hear. Kala shooed the kids to the other side of their hut.

Horca and his twenty men came into camp two days ago. The available slave women and girls have already been made aware of their way of treating women. Lena shudders, thinking of the screams and cries in the night.

"I will not submit to any man but my Tilor. He is still alive, and until I think otherwise, I am his, and he is mine."

Kala, returning to the little table they share, puts her arm around Lena. "We don't know that, Lena. I understand what you are doing and why, and I support you." She looks at Gainor for support. He nods.

"I also find that admirable, Lena. The problem is now things are changing. Deros tires of hearing your no's, and now this savage trash has entered our camp. They are our allies, and as long as they follow our rules, they are guests." Lowering his voice and moving in closer, holding her eyes, he uses a harsh whisper. "Understand, I can not protect you if they want you. I will not die for another woman, only the one I love. You understand this, right?"

The import of what he is saying starts to dawn on her. Hesitantly, "Deros?"

"He might be finished with you and offer you to Horca as a present. To have you around, the one who keeps turning him down will always eat at his mind. That and many know you deny him. It challenges his authority that a slave turns him down. No one else will protect you."

Kala hisses, "Gainor, that is harsh."

"Quiet woman, she needs to hear the truth. Her pride keeps her going, but her pride will get her handed over to those who will consider her only for what is between her legs and breasts. When they tire of her, they will sell her to another group or just slit her throat and dump her in the woods. That is the truth that she needs to think about." Both women reel from his harsh words.

The sting of the truth is worse than Lena expected. She starts to tear up from frustration, anger, and fear. Harsh laughter is heard outside of the tent. "Which one is the bitch in?"

"This one," The voice of Deros said.

The door flies open, and in come Horca and one of his men. Deros and two others are outside. Deros stands in the doorway. He says, "If you won't be mine, then you can be his."

The kids scream, Gainor stands up, Kala cries and holds Lena. Lena screams, "No, Please, No."

Gainor goes to Deros. "Deros, why? Please don't do this."

Horca laughs, "A fine present you offer, chief. I accept. Come here, woman. It's time to learn your place." He and his man move to Lena. Kala holds her still and does not let go.

Horca's man raises his hand to strike Kala when Gainor grabs his hand and throws the man into the wall. "You touch her, and I will feed your hand to the dogs."

Horca gets in Gainor's face. "You deny me my present?"

Gainor looks at Deros, who looks away. Then he looks at Kala and Lena in turn. He looks back at Horca. Slightly defiant but a little calmer, "No," Pointing at Kala, "but she is mine, and if you harm her, I will have your guts wrapped around your neck. Guest or not, you don't harm mine."

Horca, realizing he won, nods his head. "You are correct, warrior Gainor. We apologize for the insult. I will take my present and my leave of your place." He motions for his man to get Lena.

Kala is still holding her. Horca looks expectantly at Gainor. Gainor looks ill but moves to Kala's side and pulls her arms from Lena. Kala wails. Lena looks up into Gainor's eyes. They plead for forgiveness, but she gives him none.

She looks at Horca, who wears a triumphant, lecherous grin. Defiantly, she thrusts her chin out and moves of her own accord toward the door. Pass Horca without a look. She stops in front of Deros as he moves out of the way.

"So this is your honor." She spits in his face. "I am glad I gave you no comfort before the truth was known." She walks out into the night. Horca and his men are chortling their mirth.

"A feisty one."

"Wait til we getcha in da sheets. How feisty u be den."

"Too much for our friends here, you be nough for me."

With every step she takes, her stomach knots, her legs grow heavier, and her heart pounds. Others come out of the tents to see what is going on. Some look in sympathy, and others look in satisfaction that she gets what she has coming for treating their chief the way she did.

They are almost at Horca's tents when Lena's spirits rise—the distinctive whirl of Atlantean Vailixi in the distance.

A clanging noise starts, and men start running in all directions. One of the men pushes her forward, which makes her stumble. He grabs her by her hair and begins to pull her up.

She screams, but no one is paying attention. He grins at her when the first Vailixi strike occurs. The Aether blast hit near Horca's tents. They are far enough away that it is not threatening to them, but this distracts the man.

Keeping her wits and making a clear decision to die rather than let these animals have her, Lena sees her chance. His hunting knife is still in its sheath, and the man watches the incoming strikes. He holds her near him by the hair. She grabs for his knife the first time but misses.

The man notices her grab and is getting ready to strike her when another Vailixi blast near them throws them both to the ground. Lena lands on top of the guy, and as he pushes her aside, she successfully grabs his knife and quickly shoves it into his stomach.

His eyes go wide with the realization of what she has done. Lena keeps her weight on the knife, seeking to push it deeper into him. She hates him and what he wants to do to her.

Another explosion is near enough that the blast wave throws her off him. He lays there dying. Turning his head in her direction as she slowly starts to stand up. He can not move, just looking at her in shock.

She spits in his face and goes back the way they had come. She hopes to get to Kala and see if she can get her to escape during the fighting.

Lena runs past the warriors and toward the sounds of fighting. Vailixi strafes from above while a ground battle grows on the camp's perimeter. She gets to their tent and throws the door open.

The tent is dark, and no one seems to be there. Lena calls out and is about to leave and find her own way when she hears Kala.

"Lena!" Kala and her kids come from under the blankets, which look like they are in a pile. "We thought you were dead." She cries out as they all come to Lena and hug her.

"Quickly! This is our chance to escape." Lena pushes them away to get them moving to get things. "Get food, clothes, and stuff. Hurry."

Kala is confused while the children react to authority. Kala said, "Lena, we can't leave. Gainor will return."

Exasperated at Kala's thinking. "Kala, those are Atlanteans attacking here. They have Vailixi and troops outside the camp. I do not think Gainor will survive this, or if he does, he will flee or be taken prisoner."

Kala looks shocked. Even the kids slow down. Kala finds her voice and asks, "What will happen to us if Gainor is killed?"

"We will figure that out together in Atlantis. I promise I will take care of you. But we need to go now!" She pushes Kala toward the cooking area. Turning toward the kids, she motions them to return to their work. Seeing that all three are moving, she goes to the door.

The fighting is getting closer as the Vailixi strikes continue to hit the camp. People are running in all directions. She knows this is their chance to get free.

"Hurry, we need to get away."

Kala is sniffing back tears. Lena feels bad for Kala; she lost two men in a month. They can't stay here. If the Greeks win and Gainor is killed, both Lena and Kala might end up in Horca's clutches, with the fate of the kids unknown.

Kala's son Gurio approaches Lena first. "Mama, hurry up." Kara follows behind Gurio, looking shocked and scared.

Lena feels for them, too. They saw their father killed by the Greeks less than two weeks ago. Fleeing again in the dark because of another battle. Their minds are probably screaming in fear. She smiles at both of them, trying to reassure them that everything will be okay even when she does not feel that way.

She quickly checks outside. Another Vailixi explosion is close by. The ground fighting is closer, too.

They need to get out of the camp to ensure they will not be killed in the crossfire or worse. "Kala, let's go. That is enough food." She goes and grabs the woman's arm.

"I can't leave Lena in case Gainor returns. What if..." She continues. Then the slap nearly spun her around.

In an angry voice. "Think of your children, Kala. Not just yourself. If Gainor dies, you might be handed over to Horca, like me. What will happen to the kids?"

"Mama, let's go. I am afraid." Says Gurio, tears streaming down his face. Kara is staring at her mother with a look of complete terror. She grasps the clothes bag she held so tight that clothes seem coming from the top.

Lena pulls Kala along, and the kids push her and grasp her. They leave the hut and turn away from the sounds of fighting.

A Vailixi destroys a hut two down from them. Screams could be heard coming from the hut. They stop to look at the hut. Lena is battling with the idea of trying to see if anyone survived. Should they help or ignore the cries and try to escape?

Her decision is delayed when a figure emerges from the smoke toward them. It is Gainor. He recognizes them at the same time they did.

Kala comes to life and runs to him. The kids stay with Lena. Gainor is wounded and dripping with gore. He takes Kala into his arms and looks past her to Lena and the kids.

Lena worries that he will recognize they will flee and try to stop them. He looks at her and nods. She could breath again, he isn't going to stop them. Maybe even join them. They both start toward Lena and the kids when their world is changed.

Lena can barely register the blast before the blast wave knocks her and the kids off their feet. She struggles to make sense of what happened.

Dazed, her world is silent. She can only see shapes. The last thing she remembers is where the blast came from—where Kala and Gainor were standing.

Her last thought is, what happened to the children?

ALTA

The next morning, they start again. Everyone's muscles are protesting, but at least they slept well. An hour into their trek, they hear the whirl of a Vailixi again. Then another. Everyone dives for cover and listens. One Vailixi slowly passes over them, but the other stays further south. The one that passes over them goes to the northeast and then lands. Then they hear the other Vailixi come closer to them, to the southeast, and land.

Neda asks Risor, "Think they know where we are?"

The tracker, Jordon, is near them and answers, "They probably found the camp."

Risor agrees, "They probably found where we slept and realized we are in the area."

Jordon said, "If that's the case, my lord, they probably have trackers."

One of the kids asks, "Are they going to catch us?" She and some of the others look frightened.

Risor looks at Jordon, who gives a faint smile. Risor answers, "No, I think we still have the advantage, but it does mean we will need to be more careful in our movement."

They continue on a game trail for a while when one of the trackers comes running back to the main group.

"Everyone down. They are up ahead and coming our way."

The whole group moves into the brush along the game trail they follow. They move about five meters back from the path. The trackers are busy fussing with the brush on the path to conceal the team, then disappear into the bush. They wait for thirty minutes when they hear the sounds of movement ahead on the trail.

Risor tightens his grip on his spear, as does Neda beside him. He can just make out one of the troopers crouching with his spear aimed toward the path. He thinks to himself, this would be a bad place for a fight. Little visibility of the rest of the team and the bush is not enough to stop a blast of Aether from hitting someone.

The enemy troopers continue moving down the path but are not looking. Then Risor sees a tracker before them, looking at the path as the group moves along. As the tracker approaches the path where Risor's group moved off, he stops and looks intently at the ground. The troopers behind him don't seem too interested in what the tracker is doing but stop with him.

The tracker looks to the sides, peering into the brush, back at the path, then the ground. The troopers start paying more attention to the tracker while he continues investigating the area. Apparently, he has stopped many times, but not this long.

Risor worries and is almost white-knuckled, grasping his spear. There are quite a few enemies on the trail, and Risor is not sure they can kill them all quickly enough to avoid a prolonged fight before a Vailixi shows up. He prays to the Gods that his people hid their passage well enough that the tracker would move on.

One of the enemy troopers, probably the officer, said, "Madu, do you see something?"

The tracker responds, "I am not sure, my Lord. It looks like someone was hiding their trail."

All the troopers look into the bush, and some enter. There is no further talking, so Risor thinks they communicate amongst themselves via their communications link. Then Risor hears the whirling of a Vailixi coming close to them. He feels the game is up and that they have been found out.

The Vailixi moves slowly overhead while the troopers stay still. Risor hopes no one shoots. The Vailixi tries to flatten the vegetation with the power of their thrust. Risor looks and sees that many of his troopers are kneeling. The kids cower, but luckily, they are far enough off the trail that when the Vailixi exposes them, they are still behind the bushes from the enemy troopers' point of view. The Vailixi doesn't have downward-facing viewports, so they could not see anyone.

After a few minutes, the Vailixi moves off in the direction Risor's team has come, and the enemy troopers move down the trail. Risor thought this is getting crazy, they need to find shelter.

After the enemy moves down the trail, Risor signals everyone back on the trail. Talking to Gorak, "We need to find shelter. A place to rest without constant fear."

Neda breaks out the map and his seeker. The seeker is an Aether-enabled compass that can show its location on these unique maps.

"If we move south, we know we can come up against a river. We might be able to follow that to the hills and then find shelter." Neda said while still studying the map.

"How far south? If we follow this trail, what do you think?"

Neda responds, "Sir, if we follow the trail, we can move quicker."

Rinni responds, "Move quicker, ya, same with da enemy, move quicker."

Gorak nods, "My Lord, the enemy seems to be using the trail and jumping around with their Vailixi. We need to get off the trail to avoid them. Stay on the trail, we move quicker but more chance of running into them."

Many heads of the Suda and Trackers nod in agreement. Risor decides to follow their advice. His team could not go on like this for too long, they need rest. "Okay, let's cut south to get to the river as soon as possible." They then cut into the woods, going south with the Suda, hiding their tracks as much as they could.

Risor asks Gorak's men, "Did you see them?"

"No, my Lord."

"Okay, we need to pick up the pace. I want some distance between us and them."

They start to move out again. About twenty minutes later, they hear the whirling of a Vailixi behind them, and everyone freezes to listen. The whirling sounds change. Risor knows it was hovering. It's probably near the turn-off.

The whirling then starts again, getting softer. It is moving off and away. Cocking his head, Gorak says, "It's moving north, my Lord."

"Okay, let's keep going south for a while. Maybe south east, so we are still moving away from them. Gorak, can you place a trap, please."

Rinni grins at Gorak, "Getting interesting, eh?"

The terrain turns rougher as the team moves into the foothills.

"Let's keep to heavily forested areas. I don't want to take a chance of being caught exposed." Risor said.

For another hour, they move on, covering a good distance when the terrain gets hilly, and the forest starts to thin out. They have just finished crossing a clearing and hear the whirling again. Risor stops the group a little inside the forest surrounding the clearing, in a heavily bushed area.

Neda asks, "Why are we stopping, sir?"

"I want to find out what they are doing. I don't like just running and not knowing."

"Understood." Then turns to the team, Neda said, "Ten minute break."

The whirling gets louder, and then they see the Vailixi. It is heading north of their position back east along the path they had taken. Risor is about to restart the trek when he hears another whirling.

Then another. There are at least three Vailixi in the area now. One of the Vailixi is coming toward the clearing they just crossed. It moves over the clearing, running a small circle around it. It moves over their location but keeps going. Then, the worst possible thing happens.

The Vailixi lands in the clearing and disgorges twenty troopers. They span out around the clearing as the Vailixi takes off. Risor curses the Gods for their luck has turned for the worse.

He hisses, "No one moves, and by the Gods, don't shoot."

That is unnecessary as the kids are terrified, and everyone else knows what will happen if they are found. Twenty troopers in full battle armor against ten troopers and a bunch of unarmored people is not a contest.

It's not even a contest. Power spears are only accurate to about one hundred meters, and half the enemy is well beyond that range. Their numbers would overwhelm Risor's team, even without their Vailixi and the other Vailixi within support range.

A slight ache inches its way up Risor's legs as he squats in the bush, barely moving. He is sure most of the others are starting to ache as well. It could not be helped. The enemy troopers are looking around the clearing, presumably for indications that Risor's group has come through this area. Risor is thankful that Gorak's men hid their trail. Then, on the far side of the clearing, some excitement commences. It seems the troopers see some hint of Risor's team movement into the clearing—more of the troopers group around the evidence. The commander of the enemy troopers is pointing to the woods on the other side of the clearing, and the enemy starts to move off through the woods in that direction.

Risor could hear himself exhale. *It looks like they dodged another one. Maybe the Gods are testing him.* The team waits a full thirty minutes before heading off to the southeast again, away from the direction the enemy took. They continue moving in that direction for the rest of the day. Occasionally, Vailixi would be heard overhead.

After one such overflight, Risor told Neda, "I think they know we are close. Maybe three or four Vailixi are in the area."

"I think so, sir. There seem to be too many of them in the area for coincidence."

"Yes, we should keep moving late into the evening and sleep under cover when we can. I want to get as far away from here as possible."

"Yes, sir, makes sense to me."

They keep moving after dark. It is hard going, and the distance they cover is only a few kilometers, but it is a distance away from the enemy. When the moon is well overhead, they stop for the night. An exhausted Risor contacts New Altai. Tilor is on watch again.

"Sir, everything okay? Fordo told us they moved a few kilometers off the path, and they heard a bunch of Vailixi buzzing around the site where they left their heavy equipment."

Risor sighs, "Glad they left them. What is their status."

"All three groups are okay. They broke up into many smaller groups and are moving quickly. The bad thing is they have only one or two trackers or Suda. They will not be able to hide their trails that well."

"I think we are all getting a lesson in concealment now."

"It seems so. So what is your status?"

The team is in a heavy downpour, and no one is armored anymore. They are all wearing reed cloaks. Risor, Neda, Rinni, and Gorak stand in a semi-circle around one of the Suda warriors. He points to a cave entrance on a ledge about three meters above them. They all nod and move toward the path leading to the ledge.

The Suda enter the cave first. One has an Aether spear, while the other has a bow. A brown bear charges from the dark of the cave. The Suda warrior levels his Aether spear and blasts the bear. In one shot, the bear is dead.

More of the team piles into the cave.

He walks toward the bear, puts his bow away, and pulls out his knife. "It looks like meat is back on the menu."

One of the troopers says, "Good, I was getting tired of berries."

Walking up behind the trooper, looking at the kill with a critical eye, Rinni chimes in. "Ya, but ya ain't as fat anymore."

General laughter from those around the pair as the trooper takes the ribbing in stride. Rinni drops his stuff and pulls out his knife, going to the bear's carcass. The bear is a good three meters tall at the shoulders.

Neda looks around, "Should be safe for a fire. Go ahead and get one started."

The trackers and Suda dress the kill while the cooks and kids start a cooking fire.

Jana is sitting in the command seat of one of her Vailixi and talking to Lady Tomar.

After listening to Jana's report, Lady Tomar says, "You need to bring all your people back now, Commander."

A spark of anger touches Jana's eyes, but she quickly reins it in. "My Lady, if you will give me a little more time. I know they are still near."

Seeming distracted, Lady Tomar is looking at something away from the projection. "Be that as it may, we have issues you need to assist with here. It has been almost a week, and you have not had contact."

"My Lady, please. For the honor of our party. He is responsible for killing many of our soldiers."

Becoming annoyed with the pleading, she looks directly at the projection. "You will return now. Is that clear, Lady Kalin? Events here are coming to a point where I need all the force I can muster. We are calling people back from all over."

Looking at Lady Tomar for a minute, not sure of the meaning of the reference but finding no other way to argue her point. Bowing her head in subservience. "Yes, my Lady, we will return as soon as all gather."

"Good. If everything works out, you will have a chance to look again. But first, we must defend the legacy of Atlantis. Have your force proceed to Luxa when gathered."

Lady Tomar cuts the communication.

She speaks to herself, trying to imagine what is going on back there since she left. "Yes, my Lady."

Idly tracing the communicator stone, deep in thought. Luxa? There is a sizeable Shigar presence in Luxa, but no danger exists. Was it a staging ground? But to where?

THANK YOU

Thank you so much for making it this far!

I really appreciate the time you have taken to read my book. As an indie publisher, it means a lot, and I hope my story has entertained you.

If you have a few seconds, hearing your honest feedback would mean the world to me. It really helps people decide if this is a book they would want to read, and it will help me improve my next book. Please leave a review on the platform where you purchased the book. I would greatly appreciate it.

Also, join my newsletter to find out what I am inspired to write next:

https://www.author-jgrimm.com/landing-page

I plan to create smaller background stories for many of my novels. These might not be big enough to justify publishing on the retail platforms, but I want to share them with you, my readers. The smaller ones will be free to download from my store, and the larger ones that just didn't cut the grade to publish as a full novel might cost a little something.

The newsletters will also discuss current blog entries or other items I think you might like to hear about.

Finally, I will occasionally offer discounts for products on my website as another Thank You for your support.

So please click on the link above to sign up for my newsletter and join me on this adventure through imagination.

Want to make your traveling or beach reading easier and I dare say, lighter? As a purchaser of the printed version, you can get an eBook copy for a significant discount. Just go to my website and enter the code below.

Please use the code: **PowerofWater**

GLOSSARY

- Aether is a power based on drawing energy from everything and directing it as the user wishes. The gods taught humans this power.

- Alta - Continents of America.

- Alta Cieto - South America.

- Alta Falta - Region around the Gulf of Mexico and the Caribbean.

- Atlanta - The continents of Europe, Asia, and Africa are grouped together.

- Atlanta Coda - Africa below the savannahs of the Sahara

- Atlanta Luxa - North Africa above the savannahs of the Sahara and Middle East.

- Atlanta Meito - Western Europe

- Atlanta Nado - Eastern Europe

- Atlanta Rama - Indus River area, home of the Raman Empire.

- Atlanta Sangam - Southern India and Sri Lanka, home of the Sangam Empire.

- Atlanta Suna is the ice age landmass of Sundaland, which is now

Southeast Asia. This large landmass includes the island nations of Malaysia and Indonesia.

- Atlanta Questo - Northern Asia above the Himalayan Mountains.

- Blessing of Poseidon – A mystical event that occurs at sundown on clear days in Atlantis. As the light last touches the capstone, it flashes brilliantly in all directions, becoming a dazzling spectacle. The image of the God Poseidon smiling directly at the viewer, in the viewer's mind, occurs to all that look up at that moment.

- Gift of Poseidon—The average lifespan for those of ancient Atlantean bloodlines was 150 years. They remained hale until the last 20 or so years of their lives. The average non-Atlantean lived around 30-60 years.

- Mantrik – Aether adept of the Rama Empire.

- Mother Stone—A large jewel shaped by Aether. It is used by priests to concentrate Aether power and channel it into tools that use Aether. Depending on the type of tool, adepts or normal people can use it.

- Nalos – Political party of Atlantis that believes that Atlantis should be a friend to all and not try to rule the world. For the first 20,000+ years of the city-turned-empire's existence, they came as teachers and friends to the other people of the world.

- Piilo – Military unit of around 100 soldiers and part of a company.

- Poseidon's Well – The inner sanctum of Poseidon's temples where the Mother Stone is kept.

- Shigar – Political party of Atlantis that believes that Atlantis is superior to all others and all should pay tribute to Atlantis. Over the first 20,000+ years of Atlantis, there were those who reveled in the power and glory of Atlantis. They thought that Atlantis should rule the world to guide the less fortunate to civilized society.

- Shilot - A master of aether, science or medicine that is not part of the military.

- Shuma – Priest.

- Skor - Aether made metal of Atlantis, harder than today's titanium.

- Somena – Healer of Aceso.

- Tia - river

- Tia Yolan - Mississippi River

- Tes - Large bodies of water like a Sea, Gulf, or Ocean.

- Tes Atlan - Atlantic Ocean

- Tes Falta - Gulf of Mexico

- Tes Falon - Middle Caribbean Sea

- Tes Fatlan - Southern Caribbean Sea

- Tes Naldo - A large sea covering large parts of the Eastern European/Asia landmass caused by the northern ice shelf blocking northern flowing rivers.

- Tes Rama - Indian Ocean

- Tes Tira - Pacific Ocean

- Tes Zeita - Mediterranean Sea

✦

Excerpt from The Power of Blood, Book Two of The Doom of the Gods

Three Weeks Before

NEW ATLANTIS

The Prime Minister of the Atlantean Empire, Lord Tolloc, enters Lady Tomar's office, one of the top generals of the Atlantean forces. He barges in, startling most of the people in the room. She is getting a brief on the status of the war with the Rama Empire when he barges in. She, not one who startles easily, nods to those officers, and they quickly gather their stuff and leave. Before they can exit the office, Lord Tolloc takes one of their seats.

"General, I have heard that most of our forces are concentrating in Luxa. Why is that happening?" he asks.

She studies him. Well over one hundred years old, he is still a strong man. His family has the Gift of Poseidon, the gift of a long life, that many old families in Atlantis have.

"Where have you heard such rumors, my Lord?"

Waving a hand, "Never mind that, is it true?"

She gets up from behind her desk and heads to the balcony. He remains seated but is forced to turn. Out of the corner of her eye, she notes his annoyance with satisfaction.

"I thought it prudent to get most of the forces loyal to us into a staging area."

Turning her words over, recognition dawning, he gets up and quickly moves to her side near the balcony. "My Lady, the council has not agreed to such actions yet. You risk exposing us, " he hisses.

She looks at the new pyramid being built across the main plaza from the military headquarters. Soon, they will have the power to start rebuilding their military. The way Atlantis has maintained its hegemony over the world for thousands of years. The pyramids house the generating source of Aether. From the mostly completed entrance to the structure, she can see the glow of many Mother Stones.

Looking north along the plaza, to the right of the pyramid, the imperial palace is nearing completion on the outside. New Atlantis has gathered most of the Empire's priests and Mother Stones to accomplish such quick rebuilding. While most of the people live in tents, the government is being built up.

Thousands of slaves and workers wander the dirt streets below. Going about the tasks they are assigned. Soldiers walk the throngs, checking papers or motivating those moving too slowly to move faster. All kick up a little dust from those unpaved streets. The dust hangs in the air and sticks to everything. Soon, though, those too would turn to stone, and a semblance of normalcy would return. Unless the government did not see to the Shigar party's demands.

Then this great, new plaza would run with blood.

She turns to him, "On the contrary, Prime Minister, most of the council has decided. We just await your faction to join in what must be done."

Staring at her like she just grew ten heads, he is at a loss for words. His faction is the diplomatic side of the Shigar party. Some would call the Shigar, the war party, like those weak Nalos party followers. She likes to believe they are the Atlantean Empire party, the party of strength and glory to Atlantis. The world is much better under the benevolent rule of Atlantis. All of it.

Those who do not agree get to see the power of Atlantis. The might that has made Atlantis strong for most of its 30,000 years. It is sad that Atlantis had to be abandoned with the rising oceans. It also gave the Shigar a perfect opportunity to remove some of their political opponents and engineer a near takeover of the government and military.

Watching his discomfort, she continues. "Oh, and my Lord, we will not wait forever."

Finding his voice but barely above a whisper. "Wa.. what does that mean?"

"It means that you and your people need to decide soon. You are right. The others will eventually realize the build-up in Luxa and want to know why." She returns to her desk, and he meekly follows her.

His face is ash white he stands next to the desk. "My Lady, you talk of treason. We did not want to overthrow the emperor, just his government."

She rises, like a lioness lunging with her voice rising, "Do you think the others will allow that? Think the emperor will accept that? We have his cousin on our council. He will become emperor." Taking a deep breath to calm herself. "Now, we have said too much already. Prime Minister, you need to decide in the next few weeks."

She sits and then picks up a viewing tablet on her desk, waiting for her signature. The military lives on reports.

She looks up at him and smiles. "My Lord, please sit for a few minutes and regain your composure. You look like you have been scared to death. Shall I have a drink brought?"

Shaking his head in the negative. She smiles and goes back to her reports.

He sits there for a minute before realizing he is dismissed. He looks like he wants to say more but then looks down and gets up.

He gets halfway to the door. "Oh, and Prime Minister. I hope you decide the right way. Have a nice day." She goes back to her tablets.

He stares at her and the implied threat. Then walks out the door.

About the Author

He lives in Japan, the land of Anime, Samurai, the ultramodern, and the extremely old. These contrasting themes fuel his worlds. The ancient and new meld together into worlds where super-powered school kids defeat evil, forest spirits help or fight humans, and giant, futuristic robots battle to save civilization.

Where else to live for inspiration?!

James is a screenwriter and novelist living in the suburbs of Tokyo. His love of history, space, and the beauty of life inspires his tales.

Website: https://www.author-jgrimm.com/

At a train station in Kawasaki, Japan (outside of Tokyo).